THEIRS WAS A LOVE MORE RADIANT AND ENDURING THAN THE GOLD OF AN EMBATTLED EMPIRE....

HERNANDO PIZARRO—He came to pillage and to conquer, but greed was his undoing and he soon lost control.

ALONSO FALLA—An avaricious grandee, he betrayed the Alava family to the Inquisition for their fortune, then lured the exquisite Rianna to Peru—and her fate in his enemy's arms.

RIANNA ALAVA—At the mercy of Alonso, she fled her home in Madrid to find her heart a world away, to find her future in the embrace of Shalikuchima, an Incan warrior, and a fate that had been foretold.

MANCO CAPAC—Last of the Incan kings, he owed his life to Shalikuchima and his safety to the hidden city of Machu Picchu, the last refuge of his dying kingdom, from which he'd wage his final war.

CORAQUENQUE—Manco Capac's bold queen. She fought at his side with fierce loyalty until captured and forced to serve as a slave for the Castilian beauty that Lord Shalikuchima desired.

SHALIKUCHIMA—The last hope of the Incan Empire. His passion was revenge until a temptress from a foreign land stole his breath away. Their love would become legend even as a world of unparalleled splendor slipped tragically away.

TO LOVE AND TO CONQUER

TO LOVE
AND
TO CONQUER

Joyce Verrette

A DELL TRADE PAPERBACK

A DELL TRADE PAPERBACK
Published by
Dell Publishing Co., Inc.
1 Dag Hammarskjold Plaza
New York, New York 10017

Dell ® TM 681510, Dell Publishing Co., Inc.

Printed in the United States of America

First printing—October 1984

Library of Congress Cataloging in Publication Data

Verrette, Joyce.
  To love and to conquer.

  I. Title.
PS3572.E764T6   1984   813'.54   84-9540
ISBN 0-440-58677-1

For the Incas, whose courageous history inspired my story, and for Yma Sumac and Moises Vivanco, whose music set my imagination in motion

Author's Note

Because the Incas didn't have a written language as we know it, the authentic names used in this story were phonetically spelled by the Spanish explorers and should be pronounced accordingly. For example, the name Coraquenque should be pronounced "Coraqui-enqui."

TO LOVE
AND
TO CONQUER

chapter

1

The solitary Inca couldn't know he resembled a statue of an officer of ancient Greece as he stood motionless on the road from Cuzco. Shali's tunic, cloak and helmet, even his sandals bore a startling resemblance to those an Alexander or a Paris might have worn to celebrate a triumph. Though Peru and Greece were on opposite sides of the world and Shali was separated even from Alexander by more than two thousand years, Shali's insignia, the decorative details of his garments, the fact that he wore no armor were the only obvious dissimilarities. The Aegean sun would have tinted a Macedonian's skin the same gold as an Inca's. Shali's headpiece looked much like an abbreviated Trojan war helmet; and it covered all, except a few wisps of the lustrous black hair that had crept out at his temples. Though the headpiece was gold, he hoped it would shield him if the Castilians struck down at him from their horses.

A long spray of slender, crimson feathers rose from the helmet's crest, their black tips slightly curved from their length, swaying as Shali's wide-set eyes turned repeatedly in the direction he expected the cavaliers to come.

Shali wasn't nearly as at ease as his stance made him appear. His tension was revealed only by the grim lines of his mouth, which normally somehow blended a soldier's sensual directness with an incongruous tenderness that made him at moments seem vulnerable. His eyes, tilted at an angle by high, fully curved cheekbones, were as black as obsidian. Like the volcanic glass used by the Incas in jewelry for its decorative sheen as well as in dagger blades for its hard keenness, the surface of Shali's eyes seemed to mirror the late afternoon sunlight falling like dust through the trees. Their depths were impossible to fathom as they constantly shifted in search of thieves as well as one of the Pizarros' traps.

Shali was aware that being dressed in the full regalia a nobleman would have worn before the Pizarro brothers had come was enough to draw undesirable attention in these uneasy times, yet he'd deliberately put on more ornaments than he'd normally have chosen even to attend a festive state ceremony. He didn't like to stand in the road adorned with gold jewelry, the metal the Castilians valued so highly they slaughtered Peruvians wholesale to possess it. But Shali calculated that the cavaliers escorting Manco Capac, his king and cousin, wouldn't be able to resist the tempting target of a lone, weaponless Inca and would halt their horses. Though a few of Shali's men were concealed in the foliage lining both sides of the road, their orders were explicit—to effect their king's escape from his captors. If Shali became a sacrifice in the process, he would be a mourned, but dead, hero.

Because the Peruvians had no horses, they were always at a disadvantage during combat with the cavaliers. Shali had seen before how one Castilian riding a powerful, swiftly moving charger could crush a score of Incan soldiers under its hooves; but Shali had also observed that, when a man threw his weight against the metal device in a horse's mouth, entangled the creature's legs in a rope or dragged its rider from the saddle, the horse became confused, hesitant, even frightened. Then a firm hand and a calm voice were usually all that was needed to control the animal. Still, it wouldn't be a simple task to subdue the cavaliers, Shali reminded himself.

Shalikuchima had been called Shali from childhood so as not to be confused with his father. When Shali was eighteen, the illustrious Incan general had entered Cuzco on invitation from the Pizarro brothers to negotiate a truce; but instead of discussing peace, the elder

Shalikuchima had been arrested. The Castilians had charged him with heresy and fomenting a rebellion against Pizarro's rule. Shalikuchima had answered that, while he wouldn't insult a religion he didn't understand, he couldn't accept the government of his people by invaders from across an ocean. Shali had been told by someone, who'd witnessed the execution, how his father, bound to a stake in the plaza, had been offered a less painful death by strangulation if he'd been willing to accept the foreigner's religion. He was promised by the attending friar he would spend eternity in a place called heaven. When Shalikuchima had asked if the souls of his enemies went there too and the friar had answered they did, the Inca had bitterly said he didn't want to spend eternity in the same place as his murderers. He had died in the flames without making one sound to reveal his agony. Shali then had forbidden anyone to call him Shalikuchima until after his father's executioners had been killed or driven away.

Such memories made Shali's outrage become a dark fire smoldering in his eyes and he finally turned to walk a short distance up an incline in the road. Once at the top, he forced his attention to the matter at hand and peered down the tree-arched lane for a sign of the Castilians. His cape had slipped down over his broad shoulders, its scarlet folds spreading to momentarily display its border, the repeating motif of his family crest—a gold jaguar carrying a black condor. The only sign of Shali's anger his men could perceive was the sharp gesture he made as he flipped the cloak back over his shoulders; so when the cavaliers approached, they could see he hid no weapons. Shali walked back down to the lower section of the road. Although his steps appeared unhurried, his long strides covered more ground than they seemed; and like the jaguar of his crest, his movements were lithely silent. After he'd stopped, he shook his head in signal to the Incas concealed so well in the forest even he couldn't see them.

Shali reflected bitterly on how the circumstances of his people had changed in the relatively few years since the Castilians had come to ravage the Incan empire as he absently brushed dust from his tunic—creamy vicuña so finely woven a European would have mistaken its wool for silk twill intricately embroidered with red and gold, ending midthigh in a deep row of knotted crimson fringe. He shifted the gold disks that formed a belt circling his narrow waist so the tunic, a little bunched from his earlier, abrupt gesture, lay more smoothly against his flat hips. He was becoming uncomfortably warm from the weight of the jewel-woven collar that almost reached the tips of his shoulders and echoed the gleam of the wide gold wristlets whose edges were digging into the tops of his hands. The decorative knots of the scarlet cords fastened around his upper arms, insignias of his high rank, made his skin itch. He silently scolded himself for paying notice to such petty problems when his king had suffered not only discomfort, but humiliation at his captor's hands these many past months.

After killing Manco Capac's older brother, King Atahualpa, by treachery and King Huascar, next in line for the Incan throne, had suddenly and suspiciously drowned in a river, the Pizarros hadn't wanted to crown Manco Capac, a man of almost thirty. They had, instead, proclaimed Toparaca, youngest of the royal sons, Peru's king. The Pizarros had thought Toparaca was a boy they could easily manage; but he, too, had died under questionable circumstances. The Pizarros had then had no choice other than to proclaim Manco Capac king. Still, the Castilians hadn't allowed Manco to rule his people. They'd tricked him into going to Cuzco then taken him prisoner to use as a powerless figurehead in governing the Incas the way they, not he, wished. The Incas, fearing that resistance would cause Manco Capac's death, dared do nothing; there was no one left in the royal line to succeed him.

Villac Umu, a highly intelligent strategist as well as the Incas' high priest, had thought of the plan to free Manco Capac. He'd managed to persuade the Pizarros to allow him to visit his king and offer spiritual solace. Villac Umu had given Manco Capac a message revealing the plan for his freedom. The message had been in the form of a *quipu,* a sheaf of cords whose colors and the arrangement of its knots was the only form of writing used or needed by the Incas. The Pizarros, not being able to read a *quipu,* had believed Villac Umu's explanation that the knotted cords was a way of counting prayers. On a second visit, Manco had returned the *quipu* knotted into a message that agreed with the plan and added some details he'd thought of.

Manco had pretended to fall in with his captors' goals, to have become as enthralled by the lure of gold as the Pizarros. He was friendly with Hernando Pizarro and eventually told the Castilian where a cache of the valuable metal was then led him to it. Afterward, he'd told Pizarro about a life-size statue of Huayna Capac, his father, that was hidden in a cave in the Andean foothills. Pizarro couldn't resist the temptation of over six feet of solid gold and enthusiastically agreed to send Manco with an escort to get it. Shali's mouth took on a disgusted cast as he thought of how his king must bargain with an enemy for a supposed share of loot—gold that was Manco Capac's by his royal birth. The Pizarros had been taken in by the ruse. Shali's spies had reported Manco's leaving Cuzco with only two cavaliers as his escort—these to help load the statue onto the cart Manco Capac was driving and to guard it from thieves.

Shali hoped no thieves would happen upon *him* and their attack betray the rescue plan with its noise. Even more disastrous was the possibility of additional cavaliers following Manco and his escort by a more circuitous route. Then the handful of Incan soldiers, whose only weapons were the kind propelled by human strength, could find themselves facing a squad of cavalrymen carrying firearms. As he thought of the Castilians' pistols, visions of previous attacks, when Incas had been systematically cut down by cannon fire, chilled him.

The muffled sound of horses' hooves, the creakings of a heavy wagon put an end to Shali's reflections. He didn't need to signal his men; they knew from his suddenly drooping head, the slumping of his shoulders that he had begun to play his role.

When the cavaliers reached the top of the hill, they were surprised by the sight of an Incan nobleman dressed in the splendor of more prosperous days standing in the hollow. They immediately reined their horses to a stop and glanced questioningly at each other. Shali seemed not to have noticed their arrival, though he was privately cursing the distance they'd halted from him.

The Castilians' eyes were dazzled by the sun striking the gold Shali wore and both their minds flooded with the same thought. If they killed this Indian on the lonely road, they could share his jewelry with only Manco instead of surrendering it to the Pizarros, who would add it to the common hoard. One-fifth of such loot was reserved for the royal treasury in Spain; the remainder was divided among the men according to rank.

"He seems to have no weapons, Vaca," one of the cavaliers noted under his breath.

"You're thinking the same as I. We needn't share this with the Crown if Manco will agree," Vaca said quietly.

"I don't think Manco would go to Pizarro with this story. He's grown to like the weight of gold in his purse as much as we do," the first cavalier softly replied. He looked over his shoulder at the Inca sitting on the cart seat. Manco's hazel eyes were staring at the man in the road with an avid expression the Castilians mistook for greed instead of the hunger for freedom he really felt.

"What do you think that Indian is doing here, Diego? He looks peculiar, as if he's drunk or ill."

Diego hastily crossed himself at the mention of illness; smallpox brought to Peru by the Europeans occasionally reared its head among the Incas and decimated entire villages. He studied the tall Inca's face, noted his golden skin carried no telltale blemishes then called in Spanish, "Are you ill or drunk, *cochino*?"

Though Shali knew he'd been called a swine, he gave no indication of understanding the insult. Instead, he lifted deliberately unfocused eyes and muttered a slurred greeting in Quechua, his own language.

"He's drunk on *chicha*. No doubt he's spent the afternoon at some celebration," Manco said in seeming disgust.

At this confirmation of what they'd hoped, the cavaliers began to relax.

"Come here, *cochino*," Vaca directed. "Tell us where you got the maize liquor and what your people have to celebrate."

Shali stared up at him with the same blank expression.

"He doesn't speak your language," Manco commented then added disdainfully, "Even if he'd understood, he seems too drunk to take a step." Manco looked at Shali and in elegant Quechua commanded, "Approach your ruler now, shameless nobleman."

Shali hesitated a moment, as if he were trying to decide which foot would move first, then began walking slowly, unsteadily toward them. He didn't want to get too close to the cavaliers while they still were on their horses if he could avoid it. Despite his outward drunkenness, he was privately appraising the mare Vaca was riding. It was as white as the snow at the crown of the Andes and it didn't seem as wary of him as its owner was. Shali wished the Castilians would dismount and approach him. Fifteen paces away he stopped, wavering.

"He can barely stand, lest walk," Diego observed. "If he's been at a party, his host must have been very generous with the *chicha*."

"Our young men didn't always behave so," Manco Capac noted disgustedly.

"His drunkenness will make this easier than I'd hoped," Vaca commented. He looked back at Manco and asked, "You know what we plan?" Manco nodded gravely. "Do you agree?"

Manco said, "The gold might as well be ours as a fool's like him. Why should I die defending a drunk?"

"Why, indeed," Vaca agreed as he guided his horse to stop beside Shali. "This collar of emeralds and gold alone will bring a fortune in Seville," he said wonderingly.

Shali, gazing up at his enemy, merely blinked. He was aware the bits of red and blue now appearing at the forest's edge weren't all flowers, that certain patches of dark green weren't leaves but the garments of his men, who had gathered nearer. He wondered if he could later catch Vaca's horse. It would be very useful to have an animal like that under him if Manco Capac agreed with his plan to lay siege to Cuzco, the old Incan capital now held by the Pizarros.

When the Castilian admiring Shali's belt motioned for him to take it off so he could look at it more closely, Shali began to docilely unfasten the circle of gold disks. He did it slowly, awkwardly as an intoxicated man would, giving the Incas in the forest a bit more time to prepare themselves.

At Vaca's impatient gestures, Shali looked up in seeming confusion for a moment before pulling the belt from his waist. Beginning a gesture that appeared as if he were going to offer the belt, he suddenly snapped his wrist; and the gold disks whipped in a shining arc to rake the cavalier's face. Shali's seemingly slack muscles just as suddenly gathered and lengthened as he leaped up to catch Vaca's shoulders and try to drag him from the saddle.

The startled charger reared and both men fell behind its haunches to roll in the dust. Vaca, encumbered by the weight of his breastplate, was far less agile than Shali; and he was horrified when he felt the

Inca's muscles harden, his torso powerfully twist then Shali land on top of him, pinning him to the road.

"It is you, *soldadoraso,* who are a pig," Shali said in only slightly accented Spanish as he drew back his hands locked together in a double fist then swung them to strike the cavalier with all his strength. The Castilian grunted and went limp.

Shali sprang to his feet and noted his men had thrown a loop of rope around Diego and dragged him from his saddle, while another loop around the horse's neck had captured the animal as well. Manco Capac was controlling the horse that had drawn the cart with an expertise Shali envied. He turned away, intending to catch Vaca's charger if it hadn't galloped too far down the road.

As he ran fleetly around the next curve, he saw that the mare had caught her reins on a dead tree stump. She was pulling so frantically at the reins her mouth was bleeding. At Shali's appearance, her nostrils flared with even greater alarm; and she struggled harder. Shali paused and spoke soothingly in Spanish to the horse. At the sound of familiar words calmly spoken, she quieted; and Shali freed the reins.

"You're beautiful and you run like the wind," Shali said softly in Quechua as he stroked the horse's snowy neck. "That will be your new name—Wayra, the wind." The mare snorted uneasily at the strange sound of the words; and Shali smiled, adding in Spanish, "I would prefer not to have to speak always to you in the tongue of my enemies so you'll have to begin to learn some of mine." He caressed the charger's forehead a moment before turning and was relieved when the horse willingly followed to where the others were waiting.

As Shali approached Manco Capac, he began to bow; but Manco said, "How can I demand signs of homage from a cousin who has given me back my crown?"

Shali slowly straightened and came nearer. "Not your crown, my lord, but your freedom—or as much as any of us have these days."

"My freedom *is* my crown," Manco replied. He clasped Shali's arm warmly a moment then ran his fingertip pointedly over the scarlet cord fastened there. "You wear the insignia of your rank, as I'll soon again wear mine, no matter what my empire's invaders decree."

Shali advised, "We've established a camp in a nearby valley. Coraquenque is waiting to give you the *borla.*"

"Coraquenque," Manco repeated softly, lingering lovingly on each syllable of the name. "My betrothed and my crown," he added then looked at the white horse Shali had brought and commented, "That's a fine, young mare."

"I've decided to call her Wayra," Shali replied. Suddenly realizing Manco might want the mare for his own use, Shali offered his king the reins.

Manco smiled at the gesture and shook his head. He knew Shali wanted the horse for himself. "At Cuzco I made friends with the chestnut I drove here and I prefer him. Keep your Wayra. My officers should have their own horses."

"This particular officer doesn't know how to ride yet," Shali admitted, still offering the reins.

"I learned from one of Hernando Pizarro's lieutenants, who thought my lessons were amusing. I can teach you; and as we obtain more horses, you can teach others," Manco said. His smile widened as he added, "It should be interesting to watch you learn. Only have a care your lessons don't injure you as a man. Your wife wouldn't appreciate that." When Manco saw the pain flashing through his cousin's eyes like a streak of black fire, alarm replaced his humor; and he breathed, "What is it?"

The words were like ice crystals chipping against Shali's teeth, "Two seasons ago . . . Yupanqui is dead . . . and our son."

Manco caught Shali's shoulders and whispered in horror, "The Castilians?"

"They attacked Yupanqui's parents' house while she was visiting," Shali answered, his low tone throbbing with grief.

"Do you know which of our enemies led the raid?" Manco demanded. "I would order that any Inca who sees the Castilian responsible kill him, be the Inca soldier, peasant or slave."

Shali shook his head, but wouldn't raise his eyes as he answered. "I'm grateful for your offer, but I don't even know if it was one of the Pizarros or a lieutenant. There are so many Pizarro brothers, it seems, I can hardly keep up with which one is where."

"Francisco and Hernando are in Lima; Juan and Gonzalo are at Cuzco at the moment," Manco said, then fell silent, wondering if there was any way he could comfort his cousin.

But Shali took a deep breath and in a suddenly brisk voice asked, "Are you ready now, my lord, to go to our camp? What do you want to do with these cavaliers?"

Manco's first wife had been killed by the Castilians; and understanding that Shali had changed the subject so he wouldn't weep, he released his cousin. Manco thought sadly of Yupanqui; his most vivid memory was of her smiling. She'd been beautiful, vibrant and so much in love with Shali. Manco recalled the infant's merry little face and realized the baby hadn't even reached his first year. Knowing it was best for the moment to say nothing more about Shali's loss, Manco replied solemnly, "Yes, Shali, I'm ready to leave. We'll take our prisoners with us."

"Are you certain you want them to see our camp?" Shali asked.

"Is the camp extensive?"

Shali answered, "It's very large."

"Then, after they've walked home without their weapons, they can tell Pizarro how strong our forces are." Manco was thoughtful a moment before inquiring, "If only a handful of men were needed to rescue me, why did you bring so many soldiers?"

Shali hesitated, uncertain what Manco would think of his plan. Finally, he began, "From the moment the Pizarros turned their cannons on King Atahualpa's procession and killed several thousand Incas whose only purpose was to welcome them to Caxamalca, our people have wanted revenge. But he captured our king and we were afraid to act. Obedient to Atahualpa's command, we stripped many temples of gold and silver to heap at the Pizarros' feet and ransom back our king. Instead of setting Atahualpa free as he'd promised, Hernando Pizarro had him killed. It's possible the Castilians drowned King Huascar too; and because of them, young Toparaca died."

Despite Shali's determination to approach the matter calmly so he could reason with his cousin if Manco had objections to his plans, his eyes relit with growing heat as he recalled the treachery that had subjected the Incas to slavery. "The Castilians have raped our women, murdered our children and stolen so many of our possessions most of our noblemen are wandering around the land in rags. Not the lowest peasant wore rags or was hungry before these invaders came." Shali's words became softer as he spoke, though his voice was edged with hatred. "They've dragged the maidens of the sun from their convents and used them for pleasure. They've pushed old people into the streets and made their homes barracks. They've stabled horses in our temples. Our enemies think we're cowards for not resisting. We've done nothing because they've captured our kings and held them under the threat of death. They've forgotten we're a nation that made an empire of half this continent, not a deed accomplished by cowards. You're the last son of the royal house and now you're safe. We can throw their laughter back into their teeth on the points of our lances, if you'll allow us."

Shali paused to catch his breath. Though anger still ran like fire through him, he finished more quietly, "Every Inca in the land is willing to die to make Cuzco our capital again."

Manco looked past Shali a moment, as if he were considering the idea, then said, "I see our men have successfully detached my horse from that cart and are ready to march. We'll talk more about Cuzco when we're farther from this road."

Shali had no choice, but to obey his king. He went to inspect the ropes that bound the cavaliers' hands and ordered them tied together by loops around their necks. He didn't have to warn the prisoners an attempt to flee would strangle them. Finally, he gathered Wayra's reins and fell into step with Manco Capac, who was leading the copper-color horse he'd chosen.

Although Shali burned with wanting to resume their conversation, he had to wait until his king indicated the same desire. Shali took surreptitious glances at Manco from time to time as they walked and knew his royal cousin was giving the matter of Cuzco much thought. His own mind turned, as it often did, to memories of his dead wife and son.

Shali had loved Yupanqui all his life, it seemed. Even when they'd been children he'd often left games with other boys to keep her company. The boys had sometimes teased him for playing with a baby because Yupanqui was several years younger; but when her eyes, dark brown and gentle as a deer's, had looked adoringly at him, his heart had melted. As they'd grown older, his warmth for Yupanqui had become a flame singing in his being. The son they'd conceived possibly the first night of their marriage must have known how joyous the moment of their union had been for it seemed as if he'd smiled almost from his first breath.

When Shali had discovered their deaths, he'd felt as if madness, like an anaconda, was tightening its coils around him; and he'd almost been overcome with desire to butcher the Castilians the way Yupanqui and his son had been. Instead, Shali had fled to the Andes. The wind had sighed mournfully through the mountain spires and he'd thrown himself in the snow to weep until he was exhausted. The pressure of his grief had each day since swollen with anger; and like the molten rock inside the volcanoes that dotted the mountains, the heat of his anger had risen to a dangerous level. He'd become very short-tempered; and recognizing it wasn't wise for a man like him to be short-tempered, he'd struggled to contain his fury. It continued to glow redly at the edges of his spirit, always ready to leap out of control. His men knew it and walked carefully around him.

Shali's inner battle had recently begun to be complicated by his body's reminders that it had been used to making love and months had passed since the last time. He realized his passion would eventually grow into urges so powerful he'd be driven to seek a woman. But he didn't know, when that time came, how he could share such intimacy. An Incan man could take more than one wife—many of the nobles did—but Shali hadn't wanted anyone except Yupanqui. He recognized he wasn't the sort of man who could love more than one woman at a time; and he wondered how it would be possible to find physical release in another, when his love for Yupanqui hadn't faded even a little.

His soul seemed to cry silently into the mountains, "Yupanqui, how will I be able to love again when my heart is so full of you?"

When he heard Manco Capac begin to speak, he blinked rapidly, trying to clear his eyes of their bulging tears before he looked at his king.

"I tried to escape from Cuzco once," Manco was saying. "The Cañars, that tribe of savages my father had brought into the empire and had just begun to educate into some semblance of civility, found a kindred spirit in Juan Pizarro. I didn't know they were spying on me. When I'd managed to slip out of Cuzco, they told Pizarro. The Cañars, who are so wretched they've barely learned not to eat each other, led the Castilians to where I was hiding in the reeds. My brothers' murderers marched me back to Cuzco like a criminal so they could go on pretending to the Incas that orders Pizarro issued came from me."

Recognizing that Manco's bitterness matched his own, Shali declared, "None of us can know exactly what you've suffered, my lord; but every Inca feels your humiliations in his soul. We've all lost loved ones and want revenge. I for my wife and child—and my father."

"Shalikuchima honorably served my father, but he was my uncle and a friend to me as well. When I think of how he died, I feel like the Aztecs in the north, whom I'd always thought were a blood-thirsty people—I want the heart, alive and beating in my hand, of the man who lit that fire," Manco swore. "Multiply Shalikuchima's death by those of my family, the others in my court, my entire kingdom. Then you'll know how *I* feel."

"Our enemies, I've heard, are quarreling. Each wants Peru for himself to sack," Shali said.

"It's true," Manco confirmed. "Only the reports their priests must send back to their king across the ocean, fear of what he'll do if they fight among themselves and don't send him enough of our gold, are what keeps them from each other's throats. This is a propitious moment for me to have my freedom."

"Then you agree we should recapture Cuzco?" Shali asked. His heart seemed to stop beating while he awaited Manco Capac's answer.

Manco saw the fires that lit Shali's eyes and reminded himself not to allow passion to influence him into making a decision he might later regret. "If our siege would last overlong, not only the Castilians behind Cuzco's walls would be hungry. There would be famine through the land. Don't forget, our enemies have almost emptied our storehouses."

"We must starve them out of Cuzco before spring," Shali agreed, his mood becoming more subdued. "I've wondered if one of this horde of invaders would put aside his own ambitions and come to Cuzco with reinforcements for Juan Pizarro."

"If so, we might have to flee to the mountains and fight a different kind of war. Because we might not have the strength to stand and fight, we'd have to attack by surprise, do as much damage as possible, then escape before our losses become too great.'' Manco was relating the possibilities he'd considered many times during his long hours of imprisonment. ''I've thought Machu Picchu might serve us.''

Shali fell into thoughtful silence as he considered this city in the hidden valley north of Cuzco. He still was the governor of a province; Tumbez needed the protection of his men. His home was there; it was all he had left. He said slowly, ''I would hate to leave everything to live in the mountains. A lot of people depend on me.''

Manco sighed heavily. ''I have a *kingdomful* of people who depend on me. Retreating to Machu Picchu would be my last resort.''

Shali agreed, realizing the imperial army would have to have been decimated before they'd fight guerrilla style and Manco Capac would hide. Shali tried to imagine how many battles would first have to be lost to their enemies before that desperate decision would be made. The enormity of it was overwhelming. He was finally distracted from such appalling thoughts by the approach of a man he'd ordered to drop behind the group and watch for trouble.

''We're being followed by a band of Castilians,'' the scout informed him. ''I'm not sure if they know the king is with us or if they're just soldiers off duty looking for someone to rob in their spare time. There are more of them than there are of us.''

''Do they have horses?'' Shali asked.

The scout nodded, adding ominously, ''They're carrying crossbows and firearms.''

Shali's black eyes lifted to gaze thoughtfully at the mountains. The shadows of the Andes were lengthening with the approach of twilight. If they traveled much longer, it soon would be too dark to fight. ''We can't win a battle against soldiers with horses on open, level ground; but their horses would be at a disadvantage in the rocky foothills.'' His eyes narrowed as he turned to Manco. ''At Cuzco we would make good use of weapons we could capture now.''

''Let us find a place on that ridge and wait for them,'' Manco decided.

Because voices had a way of carrying far in the clarity of the mountain air, Shali dared not raise his to speak to the men. He leaped lightly onto a boulder and gave his instructions by a series of gestures. Without a word of assent or even a question, the Incas took their places.

The cavaliers still on the floor of the valley saw only that the Peruvians threading their way up the ridge disappeared one by one as they seemed to enter a canyon that formed a pass through the foothills. But as soon as Shali knew the Incas were out of sight of the valley, he dispatched several pairs of men to a slightly lower elevation. The rest of his soldiers hid between the rocks.

Having no idea the Incas knew they were following, never dreaming so small a band of Peruvians without firearms would dare turn and face them, the Castilians urged their horses up the shadowy slope. They were halfway to the canyon's mouth when they were surprised by the rattle of a rockslide.

The horses had been well-trained to ignore the roar of cannons, the scent of blood and gunpowder, even the screams of other horses wounded and dying; but fear of a landslide reached instincts deeper than training could penetrate. The chargers tried to turn. Their riders, pelted by stones, struggled fiercely to hold their mounts straight. Some of the horses half-reared in protest while others whirled, despite the cavaliers' efforts to stop them. The Castilians presented clear targets to the Incan marksmen hidden in the rocky ledges and a shower of arrows whined down from the crags. A horse, scrambling for solid footing in the loose stones, lost its balance and fell, its flailing hooves knocking down two others. All three riders tumbled among the stamping hooves. Several panicked chargers bucked until their riders were thrown. Then the animals, freed of their burdens, hastily chose their own way up the slope where Incas caught them.

When the Peruvians saw Shali's tall figure rise from between the boulders, lance in one hand, sword in the other, they caught up their own maces and spears and, letting out a wild cry, ran down the slope to attack their enemies. The Castilians, who still were mounted, were amazed that the Indians they'd thought cowards flung themselves against the powerful horses' legs to trip and confuse the animals. Others threw rope loops around the chargers' necks, while still more Incas attacked the cavaliers on foot.

Shali threw his lance, saw it bounce harmlessly off the armor of his intended victim then dashed closer to spring up and drag the soldier from his saddle. After one swing of his sword, Shali turned to see a cavalier, stooping on one knee in front of him, was aiming a pistol at Manco Capac. Shali hadn't time to do more that catch the back of the man's mail doublet and wrench him backward so the pistol discharged harmlessly at the Andes. Shali stepped onto the cavalier's shoulders; and raising his lance high, drove the point into his enemy's throat— the only place Shali could see that wasn't protected by armor. Shali stepped off the man, retrieved his lance and turned to leap at another enemy.

After the last Castilian had fallen, the Peruvians hurried to gather the weapons they'd won—swords, daggers and pikes as well as crossbows and pistols. Manco and Shali chose two other men then went to catch as many horses as possible. The Incas loaded the weapons onto the chargers; for since none except Manco yet knew how to securely sit a horse, they dared not chance riding the animals up the path through the canyon in the gathering darkness.

Shali was very satisfied with the afternoon's results. They'd not only rescued Manco Capac and captured the men escorting him; but they'd vanquished a patrol of Castilians, taken their horses and weapons; and few Incas had been lost. The echoes of Wayra's hooves, as he led her through the dusky canyon, joined the sounds the other horses made and together seemed like a drumroll heralding their triumph. During the battle, Shali had finally found himself free of grief over Yupanqui for the first time since her death. He also realized that his rising physical need for a woman had vanished. He lifted his head a little higher as he reflected on this. Perhaps the many battles he yet faced would finally give him relief from the pain of his loneliness and frustrated passion.

When the Peruvians made their way out of the last dark passage between the mountains, they finally saw in the valley below campfires the rest of the Incas had lit for the night. The lights were so many they looked like stars that somehow had been drawn to earth.

Manco Capac caught his breath in surprise at how many soldiers Shali had gathered to his cause. He stopped his horse to gaze at the scene a moment before he finally breathed, "The name of Shalikuchima yet brings the army, no matter how far our nation has fallen."

Shali looked up at his king. "It was my promise of bringing *you* back to lead them that rallied our people."

"We still don't have enough weapons or horses to fight our enemies on equal terms," Manco said regretfully.

"They know that, but are angry and eager." Shali paused and listened for a moment. Once their horses' hooves had stopped, he could hear other noises coming nearer. "It seems as if the sentries have already passed word of our arrival. I think some officers are coming to welcome you back."

Manco Capac nodded and urged his mount to resume following the path. He found himself wondering what he could say to his men; he wasn't really accustomed to being king. Having had two older brothers, Manco had never expected to inherit the crown; and after their and Toparaca's deaths, he'd been the Pizarros' prisoner with no chance to actually rule.

When they turned a bend and he saw not only a few officers and their aides, but a crowd of Incas carrying torches to light their way up the slope coming to greet him, he stopped the horse. He wasn't certain whether he should stay in the saddle or dismount. He found himself wishing he had his brother, Atahualpa's, poise and training. As the first line of torchbearers separated, Manco saw the girl he'd been planning to marry before he'd been captured. As Coraquenque came running toward Manco, he flashed Shali a smile of gratitude and swung off his horse.

Coraquenque's bright eyes lifted to meet Manco's at the same time she raised her hand to reveal the elaborately knotted gold and scarlet fringe that was his *borla,* his crown. Then Manco no longer puzzled over what his first act as king would be. He cast royal dignity aside and joyously threw his arms around her.

Watching them, Shali's dark eyes reflected the torchlight a moment then turned away. The pain silently shrieking through him told Shali he would need more than battles to ease his grief. He would need love.

chapter
2

Doña Cecilia Alava ran appraising eyes over the flower garlands festooning the veranda railings, the gaily painted lanterns strung from ornamental trees, the assortment of tables, chairs and cushioned benches and inwardly sighed. Rianna had so eagerly planned this party to celebrate her seventeenth birthday and Francisco's homecoming, but none of the noble families had chosen to attend. Cecilia had warned her daughter not to waste her invitations, but Rianna couldn't—or wouldn't—understand, though every duke, marques and lady in King Charles' court wore gems purchased from Agustín Alava and he was wealthier than many of his noble patrons, blood defined their place in Madrid's society. The Alavas were commoners, however successful Augstín was. The tables in the Alava rose garden dripped with exquisite lace, sparkled with the finest crystal and china, bore the heaviest silver service; and despite the buffet's being laden with foods the equal of King Charles' banquets, none of the nobility had come except Alonso Falla, son of the Earl of Avila, Francisco's friend since childhood.

Cecilia had sometimes wondered what her oldest son saw in Alonso. She'd never had much affection for him as a boy and even less since.

For a while, Cecilia had worried that Alonso's penchant for gambling, drinking and consorting with low women would lead Francisco astray. Just when it had begun to appear her son was growing as rakish as Alonso, Francisco had suddenly decided to embark on another kind of adventure. He had joined the cavaliers seeking fame and fortune in Peru. Although she and her husband hadn't been enthusiastic about Francisco's decision, they were relieved at this seeming confirmation he was merely sowing wild oats before he'd settle down. After three years in Peru, Francisco had returned, at only twenty-three suddenly a more quiet, mature man than even they'd wanted. Cecilia often wondered what Francisco had experienced that had made his lips tighten into a hard line at unguarded moments, as if his mouth had grown so used to frowning he now had to make a conscious effort to relax it. Cecilia remembered how close Francisco always had been to Rianna and fervently hoped the renewed contact with his sister would help erase some of the shadows Peru had gathered in his amber eyes.

"Don't you think Rianna should put her cap back on?" Agustín asked.

Cecilia looked up at her husband then across the garden at her daughter. Rianna was seated near the fountain on a cushioned bench, her azure gown looking like a circle of the noon sky that had fallen to embrace her. Although it was evening and the stars and moon were all that lit the heavens, it seemed to Cecilia that Rianna carried the sun with her whatever the hour. The light from a lantern bobbing in the rose-scented breeze touched Rianna's tawny eyes with gold flecks and made a gilt crown of her burnished hair.

Cecilia squeezed her husband's arm. "Is this really an evening for her to be so modest?"

That Agustín's eyes drew more pleasure from the sight of their daughter's richly shining curls than even from the rarest golden diamond, he couldn't deny. But instead of agreeing, he sighed. "I suppose she *has* waited long enough for this occasion. I don't want to spoil it with a reprimand, however gentle, though she's flaunting her beauty."

"She's truly unaware of how lovely she looks tonight," Cecilia denied. "See how her eyes always follow Francisco. She thinks of this party as his, not hers."

Agustín's hand on his wife's waist, tightened briefly in affection;

and she moved a fraction closer to his side. She didn't need to glance up at him to know his lips were softened by a smile, his eyes warmed by love. He was proud of their children, easier on them than she was.

The Alavas had had their first son, Francisco, after only one year of marriage; and they'd happily anticipated adding to their family at the same pace. But fate had decided differently. Rianna had been born six years later, Jacinta after another three; and the Alavas had waited a long five years for Carlo. Cecilia had feared that her children, so widely spaced, would have little in common; but her worries had been needless. The children had always been close in spirit though separated by years, as if the tardiness of each baby's arrival had made it more precious to the others. Rianna and Francisco had been particularly devoted, Francisco having immediately become his sister's companion and protector, easily graduating to confidant and hero.

Unaware of her father's scrutiny or her mother's contemplation, Rianna hadn't even noticed several thick locks of her hair had slipped from their restraining pins and fallen over her shoulder. She was so used to the rebelliousness of her curls the sensation of their tumbling loose often went unmarked. Her eyes were on Francisco's tall figure as he moved among the guests. She, too, recognized he had changed in Peru and she wondered what had happened to him there.

Rianna had barely passed her sixteenth year when she'd begun to plan her next birthday party. It wasn't because she'd been anxious to be older; in Madrid in 1540 a girl of sixteen was considered a woman ripe for marriage. It was that the Alavas had received a letter from Francisco announcing he planned to return on the next ship that left Lima and would arrive somewhere around Rianna's birthdate. Rianna had sorely missed Francisco and Doña Alava had been right when she'd concluded that her daughter's plans for this elaborate party were more to celebrate Francisco's homecoming than her birthday. Yet, when Francisco had arrived a week earlier than Rianna had dared hope, he'd seemed almost like a stranger even to her.

Studying Francisco's profile as he spoke with a guest, Rianna wondered again what Peru had done to him. It had made him leaner, she observed as her eyes moved from his face to his burgundy velvet doublet that clearly outlined the narrow span of his waist. The Andean sun had darkened his skin and his brown hair was shot with red streaks. His speech was slower, as if he cautiously weighed his words before he spoke. There was something dark and hard behind his eyes that hadn't been there before he'd left Madrid.

Rianna looked down at the bolt of cloth in her lap, Francisco's gift from Peru, minutely studying the delicately embroidered material as if she could discover something about the land that had produced it. The brightly colored cloth was called vicuña, Francisco had said, a kind of wool so fine and silky only the Incan nobility was allowed to wear it. Rianna wondered if the fabulous birds in the design depicted living creatures or were images of Peruvian fantasy. She wished they were real. The gaiety of the embroidered flowers soothed her into hoping Francisco's attitude was merely typical of travelers, whom she'd heard often seemed temporarily changed when they returned home. Rianna ran a dainty fingertip over one of the repeating designs in the cloth she knew was of real animals—a golden lissome cat Francisco had called a jaguar with a silkily embroidered bird that looked like an eagle, but Francisco had called a condor, perched on the jaguar's shoulders. The design was an Incan family crest, but the material had somehow fallen into a Castilian trader's hands. Rianna speculated on what her seamstress might make for her of the cloth. A dress would be too gaudy to be fashionable, perhaps the lining of a cloak?

"That cloth does have a certain charm, though its designs are rather barbaric."

Rianna looked up to regard Alonso, who bent slightly to inspect the vicuña more closely. His cheekbones were rather flat at the sides giving his face a narrow look further emphasized by his short beard, which was carefully clipped to a point at his chin. His mustache curved down past the corners of his mouth. Though his face was handsome, the effect was marred, in her opinion, by a certain coldness, a calculating look in his eyes that made her distrust him. Rianna often wondered if he purposely had his mustache cut to emphasize his lower lip, which was full and sensuous. Annoyed that Alonso seemed to be criticizing her brother's choice, she replied, "*I* think it's beautiful."

His lashes raised and brown eyes regarded her with a penetrating gaze, as usual, making her feel as if he missed not even the most fleeting expression that passed her face. "There's no question about its beauty," Alonso said. "I just wonder what use it can be to you,

who are so fragile in stature and features, like one of these roses." He
swept off his dark green velvet hat with an exaggerated gallant flourish
and held out a pale pink rose Rianna recognized as having been
plucked from one of the silver bowls on the tables.

Reminding herself Alonso meant only to compliment her, Rianna
accepted the flower graciously and didn't remark on its origin. When
she looked up at him with eyes like sun-warmed honey, he felt a thrill
of desire run through him. He was disappointed when she said with
seeming innocence, "I was considering having this cloth made into a
gown. I was thinking the fringe edging would make wonderful trim."

Alonso concluded that Rianna's seemingly excellent taste in fashion
must be due to her seamstress's devotion; for she appeared, after all,
to have what was in his mind a peasant's tawdry sense of color. He
said coolly, "I hardly think a gown of that cloth would become you."

As if she didn't recognize his disapproval though she was deliberately trying to pique him, Rianna replied, "Maybe a cloak with a satin
lining in bright red. I do get rather tired of the dull colors women are
wearing these days."

Alonso ran a hand through his light brown waves and couldn't bear
not remarking, "Feminine fashions are designed to gently enhance a
lady's beauty, not to shout it immodestly to the world."

"Rianna could wear one of Atahualpa's feathered cloaks and never
seem brazen," Francisco's quiet voice came from Rianna's side.

She turned to look up at her brother and smile. She extended her
hand, inviting Francisco to sit on the bench as she gathered her skirt
closer, a gesture Alonso enviously noticed she hadn't offered him.
"Tell me about Atahualpa and his cloaks," Rianna urged Francisco.
"Are they really woven of feathers from birds like these?" She
pointed to a flock of parrots embroidered on the cloth in her lap.

"Atahualpa is dead," Francisco said solemnly. He seated himself
then quickly added in a lighter tone, "Those are parrots. The mantles
and headdresses worn by Incan kings for special occasions were
sometimes made of parrot feathers, often birds like quetzals and
scarlet ibises, even cockatoos and macaws. They are gorgeous things."

"Peru seems so far away, so alien to me. Tell me about it so I can
imagine what your life there was like," Rianna begged.

The light in Francisco's eyes suddenly was extinguished as he remembered the experiences that had driven him home—the callous treatment of the Incas he hadn't been able to bear watching, lest participate in.

Recognizing the darkness that seemed to again be overwhelming her brother, Rianna hastily asked, "What are the Incan Indians like? How do they look? I've heard they're savages."

Wanting to say it was his own countrymen who were savage to the Incas, instead, Francisco gathered his thoughts and decided to describe a Peru he anticipated no one would see again—the Incan empire before the Castilians had arrived.

"The people are, on an average, taller than we," he said. "They're dark of hair and eye, but their skin is lighter than mine is now. They're very civilized. Their royal court was, I'm sure, as refined as any in Europe, though different." Warming to the subject, Francisco's tone became more enthusiastic. "I learned some of the language. It's very eloquent and musical to the ear."

"Do say something in it," Rianna begged.

Francisco told her in Quechua how glad he was to be home then added, "I spoke as the Incan nobility would, which is more elegant than common speech; but even the conversations of the peasants are very polite and discerning, pleasantly melodious."

"You returned with little of value," Alonso commented, remembering the stories he'd heard of the Incas' fabled wealth.

Francisco frowned. "I have all I need in Madrid," he answered coolly.

Noting Rianna's tension, he quickly went on, "The tales you've heard about the abundance of precious metals and gems are true." He paused, thinking how Atahualpa had filled a room seventeen by twenty-two feet almost nine feet deep with gold plus a smaller room twice over with silver to ransom his freedom and had been killed on Hernando Pizarro's order, though for appearance's sake, a trial had been held. Francisco realized the darkness had again entered his eyes and was alarming Rianna, so he shook himself free of such thoughts and said, "When the Castilians' horses wore down their shoes and the Peruvians had no iron to make new ones, silver shoes were made: the metal was that common. The Incas don't have churches as we do, but they have magnificent stone temples. The temple of the sun at Cuzco had a frieze of solid gold running around its perimeter. One of the interior walls was lined with gold carved into a sunburst; so when the sun rose on the dawn of the solstice, it fell through the doorway to shine on the sunburst side. The reflections lit the whole interior. The temple of the moon had a wall covered with silver.''

"I wonder how it would feel to own a wall made of gold," Alonso breathed, his dark eyes gleaming with avarice.

"Ask King Charles. He could have several made with all the ingots the Pizarros have so far sent him from Peru," Francisco said disgustedly.

"The gold was *melted*?" Rianna exclaimed.

Francisco nodded. "I saw many beautiful objects cut up, put in a smelter and turned into bars.''

As Francisco went on to talk about the formal gardens at Cuzco's royal palace, the decorative figures of llamas and alpacas made of solid gold placed along flower-bordered paths, a fountain generously set with emeralds from Ecuador, Alonso didn't think of the beauty Francisco and Rianna visualized, but of how he would like to get his hands on such wealth.

Alonso's mother and sister's incessant complaints about his extravagance would be silenced if he had even a small portion of the wealth Francisco was describing. Alonso hated his carping sister. He knew she'd been jealous of his title from the day she'd realized her place as a daughter was inferior to his as a son's. He would inherit the title and she would have to be content living on his largess unless she married well. How could she find a rich count or marques to wed, Alonso had sneered, when she was ugly and ill-dispositioned? Alonso thought his sister could marry a king, despite her personality, if she had Rianna's face and figure, that gloriously golden hair. Alonso had wished many times Rianna had blood suitable for a nobleman's wife. He'd desired her from the moment her childish body had first begun to hint of womanly curves.

Francisco had always thought him to be a friend while Alonso, five years his senior, had really enjoyed Francisco's looking up to him as younger boys do with older ones, especially when one was the son of a merchant, the other of an earl. At an age when Alonso's amusement at Francisco would have lessened, his interest had been caught by

Rianna's budding beauty; and he'd seemed to remain Francisco's friend while he'd wondered if he could seduce Rianna.

It had delighted Alonso to introduce Francisco to the vices available to noblemen at exclusive clubs and gambling salons. But where Alonso had anticipated a comedy of Francisco's getting drunk and foolish, Francisco had been wiser than his years in his cautious drinking. Alonso, ever hopeful of supplementing his allowance, had taught Francisco to play cards; but it had been Alonso who had lost. When Francisco finally declined to play with Alonso, saying it wasn't seemly to win so much from a friend, Alonso had turned to other, less scrupulous gambling partners. Alonso was galled to owe Francisco so large a debt he hadn't been able to repay it since before Francisco had gone to Peru. He also envied Francisco's easy charm that made most women practically beg to be bedded.

Alonso's sister, aided by their mother, had meanwhile continued to rant about his debauchery and spending until his father had added his complaints to theirs—as if he hadn't set the example Alonso had followed from the first. Only a few days before the party, Alonso's father had warned, if he didn't change his ways, he would be disowned. Alonso'd had to humiliate himself by pleading with his father and had obtained only one concession. If he repaid at least Francisco, whom the earl thought was Alonso's friend, the earl would accept this as a token of his son's good intentions. Alonso had been thinking hard about how to raise the impossible sum.

As he half-heard Francisco's description of a civilization that regarded its wealth as decorative, Alonso knew Francisco mourned the loss of the statues and carvings being turned into ingots. Francisco didn't have to think of how their value could save him from financial ruin and social disgrace, Alonso thought angrily. Alonso would gladly light the smelters if he could claim Incan treasure for himself.

It would be convenient in several respects, Alonso was thinking as he gazed down at Rianna's creamy shoulders, if the Alavas could be tumbled from the pillars of their respectability in a way that would make it impossible for him to repay Francisco, if the Alavas were stripped of their prosperity so Rianna would be available to him without the necessity of marriage. There was no force in the land Alonso could think of so powerful it could sweep away an entire family's fortune without a chorus of voices rising in outraged indignation. No force in the land except the king himself—he had no reason to punish the Alavas—or the inquisitor's tribunal . . .

Alonso's thoughts were distracted by the rattle of tambourines, a rush of clicking castanets as a troupe of colorfully garbed gypsies paraded into the garden. Surprised, he glanced at Francisco, who was looking questioningly at Rianna.

"Do you remember, Francisco, when you were twelve and I six? I wandered away from your care and you found me in a gypsy camp?" Rianna's face was alight with her recollection. "You'd feared the gypsies would carry me off: but, instead, they fed and entertained us until Father and his men arrived."

The darkness that had again gathered in Francisco's face suddenly vanished to be replaced by a smile as boyish as it had been eleven years ago. "We had a wonderful time by their campfire. You remembered and so hired gypsies to entertain us tonight?"

Rianna nodded. "It was one reason I planned this party for the evening and in the garden."

Francisco put his arm around Rianna and hugged her. The evils being done in Peru were suddenly far away. "This is just what I needed, Rianna. You're an angel to have thought of it."

Their parents, standing together under a nearby arbor covered with roses, noted Francisco's smile and, filled with gladness, caught and squeezed each other's hands.

The Alavas and their guests watched several gypsies juggle an assortment of unlikely objects while others did acrobatic tricks. After this performance, a woman with a miscellany of dogs amazed her audience with her animals' repertoire. Then, while wine was being refreshed in crystal goblets, the acrobats took up musical instruments and began to thrum the sensuous beat of these freedom-loving people that was exotic to ears used to more restrained melodies.

A young woman in a peasant's blouse and a profusion of ruffled skirts, none matching, suddenly whirled out of the shadows and spun in consecutive turns around the little fountain where the guests had clustered. As abruptly as she had appeared, she stopped whirling and stood as motionless as a statue, her arms upraised, her eyes lowered. The other gypsies as suddenly stopped playing their instruments; the garden was hushed, waiting. A rhythmic clicking sound began, at first slowly then increasing in tempo, as the girl raised her dark eyes to gaze for a moment at Francisco. Each step she took with her little boots stamping rhythm brought her nearer the bench where Rianna and Francisco sat. Though the Alavas' guests assumed it had been arranged that the girl dance for the couple the party honored, Rianna alone knew the gypsy had chosen to dance for Francisco.

Rianna glanced at her brother's face to see if he were offended at being singled out; she was surprised at the expression he wore. His smile had changed from boyish pleasure to something more manly; and his eyes, lit to deep amber streaks, were avidly watching the girl's sensuous movements, the glimpses of long, shapely legs as her skirts lifted when she swished her hips, the tightness of her blouse against her bosom as she clapped her hands.

Although Rianna too watched the dancer, she realized Francisco desired the girl. The gypsy knew the silent message Francisco's eyes were sending: it was what the dancer sought. Rianna, who had never had the chance to even kiss a man, felt a mixture of emotions. She was envious of Francisco for knowing the sensations of love at the same time she was glad his reaction was proof he'd finally forgotten whatever had so troubled him about Peru.

At the end of the dance, the gypsy plucked the rose she'd worn in her hair, kissed it and tossed the crimson blossom to Francisco. He caught it with a husky laugh then, remembering who sat at his side, looked embarrassedly at his sister.

Rianna smiled and mischieviously commented, "I'm sorry I'm just a girl, who's forced by convention to be proper. A man can do what he pleases."

Francisco's eyes melted with sympathy. "My little sister has left childhood behind and now is a woman who wants love," he said quietly.

"Your little sister has no suitors as handsome as you," Rianna joked.

Francisco put the rose in her hand. "One will come for you, Rianna. Only too soon you'll leave our home for one of your own."

Rianna returned the flower. "The gypsy meant her kiss for *you*, not me," she said saucily. "I suppose one day I'll catch a flower that holds a kiss for me or, even better, will receive the kiss directly from my—''

She stopped, distracted by a gypsy woman walking across the open space toward Jacinta.

''It is only right that a young lady so lovely should have her fortune told on this anniversary of her birth,'' the gypsy's voice floated across the perfumed air.

Realizing the woman had mistaken her sister for herself, Rianna began to rise. Then, deciding Jacinta might be amused by having her palm read, Rianna again sat down. Jacinta could tell the gypsy afterward it was Rianna's birthday.

Jacinta had raised her head to look beyond the fortune teller's shoulder and learn what Rianna wanted her to do so she didn't notice the gypsy's face suddenly pale as she stared at the girl's open palm. After Jacinta realized Rianna was signaling her to allow the fortune teller to continue, she returned her attention to the gypsy only to have the woman lay her hand back in her lap.

''You are not the girl who is celebrating her birthday,'' the gypsy said.

''My sister doesn't mind if you read my palm first,'' Jacinta answered. ''My father will pay you for reading anyone's palm here who wants you to.''

''I cannot see your future,'' the gypsy declared then hastily added, ''It is that way sometimes. The veil is not easy to withdraw for some people.'' At Jacinta's perplexed look, the woman straightened, again picked up her hand and pressed it. ''Maybe I am getting old and my sight clouded. Do not worry about this and spoil your evening,'' she assured before laying Jacinta's hand back in her lap and turning away. The gypsy pulled her ragged shawl more closely around her shoulders and ran her eyes over the crowd until she located Rianna.

Rianna watched the gypsy, who seated herself in the place Francisco had vacated. The woman's eyes closed tightly and Rianna had the impression that the gypsy had momentarily removed herself from the party simply by shutting her eyes. When the woman again regarded Rianna, she seemed weary.

''Why didn't you read my sister's palm?'' Rianna inquired curiously.

The woman shook her head as she quickly took up Rianna's hand.

"I told her I cannot see the future for some people—it is nothing—do not worry. Let me see if I can do better with yours." Although the gypsy didn't want to relate all she could perceive in Rianna's future, she peered at the girl's palm, industriously discerning what she *could* tell Rianna. At least there was *something* in this girl's future she dared mention. She kept her eyes on Rianna's small hand as she made decisions no one could know except herself.

"There is a time of trouble ahead for you. It will begin soon." At Rianna's slight tension, the gypsy fervently added, "Though the problems coming will tax you dearly, you will be equal to them. I promise you this. Remember, golden eyes, the evil *will* pass." More quietly she continued, "You will, in the midst of this trouble, find the man you are to love and who will love you. He will truly be your heart's desire and you his."

A little breathless at this revelation, Rianna asked, "Is he at this party?"

The gypsy shook her head. "You will have to travel far to find your love." The fortune teller took Rianna's face in her hands so she could look closely into her eyes. "He will not be the kind of man you may have dreamed of because he is a kind of man you have not ever seen before. But he is more a man, more true a love than you can imagine now. *Remember this through the darkness ahead,*" she said with quiet passion.

"Can't you tell me anything more about the trouble you think is coming?" Rianna asked a little fearfully.

The gypsy shook her head even while she wished that warning the girl *could* help her and those she held dear. The fortune teller released Rianna and stood up, preparing to turn away. Her gaze fell on Alonso, who had, along with the others, approached more closely. At the sight of him, all gentleness, every trace of kindness drained from her face along with her blood.

She stared at him for a long moment before she cried, "Evil one! Demon! A curse on you, misbegotten dung of the devil!" Then the gypsy spat full in Alonso's face.

She whirled away, shouting in her own language to the other gypsies, who hastily gathered their belongings. The fortune teller caught up the two smallest of her dogs and whistled the others to her heels.

She turned to flash Alonso one more withering look and vowed, "No priest will be able to give your soul peace for you will not dare confess the truth even to a holy man!"

Then she stalked after the other gypsies into the darkness, leaving the Alavas' guests shocked and silently staring after her, many of them piously crossing themselves to ward off whatever evil the fortune teller had brought to the party.

Rianna gazed at the darkness while the gypsy's promise repeated in her mind. *The evil will pass.* What evil, Rianna wondered, would befall her? Why had the woman cursed Alonso? Why hadn't she read Jacinta's palm? Rianna didn't realize she was trembling until she felt Francisco's strong arms circle her. She pressed her face against his shoulder. "What did I do by engaging those people?" she whispered. "I thought they would be entertaining. What have I done?"

Francisco alone was close enough to hear her and he tightened his grasp. "Don't blame yourself, Rianna. It was that foolish old gypsy's whim to upset us with her act. You must not take her seriously. Please, just think of the acrobats and jugglers. Remember the music and the dancer. We have our own musicians. They'll play for us now and the incident will be thought of tomorrow as a curiosity."

"I'm afraid to think of tomorrow or any future," Rianna admitted.

Francisco held her away from him so he could look into her face. "If you must think of her predictions at all, remember what she said about your finding the man who will love you. It's the only part that can be true. No one has to be a fortune teller to recognize a girl like you must deserve the love of a very special man. Didn't I say it myself before the gypsies arrived?"

Rianna nodded and Francisco released her into their mother's hands. Then he turned to signal the strolling musicians to begin a tune that held no hint of the gypsy music's beat. That done, he turned to Alonso, who was scrubbing his face with a handkerchief.

"I apologize, Alonso, for my family. We had no idea such a thing would happen," Francisco said anxiously.

Alonso nodded as he continued wiping his cheek, but he was wondering if the gypsy *had* read his thoughts. Unnerved and wanting everyone to forget the incident as quickly as possible, he thought furiously about how he might distract them. As Alonso put away his handkerchief, his fingertips touched something he'd secreted in his sleeve that gave him an idea.

"I was waiting for the right moment to give Rianna my gift. Maybe this would be the best time so she can forget what just happened, so we all can think of something more pleasant than that gypsy hag," Alonso said. He raised Rianna's hand to his lips. "Please think of this as something to brighten your eyes tonight and at any time complement your beauty."

As Alonso slipped a ring studded with sapphires and pearls on Rianna's finger, he regretted the action more than anyone could guess. It was one of his sister's rings that he'd stolen and planned to sell in the morning.

"It's beautiful, but far too costly for me to accept!" Rianna breathed.

"You must keep it," Alonso said while he wished he could snatch it back. He decided there was nothing for him to do now except carry out the plan he'd been thinking of when the gypsy had turned to curse him.

chapter
3

Through the open bedroom window Rianna could hear her father's voice drifting upstairs from the library. Cecilia's light laughter answered and Rianna could visualize her mother sitting across from Agustín, while she embroidered. Footsteps crossing the room were followed by the gentle squeak of the window being closed, the snap of the latch. Rianna was sure Carlo had closed the window against moths attracted by the candlelight. Though he'd probably been practicing his sums as he often did after dinner, he was always willing to lay them aside; but Jacinta was learning to knit and dared not pause from counting stitches before reaching the end of a row. Francisco had gone out with Alonso, but he seemed less interested, since he'd been in Peru, to spend evenings at amusements. After the downstairs window had been closed, Rianna couldn't follow the activities of her family; because few noises traveled through the thick walls of the house. The only sound Rianna heard was the friendly hum of the garden crickets through her own open window.

Rianna sighed, looked again at the sketch she'd made of a cloak and wondered if she should bring this design to her seamstress in the morning. Sorting through a sheaf of drawings, she frowned, put them all down and retrieved the bolt of vicuña that had slipped to the carpet at her feet. The cloth was so beautiful she wanted to be absolutely certain about her choice of the garment to be cut from it. Maybe it would help her decision to drape the material around her in some semblance of the cloak, she speculated and got to her feet.

After Rianna had arranged the bright cloth around her shoulders and tossed a fold over her head to simulate a hood, she looked up at the mirror and was surprised at her own reflection. The vicuña's exotic white, red and black pattern, its gold background deepened her creamy complexion almost to beige, brought her cheekbones into sharper clarity and heightened the honey tint of her eyes almost to gilt. Without realizing she was making the same gesture as a Peruvian woman, Rianna pinched her makeshift hood closer under her chin, smoothed its folds so it clung more tightly to her head. Fascinated by her reflection, she turned away to get the necklace Francisco had also brought. After she'd fastened the circle of gold birds at her throat, she looked again in her mirror. The feeling that she was staring at another woman was even stronger now; and like a little girl playing make-believe, she pretended she was an Inca, perhaps a princess or one of the maidens of the sun Francisco had described.

A poignant feeling washed over Rianna. She couldn't think of the Incas without remembering some of the things Francisco had seen in Peru he'd finally begun to describe to his family during the month since her birthday party. Rianna knew Francisco had avoided telling them the worst of it because she'd once overheard him talking to Alonso more frankly. Francisco had described Hernando Pizarro's first meeting with the Incan king, Atahualpa.

Atahualpa had been closeted due a religious fast and had bid Pizarro to go to a nearby town, Caxamalca, and make himself and his men comfortable for the night. Atahualpa had promised he would come the next day unarmed to meet with Pizarro and talk in earnest. Though Pizarro had agreed, Francisco had been stunned when, once in Caxamalca, Pizarro had commanded the men to set up cannons around the plaza. Persuaded it was a precautionary measure, Francisco had worked through the night with the other men to carry out Pizarro's orders. The next day when Atahualpa, splendidly adorned, had arrived with a procession so elaborate it numbered several thousand Incas,

43

Pizarro had waited until they all were in Caxamalca's plaza then opened fire. The helpless Peruvians had only been able to gather around their king and shield him with their own bodies while the guns had fired volley after volley into their midst. Between rounds, the Castilians had charged their horses into the Incas, slashing and stabbing with sword and pike. In less than an hour, all the Incas except Atahualpa were dead. The only Castilian suffering even a minor wound had been Pizarro himself when he'd gestured with outflung hand warning his cavaliers not to kill Atahualpa, but to take him prisoner. One of his men waving a sword had accidently cut his leader.

Francisco had told his family he'd seen such terrible things he'd regularly complained even to Pizarro himself. He'd threatened to bring charges against the Pizarros to the royal court, against Friar de Valverde for absolving the Castilians in advance of Atahualpa's ambush and later officiating at the burnings of Incas convicted of heresy. Francisco saw no rationale in charging Peruvians with heresy. They'd never even heard of Christianity before the Castilians had come; and right or wrong, the Incas had their own religion, Francisco had reasoned. He'd argued they should be persuaded to Christianity, not put to death.

Rianna sank to sit on the floor in front of her mirror as she reflected on the reasons Francisco had returned to Spain sooner than he'd planned. His complaints and warnings of charges had alarmed the conquistadors. Because Francisco hadn't traveled to Peru as part of the military, but by his own choice, as many of the adventurers had, he couldn't be silenced with martial orders. He and a number of other men, who wouldn't take part in the plundering of Incan cities, had been threatened by more devious means. One of them had been found beaten almost to death in a shadowy lane, another's feet had been burned off when he'd been caught in the stream of molten gold from an ''accidently'' overturned smelting pot. Afraid to leave Peru openly, Francisco and his friends had trekked north through the jungles and mountains to Panama, where they'd clandestinely boarded a ship bound for Seville.

Reflecting on how Francisco had already decided on the perilous journey to Panama when he'd written to his family merely that he'd planned to take the next ship bound for Spain, Rianna was awed at his courage. It was no wonder his eyes had looked haunted and he'd been so thin when he'd arrived home—he'd nearly starved in the mountains of Ecuador.

Rianna didn't hear horses entering the courtyard at the front of the house or the march of feet through the downstairs hall. Her first inkling anything was wrong was when her bedroom door flew open and three soldiers stood on her threshold. She was too amazed to move.

One of the men, a sergeant, ran his eyes appraisingly over Rianna, taking in the exotic pattern of the cloth still draped around her shoulders, the Incan necklace that lay against her bosom and commented to his companions, "It seems the accusations weren't so wild, after all. Here's proof enough of pagan influence." He nodded to one of the men, who marched across the room to catch Rianna's arm and pull her to her feet.

Insulted by this rough treatment, she demanded, "What are you talking about? Release my arm! Get out of my chamber!"

The sergeant turned away as if he hadn't heard Rianna. "Take her to the others. Make sure to bring that pagan garb," he snapped and left the room. Rianna heard his footsteps going down the hall, other doors opening and slamming as he checked the rest of the bedrooms for occupants.

She glared at the soldier holding her captive then at the other who stood in the doorway. "What is this about?" she demanded. "My father will have you in irons within the hour if you don't take your hands off me!"

The soldier holding her said, "Your father has more pressing problems." He touched one disk of her necklace then ran his fingertip suggestively along the edge of her bodice as he added, "It's such a waste that you little pagans are always so pretty."

Shocked at this stranger's audacity to actually caress her bare skin, Rianna slapped away his fingers with her free hand. Stunned that he raised his arm as if he would strike her, she flinched back.

"Never mind that. Take her downstairs," the watching soldier directed with an impatient gesture.

The man holding Rianna, obviously disappointed, pushed her roughly toward the door.

Rianna went without further protest, naïvely confident that, when they got downstairs, her father would make the soldier release her, would blister these ruffian's ears with denunciations.

But when they reached the base of the steps, Agustín was nowhere in sight—not Cecilia, *any* of the Alavas. The library door was open, the room empty. Rianna caught a glimpse of her mother's overturned embroidery frame, Jacinta's knitting needles and basket of yarn scattered. As the soldiers pushed Rianna past the parlor, she noticed that room, too, was empty. A cold sensation flooded her, as if someone had tossed a basin of icy water over her head. She tugged against the soldier's grasp, tried to dig her heels into the floor.

Resistance was fruitless. The soldier merely picked Rianna up, threw her over his shoulder and, catching both her wrists in one hand while he wrapped his free arm around her legs, carried Rianna with less effort than he might have used lugging a wriggling lamb. Rianna's head hung down his back, his leather-woven doublet chafing her face as he strode through the entrance hall, which became a blur of soldiers seen through her helpless tears.

By now Rianna was terrified and the balmy night air made her feel as if she'd been dipped in ice. She struggled to keep her teeth from chattering as she heard, but couldn't see, her mother weeping, her father's outraged protests. There was a scuffling noise, a muffled thump then Cecilia's cry. Rianna caught her breath as she realized her father had tried to struggle with someone and had been knocked down.

Casting aside fear for herself, she renewed her struggle and begged, "Let me go to my parents!"

The soldier holding Rianna surprised her by obediently setting her on her feet. She whirled to see Cecilia bent over Agustín, who was sprawled on the cobbles. Rianna immediately threw herself on her knees beside her mother.

Cecilia looked up, wiped away tears with the back of her hand and, knowing Rianna was afraid Agustín was dead, breathed, "He's unconscious—that's all."

Rianna turned to look up at the nearest soldier and began, "What do you—"

Cecilia caught Rianna's hands. "You're just a girl. What can you do? See what happened to your father? I don't understand all this either, but we'll soon learn what it's about. Don't get hurt in the meantime.''

The two women were electrified by a scream that pierced the darkness outside the circle of light the torches cast. They turned to see a pair of soldiers dragging Jacinta's slight figure toward the stable. Jacinta was begging to be released. Rianna sprang to her feet only a moment ahead of Cecilia.

"What are you doing with my sister? You let her go!'' Rianna demanded, while Cecilia seemed frozen with shock.

"Where are you taking her?'' the sergeant called.

"She can tell us which horses to harness!'' the soldier shouted back, his voice half-laughing as if he were thinking of a private joke.

The sergeant looked thoughtfully at the soldier a moment then shook his head and gestured the man to continue on his way.

Jacinta's words tumbled out between sobs, "No, no! Get your hands away from me! Don't touch me! *No!*''

"God help us,'' Cecilia cried, poised as if to run after her youngest daughter. A nearby soldier caught her shoulder and pulled her back.

In that moment Rianna, realizing they intended to rape Jacinta, leaped forward. She ran only a half-dozen paces before a soldier threw both arms around her. Lifting Rianna off her feet, he dragged her backward. As she struggled against his grip, she glimpsed Carlo racing toward Jacinta.

One of the men ran after Carlo, caught his waist and swung him off the ground.

"*Madre Maria,*'' Cecilia gasped then sobbed, "He's only ten, Jacinta not even fifteen! *Dios!* What are you doing with my children, you *diablos*?''

The soldier slung Carlo over his hip and marched across the courtyard. Without a word, he tossed the still resisting boy into the well that fed the horse watering trough.

Cecilia gave a moan of despair and collapsed beside her unconscious husband.

Rianna, too overcome with shock for an instant to move, suddenly exploded into action. She swung around to face her captor and began kicking him. He didn't feel her slippered foot through his boots and laughed at her efforts. But when Rianna bit his hand so hard she tasted blood, he cried out an epithet and drew back his fist. She struggled to pull away. An explosion sounded from behind them and the soldier suddenly crashed to the cobblestones. Rianna raised incredulous eyes to see a pair of horses galloping into the courtyard. One of them stopped, but the other continued clattering toward her.

"Francisco!" Rianna breathed.

Francisco tossed away his smoking pistol and drew his sword while, cursing vehemently, he swerved his horse toward the men dragging Jacinta.

Carlo's fading cries still echoed hollowly from the well and Rianna bolted toward them. She threw her whole being into the race and her heart seemed to be hammering at her throat when she reached the well. Sobbing with each breath, she flung the bucket into the now silent darkness and gave the well's crank a savage spin. The rope snaked down, seeming swallowed by the blackness in the well as she peered in and cried frantically to her young brother to take hold of the bucket. There was no answer, not even a splash. She could see nothing, but the faint glimmer of water far below.

"Carlo, *niño,* please—" she wept. Then she turned, wringing her hands, to shout, "Francisco, help me! Carlo is drown—" Her cry caught midword when she saw the shadow on the courtyard's far wall, hideously magnified by the torches to ten times normal size, of Francisco's plunging from his horse. She was transfixed by horror as, in the wavering light, she saw one of the soldiers pulling a spear from the mound Francisco's body made on the cobbles. One of the servants, braver than the others, ran from the shadows to throw himself across Francisco as if to save his corpse from further abuse.

The scene shimmered before Rianna's eyes. She heard a distant soldier call to another to catch her. She couldn't move one slippered foot to flee. Rianna slowly sank to the cobblestones as consciousness escaped her.

When Rianna awakened, she was lying in a place so dark she was disoriented; and she reclosed her eyes, trying to remember what had happened. Earlier, she had been in her bedroom trying to decide whether to have a cloak made of the vicuña, she recalled. Then the soldiers—no! She started again, struggling to convince herself she'd spent the evening as usual, that she was lying on her own bed having unexpectedly fallen asleep and had a nightmare. But the same memories of the horror persisted—her father sprawled unconscious, her mother collapsed, Carlo's flailing arms as he plunged into the well, Jacinta screaming as she was dragged away, Francisco . . .

Rianna turned over to bury her face in the vicuña's soft folds and muffle the sobs tearing at her soul; but some part of her mind yet able to function quickly reminded she was near hysteria, that succumbing to it would make her truly helpless. She knew she had to focus her mind on anything at all except the grief and horror; and with a supreme effort to leash her emotions, she concentrated on what she might do to help herself.

She sat up, realized she'd been lying on a lumpy cot. It smelled of mold and worse. She swung her legs off and stood up, heard a rodent's squeak in the blackness that was the floor and hurriedly sat back down to draw up her legs, tuck her skirt hem tightly around her slippers. She didn't realize her shivering was caused by exhaustion and spent nerves; she assumed the cell was cold. She wrapped the vicuña around her shoulders and silently thanked the Incan nobleman who had lost it, Francisco for giving it to her. *No.* She couldn't bear to think of Francisco or any of her family yet.

"Where am I?" Rianna asked the darkness merely to hear a human voice, not expecting an answer.

As if the place had been awaiting her question, a chorus of calls came from other cells.

"You're in the dungeon!"

"The priests have taken you for roasting!"

"You'll burn—or stay here all your life—same as we!"

Now it was impossible for Rianna to deny the truth; she was being held by the dread Office of the Inquisition. She trembled even more, but she said in a voice held firm by bravado, "I don't have to be afraid. I'm innocent."

The voices jeered that, whether she was innocent or guilty, the end was the same; she would be burned at the stake or would rot in the dungeon. Most of the voices sounded as if their unseen owners were mad and repeated the threats over and over like an insane chant that was too muddled to keep rhythm. There was wild laughter, obscene suggestions that made Rianna glad her cellmate was merely a rodent. There was weeping, so hopeless her heartstrings were wrenched anew. She covered her ears with her hands to try to block out the sounds and, failing, knew that keeping her mind busy was all that could distract her.

This was what the gypsy had read in her palm, Rianna suddenly realized. But what about Jacinta in whose hand the gypsy had perceived nothing? Rianna rocked back and forth, moaning softly in despair for her sister, though she couldn't know if Jacinta was already dead like Fran . . . No, she must not think about either of them; she'd go mad if she did. She *must* concentrate on something else. What more had the gypsy said?

Recalling the woman's promise she would survive this evil, Rianna wondered if she *wanted* to live even if her family . . . She caught herself and turned her mind to another path. She would travel far away, the gypsy had promised. She would find love . . .

A door Rianna hadn't been able to see in the darkness began to open, the wavering light on its opposite side defining its location. She blinked at the silhouette of a man standing on the cell's threshold.

"Get up, Señorita Alava," the guard said. "Come with me."

A little comforted just to hear the sound of her name, to know she wasn't going to molder away until she was as mad as so many other prisoners sounded, Rianna swung her feet off the cot. She felt something soft and furry brush her ankle and, with a little cry, ran through the doorway.

The guard caught her hand to prevent her from going farther then, realizing why she'd run, said, "There are rats out here too, señorita."

Rianna shuddered and, afraid to look at the floor in the corridor and confirm his warning, not wanting to see her surroundings at all, she fixed her eyes on the dim passageway ahead and hoped she hadn't too far to walk. The guard's lantern guided Rianna through the corridor past a stout gate, down another passageway, up a dingy stairway and into a dimly lit office.

"Mama, Papa!" Rianna ran into her parents' arms. They huddled in a common embrace, Rianna so relieved her parents were alive she didn't notice their tears smearing both her cheeks.

"Get back. That's enough," the guard said gruffly and separated them.

"We have some questions, señorita."

Rianna, still holding her parents' hands, was chilled by the voice. She turned to regard its owner and faced a figure swathed in black robes, a bony, white face, a thin, tightly pursed mouth, dark, cavernous eyes. He looked nothing like the priests she'd known all her life. Most of them had been friendly, gentle and sympathetic. There had been only one priest she'd met, who had made her uneasy; and he'd been stern, though not unkind. But *this* man's eyes were as expressionless as a corpse's. He appeared pitiless, empty of all emotion. Rianna knew, though he was called a priest and for her family's sake as well as her own she would have to address him as such, neither he nor any of the men in this place were real priests. They'd long ago lost sight of God and betrayed their vows. She realized they weren't even men; they were monsters.

"I'm Father Nuñez. These are my assistants, Fathers Xavier and Domingo." He gestured toward two other black-robed figures standing in the gloom to the side of the room. Two more monsters, Rianna silently noted, but curtsied to them.

When Rianna turned to Nuñez, though her knees were stiff with inner rebellion, she knew she must greet him properly, prove she was pious. She genuflected and remained on one knee, though she couldn't utter a word.

Nuñez approached. His voice held not a question but a command. "Where did you get this cloth and this necklace?"

"Francisco . . ." Even to say her brother's name caused Rianna's tears to run down her cheeks and she said through trembling lips, "Francisco brought them from Peru as presents for me."

Nuñez tipped Rianna's face toward his, peered at her a moment then stepped away. "Get up, señorita," he directed. After she'd obeyed, he inquired, "What were you doing when the soldiers came to your house?"

Rianna brushed away her tears with a shaking hand and whispered, "I was in my chamber, wrapping the cloth around me in different ways trying to decide if it should be made into a cloak or—"

"Isn't it true you were kneeling before your mirror praying to a pagan deity?"

The inquisitor's words were knives slicing away what was left of Rianna's courage. She stared at him, too shocked by his accusation to immediately reply. From somewhere in the prison's recesses, a scream of exquisite agony came, drawn out so long it seemed as if the passing seconds turned into hours.

Cecilia breathed, "Holy Mother, is that Jacinta?"

Agustín sprang forward, his eyes ferocious as he caught Nuñez by the front of his robe. "Tell us that isn't our Jacinta," he demanded. *"Tell us!"*

The guard rushed to free the inquisitor of Agustín's grasp.

As Agustín withdrew to again stand beside his wife, he was afraid in that one action he'd sealed his fate. "I'm sorry, reverence," he said hastily. "I'm not myself. I never would do such a thing otherwise."

The inquisitor said nothing to Agustín. He looked again at Rianna. "Isn't it fact that your brother spoke against the church's treatment of the Incas, defended heretics?"

Thinking Francisco couldn't be harmed anymore, she lied, "I don't know." If she could have thought of more to add, she wouldn't have been able to say it. She shivered while another scream traveled through the passageway beyond the office door. She looked worriedly at her mother, who was leaning against her father's chest whimpering like a small, hurt animal. Rianna moved to their side and put one hand on each of their shoulders.

"That is *not* Jacinta." Rianna's eyes looked like topaz glowing in the sun as she repeated in slow, measured words, *"Jacinta is not being tortured."* Rianna wasn't sure the screams weren't her sister's. She inwardly prayed they weren't not only for Jacinta's sake, but their own as well. Someone being so tortured, Rianna was certain, must eventually confess anything.

Oblivious to the trio's emotional state, Nuñez resumed his inquiries. "Did your brother bring a number of idolatrous objects—a ring with a pagan deity worked into its setting, a pair of bracelets decorated with other heathen deities, even a small statue?"

"A ring with a setting like a sunburst? Bracelets engraved with birds? A statue of a llama, an animal the Incas keep flocks of as we do sheep?" Rianna asked in surprise. "What's idolatrous in those?"

"Did your brother give your mother a small, carved box containing a balm reputed to have magical powers, powers that come from Hell as all magic does?"

"Perfume is what the box holds, a scent such as the Incas use. Magic? That's nonsense!" Agustín cried.

"Then what would you say this is, if not the sacrifice resulting from a pagan ritual?" the inquisitor asked coolly.

The other priests turned away to get something from a cabinet. As they carried the thing into the lamplight, Rianna saw it was the corpse of a small animal. She looked away, her lips pressed so tightly together they were white.

"It looks like . . ." Cecilia whispered then leaned against her husband, unable to say more.

"It's our—it *was* our dog," Agustín said hoarsely. "He disappeared several days ago."

"Several nights ago was the full moon," the inquisitor pointed out. "That's a time for pagan rituals. Notice the carcass's chest cavity is devoid of its heart. I know such sacrifices are made by the savages of the New World."

"*No!*" Rianna whirled to face him. "Incas don't do that sort of thing!"

"How could she know unless she'd been tutored by someone who follows pagan rituals?" the black-robed figure named Domingo asked.

Another long, wavering scream came from the prison's bowels.

After it had faded, Xavier calmly suggested, "Perhaps this girl was taught *something,* but didn't truly understand she was being indoctrinated."

"You make my son sound like a Satan worshipper," Cecilia moaned.

"How can you say such—" Agustín began.

A door on the far side of the office suddenly opened and Alonso entered the room. He was wearing a wide doublet of brown velvet, its sleeve holes faced with fur, the sleeves of the jerkin beneath slit to reveal inner sleeves heavily embroidered with green and gold. His small cap was fur trimmed. Rianna was secretly glad Alonso had dressed so lavishly for he made an imposing figure she hoped might intimidate Nuñez. Alonso went directly to the inquisitor and genuflected, keeping his head respectfully lowered until Nuñez bid him to rise.

Alonso got to his feet and said earnestly, "Reverence, I came as soon as I could. There must be some mistake in this. These people can't be guilty of heresy. I've known them almost all my life."

"You are?" Nuñez prompted.

"Alonso Falla," Alonso answered, a little put out that he hadn't been recognized.

"Falla, the Earl of Avila's son?" Nuñez inquired.

"My father is the Earl of Avila," Alonso confirmed. He realized then that this priest was of a relatively minor rank in the hierarchy of the Inquisition. For all his airs, Nuñez wasn't close enough to the head inquisitor to know it had been Alonso himself, who had given the Alava name to the tribunal. Although Alonso was chagrined, no hint of this showed as he met Nuñez with as steady a gaze. Alonso had made a bargain with the head inquisitor that Rianna would be spared if he supplied evidence of the family's heresy. It appeared Nuñez had been told nothing about this; and Alonso, instead of merely pretending, *really* would have to plead Rianna's case. Resigned, he turned from Nuñez to the Alavas, taking their hands each in turn, murmuring reassurances before he again faced the inquisitor. With an attitude that held more than a hint of annoyance, Alonso began in a deliberately patient tone, "They are good, honest, pious people. I've *never* seen them do or heard them say anything that even resembled heresy."

"How would you explain the evidence?" Nuñez gestured toward Rianna's necklace, the cloth draped over her arm, the dog's mutilated carcass and the other items taken from the Alava home that were now laid out on a table.

"None of this proves a thing," Alonso said firmly.

Nuñez was as unimpressed as Alonso had expected him to be. The inquisitor recounted what had been in his report, which was the information Alonso had supplied—Francisco's speaking against the church while he'd been in Peru and siding with the heretic Incas, the changes in his attitude since he'd returned to Madrid. The Office of the Inquisition was convinced Francisco had become a pagan and had somehow persuaded his family to follow his heresy. Nuñez finished, "When Señorita Alava was arrested, she was wrapped in that cloth with mystical creatures and plants decorating it, wearing that necklace which incorporates a design of birds the Incas hold sacred. She was on her knees praying to a pagan deity.''

"But I *wasn't* praying!" Rianna declared. "If the soldiers had examined my room more closely, they would have seen the drawings I'd made of various garments. I was going to choose one of them and take it with this cloth to my dressmaker tomorrow. I only put on the necklace to see how it looked with the cloth as a background.''

Alonso gravely nodded his head. "Rianna had asked what I thought the material could be used for.''

"I didn't know the birds were a pagan symbol," Rianna denied. "I just thought they were pretty and I'm sure that's why Francisco gave me the necklace—or any of those gifts to the rest of us.''

As if Nuñez didn't believe one word, he turned to Alonso and resumed, "Being Francisco Alava's friend, surely you noted certain changes in his outlook since he returned to Spain. The sacrifice of a household pet is in itself damning.''

Alonso was silent a moment. It had been a stroke of genius to have killed the Alava dog that way for it seemed to be the tribunal's favorite piece of evidence; but if he intended to save Rianna and a portion of the Alava fortune for himself, he must think of some way to clear her of suspicion. Finally, he said, "I have to admit Francisco did seem different when he came home, but I assumed it was because living in so barbaric a part of the world must affect anyone. Francisco is dead now and we can't question him, but I don't think the rest of his family should be tried in his place—especially Rianna, who is as innocent as a newly baptized infant.''

"Pagans are clever in concealing their perfidy," Nuñez replied.

Alonso lowered his eyes as he tried to think of how he might convince the inquisitor. His gaze touched Rianna's hand, which, by chance, wore the ring he'd given her. Suddenly he knew what he could say. "I'm of noble blood, reverence; and the Alavas are commoners. It's most unusual for a nobleman to marry a commoner's daughter; yet Rianna is betrothed to me. That ring she's wearing is proof of our betrothal.''

For the first time since any of them had entered the room, Nuñez showed a hint of emotion. For the briefest moment, he looked startled; but he quickly said, "Show me the ring in question."

Rianna, so surprised she took a second to think of what ring they meant, hastily lifted her hand for Nuñez's inspection.

He knew at a glance the ring wasn't the sort of trinket a man might present a maid to seduce her, but he didn't want to accept the explanation. He slipped the sparkling circlet from Rianna's finger to examine it minutely. He noted the Falla's family crest stamped inside the band and couldn't deny it was an heirloom, certainly not an item to lightly give away.

While Nuñez was studying the ring, another cry of pain echoed hauntingly from the dungeons. Though none of the Alavas dared speak or even move, they were tormented by the same question—was it Jacinta suffering so hideously? If not, why hadn't she been brought to the inquisitor's office as her sister and parents had? The thought of Jacinta's death was a horror not diminished by those of Carlo and Francisco or the real possibility of their own, but each of them would prefer Jacinta dead to her being strapped to the torturer's table.

Agustín had no illusions about the way the Inquisition functioned. It had begun with religious fanatics blind to all, but their own narrowly circumscribed notions. Keeping a facade of holiness, they'd become steadily more powerful because no one dared oppose them. The unscrupulous took advantage of the Inquisition to rid themselves of enemies of all kinds, even relatives who had become troublesome. Agustín had known of such cases and the result had never been based on truth. Good and evil people alike had been burned at the stake because they'd been so shocked by fear and grief they'd been unable to think of a defense against even the flimsiest evidence. Others had found some means to convince the tribunal of their innocence though the evidence against them was damning.

Recalling how in his distraught state, he'd laid hands on Nuñez, Agustín inwardly berated himself. Nuñez's personal opinion could be all that would save any of them. But who had brought his family to such straits—a business rival, a worker or a customer? He'd been fair with competitors and workers; he'd gone out of his way to satisfy customers and thought he maintained their good will. If it was Francisco's refusal to slaughter Incas that had caused this, *whose* hand was long enough to stretch across the ocean from Peru; and why wouldn't Francisco alone have been arrested? Agustín thought he would choke with grief for Francisco; but he dared not think of his eldest son or Carlo either. He *must* find a way to save the rest of his family.

Agustín considered the possibility of admitting to heresy himself; but if he, as head of the family, confessed, the inquisitor might assume he'd contaminated his wife and daughter's religious beliefs. He had to do all he could to save any of the Alavas who might have a chance to escape this nightmare. Alonso offered Rianna salvation, if Nuñez could be convinced she, at least, had someone with political power on her side. A man in love would go to great lengths to defend or avenge his beloved. If such a man had access to the royal court, as Alonso did, his protests could be highly embarrassing to the Inquisition and Nuñez.

Agustín looked down at his wife. As if Cecilia knew his desperate thoughts, her head lifted; and her eyes met his. He read in their tearful depths the same conclusion as his—Rianna might be the only one in their family with a chance to survive.

Raising his eyes to Nuñez, Agustín said, "It was a great honor to my family to have the earl's son propose marriage to my daughter."

"He gave Rianna the ring only a month ago on her birthday," Cecilia forced herself to convincingly add. "We all were so happy at their betrothal."

Alonso addressed the inquisitor solemnly. "When a man of my station decides to wed, he discreetly looks into the character of the lady he's considering. But when his bride's social status is beneath his own, his investigation must be complete in every detail." He paused to let the inquisitor consider this truth then said in an insinuating tone, "I'm satisfied with my agents' reports about Rianna. Her character is without blemish and her piousness unquestioned—until now. You can be certain I shall carry my cause to the royal court and, if necessary, to Rome. I won't rest until Rianna is declared innocent of these charges, even if this tribunal. has already dispatched her spirit to God."

Although Nuñez's expression never changed, he didn't like to think of what would happen to him if this girl was cleared of charges *after* she'd been burned at the stake under his orders. He decided he'd better release her.

"The Office of the Inquisition will continue its investigation," Nuñez warned.

"You'll find nothing to implicate Rianna," Alonso promised.

"If you're certain you're completely convinced of her innocence . . ."

"I am," Alonso insisted.

"Then I'll release the lady in your custody while the evidence is further examined. If anything suspicious is brought to light, she'll be taken back to this office—and you along with her," Nuñez cautioned.

Rianna stared incredulously at the inquisitor for a moment then turned to look at her parents. Tears again sprang to her eyes. How could she leave them in this place? Her father's eyes held a stern message to be silent. She hurried to embrace her parents; and as she did, she whispered that she and Alonso would find a way to free them as well.

Agustín and Cecilia clung to their daughter for as long as they dared. They didn't want Rianna to think it might be their farewell.

When Rianna stepped through the prison's outer doors, the sky was brightened by morning. She remembered that the dungeon, even the inquisitor's office, gave no hint of night or day. The prison was a world of its own, dark and gray, filled with pain and sorrow. The breeze was perfumed by flowers, green things growing, the cozy smoke of fires and breakfasts being cooked; but Rianna's nose was filled with the dungeon's odors—decay, mold, fear and death. As she got into Alonso's carriage, she shivered at her memories of the events that threatened to destroy her world and everyone in it she held dear.

Once inside the carriage, Rianna said nothing to Alonso. She stared at the prison as if she were aware of nothing except the horrors that lay within those dark walls, the suffering of her parents and sister. If it had been possible for her to walk through those gates, there must be a way for them too. She couldn't bear to think otherwise and retain her hold on sanity. Even after the prison was out of sight, the images of its horror were indelibly etched on Rianna's soul; and she could see nothing else.

Rianna, tightly pressed against the carriage's side, seemed so locked inside herself Alonso began to wonder if he'd rescued not the girl he desired, but a madwoman. The vehicle finally stopped and the footman opened the door. As Alonso lifted Rianna out, his misgivings grew stronger. She stared at him without recognition. She said nothing, though she leaned heavily on his arm as they entered the house.

"Señora Bovadilla, please have the guest room prepared and send Sanchez to me in the parlor," Alonso ordered a woman who stood waiting in the foyer. Hoping Rianna would respond with some hint of normalcy, he added, "Rianna, this is Señora Bovadilla. Señora, Doña Rianna will be here for a possibly extended stay. Perhaps you'll be so kind to serve as *dueña*."

Rianna nodded to the housekeeper, but remained silent.

Relieved that Rianna seemed aware enough of her surroundings to at least acknowledge the introduction, Alonso tried to slip the folded vicuña from her arm. Her grasp on the cloth tightened unyieldingly.

Looking up at Alonso with a piteous expression, Rianna finally said, "This, Francisco's gift, is all I have of him. I will not give it up."

Though Alonso was more unnerved by Rianna's insistence to cling to a length of cloth that had been used as evidence against her less than an hour before, he said nothing. He guided Rianna into the parlor, invited her to sit down, then poured generous portions of brandy. He waited, watching her closely as she sipped the drink, until she finally looked up at him.

"I'm sorry if I've seemed distracted," she said slowly. "I don't know how I can thank you for speaking on my parents' behalf and getting me out of the prison."

Glad Rianna had finally said something that made sense, Alonso waved away her apology as well as her gratitude. "It's natural for you to be upset," he observed. "My siding with your family wasn't enough to free them, but perhaps more can be done."

The brandy gave Rianna the strength to ask, "What do you think we can do?"

Alonso didn't intend to do a thing; but when he'd first thought of this scheme, he'd realized he must at least give the impression he was trying to help the Alavas. Should Rianna discover he'd been the cause of her family's downfall, he would lose her and, more important, the money he hoped to take from the Alava house as well as from Agustín's shop. He noted Sanchez, the servant he'd asked the housekeeper to send, had entered the parlor and was awaiting orders.

"There are several matters we must discuss as soon as you think you can," Alonso said to Rianna. "But first, with your permission, I'd like to send someone to your house to pack your clothes and toilet articles, any items you need or want." Alonso paused to add solemnly, "They could also get your brothers' bodies so they could be prepared for burial."

Rianna's eyes filled with tears and she lowered them to stare at her lap as she nodded agreement.

"Could you make a list now?" Alonso inquired then hastily explained, "There's need for urgency, Rianna. Forgive me for reminding you constantly of what I know is a torment. If your parents are convicted and you, a girl who can legally own nothing, are their only heir, the Alavas' valuables might go to the church. It would be wise to immediately claim what's possible—money your father may have kept in the house, jewelry or valuables that can be carried away without attracting notice."

Rianna rested her forehead on her hand. Was it true she couldn't own property because she was a woman, that the Inquisition would confiscate everything, even her brothers' corpses? She supposed it was if Alonso said so. Was it likely her parents would be convicted? She shuddered to think of it.

"Of course, if your family is released, which I'll do my best to accomplish, you can return everything to its proper place," Alonso reminded. "Your father will appreciate your foresight in secreting the family valuables."

Rianna had to agree taking such precautions was wise. She lifted her head and answered wearily, "If you'll give me some paper, I'll describe where everything is I can think of. Do you suppose the jewels in my father's shop and workrooms might also be confiscated?"

Alonso had intended to mention the shop in a moment or two, when it seemed tactful and not as if he were too anxious about her family's money. He was glad she'd brought it up first. He told Sanchez to bring the writing materials from his library then declared, "I'm certain your father's shop will be searched. Do you know where his keys are?''

"Yes, I know," Rianna answered. She stared at the paper Sanchez had laid on the table at the side of her chair. Finally, she sighed and took up the pen, having no idea that Alonso had his own purpose in getting everything he could from the Alava house and Agustín's business.

After Rianna had laboriously finished her lists and handed the sheaf of papers to Alonso, he dared do no more than glance at the first page, though he was elated at what he glimpsed on it. Alonso handed the lists to Sanchez with orders to immediately take several other servants to the Alava house then, after darkness fell, to Agustín's business.

Sanchez left the parlor without comment. He knew Alonso's plan, as he'd always known about his master's nefarious activities; because he'd aided in them and been well-paid. Sanchez was sure this was to be the most profitable of them all.

Rianna took another sip of brandy to give her the strength to say, "You promised to try to help my family. You seem to have some plan in mind."

"Yes, Rianna, I do," Alonso answered.

Pulses pounding with new hope, Rianna couldn't help bursting out, "But tell me this plan, Alonso! I beg you to tell me and ease this pain!"

"I believe, if I can't bring about their exoneration, it may be possible to help them escape," he lied.

Rianna leaped to her feet and caught his hands in hers. "Alonso, what can I say to thank you? You'll be repaid in some way: my father will give whatever reward you ask!" she cried. "Tell me how you think you can manage this escape!"

Alonso looked down into Rianna's face, so lit by false hope, and thought only that she would be his. He said, "Leave the details to me. As far as any payment is concerned, seeing you smile is enough. I want you to be happy." While he wished he could now carry her up to his room, he knew he must continue his masquerade as her mentor until they were safely out of Spain; so she couldn't bring charges against him. "I don't know what Francisco told you about Peru. Probably it wasn't very pleasant."

Confused as to why he wanted to talk about the New World, Rianna again sat down. "Mostly he said that terrible things were happening to the Incas."

"It seemed to be all he was thinking about," Alonso agreed. "You must remember those Indians are heathens; and like all heathens, they know little about gentle virtues. They're violent people, like all barbarians, and must be treated accordingly. Time has passed since Francisco was in Peru and some things have changed since. The place is becoming more civilized, so much so that King Charles soon will be encouraging migration."

"He will?" Rianna was stunned at this news.

"He's going to offer large land parcels to those willing to settle Peru. That means families, not merely adventurers," Alonso said. "It's a land that holds much promise, especially for someone who gets there before the rush of settlers. It's a fertile land rich in natural resources, a place where a man can make his fortune and people can start new lives."

Rianna was silent as she considered this. Though Francisco had denounced the conquistadors' treatment of the Incas, he'd never spoken critically about the land itself. He'd said it was lush and vibrant, majestic and wildly beautiful.

"A city has just been built on the coast. It was planned to be the center of commerce; so, of course, it isn't a rough settlement. Lima is a real city where people can enjoy civilized life," Alonso said encouragingly.

"Has peace been made with the Incas then?" Rianna asked.

"That will come soon," Alonso said confidently. "Ignorant natives always react violently to the first strangers to set foot in their land; but after settlers bring law to such wretches, they seek peace. The Incas have been all but beaten anyway. By the time settlers begin to arrive, the resistance will have died out."

Rianna didn't know what to believe—Francisco's impression, which she had to concede could be outdated, or this news Alonso claimed to have brought directly from King Charles' court. Hope for a new life for her family, a freer life in a beautiful land sprang up in her. "Father would have ample gems to fashion into beautiful jewelry in Peru," she said slowly. "I understand there's an abundance of gems."

"For myself, Rianna, I'm weary of the royal court's politics, of the gossip, the restraints life in Spain forces us to endure because of old traditions so engraved in people's minds there seem no alternatives," Alonso said. "I intend to move to Peru myself, so your family wouldn't be alone there. They'd have a friend in me."

"You *are* a friend. Truly you have proven it," Rianna said warmly. She fell silent a moment, considering the rosy picture Alonso painted then reminded herself that her parents and sister still were in the inquisitor's dungeons. She looked up at Alonso and asked solemnly, "Do you *really* think you can help my family escape?"

Alonso had already planned his answer as carefully as if he intended to help free the Alavas. "I'll try to convince the inquisitor your family is innocent. Failing that, I've learned the guards in the dungeon are greedy, willing to accept bribes and shut their eyes to disappearing prisoners. I'll send a coach to meet your family and take them to Seville. Meanwhile, I'll arrange for a ship to pick them up at the coast. There are, you know, many captains willing to make such clandestine voyages if they're paid enough. Your parents and sister could be taken to England while I conclude my affairs here. I'd book our passage to England, we'll meet your family then sail for the New World together."

Rianna took a deep breath. It seemed Alonso had thought of everything. She remembered the gypsy's saying she would have to travel far to find her love. Maybe Alonso was to be her love, despite the gypsy's strange attitude toward him. Alonso seemed to be an entirely different man from what she'd thought. Wasn't this, too, part of the fortune teller's prediction, that Rianna's love would be a different kind of man from any she'd seen before?

When Alonso's servants returned that afternoon from the Alava house, they hadn't been able to find the strongbox in Agustín's study as well as a few other items on Rianna's list; but they assumed the soldiers had taken them. Rianna was stunned to learn that Francisco and Carlo's bodies had vanished. The Alavas' servants had also disappeared. Alonso explained that the most loyal of them probably had buried Rianna's brothers secretly to prevent officers sent by the Inquisition from burning the corpses. Rianna was appalled that her brothers should be buried in unmarked graves she wouldn't be able to visit. Alonso gave her some comfort by reminding that, if the Alavas were cleared of the charges of heresy and released, such faithful servants would return and point out the graves so Francisco and Carlo could be properly buried in the family vault.

Rianna was so exhausted that night she slept soundly despite the many problems on her mind. The next morning Alonso showed her the box of gems his servants had taken from the Alava business during the night. She didn't realize it was the last she'd see of the jewels.

It took over a month for Alonso to arrange his move to Peru. Rianna never suspected that many of the gems his servants had taken from the shop, which he'd promised to keep safe for her family, were being used to pay for the preparations he was making. He also was paying his most prominent creditors so they wouldn't blacken his reputation in Spain. He wanted to favorably impress his father with his newly well-conducted financial affairs; because, after the earl's death, Alonso intended to return to Avila and claim his title as well as the family fortune.

It wasn't difficult to persuade his father that Rianna's presence in his house in Madrid was an act of compassion in memory of his friend, Francisco. Because the earl kept a mistress near Avila, he was inclined to wink at the possibility of Alonso's having made Rianna his paramour. Alonso's mother, too, accepted the idea of his having a mistress; it was what all men of means did. She had no complaints as long as Alonso was reasonably discreet.

Alonso's decision to go to Peru startled the Fallas. He painted his family a bright picture of the opportunities open to a man in the New World, but he used a different set of colors than he had with the picture he'd created for Rianna. He assured the Fallas he would amass a fortune in Peru to replace the one he'd already squandered then return to Spain. Alonso had until now sought only his own pleasures and his family had concluded he was a hopelessly extravagant rake. They hadn't expected him to change into so enterprising a man. Instead of alternately warning him then making excuses for him, the earl was suddenly proud of his newly ambitious son. Because Alonso's mother ceased her tirades about his behavior, his sister had no choice but to be silent.

During this time, Alonso maintained his role with Rianna, periodically giving her news about how the Alavas' case was proceeding, news that was part of his elaborate lie. Finally, he told Rianna her family was likely to be convicted and he would set his plan for their escape in motion.

Rianna had no reason to think Alonso wasn't going to rescue her family. Because she never left his house, she heard nothing to contradict his lies. When Alonso announced that the Alavas were safely on their way to England, Rianna felt as if a great burden had finally been lifted from her shoulders.

Alonso thought that, once Rianna was on a ship in the middle of the Atlantic, there would be nothing she could do when he told her he hadn't been able to rescue her family.

On the morning Rianna and Alonso were to board the ship for England, Rianna put on an ivory dress with wide, slashed sleeves and a tight, square-necked bodice embroidered with gold and yellow that matched the gown's under-sleeves. Instead of wearing a cap, she drew her hair from her face and bound it with satin ribbons so her curls hung in long, graceful locks down her back.

Surveying the result in her mirror, she realized she appeared more ready to attend an afternoon soirée than board a ship; but her anticipated reunion with her family made her too happy to dress in a more subdued fashion. When she went downstairs to join Alonso, who was waiting in the foyer, he looked at her with an admiring light that contradicted his comment.

"You shouldn't have worn that gown, Rianna. The sea wind will go right through it. Don't you think it's a bit frivolous for a voyage?"

"Please allow me this whim after so long a time of weeping," she answered, her tawny eyes bright with golden glimmers. She turned to take a cloak from the maid who'd been following then held up the garment for his inspection. "When I was packing, I laid aside my cape for use on the ship. See? It even has a hood."

Alonso sighed at her logic. "I'm glad you feel so cheerful. It's good to see you smile again."

He took her arm and guided her into the courtyard, where in addition to a coach, several carts piled with baggage were waiting. Because Sanchez and Señora Bovadilla were the only servants willing to undertake a voyage to Peru, after Alonso had handed Rianna into the coach, he turned to pay the other servants and give them final instructions.

Rianna arranged her skirts more comfortably on the seat as she waited and wondered at her sudden regret to leave Spain. Finally, she realized, though the terror of the Inquisition hadn't fully receded and her grief for her brothers was still a pain in her soul, the recent events couldn't blot out a lifetime of bright memories. Her gaiety became longing. as she recalled the Alavas' sunny courtyard where she'd once played with Jacinta on the cobbles, how she'd dropped her toys to race to Francisco when he'd returned from his tutor's house, her father's patient teasing when she'd climbed on his lap to beg a bedtime story, her mother's hands gently stroking her hair. Without realizing it, Rianna sighed as Alonso got into the coach.

He gave the driver his order to go then leaned forward to take Rianna's hand and ask, "Are you sad, even after all that's happened, to leave Spain?"

Rianna nodded. "I was thinking of my childhood, happier memories than . . ." She stopped. She didn't want to talk about death and mourning. She lifted her eyes and asked, "Do you suppose we could drive past my father's house, just for one last look?"

Alonso was thoughtfully silent a moment before shaking his head. "You wouldn't like it now."

Rianna suddenly realized the Alava house must be boarded up, a guard pacing at the gate. "You're right, Alonso. I don't want to take so sad a memory with me."

"Instead of dwelling on the past, think about the future in Peru," Alonso advised.

"It's difficult to imagine," Rianna said then added, "I guess I'll think about how happy we'll all be when Mother, Father and Jacinta and I are together again."

She smiled so brightly even Alonso's conscience momentarily prickled over what he'd done. He forced himself to return Rianna's smile and wondered how she'd react when she learned she'd never see her family again. His thoughts were distracted by the coach's slowing and he noticed people gathering on the street.

Alonso slid aside the communicating panel and called to the driver, "What's going on out there? Where did all these people come from?"

"They're pouring out of the houses, sir!" the driver called back. "I dare not whip up the horses or we'll trample someone."

"The man must be blind if he can sit up in the box and not see *something*," Alonso said crossly. He turned again to shout to the driver, "If we dawdle too long here, the tide may change so the ship won't be able to leave! Move on! This interfering throng of peasants will have to move!"

Rianna had been staring out the window at the direction the people were walking. "They seem to be going toward the plaza," she observed. "Sometimes, when gypsies come to the city, they perform for coins in the square. If so, I'd like to talk to that fortune teller again."

Alonso shuddered at the very idea of meeting *that* gypsy a second time much less allowing Rianna to talk with her. He said sharply, "Didn't she frighten you enough before? If that hag appeared outside this window, I'd order my driver to *aim* the horses at her. It's what she deserves for the disgusting way she behaved at your party."

Rianna assumed Alonso was angry because the fortune teller had spat on him. But as frightening as the woman's prediction had been about Rianna, it also seemed to have been accurate. Rianna wanted to ask more about her future. She leaned closer to the window, trying to see past the crowd; but she couldn't. The coach was about to enter the plaza. She hoped Alonso wouldn't realize it until they were trapped by the crowd. Then, if the gypsies were the cause of the gathering, she'd have time to speak to the fortune teller.

When Alonso noticed the coach was almost in the square, he called to the driver, "Turn away, you fool! Get us on another street before we're delayed here for hours!"

The coach began to turn, but was stopped by a knot of people crossing in front of it. The driver cursed as one of a group of passing boys slapped the lead horse's rump. The startled mare took several bounds forward, sending people scattering from her path.

Alonso groaned in despair. The horses' leaps had pulled the coach into the plaza and the crowd hemmed them in even worse than before.

Rianna again leaned closer to the window to peer into the distance. Though she could see people gathering around the center of the square, the sun glanced so brightly off the paving stones, she couldn't tell what was attracting the throng. Convinced it must be a gypsy performance drawing so much attention, Rianna threw open the carriage door and leaned out.

"Rianna, get back inside! You'll fall into the street among the rabble," Alonso warned.

"I can't see what's happening from inside," she answered and lifted a hand to shield her eyes from the glare. "If it's gypsies and we must wait, I might as well be entertained," she reasoned. "It seems as if two posts have been set up. Maybe they're making a tent for a puppet show. It would be amusing if—" She stopped abruptly as she realized the upright timbers had a far grimmer purpose. A great tangle of branches had been heaped at each of their bases.

"They're going to burn someone," she whispered; but she felt as if something commanded, compelled her to continue watching; and when Alonso began to pluck at her skirt, she shrugged off his protests. She saw the bright uniforms of the soldiers escorting the prisoners to the stakes, the black robes of the priest who led them then the tops of the prisoners' heads. A woman with a crown of shining braids the exact tint of Rianna's locks, a man with hair that shone with the same red-brown as Francisco's.

"*Madre Maria,* have pity!" Rianna gasped and, before Alonso could catch her, leaped off the coach step.

Though Rianna faced a solid wall of people, she didn't hesitate, but pushed her way into their midst. She pulled aside an old crone who stubbornly wouldn't move; and when the woman turned angrily only to see a distraught girl, her curses died on her lips. Rianna didn't notice the woman; her eyes were riveted on the center of the plaza as she fought through the crowd. A man noticing the beautiful young woman pressed against his side caught her shoulder to pull her in front of him.

"Let go of me." Rianna sobbed in his grip. "I think it's my mother and father!"

The man's eyes widened in shock. "If it is—" he began.

"I must see! I must know!" Rianna wept so pitifully the man drew her protectively behind him.

"Take a grip on my jerkin. I'll get you through," he promised then, effortlessly pushing a man out of his path, let out a bellow, "Clear a way or I'll smash you under my boots!"

Those standing directly in front of Rianna's benefactor, turned to glance at him briefly then hurried aside. He was a brawny man they recognized as a neighborhood ruffian with a short temper.

Rianna clung to his jerkin like a cocklebur as he half-dragged her through the crowd; and when he finally stopped and turned to face her, Rianna's gown was torn and spattered, her ribbons lost and her golden hair streaming loose.

"Are you *sure* you want to see, *niña*?" he asked.

"I have to know!" she cried.

He drew her in front of him to shield her from the rest of the throng. Her sharp cry of despair as she looked up at the prisoners was a sword piercing even his calloused heart.

"Mama! Papa!" Rianna burst into sobs.

"Give me a path! Let me by!" Alonso forced himself through the last of the crowd. "I know this lady. She's with me!" he told the man who held Rianna.

The stranger relinquished her to Alonso, who caught Rianna by both shoulders.

"I couldn't tell you! I dared not!" Alonso said urgently. Desperate to distract her even a little from what was about to happen, he talked fast, telling her the lies he'd planned to say later aboard the ship, "They all were put in another part of the prison where I couldn't bribe the guards. I told you they were in England to spare you."

"Where is Jacinta?" Rianna sobbed. "She *was* the girl being tortured whose screams we heard, wasn't she? Oh, God, my little sister! She died then, didn't she?"

"No, no," Alonso tried to soothe Rianna. "She caught ill."

"That's a lie! Everything you've told me were lies!" Rianna sobbed.

"No, I'm taking you to Peru as I'd promised," Alonso said frantically, wanting her to be quieter. "We'll be married."

Rianna tore free of his grasp and turned at the moment the executioner touched his torch to the faggots. Finally wordless, she stared at the little tongues of fire that crept toward her parents' feet. She lifted her gaze to their faces. They were looking at her, their eyes filled with love and sorrow.

Rianna felt as if horror was a pressure rapidly building to explosion in her brain. As her tear-streaming eyes beheld the flames leap up to make torches of her mother's ragged gown, the torn folds of her father's *zamarra*, Rianna's scream seemed to carry to the far ends of the plaza; and in a final, unendurable burst of emotion, she collapsed.

chapter

4

Shali's black eyes mirrored the flames devouring his house and, beyond the house, the city that was the capital of his province. His heart was constricted with anger and grief—first his father then his wife and son, now his home and town. Must the invaders have it *all*? Were they so greedy they must leave him with nothing of his own? Shali's fists, clenched at his sides, moved higher as his emotions grew even more intense, until his arms lifted above his head, his fists ready to threaten even the sun. The roof of his house collapsed and his eyes reflected the shower of orange sparks exploding from the fire while his fury was a demon soundlessly screaming off the mountaintops.

But Shali's cry of frustrated anger stopped in his throat as the midnight mirror of his eyes perceived a new image in the roaring flames. Was it madness born of a rage that couldn't be contained, but must? Was he seeing a vision from the nether-world such as Villac Umu sometimes did? Shali wasn't a priest; he knew nothing of the secret ceremonies the holy men conducted to evoke visions. Like his father, Shali was a nobleman, a governor and, when necessary, a soldier. He blinked rapidly; but each time he opened his eyes, their obsidian surface reflected the vision in the fire.

A young woman, more beautiful than any he'd ever seen, unlike the women of his people or any of the peoples in the empire, seemed to be standing in the middle of the burning house. Her garments, alien to him, were torn and spattered. The woman's long hair, cascading in richly gilded waves, seemed to move languorously in the wind the fire made at its heart. Her eyes seemed to gather up the rich saffron of the grass on the Andes' high slopes and somehow turn it to molten crystal. Over her cheeks streamed tears as luminous as the light that came from the sun. The girl's face was uplifted, as if she were staring at something above and beyond Shali's shoulder. Her expression was agony, as if she were caught in the maelstrom of emotions whose intensity matched his, as if she were one with him, their souls in this fleeting moment united. Her eyes lowered to gaze directly at Shali, to meet his for an electrifying instant. Then her lips moved in a silent cry, she crumpled to the ground and her shimmering form vanished.

Ruminavi, a friend of Shali's, saw Shali's tall figure swaying slightly. He quickly motioned to one of his men, Amaru, who hurried to Wayra and slipped Shali's cloak from the saddle loop then walked quickly to stoop behind Shali and smooth the scarlet cloak like a pool of blood over the grass. Shali, without glancing behind him, unaware of anyone's presence except his own, lowered himself to sit cross-legged on the cloak and think about the vision he alone had seen. His men, who recognized that something was happening to Shali they couldn't perceive, withdrew to give him privacy.

All motion in Shali's mind had stopped. He was too stunned to even wonder who the beautiful woman was and what the vision signified. His eyes stared at the image still emblazoned on his brain. The woman's soundless scream reverberated in his soul until the furor of his own emotions was exhausted in the echoes of her anguish. When he finally again became aware of himself, he was breathing fast, as if he'd run up a hill. He didn't understand what he'd seen; he couldn't imagine what it meant. It seemed that the deciphering of visions was more in a priest's realm and he decided he must ask Villac Umu.

Shali rose, his heart still fluttering in a peculiar rhythm. He turned to look at Ruminavi, who was directing the men in his stead. Flashes of blue and red tunics hurrying between the burning buildings gave evidence of their fruitless search. The people of the city had fled and left their possessions behind before the Castilians had attacked. Shali's returning anger raised his head stiffly. His eyes narrowed and looked as hard as volcanic glass. The Incas, rulers of an empire, had to flee to the jungles and mountains like scurrying animals before the seemingly endless flood of invaders.

As if Shali's anger were a live thing that reached out to touch Ruminavi, the officer turned to look at his friend; and seeing Shali's expression, he wondered what Shali had seen in the fire; but he wouldn't ask. Instead, he recalled the siege at Cuzco. It was said to have failed due to a large body of mounted Castilians arriving with supplies for Pizarro. Like Shali, Ruminavi believed it had been lost because the Incan general in charge of the battle had been too hesitant. If he'd acted faster, the Castilian reinforcements would have found Incas behind the walls manning the cannons. Shali had been so bitterly disappointed at the outcome that he'd returned to his province and continued to decline joining the resistance. Shali had feared, if he fought then returned home, he'd draw the Castilians' attention to his province, which he'd vowed to protect.

Ruminavi started toward Shali wondering, now that the city had been destroyed and Shali's own house was rapidly falling into ashes, what his friend would do.

To Ruminavi's unasked question, Shali said quietly, "I have no choice. I'll have to fight with Manco." In an unusual gesture of affection, Shali laid his arm over Ruminavi's shoulder, adding, "It's gone, all of it. I have no home, no city to govern. The people have fled my province; and they'll either hide or find Manco and join his resistance army. There's no one left here for me to protect." He took his arm from Ruminavi's shoulder and went to gather up Wayra's reins.

"Is there nothing you would have me search for in the wreckage?" Ruminavi inquired.

Shali paused beside Wayra's withers. "Would I have you poke in the ashes for some memento of a past that will only embitter me more each time I look at it?" He shook his head regretfully. "When the reigning king dies, the closing of his palace is a wise custom, one I never fully understood until now. The Shali that was is gone. This, his domain, is best forgotten. The Shali I am now will find a new place for himself.''

Ruminavi watched silently as his commander swung up into the saddle then inquired, ''Where do we find Manco Capac these days?''

Shali gazed at the mountains a moment then turned to look down at his friend. ''I must ask Villac Umu. He always knows where everyone is.'' Shali lifted a hand in a brief salute then Wayra trotted away.

Ruminavi watched Shali's receding form and thought only of how even his gesture was a replica of his father's. ''Shali had best take his father's name now, if he ever intends to call himself aright,'' Ruminavi muttered. ''His vows of revenge will likely never be fulfilled. There are too many of the enemy and I fear we'll never drive them away.''

Amaru, coming up behind Ruminavi, had heard his comment. ''Even if we can't drive the invaders away, they'll suffer greater losses now that Shali has decided to fight, that is, if the son is like the father in all ways.''

''Did you know that Shalikuchima's last words, as the flames consumed him, were a call to Pachamac to destroy the Castilians?'' Ruminavi asked.

Amaru shook his head, awed that the former commander should have still defied the enemy as he gave up his soul.

''Get your horse, Amaru, and gather up your courage as well,'' Ruminavi advised. ''The condor on Shali's crest is the king and the jaguar is the symbol of Shali's family. He's the last male of his line; he's the jaguar carrying Manco Capac, the last of our kings. Now that Shali knows his only course in protecting Manco is to fight, those Castilians will think the jaguar has landed on their naked backs.''

''But you said there were too many invaders for us to win,'' Amaru reminded.

''Driving the invaders into the ocean may not be possible to us, but Shali will find a way to save Manco and, somehow, the Incas,'' Ruminavi assured. ''The jaguar will always support the condor.''

When Cuzco was captured by the Castilians, Villac Umu retired to the city called Machu Picchu hidden in a valley surrounded by mountains. Unless he was needed elsewhere, it was where he stayed. The priest was always trying to persuade Manco to make his headquarters at

Machu Picchu; because, unless a traveler knew exactly where the valley's entrance was, no one could find it. Villac Umu was convinced Machu Picchu was the one Incan city within a reasonable distance of the sacred site of Cuzco that was safe from the invaders.

The outermost strip of Machu Picchu's valley had remained a lush jungle at the foot of the surrounding mountains. The forest was so thick anyone seeing the pass that formed the valley's entrance didn't recognize it. It appeared to be part of the jungle, the same as the surrounding area. But beyond the forested strip, the valley was a gently rolling basin fed by waterfalls made of melted snow draining from the slopes. In the center of the valley stood one majestic mountain. Its summit was almost flat, as if the peak had been sliced off. Around its base were cottages and cultivated land. The mountain rose sharply from the valley; and the only access to its top was a steep, winding road. Even if an enemy could find the valley, it was unlikely he could gain access to the city because the road was laughably easy to defend. An ascending enemy army could be disposed of with a rockslide. Higher up the slope, the incline was more gentle. Terraces were cut into the earth to grow crops.

No one knew if the mountain was really a natural plateau or if the Incas of a dim past had cut off the pinnacle to make the area where the city had been built. Machu Picchu was so old the Incas speculated if it had been engineered by the first Manco Capac, who with his wife Oello Huaco, it was said, had come from the stars to teach the savage tribes on earth. The legend claimed this first Manco Capac had taught Incan men to plant crops and build houses, temples, aqueducts and bridges. Oello Huaco had taught the women to spin, weave, sew and care properly for their families. The mysterious couple had given the Incas civilized laws and their religion, which was essentially respect for nature and reverence for life. The representative of God was the sun and the Incan name for God was Viracocha.

Shali rode unhurriedly through the valley; it was the only place now where he needn't be alert for sudden attack. He was saddened as he recalled how short a time ago no Inca feared attack anywhere he went unless it was by beasts of prey. Even the animals, though, had mostly seemed to go peacefully about their own business, perhaps because, except for an occasional hunt, the Incas didn't disturb them. The animals understood about hunting for food and held no grudges.

Wayra wound her way up the steep path to the city as calm and surefooted as if she'd traveled it all her life; and though Shali had visited the city only a few times since he'd gotten Wayra, everyone in Machu Picchu recognized the snow white horse from a great distance and knew Lord Shalikuchima was coming.

The guards at the city's entrance saluted Shali and he acknowledged their greeting with a casual wave. As Wayra paced through the streets, passersby paid Shali the deference of his rank; and he nodded politely to them, feeling as if this might soon be the only place in Peru where the ancient traditions would exist.

He stopped Wayra at Villac Umu's house; but before he had a chance to dismount, he heard a friendly call. A tall, spare man with thinning white hair and penetrating dark eyes came around the side of the house from the garden.

"I'm especially glad you've come today, Shali," Villac Umu said. "I expect Manco to arrive soon."

The smug expression in the priest's eyes made Shali curious. "There have been many times you've caused us to come to you at the same time without our realizing it, Villac Umu. I don't know how you do it; but, then, I know nothing of your priestly powers. Is this such a time?" Shali inquired as he dismounted.

The priest smiled and shook his head. "It was the will of Viracocha that you both follow the path to my door today. Manco is bringing Coraquenque with him."

Shali was very surprised at this news. "Then Manco is coming to stay?"

The priest nodded. "Since the enemy called Orgonez drove Manco from Tambo, he has been living like a hunted animal. It's no way for a king to live—nor a queen."

"It isn't how any Inca should live, yet we're forced to." Shali loosened Wayra's saddle girth then turned to Villac Umu. "I, too, no longer have a home or a province to govern."

"You have a home at Machu Picchu, as do your men who are following," the priest said.

Shali sighed. "You knew what happened at Tumbez before I spoke."

Villac Umu inclined his head. "Bring Wayra around to the back of my house, where a servant will tend her. Then you and I can talk about matters other than war. I know you have more on your mind than Castilians and you and Manco will discuss the enemy enough after he arrives."

Shali obeyed the priest. He was, it seemed, a crystal Villac Umu could look through whenever he chose. Shali was glad the priest respected privacy or he would know every impulse that passed through Shali's brain.

After the men were comfortably seated in the shade of Villac Umu's house, the priest signaled a servant to bring refreshments. He said nothing of importance until after the servant had furnished them with fruit drinks cooled by snow brought from the surrounding peaks. Then he observed, "Something has happened that confuses and excites you at the same time. This much I perceive, but you must describe the incident to me."

Shali wondered if the priest might think the vision a momentary madness. He'd seen several Incas who had been overwhelmed by the pain of the recent events and whose minds had snapped. The idea of his losing control of his own thoughts was more fearful to him than dying. He took a deep breath and resignedly described what had happened at his house in faithful detail that left out nothing.

After Shali had finished, Villac Umu was silent for so long a time Shali declared, "I'm not given to visions so it might have been an illusion caused by my anger, yet what I saw haunts me incessantly. The golden hair and eyes of that woman makes me wonder if I've somehow seen a handmaiden of the sun, if she's a ghost or a goddess. Tell me what you think and don't spare my feelings. If I've become mad, say that too; for a madman is of no use to his king."

Villac Umu raised his eyes and said slowly, "You aren't mad, but I believe the heat of your temper somehow caused the vision. A ghost returns to a place that had meaning during its former life, appears to someone it was attached to; so I don't think this strange woman was a ghost. A goddess doesn't wear torn, spattered garments. A handmaiden of the sun has no need to weep."

"Not even for the downfall of our people?" Shali asked bitterly.

"If she wouldn't weep for my sorrow, wouldn't she weep for the Incas?"

"Perhaps she wept for a reason of her own we can't know," the priest answered.

Shali was stunned. "You're saying, then, she could be a mortal woman? It isn't possible!"

"I wonder if you saw the image of a woman who's not one of our kind, an alien, suffering the same as you, but from some different fire. It's possible your souls have some connection and your mutual pain at simultaneous moments united you."

Shali stared at Villac Umu. It was seldom the wise priest was as baffled as he now appeared. "If this woman is a human being, a woman of flesh and blood, she's like none I'd dared dream of even in my wildest fantasies," he whispered.

The priest shook his head in obvious bewilderment. "The incident is like nothing I've ever heard. I can only think, because this vision is so vivid, so forceful, it's the beginning of something you can't avoid. I think she isn't evil because those who are evil don't weep with their hearts. Perhaps you'll experience another vision. If you do, tell me about it. We might learn more from it."

Shali promised he would tell the priest; but he privately doubted the golden-eyed woman was, as Villac Umu had suggested, human. If she were and he met her in the flesh, Shali was thinking, he could only hope she wasn't evil. She was a woman Shali knew could make him finally lay aside his love for his dead Yupanqui, make him forget the past, *everything,* except that he was a man. He was so immersed in his thoughts he didn't notice Villac Umu's head lift in sudden alertness.

Shali still didn't realize what was happening until the priest stood up and announced, "Manco has entered the city. He'll come directly here."

An Incan king only a few years ago would have traveled with an entourage of personal, as well as official attendants, almost equal in number to the royal guards. He would have been accompanied by record-keepers, envoys, myriad assistants, entertainers and many noblemen. He and the queen, adorned with jewels and magnificently feathered capes, would have ridden in comfortable litters.

Manco Capac and Coraquenque arrived at Machu Picchu sharing the copper-color horse he'd taken from the Castilians and accompanied only by a score of personal guards, having left the rest of the soldiers to camp in the valley below. The people of Machu Picchu crowded the streets, threw flowers and showed their obeisance as the royal couple passed; but Shali was saddened, as they all were, by the changes forced on them.

Later, after the king and queen had bathed and rested, they rejoined Shali and Villac Umu—and Ruminavi, who had since arrived—for dinner. The table was prepared in the garden under an arbor made of interlacing tree branches and flowers that showered them with a sweet perfume to help them forget melancholy. None of their conversation hinted of the trouble that was tearing the empire apart because dinner was a time to relax. The talk was limited to the plans the royal couple must make for settling in the city. Manco asked Villac Umu about the condition of the palace, which in this city had long been vacant. Coraquenque asked Villac Umu where she could find servants for their personal needs. Manco invited Shali to move into an apartment in the palace. All the nobility close to the king's confidence, who came to Machu Picchu, would stay in the palace, Manco advised. There wasn't room enough for them in the city unless they displaced its regular inhabitants.

Shali tried to imagine what the city on the mountain might be like if it was rebuilt to house the court. However beautiful the result, he wondered if he'd prefer to live in the privacy of the valley away from the other noblemen.

Villac Umu's garden was at the edge of the plateau; and beyond the wall, the mountains across the valley were violet in the twilight. As the slopes darkened to imposingly massive shadows and their peaks began to sparkle with moonlight, Villac Umu's servant brought chocolate in steaming bowls. Somewhere in the valley a shepherd played haunting melodies on panpipes to his flock of llamas.

Coraquenque finished her chocolate and rose, saying she was becoming chilled from the night and was weary from her travels. The men wished her fair dreams and knew she'd left them to talk of battles past and yet to come.

Manco looked at each of them with a faint smile. "She might as well have stayed to join our conversation. She'll awaken later and keep me from sleeping asking about what was said.''

"Coraquenque is interested in such things?" Shali was surprised.

"Don't let her seemingly gentle eyes or that fragile-looking face fool you, my cousin. My wife is a warrior-queen," Manco advised. "I would have left her somewhere safer after I had to flee Tambo, but she wouldn't allow it. She stole one of the Castilian's horses and rode at my side. Where she'd learned to ride a horse, much less steal one, is a mystery to me. She shared my mount coming into the city only because she'd loaned hers to one of my lieutenants who has a wounded leg and can't walk with the others.''

"Our queen is an unusual woman," Shali agreed.

"The Castilians' women ride horses, I've heard," Manco said then added proudly, "If they can, I suppose an Incan woman can do it too."

Ruminavi frowned when he thought of Castilian women riding horses for sport when Incan soldiers so desperately needed them for battle.

"I've never seen one of our enemy's women. I wonder what they look like," Shali speculated.

"Perhaps they have hair growing on their chins as their men do," Villac Umu quipped.

Shali's own smile surprised him and he commented, "The only Castilians I've seen deprived of their armor were those guards we attacked on the road and they appeared hairy all over."

"If their women are the same, they must be like sleeping with a ring-eyed bear," Ruminavi remarked.

Manco smiled at the idea, but said, "It's true the men grow much more hair around their mouths and on their chins than we do; but while I was forced to live among them in Cuzco, I did see a few of their women. Though the ones I saw seemed to be of low status, judging from the way the men behaved toward them, they didn't have face hair and some were quite pretty. I remember one with eyes as blue as a mountain lake and hair the same color as my horse's mane."

Shali's eyes widened in shock. The woman of his vision had hair of a more tawny hue, but the lightness of the color Manco described seemed as unlikely. "Such hair *exists*?" he breathed then couldn't resist asking, "Have you ever seen hair the shade of honey?" After Manco had said he'd seen Castilians with similar hair tints, Shali persisted, "What of eyes that color?"

Manco shook his head. "Never among even them have I seen golden eyes."

Villac Umu knew what Shali was thinking, but said nothing in front of the others. Instead, he commented, "If they bring women, it seems they intend to stay."

"More women are coming," Manco said in a solemn tone.

"How did you learn this?" Shali asked in alarm.

"Equal in wonder to Coraquenque's courage is her ability to learn quickly. Ever since I taught her what I'd learned of the enemy's language while I was at Cuzco, she's insisted on periodically going into whichever city we're near dressed as a blind peasant so she can listen to the conversations of passing Castilians while begging for coins. Her seeming lack of sight keeps the Castilians from molesting her; for they fear people with such afflictions, a strange attitude," Manco said thoughtfully.

"Coraquenque is a queen like Oello Huaco," Villac Umu said slowly.

"Such spying is extremely dangerous," Ruminavi breathed.

"She's taking a grave risk," Shali agreed.

"If my royal command doesn't stop her, what is there to do other than keep her like a prisoner? I know of nothing else," Manco said worriedly. "She answers always that to be Inca these days is to be in danger. She's right about that and she's given me valuable information each time she returns from the city. I've thought of dressing similarly and going with her, but she fears for my life more than her own. She says the royal line comes through my blood. I *must* live, even if I marry another wife to bear the next king. She always manages to sneak away without my discovering her absence until it's too late to follow."

"If all Incas, even those who can't go to battle, showed her spirit, the invaders wouldn't have a chance," Shali commented.

"Our people need weapons like the Castilians—and more horses," Ruminavi declared. "We're always at a disadvantage, even if there are more of us than the enemy. Our soldiers are being slaughtered in appalling numbers."

"We'll have to learn how to turn the advantage to ourselves, use a different strategy than our enemy is trained to follow," Shali said thoughtfully. "We've learned we can't defend a city from them because their cannons can destroy its gates. We can't fight them openly on the plains because we haven't enough horses. I think we must meet them in the swamps and jungles, in the hills where their horses can't maneuver or become frightened by their surroundings."

"I'm finally hearing the voice of Shalikuchima!" Villac Umu declared.

Shali passed him a grim look. "I can't bring myself to use the name my father passed to me while the empire is so endangered and I haven't yet avenged his death."

"You speak as if you allowed him to die, but there was nothing you could have done," Manco said. "I saw three brothers killed before the crown passed to me and I couldn't prevent it."

"It's Viracocha's choice who lives or dies," Villac Umu reminded.

"It's the will of Viracocha only that we're born. That we've behaved like fools can be blamed on no one, but ourselves!" Manco burst out. Seeing their shock, he explained, "When Hernando Pizarro promised Atahualpa they would meet in peace, Atahualpa expected him to keep his word as we would; so my brother was captured. When Pizarro said he would release Atahualpa for the gold, my brother thought they'd struck a bargain and died for his innocence. I will *not ever* believe a word that comes from any Castilian's mouth. They're so greedy and treacherous they're arguing among themselves. Mark what I say—they'll soon begin to kill each other!"

"If more of their women come, they'll soon have families. Then their quarrels with each other will be forgotten. They'll face us in a united cause, to defend their women and children as we do ours," Shali warned. "What we must do, before this happens, is to make the resistance so violent they dare not bring more women."

"I thought you were intent on defending your own province, but you sound as if you want to expand your war," Manco commented.

"Didn't you hear they've burned my house and city, that Tumbez is a shambles and my people are either hiding or furious to fight?" Shali asked.

Manco shook his head. "I thought you were at Machu Picchu only for a visit."

"I have nothing to go back to. What you see me wearing is all I now possess," Shali said. His temper rising, he demanded, "What else can I do, but fight? Shall I wander around the countryside like some of the other nobles until my garments are in rags and I so starved I'll be too weak to lift my hand, lest a sword? There's nothing for me, for any of us to do except fight." Shali's eyes reflected the torchlight like glittering black mirrors and the forces raging in him were as tangible as those in the air before a lightning storm. "I believe we must lay aside our scruples. If we speak to any of their leaders, our every word must be a lie. The only way to defeat this enemy is to destroy it as quickly as possible and with as little loss to ourselves as we can manage. We must steal every horse we can, every firearm and crossbow. Above all, we must show these Castilians more violence than they have to us and we must give them even less mercy."

chapter
5

After Rianna had collapsed at the foot of her parents' pyres, she had to be carried from the plaza and put into Alonso's coach. She didn't regain consciousness until the vehicle was moving briskly through the outskirts of Madrid. Then she immediately opened the coach door and started to get out. Assuming in her distress she intended to dash herself to the road, Alonso quickly pulled Rianna back inside. But he was more chilled by her expression than he'd been by the idea of her wanting to commit suicide. Rianna's eyes were as vacant and lifeless as the Alava house. He soon learned she had no idea where she was and no memory of what had happened. She couldn't even recall her name.

Alonso didn't look forward to traveling to Seville with an unpredictable, mind-shattered girl; but he had no choice. He wished he could order the coach to stop, put Rianna out and let someone else who passed later take her in; but Señora Bovadilla and the coachman's presence prevented it. Unlike Sanchez, neither knew about his schemes; and though Alonso might have tried to bribe the coachman, he realized he wouldn't be likely to succeed in buying the *dueña's* silence. To put the woman out of the coach with Rianna would assure her going directly to the authorities. There was only one way to rid himself of the two women that Alonso could think of and he was sure the coachman wouldn't stand aside for it.

The housekeeper turned *dueña*, meanwhile, showed a sympathy for Rianna's plight that surprised Alonso, for she was normally a stern, tight-lipped woman. He knew she'd agreed to go to Peru only because he paid her well and she had no family in Spain. Señora Bovadilla persuaded Rianna to rest her head on a small traveling pillow she'd brought for her own use, drew Rianna's cape over her lap and gently urged her to sleep. When the coach stopped at an inn for the night, the *dueña* led Rianna out, coaxed the girl to take a few bites of her meal, prepared her for the night and dressed her in the morning. Rianna did whatever the woman asked and said nothing. The past seemed to have dropped out of her consciousness.

When the group boarded the ship at Seville, Rianna was still in a walking stupor. Señora Bovadilla had to guide her every move, tell her when to stop or turn or step over something. Rianna's poignant beauty was eye-catching; but when a young gallant bowed over her hand, he was startled by her vacant gaze. Even the captain's greeting went unanswered. It was so obvious something was wrong with Rianna that the other passengers and even the crewmen stared. Nonplussed by the whispers and gawking Alonso was sure he'd have to endure during the entire voyage, he decided the less anyone on the ship saw Rianna, the better. To give everyone a good opinion of his own motives, Alonso told the captain Rianna's family had been charged with heresy and, despite his efforts, convicted. Then Alonso hurried Rianna to the cabin she would share with Señora Bovadilla and told the *dueña* to keep her charge inside.

It took only a few hours for the news to spread over the ship and fearful glances changed to sympathetic comments. There was not, he soon learned, one person on the ship who believed the Inquisition was proper or holy; and he congratulated himself on telling that much of the truth about Rianna's illness. Everyone thought he was extraordinarily kind and generous. No one had an inkling it was Alonso's plot that had brought Rianna to this state.

The ship's Dr. Gonzales volunteered to examine Rianna and, afterward, concluded she was physically healthy. Having never seen a case like hers, he admitted he didn't know if she'd return to normal and left the cabin muttering angrily about the tribunal.

Father Aquinas, a priest on a mission to Panama, asked if he might help. Señora Bovadilla was ready to redden his ears with complaints that it had been other priests who had caused Rianna's illness; but as she looked into Father Aquinas' gentle eyes, she realized he was nothing like the ecclesiastics connected with the Inquisition. His accent was that of a province known for its people's simple, honest faith; and she decided to admit him to the cabin. At the sight of his cassock, Rianna's previously dull eyes flared with a blaze of gold lights. She sprang to her feet and screamed incoherently until the priest left. Then, as abruptly as if she'd been struck down, she collapsed.

Rianna was unconscious for several days. Dr. Gonzales was summoned, but he could offer no advice. Father Aquinas begged to be allowed to pray for Rianna. The *dueña* reasoned that, as long as Rianna wasn't conscious, the priest's presence couldn't upset her and decided to allow him to come in. He knelt on the floor by Rianna's bedside and unobtrusively prayed for several hours. He returned the next day and the next until Rianna showed signs of stirring. Then he left hastily so the sight of his cassock wouldn't again make her hysterical.

After Rianna awakened, her condition seemed little improved. The recovery of her memory only brought new pain and she alternated periods of wild sobbing with silent withdrawal that was more unnerving to Alonso than her previous stupor. Several weeks passed before Rianna's uncontrolled weeping began to subside; but then she grew more retired, as if she were mentally shutting herself away.

Months later, after the ship had docked in Panama, Alonso had to make arrangements for the rest of the trip to Lima. As he found himself having to explain over and over about Rianna's condition, he wished even more fervently he'd been able to think of a way to get her off his hands in Spain. It was necessary to travel overland to the west coast of the isthmus then take another ship to Lima. The terrain was rugged; and when Alonso considered the dangers of the journey, he often found himself hoping, if Rianna didn't regain normalcy, she might have an accident or contract one of the tropical fevers that were killing so many Spaniards in Panama. Although Alonso had begun this adventure wanting the Alavas disgraced and Rianna helpless, his most important goals had been to repay his creditors and redeem himself in his father's eyes then to make a new fortune of his own in Peru and return to Spain. Alonso still desired the Rianna he'd known in Madrid; but now she seemed like another person. Her pallor and the wistful expression she almost constantly wore made her even more lovely; but it was a fragile, unearthly beauty.

Alonso's fears at having to journey with Rianna in her seemingly unpredictable state were, in reality, groundless. Although she still appeared to be as mentally isolated as before, she was beginning to recover. Her grief hadn't diminished, but she was trying to come to terms with her loss.

When the travelers finally reached the west coast of the isthmus, Rianna gazed impassively at the Pacific's rolling waves, inwardly reflecting there was no purpose in wishing what had happened could be changed. She must somehow make another life for herself. If that life must be in Peru, she would have to adjust to the changes it would impose on her. If it seemed marriage to Alonso, as he'd offered, was her only course, she would marry him. Otherwise, she would tell Alonso to give back the box of gems and the money he was keeping for her; and she would find a way to manage on her own.

The final leg of the trip, the relatively short voyage to Lima, promised to be uneventful. The sky was clear and the ship clung to the peaceful waters near the coast. After the arduous journey across Panama, everyone in the traveling party was exhausted and used this quiet interval to rest; and it was easy for Rianna to leave the cabin she again shared with the *dueña*. Because Rianna's behavior crossing the isthmus had given no one cause for alarm, Alonso and Señora Bovadilla no longer apprehensively watched her every move. Rianna spent much of her time at the ship's rail observing the coastline that slid past. Francisco had described Peru as beautiful and vibrant, but the land she was seeing appeared as forbidding as Panama. It seemed to be a maze of impenetrable jungles, massive forests and ominous swamps.

"We're north of Peru, Doña Rianna. Don't worry. Our destination is not like this."

Rianna glanced sideways at Señora Bovadilla, who had approached. "I hope not." She returned her attention to the coast.

"I asked the captain, who assured me Peru is much more civilized," the woman added. She was silent for a time, hoping Rianna would say something of her own choosing; but when she didn't, the *dueña* finally sighed and commented, "You're behaving exactly the way I did when I lost my husband." Not a flicker of interest passed Rianna's face. Concerned with the girl's seeming preoccupation with mourning, Señora Bovadilla thought Rianna must soon begin to take interest in other matters. She was afraid to prod the girl and make her weep, but she thought she should do something. Finally, the *dueña* said cautiously, "Doña Rianna, I know how awful it was to see what you did in Madrid."

Rianna turned to regard the woman and replied bitterly, "No one can know what it's like to see someone you dearly love burned alive unless—"

"Unless you experience it yourself, as I did," Señora Bovadilla finished. At Rianna's speechlessness, the woman continued, "My husband died the same way. I never forgave the inquisitor, though I no longer condemn all priests for what happened. You thought I was a stern, unbending person; because you've never seen me smile or my mood lighten. It isn't because I was born humorless, but I mourned my husband for so long a time I forgot how to do much else."

"I never knew, Señora Bovadilla," Rianna breathed. "Forgive me for—"

"For thinking me to be what I really have become? No, Doña Rianna. You need no forgiveness. I'm a dour, unhappy person; and I'm not likely to change," the *dueña* said. "I'm telling you this because I want you to avoid the pit I fell into. Don't mourn so deeply you begin to cherish the pain more than look forward to recovering from it. Don't throw away your life by making yourself a living martyr."

Rianna didn't know what to say. Finally, she put her hand over the *dueña's* and pressed it. "I can assure you, Señora Bovadilla, I have no intention of becoming any kind of martyr."

The woman realized then that Rianna hadn't been as mindless as they'd thought. She was relieved; and despite her habit of keeping a certain distance between herself and others, she impulsively asked,

"Do you think, Doña Rianna, that you might now call me Beatriz instead of Señora Bovadilla?"

For the first time in almost a year, Rianna's lips curved in a smile. "Of course, Beatriz. Thank you for worrying about me all this time." Rianna caught the woman's shoulders and warmly hugged her; but she could feel Beatriz stiffen in the embrace, as if she were made uncomfortable by physical contact. Rianna quickly stepped away.

Despite Beatriz's confiding in Rianna, the woman made no further gestures toward friendship and seemed not to notice Rianna's attempts to reopen the subject. The *dueña* went about her tasks for the next several days with the same business-like air as before. Rianna concluded that Beatriz, as she'd admitted, really had been humorless so long she didn't know how to unbend. It was sad, Rianna observed, that the two people on the ship who could understand each other's situation best, who needed a friend most, were held apart by the prison Beatriz had made for herself.

Alonso, still wary of Rianna because of her previous hysterics, didn't seek her out. Though Rianna saw him every evening at dinner and at odd moments during the day, she made no effort to talk with him. She knew she'd be in his company almost constantly in Lima; and she saw this part of the trip as an opportunity to continue sorting out her own thoughts. To Alonso, Rianna appeared as distant as before; but as the days passed, he was relieved that her tempests of weeping seemed more and more to be a thing of the past.

The swamps and jungles of the coast gradually became forests then beaches with cultivated fields beyond. The fields narrowed as the mountains crept closer to the sea. As the ship drew nearer its destination, Rianna found anticipation rising in her, an eagerness to reach out to this land, to begin to explore her new life, find friends and perhaps even love.

The last night on the ship Rianna's anticipation budded into excitement and she couldn't sleep for trying to imagine what it would be like to live in Peru.

The gypsy's predictions in Madrid that Rianna would find her love had been a constant whisper in the back of her mind. Now it became a brightening song. The fortune teller had been only too tragically accurate so far, Rianna reasoned; so she hoped the happy part of the prophecy would now begin to unfold. Rianna didn't realize it was well before dawn when she finally gave up her effort to sleep and got out of bed.

She dressed as quietly as possible, but she wasn't overly worried that the soft sounds she made fumbling in the dark would awaken Beatriz. Though the *dueña's* bed was only a few steps from Rianna's in the cramped cabin, Beatriz was a very sound sleeper. It wasn't possible for Rianna to complete a proper toilette in the shadowy compartment, but she managed as best she could. Unable to do much with her rebellious hair in the dark, she ended by tying it back with a ribbon.

Rianna groped in her trunk for a cape. Her fingertips recognized the soft folds of the vicuña and she hesitated. She hadn't looked at Francisco's gift since the morning she'd left the inquisitor's office. Rianna finally decided that nothing was more suitable to keep the chill of a Peruvian morning from her than this cloth made for an Incan nobleman. She pulled out the vicuña, draped it over her shoulders and left the cabin knowing Francisco would have applauded her decision.

Sometime during the night the ship had entered the river that flowed through Lima to the ocean; and not wanting to navigate the waterway in the dark, the captain had ordered the ship anchored till morning. Except for a sailor who stood watch, the crew was in its quarters. The seaman's job was to be alert for the ship's safety, not a sleepless passenger; so he ignored Rianna. She felt as solitary on deck as if he didn't exist.

The wind blowing up the river from the ocean was chillingly sharp compared to the daytime's languid breezes and it tugged persistently at Rianna's curls. She turned into a nook to pause and catch her breath, but the capricious wind changed its direction as if it deliberately followed her. Rianna pulled a fold of the vicuña over her head and, holding it snugly closed at her throat, resumed walking. When she stepped around a corner to the side of the ship facing the shore, she stopped abruptly, her discomfort and coiffure forgotten.

Peru was yet so deeply swathed in night the only hint Rianna had of where the sky began and the land ended was that the blackness above held a glittering sweep of stars. The darkness was so complete she had an eerie feeling there was no land at all; she was enveloped by the sky. She reached out to cling to the rail. It and the deck's solid feel under her slippers assured her of the ship's reality. The sensation of being disoriented slowly passed, leaving Rianna wondering if standing on a safely familiar deck was preferable to the breathless excitement of being thrust into the unknown. She hadn't long to think about it before the beauty of the beginning sunrise caught her in its spell.

A thin red line suddenly appeared and ran jaggedly across the sky. During the moment it took Rianna to realize this first messenger of the Peruvian morning was outlining the mountains, the glow brightened and spread into the cleft between two crags that dipped closer to earth than the others. The light increased until it became a flare that momentarily cut a path across the water and bathed the deck with sudden radiance. The shining edge of the sun sent its fire along the peaks and dazzled the snow-crowned Andes with crimson. As the light in the sky softened to luminous coral, the sparkle at the tops of the mountains moderated to an orange blush. Then the sun soared above the summits, turning them into gold frost that reflected fingers of light into the purple shadows of the land.

Rianna glimpsed a string of crystal beads that was a distant waterfall tumbling from a cliff. Dark masses of trees became orchards and fields of corn emerged from shadow. Here and there the morning glanced off the white walls of a solitary house with a cozily angled thatched roof. Finally, tucked between the bosom of the mountains, Rianna saw Lima.

Though the city was still veiled by shadows and no life seemed to be yet stirring in it, Rianna was disappointed that it looked much like any seaport she might have entered in Spain. She thought about this and wondered why she should have expected a city in Peru built by Spaniards to be different from those in Spain. As Lima grew clearer in the light, she realized what she'd wanted to see was an Incan city.

Rianna's eyes rose again to the foothills to gaze at the thatched roof houses she rightly assumed were the homes of Peruvian peasants. Her attention moved, fixed itself to the mountains beyond the farmland, as if somehow her eyes might penetrate the distant granite spires and find the exotic city she sought. Rianna was so absorbed in her quest she didn't notice the vicuña folds had slid from her hair, the breezes had undone the ribbon and her rich curls tumbled free. The dawn light made a gilt banner of Rianna's hair and gathered gold dust in her luminous eyes. It caressed the vicuña enfolding her, as if congratulating the embroidered jaguar for its safe return home—as if welcoming the woman wrapped within it.

chapter

6

It was midmorning before the deckhands tossed lines to men on the wharf. A crowd had gathered to watch the ship draw into port. Some were awaiting friends or relatives, most hoped to get letters or packages from home, but the rare arrival of any vessel was cause enough for a man to lay aside whatever he was doing, to come and gape.

Rianna scanned the faces in the crowd and was glad to note a squad of soldiers cordoning off the section of the wharf nearest the ship. Aside from dock workers and the impassive faces of a few Peruvians, the onlookers appeared to consist of rough-looking men; and she was aware of the hungry stares fixed on her. Rianna was happy to step aside and let Sanchez precede her down the passageway; and Alonso's arm firmly guiding her was reassuring.

An officer in a scarlet uniform glanced at the passengers; and recognizing Alonso, exclaimed, "Alonso Falla! What are you doing here?" He walked quickly to face Alonso and grasp his shoulder in welcome. "The last time I saw you was in a posh—"

Alonso, obviously surprised to see the officer, smiled, clasped his hand and declared, "It's good to see you, Nicasio. I didn't know you'd been assigned to Lima."

The officer grinned . "A small problem made it expedient to come here a while." He looked questioningly at Rianna. "Don't tell me the bachelor of Madrid has finally surrendered to marriage!"

Alonso shook his head. "Not quite yet, Nicasio. Let me introduce you to Señorita Rianna Alava. Rianna, my old friend, Captain Nicasio Montesinos."

Montesinos swept off his plumed hat and his dark curls bent over Rianna's hand as he brushed his lips to her fingers. When his eyes lifted to meet hers, they were openly admiring. "Doña Rianna, forgive my staring. It's been several years since I've had the pleasure of meeting a lady from home. So beautiful a lady is a doubly welcome sight."

"Thank you, Captain Montesinos," Rianna answered. "It's a pleasure to meet a friend of Alonso's."

Not having missed Rianna's apprehensive glances at the men on the dock, Nicasio said, "Lima's population consists mostly of soldiers and civilian adventurers with a few priests sprinkled in to remind them of God. Although some of the officers' wives have recently come, there aren't many Spanish women here and even fewer ladies like yourself. This will change, Doña Rianna, because settlers will soon begin to arrive." He gestured toward the onlookers with a flourish, adding, "Despite the rudeness of their stares, you're quite safe."

"You're kind as well as charming, Captain. I'm reassured by your company," Rianna answered.

Alonso watched Rianna and listened to her with great interest. Her manners recalled the Rianna he'd known in Spain and he was becoming increasingly hopeful she'd finally recovered.

"Nicasio, you may remember Sanchez. And this is my housekeeper who's acting as Rianna's *dueña*, Señora Bovadilla," Alonso introduced.

Nicasio greeted the couple politely then again turned to Alonso. "Where may I escort you? Have you arranged where you'll stay?"

"I'm afraid any letters I might have sent to secure accommodations would have arrived on the same ship as I," Alonso answered. "Perhaps you can suggest a comfortable inn, Nicasio?"

Montesinos shook his head. "There's no inn suitable for Doña Rianna," he replied. "But I insist you be my guests while you decide what you wish to do." Nicasio shrugged off Alonso's protest. "I know you think a captain must either live at military headquarters or rent some tiny hovel, but Lima isn't Madrid. I don't have to depend on my father's stingy allowance or live on a captain's pay. My share of the gold we've taken has amounted to a considerable sum and it's been my good fortune to obtain a house. Your stay there will be more comfortable than any other temporary arrangement you could make.''

"You're generous," Alonso said.

Nicasio chuckled. "I owe you a debt, if you recall. Consider your stay my payment, if you wish.''

"A debt, captain?" Rianna inquired.

"A wager, Doña Rianna, for sport," Nicasio explained before again regarding Alonso. "The matter is settled. You must come to my house. Don't forget, I've been here a long time and I intend to take advantage of your company to learn all the news of Madrid I've missed.''

Nicasio left no room for refusals and Alonso finally accepted the invitation. He'd really intended to agree at Nicasio's first mention of it and had only politely protested. While Alonso was willing to tell Nicasio Madrid's gossip, he also planned to learn all he could about Lima. Alonso couldn't think of a man he'd rather get information from than Montesinos. Nicasio was privy to the military's plans and attitudes about the entire area; but he also was a scoundrel, who quickly learned how to maneuver himself into almost every layer of society wherever he was.

While Alonso and Rianna waited for their belongings to be unloaded from the ship, Nicasio obligingly sent one of his men for a carriage. The soldier returned so promptly the cargo was only half-unloaded; but Nicasio assured Alonso their baggage would be delivered to his house. Alonso directed Sanchez to remain and point out their items. Then Nicasio took Alonso and the women to the carriage.

Alonso and Nicasio chatted the way friends will, who haven't seen each other a long time; and Rianna paid little notice to their conversation. She was looking at the neighborhoods the carriage passed.

After seeing the rough-looking crowd that had greeted them on the wharf, Rianna had become uneasy about living in Lima; but the city appeared civilized enough. The houses were mostly made of sun-dried bricks and wood, but the larger ones had walled-in courtyards. Where the gates had been left open, Rianna could see flower beds and shrubbery as in Madrid. The streets were straight and neatly set at right angles to each other and there were little green parks like islands of trees at regular intervals. As the carriage passed the center of town, Rianna observed the plaza was lined by official-looking stone buildings. She was sure that, as in Spain, such buildings housed the city government. There was a cathedral, as stately as any she'd seen in Madrid, though not as ornate. When a couple of priests stepped out of the church, Rianna's heart gave a lurch; but she did nothing to reveal it. She was aware of Alonso's eyes warily watching, of his relief when she seemed undisturbed; and she was glad she at last was able to control her reactions if not her emotions.

The marketplace held carts and tables displaying fruits, vegetables and a variety of other merchandise. Most of the sellers were Peruvians, who were shabbily but cleanly dressed. Rianna noticed that their faces were either expressionless or sullen; and she wondered if they resented selling their produce to Spaniards or were a naturally taciturn people. Pairs of European women, who appeared to be servants shopping for their households, were always accompanied by a male escort, Rianna noted and wondered if the women were afraid of the Peruvians, the sort of men she'd seen on the docks or both. Rianna concluded there seemed little danger from either group. The marketplace was as orderly and peaceful as any, though shoppers in Madrid had a happier air than those in Lima.

The carriage passed through the entire city before they finally approached a high stone wall Montesinos said enclosed his home. Looking down the length of the wall, Rianna was impressed at the size of the captain's property and decided he hadn't been boasting when he'd described his home. She wondered if, during their stay, it would be possible for her and Alonso to borrow horses and take a ride in the nearby Andean foothills.

When the carriage rolled into the courtyard, Rianna saw that the house was made of stone blocks, its roof thatched, not tiled as it would have been in Spain. The house had only one floor, but it covered so much ground Rianna guessed the rooms were spacious. The paved courtyard was small, but at the far side of the house she glimpsed an extensive garden.

"I see you're curious about the unusual design of my house," Nicasio commented as he helped Rianna from the carriage. "It's an Incan building that was used as a resting place for travelers. The entrance was at the opposite end of the building, where the gardens are."

"This was an inn?" Rianna asked.

"Not as we think of inns because the rooms weren't rented," Nicasio replied. "The place was a convenience for anyone who needed to stop for a night. The storehouses always held food and whatever else was necessary. Because royalty, noblemen or other officials did most of the traveling, the accommodations were very comfortable."

"Who owned it?" Alonso inquired.

"The king owned it and the storehouses were kept supplied by his agents. Travelers had their own servants to look after their needs, so these places had no regular staff," Nicasio answered. "The Incas stopped using the building before we began building Lima. I took a fancy to it and claimed it for myself. You'll find it's a little different from the kind of houses you're used to. Come inside and have a glass of wine while your rooms are being prepared."

Rianna discovered that the main part of the house was a comfortably furnished hall large enough to have held a banquet. Nicasio invited them to be seated on furniture it appeared he'd brought from Spain. She was disappointed that, aside from the odd design of the house, there was nothing to hint of its former furnishings. Nicasio explained that a second, smaller hall had to be used as a dining room and the kitchen was in one of the outbuildings. Since the bedrooms had once been used as temporary living quarters for a variety of people who might arrive at the same time, they could be entered only from the garden. Each room had a private bathroom with heated or cold water piped in.

Alonso was highly impressed by these comforts and remarked on the ingenuity of the Peruvians, whom he'd thought were ignorant heathens.

Rianna was embarrassed Alonso and Nicasio spoke so insensitively within hearing of a Peruvian servant who was pouring their wine. The Incan boy's eyes remained downcast when he handed each of them a goblet, but Rianna could sense his resentment. When he moved to the far side of the room to await further orders, he stood in a direct line with her gaze; and she could look at him without rudely staring. She noted, though Topa was in his teens, he was the height of a full-grown man; and she wondered if all Incas were so tall, so long-limbed. The boy's hair was straight, black and clipped level with his shoulders. Topa's dark eyes, when he raised them, were momentarily sullen before he hid his inner feelings with an impassive mask. Men in Europe wore tight-fitting doublets, loose, coatlike garments called *zamarras,* short pantaloons puffed at the hips and snugly bound at their upper thighs while their legs were sheathed in long hose. The Peruvian boy's garments were odd to Rianna's eyes, a simple white cotton jerkin that skimmed the lines of his body, long-legged breeches that were neither tight nor loose, but outlined his limbs to his ankles. Slippers, which looked like felt, were as silent on the wooden floors as a shadow.

"If you think Peruvians are clever in the way they build their hostels, their battle tactics are brilliant," Nicasio was telling Alonso. "At first they seemed to have a mild temperament, but that was only while the Pizarros were holding one or another of their kings. Their present king, Manco Capac, escaped and he's been causing a lot of trouble. One of his generals, Shalikuchima, who had been staying mostly to himself, finally joined the resistance. Manco made him military commander and he's been a terror to us."

"But how can these natives match our soldiers when we have guns and I've heard they don't?" Alonso asked in obvious surprise.

"They ambush patrols and travelers and *take* our guns. They've been clever enough to figure out how to use them too!" Nicasio exclaimed.

"Isn't that like a horse learning to put its harness on a man?" Alonso asked disdainfully.

Rianna glanced at Topa and noted he hadn't missed the insult, but he quickly lowered his eyes when he realized she was watching.

"Manco Capac's army has shown a discipline I wouldn't have believed. They never retreat even if they're losing, unless they're given the order. They'll fight till they've been killed to the last man," Nicasio said. "This General Shalikuchima attacks only where our mounts are at a disadvantage. His men drag trees or make other barricades on the road so our soldiers must stop to pull them away.

Then the Incas leap out of the bushes and, if necessary, throw themselves at our horses' legs to stop the animals. They toss ropes with a sliding loop over our horses' necks or even our soldiers and drag them from the saddle. They'll face our pistols with only swords and maces, our cannons with lances and slings. Their aim with a simple longbow is deadly; but when one of them gets a gun or a crossbow in his hands, he quickly learns to use it as accurately. They're always after our weapons and horses, which they learn to ride as fast as they steal them. Shalikuchima has a way of seeming to drop out of the sky, fight like a devil then disappear. It's said he loves his sword and longbow like other men love their women.''

"They sound like a formidable foe," Alonso said slowly then added in obvious disappointment, "I meant to seek a fortune here, but how can I if these wild people are ready to ambush a man at every turn?"

"There's still plenty of gold around; but you'll have to go to one of the areas still plagued by the Incas, which is dangerous," Nicasio observed. "You'd have to hire men such as you saw on the wharf to protect you, promise them a share of what you get. Cuzco is a better place to find such men. Those now in Lima have mostly made their fortune and are ready to return to Spain or they're waiting for women to come so they can establish a home and family here." Nicasio signaled the servant to refill their glasses.

Alonso slowly asked, "What is the political situation, Nicasio? How firmly established are the Pizarros?"

"You're as shrewd as ever." The captain grinned. "You always want to know who's *really* in power and how far bribes and intrigues can carry you." Nicasio's face sobered as he considered the situation. "Francisco Pizarro sent his brother, Gonzalo, north to find a place called 'the land of cinnamon.' I don't think that was wise while his other brother, Hernando, is back in Spain. Francisco behaves like a king, but he's made enemies. He had a falling-out with Almagro and arrested him. After a trial that was a farce, Almagro was executed.''

"But I'd thought the Pizarros and Almagro were friends," Alonso said in surprise.

"The lust for power has undone many friendships." Nicasio shrugged then continued, "Almagro's son Diego is bitter, but hasn't caused trouble so far. The men Almagro used to command are another story. They played a large part in the exploration of Peru from the beginning, yet Francisco Pizarro has discharged most of them and demoted others to the lowest rank. He's even confiscated the share of gold they'd earned.''

''Pizarro has to expect those men to be angry,'' Alonso commented.

''In my opinion, Almagro's execution was an act of mercy,'' Nicasio remarked. ''He was riddled with disease and could hardly think. He was so weak he had to be carried everywhere in a litter.''

''What disease?'' Alonso asked in alarm.

''The kind a man gets from lying with prostitutes,'' Nicasio answered with a sneer. ''Almagro had it long before he came to Peru.''

Reassured that no epidemic had seized Peru, Alonso's mind again turned to the possibility of violence. ''How great is the threat from Almagro's men?''

''No one speaks openly of it because Pizarro doesn't want to hear opinions; but I think that so many soldiers with no jobs to do, who have had everything they've worked for taken from them with little chance of their complaints being heard, are a potential danger,'' Nicasio replied. He shook his head in wonder that Francisco Pizarro had behaved so foolishly, adding, ''This all could have been avoided if Pizarro had made it appear Almagro was killed by an Inca. But Pizarro seems to think he's invincible.''

''Even kings can be assassinated,'' Alonso observed.

Nicasio was about to say more, but there was a commotion in the hall, and he gestured Topa to open the door.

A soldier entered the room pushing a young Incan woman roughly before him. ''Captain Montesinos, this Indian was in the plaza pretending to be a blind beggar. I've discovered her eyes work as well as mine and I think she's either someone's escaped slave or a spy.''

The Inca's amber eyes traveled first over Nicasio then Alonso as if swiftly taking their measure. Finally, her gaze rested on Rianna. She looked surprised and exclaimed in Quechua.

''Don't let her fool you, sir,'' the soldier warned. ''She can speak Spanish almost as well as I.''

''There was no deception in what I said!'' The Inca quickly denied in Spanish. ''It's just that I was surprised at this lady's hair and eyes. She has the colors of a handmaiden of the sun.''

"Don't contaminate Doña Rianna's ears with your heathen ideas," Nicasio said harshly. "Just tell me why you were pretending to be a blind beggar."

"Aren't all Incas beggars since you came?" she inquired coolly.

Nicasio ignored that and demanded, "How did you learn Spanish?"

"I lived for a year with one of your soldiers," she lied. "He was killed and I couldn't go back to my own people. I had to become a beggar to survive. I pretended to be blind so people would have more pity and I more coins."

"She's lying, Captain. I'm sure of it," the soldier insisted.

"He says that because he wants me for his bed!" the Inca spat, her eyes flashing with a mixture of anger and fear. "If you decide I'm a spy, he'll pretend to take me to be executed; but he'll lock me in his quarters."

"All these Indians do is lie," the soldier said angrily.

"Are such things done?" Rianna was shocked.

Nicasio knew they were, but didn't want to admit it. Instead of answering Rianna, he asked the Inca, "What are you called?"

"Coraquenque," she answered promptly, knowing it wasn't likely any of these Castilians had heard the name of Manco Capac's wife.

"Captain Montesinos, is it possible for Coraquenque to be executed on the decision of only one officer?" Rianna asked in an icy tone.

Nicasio didn't know what to say. Though he hadn't learned what Rianna's relationship was with Alonso, he knew they weren't married; and he didn't want to ruin any chance he might have with her. Finally, very reluctantly, he nodded.

"It appears life is held in even cheaper regard here than in Spain," Rianna commented.

"Not by me, Doña Rianna," Nicasio quickly denied. "I'm not convinced she's a spy anyway."

"But, Captain, you can't free this Indian, whose purpose on the street was in itself deceiving," the waiting soldier declared.

"I didn't say she was free to go; and I'll decide what to do with her, Private Sarabia," Nicasio snapped. He turned to Alonso and inquired, "You've brought no servants other than Sanchez and Bovadilla?" Alonso nodded and Nicasio said, "You'll need more; and if Doña Rianna has taken a liking to this Inca, perhaps she could be used as a maid. If she does anything suspicious, someone else can be found.''

"I suppose a native servant requires less pay than—"

Alonso was interrupted by Coraquenque's bitter laugh. "The captain isn't talking about a servant, but a slave. Or didn't you know your government awards you an allotment of captured Incas as slaves?'' Coraquenque inquired in a tone dripping sarcasm.

"That can't be!'' Rianna breathed. Her eyes fell on the Incan boy standing across the room, who nodded. She turned to Nicasio. "I don't want a slave.''

Nicasio said placatingly, "It's better for their criminals to serve us than be locked in prisons. We don't have enough prisons anyway.''

"The criminals the captain means are Incan men, captured while fighting for our own king, and any of our women your soldiers notice and desire.'' Coraquenque's eyes glittered with resentment.

"This girl is very rebellious. She may be more difficult to manage than her service is worth,'' Alonso speculated.

Although Rianna was disgusted at the idea of owning a person, she was sure the Incan girl's fate would be worse if she were rejected. "I will need a maid, Alonso; and though I find the idea of slavery distasteful, if this is how things are done in Lima . . .'' Rianna shrugged as if resigning herself to the situation.

"Maybe a more docile slave would be better,'' Alonso said.

When Coraquenque had been brought to Montesinos' house, she'd been certain he would hand her over to Sarabia; but she'd begun to hope she'd be given to Rianna. Coraquenque could see several advantages in being Rianna's slave. This golden-eyed Castilian girl would be an infinitely better mistress than Sarabia a master, who would ravish and beat her until he tired of her and belatedly carried out her execution. Coraquenque wondered, too, if she remained in this captain's house, whether she might learn information she could carry back to Manco if she saw an opportunity to escape. Now she realized her own defiance might put her back in Sarabia's hands. There was only one way to avoid this disaster she could think of, to behave as if her spirit had finally drained out of her and beg for mercy. Inwardly disgusted at how she must debase herself, Coraquenque sank to kneel at Rianna's feet.

"Please don't turn me away. It will mean my death. If you'll let me serve you, I won't cause trouble," Coraquenque implored.

Rianna wasn't fooled by the Inca's sudden show of humility, but she understood only too well the girl's reason. The memory of her own lie to escape the inquisitor's office vividly burned in her memory. Rianna said firmly, "I've decided I want her for my maid."

While Alonso still hesitated, Nicasio took advantage of this chance to win Rianna's good opinion by siding with her. "Let Doña Rianna have this Indian, Alonso," he urged. "If the slave causes trouble, we can correct it easily enough."

Alonso had noted Nicasio's interest in Rianna and knew the captain wanted to make a good impression on her. He turned to Rianna and smiled. "You may have her, my dear. I just want to be sure of your own safety and happiness. If this maid gives you even the slightest reason to feel uneasy, you must tell me."

"I will, Alonso," Rianna promised and, glancing at Nicasio, added, "Thank you both."

Satisfied that he'd regained Rianna's good will, Nicasio suggested, "Perhaps you'd like to go to your room, Doña Rianna. Your bathwater must be warm by now and I'm sure you'd like to get settled. Topa can show you the way."

"Thank you, Captain," Rianna replied. She looked at Coraquenque and remarked, "I don't know how to address a slave, seeing as how you're the first I've had."

Coraquenque lowered her eyes to hide their humor as she thought of what the Incan boy, who knew who she really was, must think of her charade. "It's a new experience for me to be a slave, so I'm afraid I can't instruct you," she answered.

"I suppose we'll have to learn together," Rianna said and turned to follow Topa.

She was escorted through a corridor then outside. A wide, stone-paved walkway ran parallel to the building with a latticed roof protecting it from direct sun. Leafy vines wove through the wood strips and dropped star-shaped golden flowers with cinnamon-color throats at Rianna's feet as she walked. They passed several doors, rows of shuttered windows; until Topa stopped to open shutters and unlatch a door. Rianna turned to look at the garden and glimpsed paths curving through the foliage and flowers, heard a fountain's spray from somewhere beyond a grove of trees.

She inhaled the fragrant air and sighed. "This will be a pleasant view from my bedroom each morning."

"My people once appreciated the beauty of this garden," Coraquenque said, wistfully remembering times she, Manco and the other Incan nobility had stayed at this hostel. Then noticing that Topa waited beside the open door, she added tartly, "But they're too busy fighting or being slaves to enjoy much of anything these days."

Rianna turned to follow Coraquenque into the room. "I've done nothing to your people and I'm not here by choice," she commented. "In a way, our situations are very similar."

Coraquenque flashed her a surprised glance, but Rianna was studying her temporary quarters and didn't notice.

Like the room where they'd left Alonso and Nicasio, this chamber held furniture Rianna was sure had been shipped from Spain. A bed of dark, carved wood supported a ruby-color brocade canopy that matched the drapes the Incan boy drew aside to reveal a row of windows overlooking the gardens. Carved, wooden cabinets lined one wall. There was a dressing table with a gilt-framed mirror, several chairs and a gold-flowered divan. Moorish rugs in a variety of designs had been scattered over the wooden floor. Rianna approached a doorway and discovered a more simply furnished room she assumed was meant for a maid's use. The only other door opened onto the bathing room and she stepped inside to look with open curiosity at its furnishings.

The floor was made of polished stone and, at the center of the chamber, formed a low platform. When Rianna went nearer, she saw a rectangular opening in the stones filled with steaming, flower-scented water. She wondered at its purpose and looked questioningly at the Incas.

Coraquenque spoke rapidly to Topa, who quickly left the suite. Noting Rianna's confusion, Coraquenque asked, "I understood you wished to bathe. Was I mistaken?"

"But this *little* opening can't be a bath!" Rianna said incredulously.

"Incas don't sit, but stand, in their baths," Coraquenque advised. She came nearer. "Will you show me how to unfasten your garments? They're different from ours and appear complicated."

Rianna looked uncertainly at the bath a moment more before answering, "I'll undress myself, but you show me how to get in and out of this bath."

Coraquenque laughed softly. "Don't worry, Doña Rianna. My people are no more interested in drowning than you. There are little steps cut in the stone you'll see when you go closer."

Having something more important on her mind than the way she would bathe, Rianna turned to face Coraquenque. "Will you answer me truthfully?" she asked. When Coraquenque looked hesitant, Rianna explained, "I've only arrived in Lima and am ignorant how things are done here. For my own education, I need to know the truth. Could the captain have sentenced you to death on no more evidence than Private Sarabia's word that you were spying?"

Coraquenque nodded. "It has often been done to others of my people."

Rianna's eyes hardened with anger, but she persisted, "Do you truly think the private would have taken you to his quarters instead of carrying out the sentence?"

The Incan girl sighed. "I noticed him watching me this morning and knew he desired me, but I had to pretend I was blind and couldn't see his stares." Coraquenque looked away, as if she were shamed by what happened next. "Finally, he came across the street, pulled me into a doorway and started fondling me. He said he was going to take me to his room; and if I didn't go quietly, he would just pretend he'd arrested me. I managed to break away and started to run. He caught me, but he knew from the way I ran I wasn't blind."

Rianna took Coraquenque's hand and squeezed it. "If anyone else tries to molest you, tell me. I'll make sure he's punished."

"You believe me?" Coraquenque was surprised.

"I saw my sister dragged away to be raped by soldiers—my brother, who was only a boy, thrown down a well and drowned—my other brother impaled on a spear." Rianna's eyes flooded with tears as she fought to hold her voice steady so she could finish, "My parents were burned at the stake in Madrid." She wiped away her tears then reached to begin unfastening the back of her dress. "I've looked into my mirror too many times and saw fear in my eyes not to recognize it in yours as you spoke."

"I didn't know your people treat each other even as they do us," Coraquenque breathed, awed at what Rianna had suffered. Noting Rianna's fingers were trembling too much to unhook the dress, Coraquenque came closer to help.

When Rianna felt the Inca's nimble fingers start unfastening the hooks, she commented, "It's odd I can tell you these things with no more than a few quiet tears. Before now, I couldn't speak of my family without a storm of weeping overwhelming me."

"There is much for you, as well as me, to learn about you," Coraquenque said quietly.

Rianna took a deep breath. "I have a lot to learn about you and your people."

"You *want* to know about my people?" Coraquenque asked in surprise.

Rianna nodded. She felt the Inca's fingers pause in her work, sensed her trembling and quickly said, "This situation is awkward for us both, but let's try to make it as pleasant as possible."

While she thought about Rianna's attitude, which was so different from that of the other Castilians, Coraquenque worked on the remaining hooks. Finally, she inquired, "Shall I call you 'mistress' or will 'doña' be enough?"

"When we're with others, I suppose you must say doña. Otherwise, Rianna will do." Rianna stepped out of her dress and turned. She noticed Coraquenque's eyes were blurred by tears before she hastily lowered them. She patted the Inca's arm sympathetically. "You were lying when you said you couldn't go back to your people. Your tears tell me someone loves you and is awaiting your return."

Coraquenque glanced up in surprise and alarm.

"Your secret is safe with me," Rianna assured. "Maybe we can find a way for you to go back to him."

Coraquenque shook her head and replied, "I can't run away unless I can be certain of escape. Your people send dogs after runaway slaves."

Rianna shuddered at the thought, but insisted, "We *will* find a way."

Still amazed at Rianna's offer to try to help, Coraquenque blinked away her tears and decided she'd best change the subject. Rianna already knew too much about her.

*   *   *

Shali remained in the saddle until after his soldiers had left the palace courtyard to go to their own quarters. Then he turned Wayra into a shadowy alcove near the entrance to his rooms. He dismounted slowly, taking care to avoid disturbing the wound in his thigh any more than necessary; but the instant he put his weight on that leg the stabbing pain made him catch his breath. Wayra tensed and he laid his arm over her withers to calm the horse as well as steady himself.

"It isn't a serious wound, Wayra. It just hurts," he said softly. "Stand quietly a moment while I rest against you."

As if the horse understood and answered, she turned her head to touch his cheek so lightly he felt only her silky whiskers, her warm breath. A wave of dizziness came over him and he leaned his forehead against the saddle while he fought it. Aside from her one affectionate gesture, the mare stood as motionless as if she'd turned into a statue carved of moonlight.

Shali felt a warm trickle of blood making its way past his knee and sighed. He'd hidden the wound from his men by tucking the edge of his cloak between his leg and the saddle. If they'd known he'd been hurt, they'd have clustered around him, endangered themselves even more by trying to shield him; and the struggle with the Castilians had been a near enough thing.

It had been as much a surprise to the Incas as to the Castilians when they'd suddenly come face to face in the clearing. The relatively small patrol of Peruvians had been outnumbered and they'd had to use every trick they knew to put their enemy to flight. Although neither force ordinarily engaged in combat after dark because it was so difficult to see what they were doing, Shali had discovered that the night had given the Incas some advantage. Unlike the Castilians, they wore no armor to shine in the moonlight and mark their changing positions or to encumber them with its weight. They'd moved quickly and kept in motion throughout the brief, ferocious battle. The Incas had captured several more horses, a dozen crossbows and a few pistols. But Wayra's snowy coat had been like a light in the darkness and it had been too easy for the enemy to see Shali. It was only because the mare had suddenly reared that the arrow had pierced Shali's thigh instead of his heart. He'd immediately pulled out the arrow and thrown it aside and the pressure of his leg against the saddle had slowed the flow of blood, but the wound had been seeping steadily all the way back to Machu Picchu.

"You're hurt."

At the sound of the soft voice, Shali lifted his head to face Suya, his dead wife's sister who, like him, had been widowed by the Castilians. "Please don't awaken anyone," he said softly.

"But you need attention," she whispered. He shook his head and she asked anxiously, "Why don't you want anyone to know?"

Shali tried to put a little weight on that leg to reassure her, but he couldn't prevent his gasp. "It's more painful than serious," he said quickly, again leaning on Wayra. "If you arouse anyone, Manco will learn of it and confine me to my quarters for twice as long as necessary. I don't intend to be left out of a raid because of a minor wound."

Suya knew Shali would be angry if she called for help. Instead, she asked, "Do you intend to stand against Wayra and bleed all night because this wound is too painful to walk to your chamber by yourself?"

Shali knew she was right; he couldn't manage alone. "Find me something I can use as a walking stick," he said more curtly than he intended.

Suya knew his harsh tone was inspired by pain and ignored it. She slid her arm around his waist and urged, "Lean on me. I'll help you inside."

He looked down at her and said more gently, "I'm sorry for answering so sharply."

Suya nodded and Shali put his arm around her shoulders. Although his door wasn't far and he put as little weight on her as possible, she was panting by the time he reached his bed-mat and sat down.

Suya dropped to her knees and tore open the leg of his breeches to peer at the wound. She finally said, "It's very deep."

"If you'll get me some clean cloths, I'll bind it," Shali replied.

Her dark eyes looked up into his. "Are you afraid of my touching you?" Suya's question held more meaning than she knew Shali would acknowledge.

"Someone may question Wayra's being left saddled outside," he said quickly. "If you'll take her to the stable, I'll clean the wound and try to slow the bleeding. You can wrap it when you come back, if you're willing.''

"You know I am," she answered and got to her feet.

After Suya had left, Shali bathed the wound carefully; but his mind was filled with the memory of her sinuous movements as she'd brought the basin of water, the lengths of her long, black hair shifting with her steps, the way her dress had clung to her body as she'd stooped to get cloths from the cabinet, the scent of her skin as she'd bent to put the towels beside him. Like Shali, Suya's loss of her mate had been agonizing; but she'd lately begun to long for another husband and hinted strongly she wanted him. She'd assumed his seeming lack of response was because his military duties absorbed all his energy, but this wasn't true. Shali's instincts were powerful and his attraction to Suya a thing he often fought. His grief for Yupanqui had finally dulled; but when he'd become aware of Suya's interest, he'd decided she reminded him too much of her sister. Making love to Suya would be like coupling with a ghost.

The door opened and Shali glanced up in alarm. Relieved it was Suya, not Amaru who might have noticed his lamp still burning, Shali quickly returned his attention to staunching his bleeding. He didn't want Suya to see the desire he knew his eyes held despite his resolution. It wasn't until she approached with a needle and thread that he dared look up.

"You'd best lie back so your leg will be steady," she suggested.

Shali gingerly pulled himself farther on the bed and lay down. Suya knelt on the edge of the mat and bent over the wound.

Shali closed his eyes and tried to think of something to occupy his mind that would distract him from the pain. His thoughts turned to the vision of the golden-eyed woman he'd believed was fantasy and Villac Umu had insisted was real. Shali wondered again if she were a living human being, if he'd ever meet her. But if he didn't, why should he have seen her at all? What had the incident meant? It was a riddle for which he could find no answer. Though the needle passing through his flesh made beads of moisture break out on his face, he remained silent and motionless as he puzzled over the enigma.

While Suya was bandaging Shali's leg, he was remembering the vision so vividly he could feel again the golden-eyed woman's grief and was saddened by her weeping. Lost in the memory, he again felt an impulse to draw her into his arms. He could almost imagine he felt her head on his shoulder, her cheek as soft as a flower petal against his throat, her hair sliding through his fingers as she tilted her face to look up at him. Her mouth no longer was crying out in pain; it was like a blossom budding.

Suya had straightened to look at Shali. In the wavering lamplight, the angles of his face were sharpened, though his helplessness gave him a boyish look. She blotted his damp forehead with a cloth then bent to kiss it. When she withdrew, his eyes were open; and she wondered at the emotions hidden behind their black surface. Suya couldn't know that, with the lamp burning behind her, she was only a silhouette; and Shali was still lost in memories. She impulsively leaned closer to touch her lips to his and discovered his mouth, which had held so grim a set since Yupanqui had died, was softer than she'd dreamed. She felt his hands at her temples gently coaxing her face closer while his lips grew firmer and his kiss changed from passive acceptance to sensual exploration. Shali's mouth began to move against Suya's so insistently her body was charged with sudden fire. But when her fingers slid into his thick hair, his eyes focused, his lips grew rigid and he turned his face aside.

"Why?" she whispered. "Your leg needn't be disturbed by making love."

Shali didn't look at Suya as he answered, "A man should desire you for yourself, not a vision."

Suya assumed Shali meant Yupanqui. "It was *my* mouth you've fired with passion, not a ghost's! It was *me* you wanted to hold closer, not Yupanqui!" she breathed.

When Shali turned his head to look at her, she saw that his eyes were clear. His desire had been leashed. Disappointed, she raised her head to stare into space while her heart resumed a slower beat.

"You would, I think, learn the difference between me and Yupanqui; but maybe, though you need a woman, you don't want me," Suya murmured.

If he couldn't explain the vision, Shali thought he might make an effort to at least soothe Suya's hurt feelings and began, "You're as beautiful, as desirable a woman as . . ."

There was a quick, impatient knock; but before Shali could call out, the door opened. Manco stepped inside.

"I saw your light and thought . . ." Manco's eyes fastened on Suya and he fell silent. Had he walked in on a lover's tryst? Then his gaze took in the basin of bloodied water, the crimson-stained cloths; and he quickly came nearer to say in concern, "Amaru didn't tell me you'd been wounded."

"I didn't want him or any of them to know it for precisely that reason," Shali replied. "It isn't serious enough to worry about. Suya helped me bandage it."

Manco gave Suya a penetrating glare. "Is it true the wound's not serious?"

Suya dared not lie to Manco Capac, but she didn't want to anger Shali. She finally compromised by saying, "It bled freely, but it's stopped now."

Manco's frown deepened. "How long will it be until he can walk, do you think?"

"I'm not unconscious that you need to talk past me!" Shali declared. "I heal quickly. I'll be on my feet in the morning."

Manco glowered at Suya and she helplessly shook her head. He said more quietly, "Tell the truth, Shali. I need to know what I can plan on."

Surprised at Manco's worried tone, Shali thought a moment then answered more accurately, "I'll be on my feet tomorrow if I use a cane, but I won't be able to move around much for the next couple of days." He sighed at Manco's expression and admitted, "I doubt I'll get up on Wayra for a week."

"How soon could you ride in a cart?" Manco inquired.

"I should be able to manage that in a couple of days." Shali knew his cousin wouldn't press him unless he had an important reason and he asked, "What's wrong?"

"Coraquenque slipped away again. I think this time I must find her," Manco said tightly.

Shali glanced up at his friend in alarm then turned to Suya. "Would you pour us some *chicha*? My leg aches and Manco looks like he needs calming." Suya nodded and immediately rose. Shali asked, "Where do you think Coraquenque went?"

Manco sank down to sit cross-legged on one of the floor cushions that served the Incas as chairs before he began, "She left soon after you did."

"She's been gone almost a month?" Shali exclaimed.

Manco nodded. "I think she went to Lima to learn how many soldiers came off a ship that was reported sailing along our coast. I'm terrified she's been captured."

"But if you go, you'll be caught too!" Suya burst out as she put down their cups.

Shali looked up at her. "Not if we dress like peasants and ride in an ox-drawn cart piled with squash and potatoes," he said. He looked at Manco and inquired, "That *is* what you had in mind, isn't it?"

Manco took a sip of *chicha*. "If any Incas recognize us, they may show us deference out of habit; so our disguise will have to deceive them as well as the enemy."

Shali was solemn. "That can be done if we dress poorly enough and remember with every breath to speak like peasants. But what chance would we have if we're discovered? My leg won't be strong enough for me to defend you very well. We should take Ruminavi with us."

"Adding another man increases our chances of making a mistake or being noticed," Manco argued. "Besides, who will associate Shalikuchima with a limping peasant or believe Manco Capac would ride in an ox-cart on a load of squash?"

"And if you don't find Coraquenque?" Suya breathed.

"We *must*." Manco's eyes were bleak with fear for his wife.

"We'll find her if we have to search every alley in Lima," Shali said in a quietly determined tone.

chapter
7

"How can you expect me to be content when there's nothing for me to do? Shall I sit day after day with my hands folded in my lap waiting for you and Nicasio to return and tell me what's happening beyond his gates?" Rianna asked unhappily.

Alonso turned away to signal Topa to pour wine for them. The interval gave him a moment to consider his answer. Rianna's complaints were justified, but he didn't want her to think so. Aware that a beautiful young woman would certainly draw attention in Peru, Alonso had decided even while they were on the ship that he'd have to keep Rianna from having contact with the Spaniards who lived in Lima. He'd also realized he'd have to give some explanation of his and Rianna's relationship. If he'd said Rianna was his fiancée, the women would ask Rianna about wedding plans and, discovering there were none, encourage Rianna to initiate some. But Alonso didn't want to marry, only bed, her. If he'd said Rianna was an orphan and he her protector, visitors would offer sympathy and ask too many questions about the past while bachelors looking for wives would call on Rianna with hope in their eyes and gifts in their hands. The only way Alonso had been able to think of to explain Rianna's coming to Peru and still avoid too-friendly or too-curious visitors was to give the impression she was his mistress. Alonso hoped respectable women would shun Rianna, that men would consider her already claimed as a paramour and unacceptable as a bride.

Alonso's plan had worked perfectly and would continue to succeed as long as Rianna didn't get a chance to speak privately with anyone. Even Nicasio, who was attracted to Rianna despite thinking she was Alonso's lover, had no opportunity to see her alone. While Alonso made inquiries about the best areas to find Incan treasure, Nicasio went into town every day to attend to his military duties. Alonso merely had to be sure he returned from town before Nicasio. Señora Bovadilla inadvertently acted as an extension of Alonso's eyes and ears by always accompanying Rianna except in her own room. The *dueña's* vigilance prevented even Alonso from making romantic overtures; and though he desired Rianna now as much as he had in Madrid, he'd resigned himself to waiting until after they'd left Lima to possess her. He was sure he could find some way to rid himself of Señora Bovadilla once they'd started the trek.

Alonso's lies had worked so well no one in Lima inquired a second time about Rianna and he was sure they wouldn't question the propriety of his taking her into the wilds on his fortune hunt. Neither would anyone care when, after a few years, he boarded a ship to Spain and left Rianna behind.

The only problem he had was to keep Rianna from complaining too much or too loudly. He had to convince her that staying on Nicasio's property was paramount to her safety and her complaints were exaggerated.

Alonso took a sip of his wine and finally said in a deliberately patient tone, "Other women find things to do at home. Why don't you pass some time with needlework, as Señora Bovadilla does? Don't women have things to do with their clothes, spend hours experimenting with new hair arrangements? Why don't you read something?"

Rianna sank into a chair and sighed as she accepted the wine Topa offered; but instead of taking a sip, she stared into the liquid's crystal depths and nervously fingered the goblet. "Santa Maria knows I've been through the house enough times looking for books; Nicasio has none. I've gotten so tired of doing nothing I've asked Coraquenque to teach me something of her language. I'm not used to such indolence, Alonso. This confinement makes me feel like a prisoner."

"What do you want to do?" Alonso asked.

Rianna put the goblet on a table and got to her feet to face him determinedly. "I want to go for a ride in the foothills and look at the countryside. I'm curious to see the old Incan road that passes near here. I'd like to go into Lima to visit the shops. I wish I could talk to someone who lives outside this house."

"There are only servants, soldiers and Incas in the marketplace. The few Castilian women in Lima don't go about as freely as you did in Madrid. It's too dangerous," Alonso replied. "Riding in the foothills is even more a risk. What would you do if you met one of those murdering rebels?"

Rianna's eyes flickered with exasperation. "Why can't someone go with me? Nicasio has offered several times, but you've always declined for me on one or another excuse. Riding with an army captain as escort should be safe enough," she insisted.

Alonso came closer to warn in a lowered tone, "I don't want Nicasio to overhear you and think we're ungrateful for his hospitality, that we gossip behind his back. Remember, Topa is his servant."

"Topa is a slave, not a servant, and has no reason to care about Nicasio's feelings or look after his interests. In any event, we aren't gossiping," Rianna said sharply. Then, not wanting to make Alonso angry so he wouldn't listen at all, she suggested, "Why don't *you* go riding with me or take me into Lima?"

"If I want Incan gold, I'll have to go deeper into the country. You know how occupied I've been making inquiries about other possible areas," Alonso answered wearily.

"While you're gathering information about Cuzco, Caxamalca, even the borders of Ecuador and Chile, I can't learn what Lima, a stone's throw away, has to offer," Rianna complained.

"Leave the decision of where we'll live to me," Alonso said shortly.

Rianna stared up at him in surprise. Having no idea Alonso considered her to be almost on the same level as Coraquenque or Topa, that he had no intention of marrying her, Rianna was annoyed at his seeming to have assumed she'd accepted his proposal. She didn't want to appear unappreciative of the help he'd seemed to have given her so far, but she didn't intend to offer herself in marriage to thank him. It was Alonso's turn to be surprised at Rianna's spirit as she said coolly, "I haven't given an answer to your proposal. I can't stay under Nicasio's roof while I'm making my decision and you're in the jungle looking for gold. I must ask you now to return the money and gems you've been keeping for me so I can rent or buy a little house."

Alonso's eyes had become wider and darker with her words, his skin paling until even his light brown beard stood out starkly against his skin. Shocked at her effrontery and at the same time knowing he couldn't return her money and jewels because he'd spent so much of it, he said angrily, "The same government runs Peru as Madrid and the laws are the same. As a woman, you have no legal rights. If I were foolish enough to give back your money, you'd find you can't buy a thing with it. If you tried, the seller would come here to get my approval. I wouldn't give this approval for your own protection. If you were to move into a house of your own, you'd have every soldier and adventurer in Lima knocking on your door for only one reason— they'd assume you're a prostitute because no lady lives alone."

Stung to the spirit by such an idea, angry that it seemed she was little more than a prisoner, Rianna also realized, if she argued the matter, her temper might cause her to say something she might later regret if her position were truly so helpless. Rianna spun on her heel and marched to the doorway. There she paused to say over her shoulder, "You needn't follow me, Beatriz. I'm going to my room where I intend to remain all day."

"Rianna," Alonso began, but she marched haughtily from the room with even her skirts seeming to rustle from indignation.

Coraquenque, who had listened to the conversation without revealing a hint of her opinion, hurried after her mistress. She thought Rianna would be weeping; but when she entered Rianna's room, she found her mistress standing stiffly before the window angrily staring at the garden.

"It seems as if you and I have something more in common," Coraquenque remarked.

Rianna's glance flashed with gold fire as she agreed, "It looks to *me* as if we're both slaves."

"At least I can dream of possible escape, but what can you dream of?" Coraquenque observed.

"A man who doesn't use the law for his own purpose," Rianna bitterly answered.

"Then you'll have to find an Inca to love," Coraquenque advised.

"Incas don't think their women are children and can't be trusted with money?" Rianna asked sarcastically.

Coraquenque replied, "Incan men aren't interested in making love with female children. And we don't have money."

"But I've heard your people are wealthy!" Rianna declared in surprise.

"Wealthy in many ways, yes, and prosperous too," Coraquenque agreed. "I've come to realize I need this thing called money to live among your people, but I don't know why your people worship those hard little disks of metal almost as we revere the sun. Though gold and silver are beautiful, I think the sun is also beautiful and surely more useful. All your people do seems to be measured in terms of money. They seem to value each other first by how many coins each has and second for personal qualities. Even your maidens' fathers pay money to their bridegrooms, as if their daughters are so much a trial they can only be gotten rid of by paying a husband to mate with them."

"Incas don't have dowries?" Rianna asked in wonder.

Coraquenque shook her head. "Incas have love and passion."

A shock wave of emotion ran through Rianna as she thought of how it would be to have such a man want her. She said slowly, "Perhaps I should arrange your escape and my own as well."

"Maybe, if you came with me, the authorities wouldn't send dogs after us," Coraquenque speculated.

Rianna shivered at the idea. "It's still hard for me to believe such things are done."

"That's because you've never gone past the gates of this house," Coraquenque said angrily. "You never saw the dogs being trained for hunts by using my people as bait." Rianna turned to look at Coraquenque in horror. The Inca nodded as if to assure Rianna this was true, adding, "Such training sessions are considered great sport and wagers are made."

Rianna turned away and put her face in her hands. Coraquenque knew she was weeping and stepped around Rianna to draw her into her arms.

"I'm sorry I told you. It's painful to learn such hard things about your people and you already have enough to worry about," Coraquenque apologized.

"What Francisco said about what was happening in Peru should have prepared me. It's just that all my people don't behave that way. I hope you can believe most of us are decent and kind."

"I know your people aren't all like the men who have come to Peru," Coraquenque said quietly. "I know *you;* and from what you've told me of your family, I know they were kind and good."

"I'm glad you realize that." Rianna lifted her head. "But tell me, has Nicasio treated Incas so?"

Coraquenque looked into Rianna's tear-starred eyes and didn't want to answer.

"It is true, isn't it? He's made such wagers."

Coraquenque nodded. "The captain has a certain dog he values highly because it's won many prizes for him."

"If he and Alonso are such good friends, Alonso must be as bad as he." Rianna turned away. "I can't bear to stay under Nicasio's roof," she breathed.

"There's nothing you can do about it unless you run away for good. To succeed in that, you'd need a carefully thought-out plan, not the impulse borne of a moment of anger," Coraquenque reminded.

"I must get out of here for a little while, at least," Rianna insisted. She again faced Coraquenque. "Alonso and Nicasio will soon leave the house for the day. After they're gone, couldn't we sneak out to just visit the marketplace? Couldn't I dress like you and both of us pretend we're servants doing the shopping? We wouldn't have to worry about how we'd get horses out of the stable because servants would be likely to walk, wouldn't they?"

Coraquenque let out a breath. "Incan slaves are never allowed to be alone with a horse."

"I'd have to tell Beatriz what we plan; so if our absence is discovered, she can explain we haven't really run away," Rianna said. "You wouldn't have to worry about our being hunted then."

"She wouldn't approve."

"It doesn't matter. What could she do to stop us?" Rianna reasoned.

"She could send a message to Alonso or Nicasio," Coraquenque warned.

Rianna considered this possibility and, recalling what Beatriz had said on the ship, shook her head. "Beatriz has reason to understand how I feel. She won't like my going out, but I think she won't betray me." Rianna looked up at Coraquenque and the Inca could see from her expression there was no point in arguing. Rianna said, "We're the same height and size. Your clothes should fit me. What can I borrow?"

Coraquenque sighed. "If we were in my own house, I could offer you a choice, but here I have only one blouse and a skirt besides what I'm wearing. It's a pity because you would be beautiful in an Incan woman's dress. Here you must put on clothes I got from one of your people, a beggar's garments." She produced a plain black skirt made from roughly woven cotton, a simple white blouse such as peasants wore in Spain when they worked in the fields.

"It will do," Rianna said, measuring the skirt to her waist. As Coraquenque started to unfasten the hooks on Rianna's morning dress, Rianna asked curiously, "How do Incan women dress?"

Coraquenque was silent a moment. She dared not exactly describe the garments of Manco Capac's wife. Finally, she said, "I have a dress made of soft wool that would suit you. It's white with a yellow and red design of birds sewn into it. The dress isn't tight at the waist like the ones you wear. It caresses the body and ends at the ankles. You have a slender figure that's nicely curved and pretty ankles so it would become you." Coraquenque neglected to say that the yellow threads were spun gold and the scarlet design was feathers of the rare bird she'd been named after. The dress was silky vicuña, not wool; and the jewelry worn with it was beaten gold.

She smiled as Rianna stepped out of her petticoats and advised, "If you would pretend to be Inca, you must remove your undergarments." Rianna looked up at her friend in surprise and Coraquenque's brows lifted in humor as she noted, "Incas don't wear corsets."

After Rianna had finished changing, Coraquenque carefully drew her curls from her face and bound them at the nape of her neck. "What shawl can you wear to hide every wisp of that hair?" she asked.

Rianna considered this only a moment before she answered. "My brother brought some cloth from Peru as a gift for me. If we cut a corner from it, I think it would make a very suitable shawl." She went to a little trunk Coraquenque had never seen her open before.

The Inca watched curiously; but when Rianna pulled out the vicuña cloth, Rianna heard Coraquenque's quick intake of breath and was confused by her expression as she came nearer to examine the cloth more closely.

"What's wrong, Coraquenque?" Rianna asked. "Can't I use this to cover my hair?"

"Nothing is wrong," Coraquenque said quickly. "I just was surprised you would own such a thing. This cloth comes from a nobleman's house. His family's insignia is sewn into the border. It's the jaguar and the condor."

"Is the nobleman someone you know?" Rianna asked hesitantly.

"He was one of the king's best and bravest generals. He's dead now; but his son has taken his place, I hear," Coraquenque answered as cautiously as she could.

"Francisco got this cloth from a Castilian merchant," Rianna said. "I wonder how it came into the trader's possession."

"Many Incan things have passed to the Castilians. Maybe the cloth was among the general's possessions when he was taken prisoner or it could have been taken from his son's house before it was burned," Coraquenque said sadly.

Rianna looked guiltily at the cloth then offered it reluctantly to the Inca. "Perhaps you have more right to it than I."

"Viracocha put it in your brother's hands and it was his gift of love to you," Coraquenque said. "You must keep it."

"I've always felt it was lucky, but I suppose it's dear because Francisco gave it to me," Rianna commented.

"Then we'll cut an end from it and you can wear it today," Coraquenque decided. "Maybe the spirit of your brother as well as our general's will protect us from discovery or, at least, from too harsh a punishment if we're discovered."

Despite the possibility of being discovered, Rianna was so happy to be out of the house it was only Coraquenque's frequent reminders that

kept her eyes lowered. Not only was it necessary for Rianna to hide
their curious color, but she had to imitate the humble attitude of a
slave. Rianna was so elated by her tenuous freedom she could hardly
bear to walk quietly beside Coraquenque. She would have liked to
sweep off the cloth that covered her head and let her hair blow free,
the sun warm her face. It was a nuisance to hold the shawl over the
lower half of her face with one hand and grasp a market basket with
the other, so it was impossible for her to do anything more than look
at the merchandise on the tables and carts.

Because she'd learned only a few words in Quechua, she wasn't
able to do more than greet the Incan traders; but she was satisfied
merely to listen to them chatter among themselves and with customers.
Though she didn't understand the conversations, she was glad to hear
voices other than those in Nicasio's house.

Rianna had given Coraquenque a few pennies from the small cache
of coins she had left and the Inca bought a fragrant mixture of rice,
beans and a savory red vegetable served on a large leaf from a pot
stirred by a smiling woman for their lunch. Then she and Rianna
found a place to sit on the grass under a solitary palm to eat. Their
care to remain apart from the others, while Rianna's face was uncovered,
drew no suspicious glances. The Castilians had brought smallpox to
Peru and some of the Indians bore scars they hid in public. The Incas
understood and avoided staring so as not to embarrass the young
woman who seemed so shy she never said more than a brief greeting.

After they'd finished their rice, Coraquenque told Rianna she would
buy some fruit. Rianna carefully recovered her face before turning so
she could watch Coraquenque bargain for a melon. Having enjoyed
her adventure so far, Rianna reflected that she even liked the way the
Incas traded. They didn't behave as if one's purpose was to cheat the
other, but bargained with a friendly, open attitude, as if both were sure
they'd benefit from whatever agreement was made.

Rianna noticed Coraquenque's sudden tension. Alarmed, Rianna's
gaze followed the direction her friend was looking and saw two Incan
men near a cart piled with squash. They were dressed in loose shirts
and tapering breeches like Topa usually wore, but of a much poorer
quality and of a blotchy brown color that said the cloth had been
hastily dyed in a vat too small. They wore faded blue hats of coarsely

woven wool that were pulled so tightly down their hair was hidden and Rianna could only see their mouths and chins clearly. One of the men was smiling so widely at Coraquenque Rianna could see his teeth, straight and white against his golden skin. The other's mouth held a solemn expression and Rianna felt that he was carefully watching the crowd. Coraquenque seemed poised to go to them; then, as if suddenly remembering Rianna was waiting, she put the melon back in the trader's hands, hurriedly said something to him and quickly returned to Rianna.

"Who are they?" Rianna asked as she got to her feet.

"Please let me go and speak with them," Coraquenque said softly, but urgently. "The one who's smiling is my husband."

"Your husband!" Rianna breathed. She looked again at the men. Although they were trying to appear as if they were loiterers, she could sense their tension. The man, who'd been smiling at Coraquenque, nodded as if to coax Rianna to agree to approach them. His companion continued staring in the other direction and Rianna again had the feeling he was alertly watching the crowd. Puzzled by his attitude, suspicious they might be rebels who were afraid to be recognized by one of the soldiers mingling with the shoppers, Rianna felt her heart take on a faster beat.

"Are they members of the resistance?" she whispered.

Coraquenque was silent a moment, reluctant to admit, "All Incas *must* resist."

"But the one is your husband," Rianna said slowly, thoughtfully.

"He hasn't known all this time what had happened to me," Coraquenque whispered. "He's taken a very great risk to come in search of me."

"Yes. I suppose he has," Rianna replied. Still afraid of discovery, she hesitated while she glanced at the men again. Coraquenque's husband was staring openly at them, as if he no longer cared about being noticed, as if a moment with his wife was worth any chance he was taking. Rianna recalled what Coraquenque had previously said— Incas married for love and passion—and knew the hazel eyes watching her friend held both. Rianna's heart melted and fear for herself faded to nothing.

"If I had a husband who looked at me that way, I wouldn't ask

122

someone else if I could go to him. No one would hold me back,'' Rianna breathed as she took Coraquenque's arm and began toward the men.

Rianna didn't need Coraquenque's warning to keep her eyes lowered as they walked across the marketplace. She knew, if she caught anyone's attention now, it could mean discovery and death for Coraquenque's husband as well as his companion. She carefully held the shawl over the lower half of her face, kept her eyes down and her brief greeting to the men was muffled. Though Rianna was curious to see what Coraquenque's husband looked like, she dared not even glance up at him. Instead, she turned partially away from the pair and tried to appear as if she were idly waiting. But from beneath her lashes, she was watching the movements of the soldiers she could see.

Aware of the other Inca's turning to an angle so he had a view of the opposite side of the marketplace, Rianna wondered at the man's identity. Having acknowledged her greeting with a distracted nod, he'd silently become Rianna's partner in trying to safe-guard them all. The Inca was so tall the top of her head barely reached his shoulder. The way he moved and held himself revealed an innate personal power that conflicted with his shabby garments. As inexperienced with men as Rianna was, she was aware that he had an almost animal-like confidence in his body's reactions and strength. He was standing so close she could feel his warmth radiating out to her and she was drawn to him. She'd seen no more of his face than his mouth; and her attention strayed from watching for soldiers to reflecting on the grave set of his mouth, despite the tenderness of its shape, the sensuality of his lips' roundness.

Surprised at where her thoughts were straying, that she had an impulse to lean against this man, who was a stranger and a dangerous one besides, Rianna concentrated on Coraquenque's conversation with her husband.

They were speaking barely above a whisper; and though Rianna had learned too few words to understand the lilting Quechua, she did recognize a difference between this flow of sounds and those spoken by the servants in Nicasio's house. Where the servants' accents had been rhythmic, Coraquenque and her husband's were music. At times when the servants would have used a tighter meter, this Quechua was crisp and clean. Rianna could see that the couple were holding hands close to the folds of Coraquenque's skirt, hiding their affectionate contact. Rianna reflected that concealing one small gesture couldn't dim the glow of the love that seemed to illuminate the air around them.

Rianna became aware of the other Incan man turning a bit more toward her, his hand at her side raising slowly, hesitantly. She shifted her gaze to see long, tapering golden fingers brush the hem of her makeshift shawl, touch an embroidered jaguar. Though she dared not lift her eyes to look at his face, she wished she knew enough of his language to ask why he touched the cloth so tentatively. She remembered what Coraquenque had said about its origin and realized this Inca must have recognized the insignia on it. She wondered if her disguise was so complete he thought she was a member of the dead nobleman's household.

Rianna couldn't know Shali was remembering that the cloth had been woven and embroidered in his home. It had been planned to be used as a dress for Yupanqui before it had been stolen and she'd been killed. If Rianna had looked up at him, she would have seen that his eyes had taken on the liquid glimmer of a lake on a moonless night.

"What are you doing here, you little slut?"

At the sound of Alonso's voice, Rianna whirled to see him making his way across the marketplace. His face was flushed, contorted with his temper; and his eyes were narrowed from fury.

"I can't leave the house for an hour and you sneak out! Dressed in these rags! I take every care to treat you like a lady and you make a fool of me by coming here to flirt with these heathen Indians! Were they inviting you to have a cup of *chicha* with them? How peasant blood always reveals itself, after all! You *are* a commoner—and common besides!" Alonso shouted.

Though Rianna was insulted, she was terrified that Coraquenque's husband would be recognized and captured. Hoping to draw attention from the Incas, she stamped her foot and glared defiantly at Alonso. "How dare you speak to me in that way even in the most discreet tones and in private? But to *shout* such accusations in public is unforgivable. You call *me* a commoner, accuse *me* of making you a

fool? I need not. You have done it yourself," she said in so contemptu-
ous a tone it was like a lash stripping away Alonso's arrogance.

Unaware that both Shali and Manco understood her words and were
afraid to leave lest Alonso harm her, Rianna wondered why they
didn't take advantage of the moment to flee. She glared at Alonso and
demanded, "How could you think you'd keep me in that house like a
prisoner? What gives you the right to tell me what to do and where to
go? If anyone ever had that right—"

What Rianna would have said was stopped by her gasp of horror.
Alonso was carrying a riding whip; and infuriated by her defiance, he
raised it high. Aghast that he might strike her, she was too shocked to
move as the whip whistled past her to hit Coraquenque's husband.

Several more strokes followed in quick succession, but Shali leaped
in front of Manco. Protecting his king with his own body, he raised
his arms to cover his face lest he lose an eye. As enraged as Shali was,
he dared not strike back; or the soldiers, who had gathered to watch,
wouldn't wait for Alonso's order to arrest Shali—they would kill him
and Manco. Shali had no choice, but to behave like a cringing slave so
no one would guess he was Shalikuchima sheltering Manco Capac. As
a new barrage of blows struck Shali's shoulders, raked his forearms
with welts, he muttered a curse in the accents of the lowest Incan
goatherd and backed into Manco, crowding against him, forcing him
into unwilling retreat.

Rianna, meanwhile, not only had recovered her wits; but her anger
had turned into a storm of loathing. "Stop it, Alonso!" she cried and
threw herself against him. "How can you do this? Stop!"

Alonso paused to loosen Rianna's grip on him. He pushed her away
so roughly she fell against Shali, who caught her shoulders to steady
her. Alonso's last stroke struck Rianna and she cried out in pain.
Shali's arms immediately closed around Rianna to protect her from
more lashes. When they didn't come, he released her.

Rianna's forgotten head-covering had fallen to the dust and her
bright curls tumbled around her shoulders. She looked up at Shali's
face. He stared into her golden eyes, saw the tear-trails glistening on
her cheeks and was stunned. This child of his enemies was the
duplicate of his vision! He couldn't move or speak in Quechua or
Castilian. For a long moment he stood as rigidly as a statue.

Alonso caught Rianna's arm and pulled her back. She spun around to face him. "Is this what an earl's son does, beat a woman he pledged to protect?" she taunted through her tears. "If there was doubt in anyone's mind about who's noble and who low-born, this morning you've shown everyone how base you are!"

Noting that the Castilian man glanced embarrassedly at the watching crowd and now might relent, Manco said hastily in Quechua, "We only asked these ladies the direction to a certain house and meant no offense."

Coraquenque hurriedly translated for Alonso.

Shali realized, as revolting as it was for Manco to apologize to Alonso, it was what a poor Inca would do. "I most humbly beg your pardon, exalted lord. The offense was inspired by my own ignorance and not intended to insult the lady," he added, pushing Manco farther back, hoping they might escape.

"I should—" Alonso started again to raise the whip.

"Don't you think you've made yourself odious enough?" Rianna asked derisively as she brushed away her tears.

Alonso slowly lowered the whip and Rianna immediately stepped between him and the Incas. "Get out of here," she urged. "Coraquenque, tell them to go *now*!"

Coraquenque didn't need to translate or even have a chance to speak.

Shali apologized again in the most humble Quechua and said a hurried thanks as he bent to retrieve the shawl Rianna had dropped. He handed it to her, gave her one last lingering look then turned to leave.

Rianna recognized that the Inca's tone had been saturated with servility, but it didn't match the expression in his eyes. Though she couldn't fully read their emotions, she knew those blackly glimmering depths held anything, but meekness, as he limped away.

As soon as Shali and Manco were far enough away so that no one in the marketplace could see them, Shali stopped walking and faced his cousin.

"This is as safe a place as any," he advised then asked, "Will you wait here?"

Manco nodded. He'd seen Shali's expression when the woman with hair like the sun had looked up at him. Manco knew Shali intended to follow the evil-tempered Castilian and learn where he took the woman whose intervention had saved them.

chapter
8

When Alonso offered to lift Rianna to his saddle and take her home, she angrily shrugged him away. "I prefer walking beside Coraquenque to riding with you," she snapped.

The little group arrived at Nicasio's house so soon after the captain had come home he was in the courtyard still astride his horse. Surprised at Rianna's appearance and that she was walking in the dust before Alonso's mount like a captured slave, Nicasio swung from his saddle and hurried closer.

"What happened, Doña Rianna?" he asked concernedly.

Rianna thought of the dog Nicasio used to win wagers hunting human beings, gave him a scornful look and marched silently into the house.

Beatriz was anxiously waiting in the main hall. She saw the tear in Rianna's blouse and knew Alonso had left in such a rage he'd been capable of striking the girl. *"Dios!"* Beatriz gasped. "Doña Rianna, has Señor Falla done this?" At Rianna's nod, the *dueña* breathed, "I'm sorry, so, so sorry. I *had* to tell him where you'd gone. Please, Doña, come with me. Let me look at your shoulder."

Rianna patted the woman's arm. "It's all right, Beatriz. I expected you to tell him where I'd gone if he came back too soon. I don't blame you.'' She flashed an angry glance at Alonso, who'd just followed them into the room, adding loudly enough so he could hear, "If you hadn't told that beast where to find me, he probably would have set Nicasio's dogs on our trail.''

"Dogs!'' the *dueña* exclaimed in horror.

"They do that to escaped slaves, you know. And that's what I seem to have become, Beatriz, a slave,'' Rianna said bitterly. She gave the woman one more pat, adding, "Don't worry about me. All I need is a bath and Coraquenque can see to that.'' Then Rianna turned and stalked from the room with Coraquenque close at her heels.

After they were in Rianna's chamber, Coraquenque turned to her and began, "I'm grateful for what you—''

Rianna hurriedly motioned for her to be silent while she latched the door and closed the shutters. After she'd smartly snapped their locks in place, she turned to the Inca and warned, "We must not speak within anyone's possible hearing.''

Coraquenque nodded and wondered what Rianna would think if she knew whom she'd protected that afternoon. For a moment, Coraquenque was very tempted to tell her friend the peasants had been Manco Capac and Shalikuchima in disguise, that she was Manco's consort; but to do so would be to confess to spying. The less Rianna knew about that, the better for her own sake, Coraquenque decided.

Finally, she said, "You saved my husband and his friend's lives by keeping Alonso angry with you.''

Rianna smiled wanly as she painfully pulled off her blouse. "I think Alonso's anger wasn't aimed solely at me. I was struck only once, your husband several times and his friend a dozen strokes.'' She looked back at her shoulder and winced over the red welt she glimpsed.

"Alonso wanted to beat *you* and dared not in public so he made them a substitute,'' Coraquenque reasoned as she peered at Rianna's welt. "If I were at home, I would have an ointment to put on that.''

"A cold cloth will do,'' Rianna advised.

As Coraquenque filled a basin with water, she said, "The soldiers were so amused by Alonso they didn't look at my husband and his friend. If they had and recognized them, their heads would now be displayed on pikes by Lima's gates.''

Rianna shuddered at the thought. "Your husband must be a famous desperado to warrant that," she finally commented. When she saw the alarm that momentarily flashed through Coraquenque's eyes, she sighed, "I don't care if your husband is the leader of the resistance and his friend is second in command. I couldn't bear to see them captured or killed."

"I owe you a debt I can only hope to repay," Coraquenque said with quiet sincerity as she brought the cloth for Rianna's shoulder. She was silent as she patted it in place then warned, "You'll have to be careful not to anger Alonso too much if you're alone with him."

"I know," Rianna gravely acknowledged. "But you or Beatriz or both of you are always with me."

"I'm an Inca so my presence doesn't matter to him," Coraquenque reminded. "He would no more hesitate to beat me than he did my husband."

"We'd find some way to stop him," Rianna promised.

After this afternoon's events, Coraquenque knew what Rianna said was sincere; and she quietly admitted, "I did once think all your people were the same, cruel and greedy, until I met you."

"Many of the Spaniards, who came to Peru, were lured by gold; but others, like my brother, were young and looking for adventure. After Francisco learned what was happening here, he tried to stop it and couldn't. He and some friends, who felt the same as he, had to flee for their lives," Rianna said slowly. "The conquistadors are the dregs of our society. What they've done here no more represent the people of Spain than the Inquisition does. Decent Spaniards are terrified of both." She looked up at Coraquenque and saw tears in the Peruvian's amber eyes. Rianna said comfortingly, "We'll think of some way for you to escape."

Coraquenque shook her head. "When Incas have a debt of honor, they repay it. Before I leave, I must find some way to help *you*."

Rianna impulsively put her arms around her friend, having no idea she was embracing Manco Capac's queen.

Rianna couldn't stop thinking of how Alonso had acted in the marketplace and comparing his behavior to the tall Inca's. Where Alonso's mask of gentility had disintegrated to reveal his vile character and shallowness of soul, the Peruvian hadn't leashed his anger out of fear for himself; he'd safe-guarded Coraquenque's husband. Rianna wondered again about their positions in the Peruvian chain of command, but she couldn't speculate too long on this. Her thoughts swiftly revolved back to the man who had protected her from Alonso's violence.

When the Inca's arms had enfolded Rianna, she'd sensed Alonso's whip strokes had stung not only his flesh, but his pride. Despite his inner rage, he'd held her gently; and Rianna's trembling hadn't been caused only by Alonso's shocking behavior. The Inca's touch had made her feel, despite her fear, as if little fires had spread along her nerves. After Rianna had stepped away and looked up for the first time at him, she hadn't been able to tell quite what he might do. Had his eyes, narrowed by anger, gazed down at her in surprise? Bewilderment? She didn't know which or even if it was something altogether different. As if he were used to hiding his feelings, the black depths of his eyes had immediately hardened; the emotion in them had vanished and she could see only her reflection on their surface when he'd faced Alonso.

Although Rianna had learned only a few words in Quechua and couldn't know exactly what the Inca had said, she'd realized he'd very humbly apologized at the same time the air had almost crackled with his fury. She couldn't blame the Inca for his feelings. Her revulsion at the way Alonso had behaved toward the Peruvians, as if they were chattel, added to her anger over the vulgar accusations Alonso had hurled at her, was like a wheel of sparks spinning through her spirit. She didn't leave her room for the rest of the day because she knew the mere sight of Alonso would cause her to say or do something that would provoke him again.

Reasoning that she couldn't avoid Alonso forever and couldn't pretend to act subdued to keep peace, Rianna knew she must think of a way to survive without him.

She wasn't certain he'd told the truth when he'd said a woman couldn't own property, but one thing was sure—Alonso had the money and gems his men had taken from the Alava house and business. Unless Rianna could persuade him to give back what had become her only inheritance, it might as well not be hers.

Even after Rianna had gone to bed, she couldn't close her eyes because of her disturbing thoughts. She lay staring up at the dark ceiling wondering if she could locate the box where Alonso had locked her valuables and break it open. If Alonso hadn't lied about the law and she really couldn't buy a house, could she rent one? She knew he was right about the gossip that would be caused by her living alone. She'd have to learn to ignore it, to endure being shunned even by her own countrywomen. She decided, too, that she'd have to learn how to deal with the men who, thinking she was a whore, would feel free to make lewd advances. Rianna turned to her side to gaze at the moonlight that filtered through the shutters in luminous patterns on the floor as she reflected on the dreariness of such a future. It was all she could hope for, she reminded herself, unless she returned to Spain. But Alonso, ever mindful of his title and his father's opinion, couldn't allow Rianna to bring back reports of how he'd taken her money and tried to beat her, that he intended to kill Incas for their gold.

Finally, Rianna threw her blanket aside and swung her feet to the floor. Haunted by memories of the life she'd once led, when she'd been part of a loving family, she put her face in her hands while a torrent of grief and despair flooded her. What evil star hung over her destiny so all her dreams had been destroyed? Even those who'd loved her had perished. Great sobs welled from her heart, yet she found she couldn't weep. Her tears seemed to have shriveled away in the desolation her life had become.

An overpowering need to get away filled Rianna. Though she knew that, for the present, her escape could be only temporary and she could go only as far as the garden, she got out of bed and groped around in the darkness for her robe. After she'd put it on, she tiptoed to the door, lifted the latch and went outside.

Rianna didn't pause beside the moonswept veil the fountain's spray had become. She took no notice of the trees whispering against the star-scattered arch of the sky, the flowers lining the stone-paved paths, the varying bouquets of fragrance the shifting breeze offered as if trying to tempt her from melancholy. When Rianna sat on the low wall of stones bordering a fishpond that once had belonged to the Incan king, she was deaf to the exotic calls of the nightbirds.

Staring into the water, Rianna silently cursed the gypsy woman who had prophesied this horrendous chain of events, but hadn't told the truth of their outcome. The gypsy shouldn't have given her hope by predicting she would find love in a distant land, Rianna thought bitterly. If the gypsy had been honest about her future—the anger, unhappiness and grief following relentlessly on her heels—Rianna knew she wouldn't have lied to save herself from the stake. She'd have gone to the fire with her parents. She gazed dejectedly into the water until dawn began to tint the sky with a deep crimson light that turned the fishpond into a goblet of dark wine.

She was startled when a shadowy reflection appeared behind hers and said softly, "Your man doesn't treat you very well."

Rianna turned quickly; and her heart gave a lurch as she looked up at the Inca, whose arms had sheltered her from Alonso's lash. She was too surprised by his presence to question his having spoken in Spanish, but she answered sharply, "I'm *not* Alonso's wife." Then, realizing what the Inca might conclude, her face flaming with embarrassment, she added quickly, "I'm not his mistress either."

"I'm glad to know that," the Inca said quietly then fell silent.

She continued staring up at him, unsure what to do or say.

He wore a roughly woven cloak, but now his head was uncovered. His hair was straight, clipped shorter than other Incan peasants Rianna had seen. It was even with his jaw and its growth so luxurious it reminded her of long, black fur ruffled by the breeze. The dawn-fading moonlight revealed his face, but not his purpose. His features seemed chiseled from granite; and while his eyes were as unreadable as a statue's, his mouth was tender, questioning, unguarded.

The Inca sat beside her on the low stone wall. In Castilian that took on the lilting accent of Quechua, he finally said, "That man isn't deserving of a woman so . . ." He searched for a word to translate his thoughts and finally explained, "In my language we would say finely born, but it doesn't mean quite the same in Spanish."

Rianna smiled wanly in spite of her previous despair. "How aghast Alonso would be to hear you say that," she commented. "He prides himself on his father's title and thinks he's superior to me because my father was a merchant and my family not in the king's register."

The Peruvian reached up and tentatively touched her hair. He lightly grasped a lock between two fingers and ran them down to its end, slowly, as if gauging its silk, before he said, "Now I finally understand why my people cannot successfully negotiate with yours—everything in your land is opposite of mine. Those among you, whose characters have little merit, are the ruling class while those, whose qualities we hold in highest regard, are the ruled.''

Rianna didn't know what to answer. In one sentence he had pulled together all the elements of the society that had brought her to this misery. He'd made sense of her own tortured questions.

''My name is Shali,'' he said then asked concernedly, ''Does your shoulder pain you too much to sleep?''

Rianna shook her head. ''I have other reasons to be awake, Shali.'' She told him her name and reminded, ''You took most of Alonso's blows. How are you and Coraquenque's husband?''

''We bathed in a cold stream. He's a little stiff, but he'll be all right.'' Shali shrugged off his own welts.

''But you were limping,'' Rianna noted. ''Did the whip hurt your leg?''

''That's from another injury almost healed,'' Shali replied then, wanting to draw her attention from a wound he'd gotten in battle, quickly asked, ''Why do you stay with that man?''

Unused to people being so direct, Rianna hesitated a moment. But when she thought of her situation, of Alonso's having the power to manipulate her life, the anger in her burst out to answer sharply, ''He has my money and won't give it back!''

''Where is your father? Have you no brothers to defend you?'' Shali asked quietly.

Rianna felt the tears that wouldn't flow before begin to gather in her eyes. Though she would have lowered her head to hide her emotions, had anyone else asked such a thing, she couldn't tear her gaze from Shali's. She looked helplessly up at him while her tears overflowed her lashes and trickled down her cheeks. ''The Holy Inquisition killed them all!'' she breathed.

Shali frowned. ''This inquiring institution, why do you call it holy? It sounds to me as unholy as it's possible to be if it would kill the family of one such as you.''

''It has become a curse on my people,'' she said bitterly.

Shali commented, ''And your people say *our* beliefs are evil.'' He was silent while he wondered if the horror of this experience had somehow linked their thoughts, as Villac Umu had insisted, and brought him the vision. He returned his gaze to her and asked, "How did they die?"

Rianna caught her breath as her tears accelerated, though she couldn't take her eyes from his. "My parents were burned at the stake," she whispered.

There was the link with the fire in his vision, Shali concluded. He took her hands in his and gently urged, "Tell me what happened. I would repeat it to a very wise man I know. He might think of a way to help you, if I can't."

Rianna's hesitation faded in the face of his sympathy. Intending to tell Shali only the barest details, as she had Coraquenque, she found herself pouring out her heartache. As she finished, she was overwhelmed by sobs.

Afraid someone might hear her weeping in the dawn and come to discover them, Shali put his arms around Rianna and drew her face to his shoulder to muffle her sobs. After a time, Rianna's weeping lessened; and he loosened his hold on her; but she clung to him as if there were nothing else in her life solid enough to sustain her.

Finally, Rianna stopped trembling and lifted her head to look up at Shali. He was a silhouette against the growing flame of the dawn and she couldn't see his face. Though he said nothing, she could feel anger radiating from him like invisible waves of light; but his hands on her shoulders were gentle.

"I'm sorry, Shali. I shouldn't have bothered you with this," Rianna began to whisper.

But Shali leaned closer and, by kissing the corner of her mouth, stopped her. She caught her breath in surprise as his lips, delicately brushing over her skin, moved to her cheek.

Shali had meant to kiss Rianna tenderly, as he would a child, to comfort her. But as he caressed her cheek, absorbed the sweet, warm scent of her skin, he found his purpose changing. Shali's lips moved slowly, experimentally to her temple, where a silky strand of her hair lit a spark in him. His mouth traveled back to Rianna's and warmly covered it, while his arms drew her against him. Her breathing quickened and his lips moved on hers more eloquently until her hands against his chest warned him away. He looked at her wonderingly.

This woman of his vision he'd thought he'd never see in the flesh was gazing at him from eyes so bright a gold they seemed to illuminate every shadow in the garden. Her face was lit with the meaning of the song his blood was singing.

Flushed and breathless, Rianna looked up at Shali and whispered, "I shouldn't do this. A lady of Madrid doesn't kiss strangers."

Shali considered this news silently a moment before he said, "We have never been strangers, *chinita*." He paused then observed, "Among my people, it's the custom for a man, who is drawn to a woman, to embrace and kiss her; but perhaps this is another way our people differ."

Rianna lowered her eyes and said hesitantly, "Men and women in Spain hardly ever kiss until after they're married. A lady is never allowed to be alone with a man, even after they're betrothed. She's always accompanied by a *dueña*, who insures her innocence isn't taken advantage of and she isn't tempted into sin."

Shali's fingers under Rianna's chin tipped her face toward his. "I'm glad for this custom only because I suspect Alonso might try to take you against your will if you had no *dueña*. But among Incas, such guardians aren't necessary or wanted. Making love isn't wrong if both the man and woman are willing and free to love. I'm an Inca; I'm free to do as I wish. I think you want to kiss me."

Shali again started to lean closer; but needing a moment to delay him so she could order her spinning thoughts, Rianna hastily said, "I didn't know your people kissed."

As if Shali knew her purpose was to buy time and it amused him, a small smile played over his mouth as he inquired, "What did you think we do, *chinita*?"

After a long moment of awkward silence, Rianna said lamely, "I don't know."

Shali's face was so near she could feel his breath warmly on her cheek as he murmured, "Maybe Incas do more than your people."

Rianna had assumed Shali would now kiss her as firmly as when she'd pushed him away. He surprised her by lightly kissing one corner of her mouth then moving unhurriedly along the edge of her upper lip, making an exploration of his caress. Instead of relighting the flame that had swept through Rianna before and frightened her, Shali kissed the other corner of her mouth, arousing only a glow that warmed her, but threatened nothing. The rules of propriety she'd been taught in the past seemed not so badly endangered when he nibbled her lower lip so delicately the caress seemed to be only a harmless, soft fluttering against her skin. When he again reached the corner of her mouth and she expected him to kiss it as lightly as before, the tip of his tongue surprised her with a dot of fire.

Then his hands were at her temples and he tilted her face so his lips could claim hers. Shali's mouth was firm and eager now; and he kissed her searchingly, savoring her response, challenging Rianna to deny what she was feeling. He nipped her with sweet savagery, moving quickly from one lip to the other, again and again, until her heart leaped into a new, exciting pace.

Intoxicated with the pleasure his kisses were giving her, Rianna momentarily forgot what she'd been taught about restraint. Shali's cloak had fallen open and she reached between the folds to put her arms around him. His hands left her temples and wove into the opening of her robe, spreading it wide as his arms slid around her. As he drew her firmly against him, the fragile silk of Rianna's nightdress, the flimsy cotton of his shirt, seemed to vanish between them. She melted against the taut muscles of his body.

Shali's instincts perceived Rianna's possible surrender and his long pent-up passion flared higher. His lips stroked, nibbled and tantalized then covered hers in a kiss so demanding she felt as if her life, all her world, depended on this man and this moment. She became aware of his hands at her breasts caressing her through the nightdress. His mouth released hers and he bent to nibble a fiery path along her throat. When she dipped her head to lay her cheek caressingly against his hair, she felt his smile against her bosom. Then his lips were at her breast, nuzzling, restlessly moving, enticing her nipple even through the silk of her gown, until so exquisite a sensation rushed through her she caught her breath. The small sound Rianna made shocked her and she pulled away. She was stunned at the liberties she'd allowed him, but her mind was still too muddled for her to say a word.

Shali's eyes shifted with reflections of dawnlight and whirling stars then focused. With a swift, graceful movement, he got to his feet and looked down at her silently for a long moment. Finally, he said slowly, as if he were very carefully choosing his words, "The customs of your people have stepped between us; but for a woman with passions as strong as yours, they must be a heavy burden."

"They never were until now," Rianna admitted with a sigh. She accepted the hand Shali offered and got to her feet. She could feel his magnetism pulling at her, became aware of swaying toward him. Resisting the temptation of his nearness, she stepped away and looked up at him.

"I've known since the first time I saw you, if it would ever be possible to take you in my arms, I would forget everything else; but how could I know you'd been taught to avoid being a woman?" he said quietly. A dark glimmer passed through his eyes and he added, "Still, I think there will come a time when you'll discard those teachings, *chinita*."

Needing to say *something*, she hastily asked, "What was it you called me—*chinita*? What does it mean?"

"*Chicha* is a girl, also a beverage that can intoxicate a man. *Chinita* means a small, lovely girl," Shali answered softly. "Next to me you are small in stature. You're also beautiful and intoxicating."

Rianna said nothing and the tension between them heightened. Shali put his hands on her shoulders. She knew, if he tried to kiss her again, she wouldn't have the strength to refuse him; but if she allowed the feelings he aroused in her to rise as before, they would overwhelm her.

She was startled from her thoughts by the sudden, frenzied barking of a dog near the house. Shali released her and she turned to look fearfully in the direction of the sound. Rianna knew that if someone awakened and ordered a guard to check the grounds for intruders, Shali would be captured. Her heart seemed to become a lifeless, heavy thing in her breast as she waited until the barking finally ceased. Still frozen with dread, she continued to listen and watch for Nicasio's guards. When the dog remained silent and no one came stamping down the path, Rianna's heart finally resumed its beat.

As she turned, she whispered, "It must have been—"

But Shali had vanished.

Rianna turned slowly to scan the shrubbery and wondered if the bushes' slight movement was from the breeze or Shali's concealing himself. She approached the greenery, but saw no hint of him.

"Shali, Shali?" she whispered as loudly as she dared. There was no answer; but she tried again, waited a little longer then finally turned to go dejectedly back to the house.

Although it wasn't Rianna's habit to awaken before the sun showed its fiery edge over the treetops and she didn't want to draw attention to herself by behaving in any unusual way Alonso might question, it wasn't possible for her to sleep. She was too restless to even lie in bed. She decided to bathe quietly so she wouldn't awaken Coraquenque because she didn't want her friend to ask questions she couldn't answer even for herself.

Despite the scare Rianna had suffered when she'd thought guards might discover her and Shali together, though she'd somehow found the strength to resist his magnetism, her desire had flooded back like a stream of fire flowing through her veins.

She filled the bathing tub with cold water in the hope that its shock would distract her from the memory of Shali's kisses; but she was disappointed. After her body adjusted itself to the chill, her inner heat returned; and she knew that shutting Shali out of her thoughts was going to be a long and arduous task.

Rianna's resolve failed her. She thought about Shali throughout the day and twilight found her sitting in the garden by the fishpond hoping he might return at the same time she was chagrined by her attitude.

When Rianna saw a shadowy figure coming down the path, her heart leaped with anticipation then fell as the figure came closer and she recognized Coraquenque.

Coraquenque studied Rianna for a moment wondering, as she had many times that day, why her friend was so withdrawn, if the incident in the marketplace had made her moody. Finally, Coraquenque sat beside Rianna and said, "I thought you'd want to know something I just overheard Alonso telling Nicasio." Rianna merely nodded in answer; and Coraquenque, grasping at straws, asked, "Are you ill?"

Rianna lifted her head and looked at her friend with haunted eyes. "What did you come to tell me?"

"I hate to give you more to worry about, especially if you aren't feeling well," Coraquenque said slowly.

"I'm not ill and I believe I'm already past my capacity to worry. One more problem hardly matters," Rianna drearily replied. "Seeing as how I've successfully avoided Alonso all day, I suppose I should know anything you've learned about what he's thinking."

Coraquenque doubted Rianna would welcome the information she had. "Alonso has decided to go to Cuzco."

This news immediately caught Rianna's full attention. "But I'd thought Cuzco had already been stripped of gold!"

"Alonso has learned there are towns in the mountains nearby that still haven't been looted because they're so hard to find," Coraquenque explained. "He wants to live in Cuzco while he searches for those towns."

"Did he say when he intends to move?" Rianna was alarmed that Alonso might drag her away before she had a chance to find the gems he'd hidden from her. She was sure, once Alonso had taken her into the mountains, there'd be little chance of escaping him.

Coraquenque said, "He only talked about starting to gather supplies he'll need for the journey and beginning to choose the men to go with him." She paused before adding, "I think that will take less than a month."

"Then I'll have to find my father's gems quickly," Rianna said anxiously. "Alonso often ignores the presence of an Inca in the same room with him and I wonder if Topa or any of the other servants have ever seen that box he keeps my father's jewels in. Do you suppose they'd tell you if you asked?"

"I've already questioned them and learned nothing," Coraquenque said. "While Nicasio and Alonso were gone, the Incan servants searched the house, but found nothing."

Rianna looked at Coraquenque in surprise. "You had them search?" she breathed. "Didn't they mind? Are you sure you can trust them not to mention it to Nicasio?"

Coraquenque recalled how eagerly the Incas obeyed an order from their queen and struggled not to smile. Though she couldn't tell Rianna who she was even to assure her, Coraquenque promised, "No more thorough search could be made and not a word will reach Nicasio or Alonso's ears." Hating to say this, but realizing Rianna should know her position, Coraquenque said slowly, "I think you shouldn't count too much on finding what you seek."

Rianna surprised Coraquenque when she lifted her head and firmly answered, "I may as well forget recovering those jewels or any money at all. I think Alonso sold the gems in Spain; there's no way I can tell one doubloon from another and claim it as mine."

"Maybe you should just take whatever money we can find," Coraquenque suggested.

"If we could find any and I took it, Alonso might call me a thief and have me arrested," Rianna answered.

"Perhaps you should seek refuge with my people."

Rianna considered this possibility a moment before answering, "Your ways are different from mine."

"The Incas were happy enough before the Castilians came," Coraquenque recalled. "I'm sorry I can't promise what the future will be."

Rianna said hastily, "I'm not hesitating because I anticipate your people's destiny is to become slaves or be destroyed. Neither do I mean life in Spain is superior to yours. Please don't think that."

Coraquenque patted Rianna's hand. "I know you better than that, my friend." She paused thoughtfully then concluded, "You know so little about Incas. I admit you'd have to accept or tolerate many differences between our societies. It isn't possible to predict how you'd react to some of our beliefs, but I promise we aren't savages or cruel."

"I understand that, Coraquenque, but . . ."

"In order to build any kind of life with us, you'd have to put out roots, make friends among us," Coraquenque said. "Perhaps you'd fall in love with an Inca. Then you'd have to deny your love or forget all possibility of returning to your homeland."

Rianna bowed to Coraquenque's logic and inwardly wondered if she'd already fallen in love with an Inca and must deny it.

That night Rianna again faced sleeplessness; but this time she refused to give in to the temptation to leave her room. If Shali was in the garden, she dared not meet him. Should he kiss and caress her as he had the previous night, the risk was too great that she would surrender to the passion he aroused in her. It was impossible for Rianna to separate love and its physical expression. To her mind one was melded to the other; she was determined not to love an Inca unless she could, as Coraquenque had pointed out, accept a civilization so different from her own and forget returning to Spain.

But try as she might to put Shali from her mind, his image persisted in her memory. The shape of his face outlined by his hair, hair that had felt so luxurious and soft against her cheek, the freshly washed scent of it, the warm, slightly musky fragrance of his golden skin. Shali's eyes seemed to look at Rianna from the shadows of her room and she remembered how they'd flashed with dark fire after he'd kissed her passionately. Angry at her musings, Rianna struggled to turn her thoughts to what she might do to avoid going with Alonso to Cuzco; but she heard again Shali's voice warmly coaxing to pour out her troubles, felt his cloak's texture against her face as she'd wept on his shoulder. His shoulders were so broad, she remembered, his body trim and tightly muscled.

Rianna was alarmed at how her thoughts persistently led her back to the desire she'd felt in his arms, the exquisite sensations his touch could arouse in her.

Finally, Rianna sat up in bed and stared at the moonlight pouring through the shutters, wondering if he were in the garden waiting for her to come to him. Furious at how her body could betray resolution, she again lay down, this time with her back to the windows, and determinedly shut her eyes.

But Rianna couldn't help wondering why Shali had risked his life the night before by coming to Nicasio's garden. He couldn't have anticipated her going outside. She was haunted by the feeling that he'd intended to steal into her room. When she finally fell asleep, her dreams were filled with fantasies about Shali's coming soundlessly to her bed and spending the night making love.

chapter
9

Coraquenque slowed her horse to a walk and turned him off the Incan road onto a trail that wound into the foothills like a snake. Noting that Rianna's mount fell into step behind hers, she turned in the saddle and called back, "This path is wide enough for both horses." After Rianna had guided her animal forward so they rode abreast, Coraquenque said encouragingly, "You needn't worry about this trail. It goes around the base of the slopes and our horses won't have to do any real climbing." Rianna nodded, but Coraquenque knew she still was very uneasy and remarked, "I thought you'd be glad to get out of the house for a few hours. Are you afraid we'll be caught?"

"It doesn't seem likely," Rianna answered. "Alonso should be busy all day choosing the men who'll go with us to Cuzco. Nicasio's being with him makes it doubtful they'd return to the house early because they'll find most of the men in taverns and I've noticed Nicasio is never in a hurry to leave a place where he can have a drink or two."

"You've stayed in your room and avoided them so completely this past week, even if they did come back early, I doubt they'd miss seeing you," Coraquenque observed. "Beatriz was still asleep when we left so she wouldn't be able to tell them anything if they'd think of asking. Only Topa knows we've gone because he saddled the horses and sneaked them out to us, but he wouldn't tell Alonso even if Nicasio has him beaten to death.''

From time to time Rianna had privately marveled at Topa's friendship. The boy seemed willing to do anything for Coraquenque if she only hinted she had a task. Rianna couldn't know Topa was obeying his queen and could have died for her, as the Incas in Atahualpa's procession had sacrificed themselves to shield him from Pizarro's cannons and swords.

Aloud, Rianna had to concede, "You've seemed to have thought of everything. I was surprised when you showed me that the old Incan gates at the back of Nicasio's garden only appear to still be sealed. You could leave Nicasio's house any time you choose, especially if Topa will saddle a horse for you.''

"I promised to help you before I leave. Such a promise is sacred to an Inca,'' Coraquenque insisted. She was silent a moment before adding with a sigh, "Topa can't sneak a horse out of the stable *any* time I ask. He could manage it today only because Nicasio's guards know he and Alonso won't come back till after nightfall and can relax without fearing punishment. Everything fell in place to give me a chance to see my husband and tell him I'll be going to Cuzco with you.''

"As well as give him any other information you've learned about what's happening in Lima?'' Rianna ventured. At Coraquenque's silence she added, "I've noticed you've avoided mentioning your husband's name; so I've concluded he must be very famous if you think even *I'd* recognize it. Don't answer, my friend. I respect your reasons for what you're doing. Besides, I can hardly admire what my countrymen are doing to your people. I can only say I realize you're going to tell your husband what you've heard Nicasio say about military plans and that the men who were under the late Almagro's command have become so disgruntled they may cause trouble soon.''

"I should have known you'd have thought all this out,'' Coraquenque admitted. "But you'll be safer if you don't learn more about my husband or what I'm doing.'' When Rianna said nothing, Coraquenque asked, "Is that why you've been so nervous today?''

"Going to the hills with a spy to meet one of the leaders of a resisting army is hardly what I'd call merely a pleasant ride," Rianna observed. "I suppose Shali will be with your husband."

Coraquenque didn't miss the cautious note in Rianna's voice when she mentioned Shali. It occurred to her that Rianna had also casually inquired about Shali several times during the past few days. Coraquenque hadn't wanted to say anything that would have revealed Shali's identity as Shalikuchima so her answers had been as obtuse as anything she'd have said about Manco. She turned to look at Rianna as she replied, "Yes, Shali will probably come along. Will you mind his company for a while? My husband and I would like to go off by ourselves." Coraquenque saw the surprise flash across Rianna's face and added, "Though Shali often seems reserved, you'll find he isn't at all shy and can be pleasant company. He speaks your language very well so you can pass the time with conversation if you wish."

"I know," Rianna replied.

Suddenly Coraquenque realized it had been *Rianna* who'd mentioned Shali's name first and she hadn't introduced them in Lima. She recalled that Shali had spoken only Quechua in the marketplace; Rianna couldn't know he understood Spanish unless they'd met since. Rianna hadn't been anywhere she might have met Shali by accident. He must have come to the house, Coraquenque concluded. There was only one reason Shali would have taken such a risk—he was attracted to Rianna. Coraquenque thought a secret, romantic meeting with Shali would explain why Rianna had been so moody lately. She understood Rianna didn't want to talk about her feelings and decided not to say more.

Coraquenque tilted her face to the sun a moment then pulled her shawl over her darkly shining hair and commented off-handedly, "The breeze from the mountains carries a sweet, fresh scent; but it's chilling. Maybe you should cover your head too."

Rianna pulled the vicuña cloth over her hair, not knowing wearing Shali's insignia told Manco, who was watching from a rocky ledge, that no one had followed them from Lima.

The path ahead narrowed to thread between two lofty slabs of granite. Rianna held her horse back behind Coraquenque's mount.

145

Walking single file made conversation awkward and Rianna welcomed the opportunity to compose herself.

Since that dawn a week ago when she'd met Shali in the garden, Rianna had valiantly struggled to put him out of her mind. She'd thought she'd been making a little progress until the previous night, when Coraquenque had awakened her.

A message had come from Coraquenque's husband asking her to meet him in the foothills. Rianna had assumed Shali was the courier; and when she'd realized he must be waiting for the answer outside the bedroom door, her heart had started pounding wildly. She'd known she must accompany Coraquenque; because, if the Inca went alone and accidently met a Spaniard on the trail, he'd assume she was an escaped slave and take her prisoner. Rianna had decided she would have to control her feelings for Shali, but then she'd thought she and Shali would be in Coraquenque and her husband's company. Having learned now she and Shali must be alone together, her pulses sang with an excitement she couldn't deny. She was angry at her inability to control her feelings for this man, who was unsuitable for so many reasons.

Coraquenque passed the end of the rocky corridor and drew her horse to one side so Rianna's mount paused too. Rianna's inner struggle came to an abrupt halt as her eyes fell on the scene before her.

The granite slopes had withdrawn like arms that opened to reveal the meadow they had hidden in their embrace. The rising and falling wind turned the long grass into green waves so it seemed as if the valley was filled by a rolling emerald sea. In the distance the grass disappeared into the shady avenues of a grove of trees that swayed against the silvery-gray walls forming the foot of the Andes. Rianna lifted her eyes to the surrounding peaks, towers of granite capped with snow. Curls of gray smoke from a drowsing volcano joined the white cloudbanks being blown across the bright arch of blue sky. Despite the moving clouds, the sun was a dazzling gold disk that turned the Andes' frosty tops into shimmering crowns.

Noting the rapt expression on Rianna's face, Coraquenque said quietly, "Now you can feel in your own heart why we fight to keep our land."

"It's as if this place has a life of its own. I can almost hear its heartbeat," Rianna breathed.

"Have a care the friar in Lima doesn't hear you say such things," Coraquenque warned. "They come too near Incan thought and the foundations of our religion."

Surprised, Rianna looked up at her friend and didn't know how to reply. But beyond Coraquenque's shoulder she suddenly noticed two horses grazing on the distant floor of the valley. One of them was a coppery flame in the sun, the other as dazzling white as the mountain summits. Alarm was a stream of icy water abruptly flooding her veins. "Horses!" she exclaimed. "Have we been followed and a trap somehow laid?"

"Those are my husband and Shali's mounts," Coraquenque said.

Rianna returned her gaze to the horses wondering that men, who'd appeared as impoverished as Shali and Coraquenque's husband in the marketplace, could possess such fine-looking animals. Then she remembered they'd had to have captured the horses; there was no other way Peruvians could get them. Her thoughts were interrupted by Coraquenque's horse suddenly bounding forward and she realized Coraquenque was eager to see her husband. Rianna gave her mount the signal to follow, but they trailed behind Coraquenque. She was surprised when Coraquenque veered her horse toward the trees before she noticed the distant chestnut galloping in the same direction. When Rianna understood the Incan couple were racing off to be alone, she slowed her horse to a trot.

Shali, who'd been sitting in the grass, had risen and was watching the couple. Rianna noted that the longbow he held had an arrow already fitted to its string and a case of more arrows was slung over his shoulder. She knew that, even here in this hidden valley, he was alert for an enemy. Not until after Coraquenque and her husband had disappeared under the trees, did Shali turn his dark gaze on Rianna.

Feeling excitement already rising in her, wanting to delay their meeting so she could regain her self-possession, she slowed her horse to a plodding walk. But she couldn't tear her eyes from the tall figure moving with such effortless grace to the white horse to tie the weapons to the saddle then turn to await her. As she came nearer, she noticed, instead of the cracked sandals of before, Shali now wore boots that seemed to be sewn of gray suede. His dark green jerkin skimmed over the hard lines of his body to his narrow waist where he'd knotted a slim, black sash. Black breeches outlined the length of his legs to his ankles and covered the tops of his boots. A sheath holding a long dagger clung to his flat hip. When Rianna stopped her horse and looked down into Shali's face, she recognized the tension in his features, the streak of dark fire that shot across his eyes before they hardened into unfathomable black pools. He raised his hands, offering to help her down.

When she didn't move, he asked, "Do you prefer to remain on your horse?" She continued to look silently at him and he added, "Coraquenque will be some time returning and I think you'll get tired in the saddle."

Rianna leaned forward and self-consciously put her hands on his shoulders. They were so firm and warm, his hands at her waist so gentle in their strength as he eased her from the horse. Her breasts brushed his chest; and when he set her on her feet, she was little more than a breath from his embrace. Rianna felt Shali's magnetism pulling at her, though he only gave her a long, thoughtful look before releasing her waist. Without a word, he took her hands from his shoulders and turned away.

Rianna watched his long, smooth strides, the graceful way he moved unhurriedly, almost lazily away; and she wondered what he intended. Unlike their meeting in the garden when his attitude had been open and warm, Shali now seemed distant, even cold, though the dark gleam in his eyes had a moment ago belied this. When he stopped walking, she expected him to turn and face her, say something; but he lifted his head to look at the distant mountain spires; and the wind's whispering was the only sound besides the pulse beating against her temple.

Though Shali seemed to ignore Rianna, his own emotions ran so high he closed his eyes while he tilted his face to the wind and wished fervently he could erase from his memory the vision Rianna had made. The shawl had slipped back from her head as she'd ridden across the valley. Her curls had loosened to scatter like silk rings thrown to the sun and her eyes had seemed to gather the light, becoming as gold as topaz at noon. While he struggled to suppress his feelings and wondered if his passion for Rianna was as indelibly inscribed on his face as it was in his being, he wasn't conscious of defiantly straightening his shoulders and drawing himself even more proudly erect. He didn't know that, to Rianna's watching eyes, his high-flung head made him appear more a prince than a soldier, that she was thinking he was an Inca, whose heritage was woven into the mists of the ageless mountains. He was in his element, part of a world that seemed so alien to her she couldn't guess his thoughts.

Finally, sensing Rianna's tension, Shali opened his eyes. Though he still didn't turn to look at her, he asked quietly, "Are you uneasy because you aren't used to mountains or because you're alone with me?"

The forgotten reins slipped from Rianna's fingers and she approached Shali hesitantly. "I think this is the loveliest place I've ever seen," she answered. Irritated with herself for implying she was nervous in his company, but not knowing what else to say, she helplessly stared up at the strong lines of his profile and tried to order her discordant thoughts.

Shali's eyes remained fixed on the mountaintops and his mouth was set in the same hard line as when he'd helped Rianna down from her horse. "Then it's my presence disturbing you," he surmised. He waited a moment and, when she didn't reply, turned his head to look down at her and almost harshly say, "I told you before you have nothing to fear from me."

"I'm not afraid of you," Rianna denied.

"Then you must be frightened of the way you feel about me," Shali concluded.

"It's only that—I just—" She fell lamely silent a moment before finishing in a burst, "You *can't* understand how I feel! Your world is too different from mine. We're too different from each other!"

Shali's hands abruptly gripped Rianna's shoulders and he firmly turned her to face him. His eyes were narrow and gleaming with angry light as he demanded, "How can *my* world be so fearful when it was *your* world that killed your family? A man of *your* world is holding you prisoner but I never considered doing anything against your will.'' Realizing he'd defeated his own purpose, that his first words had revealed how he wanted her, Shali loosened his grip on her shoulders. ''Though you turned me away, I came back the following night and again the night after hoping you would change your mind and come out to me.''

Having no idea that royal blood flowed in Shali's veins, that he'd have been a duke if he'd been born cousin to the Spanish king, not knowing what a concession such an admittance was to an Incan nobleman, Rianna exclaimed, ''What would I have done, made love with you in the grass like an animal? Are you so used to base-born women you think a lady's no different? Or is Coraquenque a rare exception among your people?''

Shali stared at her a long moment, so infuriated he was speechless. Then, realizing Rianna had no more inkling of who and what he was than how an Incan courtship was conducted, Shali leashed his temper and said mockingly, ''Even the ignorant Indian you think I am would be a fool to make himself vulnerable to capture by losing himself in a woman's body in his enemy's garden.'' He paused then added coolly, ''And I have never touched what you call a 'base-born' woman.''

Rianna was as aghast at her outburst as he. Shali hadn't tried to force her to do anything and she had no right to insult him, she reminded herself. She'd just proven she was afraid of her own emotions. Her cheeks flamed and, feeling wretched, Rianna lowered her eyes. ''I'm sorry. I've assumed so much, too much, about many things,'' she stammered. He released her shoulders, but didn't turn away. Despite her apology, she was wary when she felt his fingers under her chin tilting her face toward his.

But Shali merely looked down at her appraisingly a moment before his expression finally softened and he observed, ''The first time I saw you I wondered if the color of your eyes and hair meant you were a handmaiden of the sun. Now your skin adds to the effect.''

Wishing she could turn away, Rianna said helplessly, ''I'm blushing! Haven't you ever seen a woman blush with embarrassment?''

The corners of Shali's mouth tipped in a restrained smile as he answered, ''No, *chinita*. It's a thing my people don't seem to do.'' He released her, adding, "That you blush and I don't is only one of the many things we can learn about each other if you're willing."

"I suppose there is a lot we don't know."

Shali's fingers lightly closed around hers and he said more casually than he was inclined, "Come with me, *chinita*, to sit in the grass and look at the mountains while we talk. I'll answer whatever I can about me and my people and perhaps ask a question or two about yours."

Rianna studied Shali's face. His expression was without guile, his eyes open and unguarded. At the same time she decided to do as he'd suggested, she also resolved to keep her emotions under better control.

Shali's hand steadied Rianna as she settled herself in the grass. In one lithe, easy movement he lowered himself to sit beside her then again took her hand in his. Just that casual touch seemed to start a current flowing through her blood. Wishing she could snatch away her hand, but not wanting him to know how he affected her, she stared at the slender fingers weaving through hers and asked the first question that came to mind. "How did you learn to speak my language so well?"

Shali's eyes took on the unfocused look of someone staring into the past as he said, "I was living near Tumbez when Francisco Pizarro first came to Peru. A number of his men were weak from hunger and they needed a place to rest from their travels. They behaved well in those days and their visit appeared friendly so they were allowed to remain. Several officers were guests in my parents' house and I learned enough of their language to make their needs understood. Pizarro decided to return to Spain and asked if a few of our people could go with him. My father foresaw having more traffic with these aliens and thought it might be good for me to learn about your land, but he insisted Pizarro leave a number of his men behind to ensure bringing me back."

Not aware that Pizarro had brought Incas to the Spanish court, Rianna said, "Perhaps you won't have so many questions to ask me if you've already visited Spain."

"Maybe not about your land, but there still is much for me to learn about you," Shali replied. As if he weren't ready just yet to voice questions about Rianna, he continued, "I became fluent in your language and learned to read and write. I was surprised when I later discovered Francisco Pizarro can't read, though he calls us savages."

"How do you know he can't read?" Rianna inquired, herself surprised at this information.

"While Atahualpa was imprisoned, he came to suspect it and had one of his guards scratch the name of your god on a nail he'd found then presented it to Pizarro and asked what the markings meant. Pizarro said the scratchings had no meaning," Shali recounted.

Rianna shook her head in dismay that the leader of the Castilians in Peru knew less than Shali, an Incan peasant. "I wish I could speak your language," she said.

"I would teach you, but we'll never have enough time together unless . . ." he began then hastily suggested, "Coraquenque could teach you."

"She has, a little; but sometimes she seems to put me off. I've wondered if she dislikes the task or would rather I don't learn enough to understand what she says to the other Incas in Nicasio's house. She goes to some lengths to avoid mentioning even her husband's name," Rianna said. She paused and looked slyly at Shali. "I don't suppose you would tell me his name?"

"I wouldn't want you to have to constantly worry about being overheard if you impulsively mentioned it, of having to remember to keep a bland expression on your face if Nicasio should bring news about him that makes you happy, sad or angry." Shali laid his hands on Rianna's shoulders. "Nicasio would do anything to learn where Coraquenque's husband is hiding—*anything*."

Rianna concluded, "Nicasio would torture us both."

"Since Coraquenque would never betray her husband and you have no idea where he is, Nicasio would torment you to your deaths." Shali leaned closer. "I can't risk telling you not only for your and Coraquenque's sake, but for her husband and my sake as well."

"Of course you must think of your army and your own survival."

"I wasn't thinking of that, *chinita*," he said softly.

Rianna looked up at him, wondering at his meaning.

"Coraquenque's husband loves her and I . . ." He didn't know how to finish.

Rianna stared at Shali. "But what do you mean?" she breathed, feeling as if she were on the edge of a precipice as she waited for his answer.

Shali's black eyes gave back her steady reflection as he said, "I'm not a man to make hasty decisions so I can't be certain yet, but I suspect I love you."

Rianna's lips parted in surprise. Above the thunder of her heartbeat she suddenly again heard the gypsy fortune teller's voice. *Not the kind of man you may have dreamed of, a kind of man you have not ever seen before, more a man, more true a love than you can imagine.*

Shali's fingers curved around Rianna's shoulders and he drew her closer. When he felt Rianna's hands at his waist, he brought his lips to hers and kissed her tenderly rather than with passion. Shali wasn't sure if Rianna would react as she had in the garden, with the fear someone else had taught her. He hoped, if he were careful to contain his own passion, he might not alarm her before he had a chance to teach her that love-making wasn't something a woman must endure because of a bargain made between two families.

Shali didn't know propriety and passion had been waging a battle in Rianna all this time; and when he kissed her, prudish tradition retreated before love. Rianna's mouth was willingly offered up like a gift to the sun and the mountains and the sky that stood over them. Shali could hardly believe it when, without his guiding them, her hands moved up from his waist to his sides and clung to him. He was gladdened by this sign of her coming triumph over fear; and his lips happily wandered over her face, softly kissed her eyelids, nibbled the curls that fell over her temples. When his tonguetip began to explore the patterns of her ear, he felt her body tense; he was afraid she would end this now. But Rianna didn't move away or give any sign she wanted him to stop. Encouraged, Shali lifted her hair; and Rianna turned her head languidly as he followed its curve to kiss her nape. His mouth moved again to caress the side of her neck to its base, where his tongue tasted her skin and found it as sweet as the nectar in a dew-kissed flower. He dipped his head to the lacy edge of her bodice, traced her skin with a line of kisses.

Shali's hands slipped from Rianna's shoulders to cup her breasts. They made creamy mounds above her bodice his kisses could explore, his tonguetip burrow momentarily between, follow their valley to its end and travel up her throat to again find her lips. Aware of Rianna's quickened breath, Shali trusted the instinct that told him she wouldn't push him away as she had in the garden. His fingertips found the buds of her nipples, lightly caressed them through the thin cotton gown until they bloomed and she trembled. When her lips clung more hungrily to his, a flash of fire swept through his nerves.

He kissed her forehead then moved away to wait until the flame in his being dwindled to a more manageable heat. When he took her hands in his and she looked up at him, her eyes seemed to be molten gold begging to be stamped into his design.

Still wary of frightening her and losing all he'd finally gained, he said softly, "I can't know what will offend or alarm you. Tell me if I do anything you object to. Don't push me away in anger or fear."

But Rianna had already discovered she didn't want to make decisions. She wanted to cast aside all the rules she'd been taught, like old petticoats she knew she no longer wanted and didn't care to even look at again. She wanted to be swept away on the feelings Shali aroused in her. She touched his cheek and felt, even in that small gesture, as if she were begging to become part of him.

When Shali asked her to lie down, Rianna sank to the grass with an ease that surprised the part of her mind still able to judge what was happening. But it didn't protest. When his arms cradled her shoulders and his hands cupped her head to tilt her face to his, she nestled closer.

With Rianna's bosom pressing his chest, the contours of her hip and leg warmly against his, Shali was too distracted to be cautious. His lips caressed hers with more fire than he'd planned; but Rianna's mouth moved urgently, hungrily, with his. Startled by her new abandon, Shali opened his eyes to find hers like golden lamps lighting the darkness he'd lived in so long.

Now the spirals of sparks rising in Shali ignited the shadows in his eyes and revealed the path to his soul. The last shreds of Rianna's inhibitions dissolved, leaving her like an empty vessel waiting to be filled.

The desire Shali had denied himself surged through him with such power his mouth took Rianna's in a fiery compulsion he couldn't withhold. His body swung over hers and even through their clothes they were captured by an almost unbearable need. He moved persuasively, tantalizingly against her, until the forces raging in him were so compelling he forgot all else. He moved aside and sat up. Intending to strip off her clothes, he suddenly realized he didn't know how her alien garments were fastened.

Rianna stared up at Shali. His features were taut with desire, but the moment had given Shali's mind a chance to function again. He turned his face aside to take several deep breaths and collect himself. When he again looked at her, his mind was clear; and his eyes had lost their wild look.

Shali coaxed Rianna to sit up then guided her until she was half-lying across his lap. He felt her trembling and drew her closer, until she rested her cheek against his chest. He kissed the top of her head and whispered into her hair, "My heart was too quickly filled with you."

"I couldn't think of a thing except what I was feeling," she said wonderingly.

He lifted his head to gaze at the Andes as he softly said, "I would like nothing more than making love to you in this valley, especially for this, our first, time." Shali felt the shiver that went through Rianna and knew she'd been too absorbed by the discovery of her passion to think of the enormity of repeating tomorrows. "You do realize these feelings we share are not the kind to be quickly ended," he warned.

"Maybe that's what frightened me from the beginning," she admitted. She thought about how great a change he'd caused in her, smiled ruefully and said, "A short time ago I accused you of wanting to make love in the grass like an animal, but you had to stop *me* from doing just that."

"I like making love in the grass," Shali remarked then added, "but I don't want Coraquenque and her husband to return and find us in the midst of it." He was silent a moment as he thought of how it could have been if they'd had more time. He realized he wouldn't even be able to tell Rianna with any certainty when they would see each other again. He sighed and said, "The circumstances of our lives make pledges impossible. I can only promise I'll come to you as soon as I can—unless you meanwhile change your mind."

She could hear his heart beating strongly in her ear and knew he was afraid she'd deny him. She lifted her head and looked up at his face. His eyes moved down to meet hers; and once again, they were impenetrable, guarded. Suddenly she realized how deeply his emotions ran, how sensitive he was that he had so great a need to conceal his feelings. She said slowly, "If I had friends among my people I could confide in, none of them would think I'm wise. Only one person might have understood, though he wouldn't approve—my brother Francisco."

Shali bent his head to kiss her tenderly. Then he said softly against her lips, "It will sometimes seem as if what we want is impossible. There may come times when you'll question my purpose; but always remember this, *chinita*. The circumstances may disappoint you, but my motives won't. Despite the troubles ahead, you'll have to trust me."

Because all the obstacles they might have to face seemed less real than their immediate problem of finding a way to be together again, Rianna solemnly, but readily, agreed.

When Manco and Coraquenque returned a short time later, they found Shali and Rianna sitting side by side in the grass. That Rianna's head rested on Shali's shoulder and his arm was snugly around her waist answered any questions Coraquenque may have had. When Shali looked up, Manco regretfully said they should get ready to leave the valley. Shali reluctantly obeyed and helped Rianna to her feet. Because she wanted to preserve her and Shali's closeness as long as possible, she went with him to get the horses, which had wandered across the meadow as they'd grazed.

Shali's low call caught Wayra's attention, but she came directly to Rianna. The mare lowered her snowy head and touched her nose to Rianna's cheek to softly blow on her. Rianna smiled and lifted a hand to caress Wayra's silky neck.

Shali looked on in amazement a moment before commenting, "Wayra comes to no one that way except me."

At the sound of Shali's voice, Wayra turned her head to look at him; but she didn't move away from Rianna.

"She knows I'm a friend," Rianna said as she brushed her cheek against one velvet ear.

"It appears she thinks of you as more than a friend," Shali observed, looking thoughtful.

"Sometimes a horse can sense a special bond with a person even at their first meeting," Rianna said quietly as she watched Shali swing up into his saddle.

Shali gathered the reins in his hands then looked at Rianna silently a long moment. "Sometimes a man can sense an even more precious bond with a woman the first time he sees her." He kissed his fingers and reached down to transfer the kiss to her lips. His fingertips lingered to softly trace the outline of her mouth, showing in his gesture how passionately he wanted to stay.

Then he turned Wayra, nudged her sides and galloped away leaving Rianna looking after him with such open longing Coraquenque felt almost as if Rianna might run after him.

"Shali isn't the kind of man to offer his heart lightly," Coraquenque said softly.

Rianna glanced at her friend from eyes glistening with tears and couldn't answer.

"You want him as much as I want my love," Coraquenque surmised then added encouragingly, "I think it won't be long until they return."

"But how can they?" Rianna breathed.

"They'll find a way," Coraquenque replied.

She put her arm around Rianna's waist and they watched until the horses vanished in the distance.

Rianna repeated Shali's promise over and over in her mind all the way back to Nicasio's house until it became a litany, a prayer. To Shali's god or hers, she wondered, or were they the same?

Rianna spent what was left of the afternoon sitting in the garden by the fishpond letting memories of the afternoon overwhelm her. When Coraquenque came to remind her Alonso and Nicasio would soon be home, Rianna sought seclusion in her room.

Neither Rianna nor Coraquenque had an appetite for dinner. Though they knew sleep was unlikely, both wanted to cherish their memories of the afternoon in the quiet of their own beds; and they prepared to retire even before the sun's last rays had faded from the sky. After bidding Rianna good night, Coraquenque went to her adjoining room.

Having anticipated a restless night, Rianna was surprised by drowsiness. She concluded that the long ride and the mountain air had been tiring. She closed her eyes to envision Shali standing in the meadow staring at the snow-capped Andes, his hair ruffled by the wind, his back defiant with anger. When slumber overtook Rianna, her memories became dreams.

Once again Rianna was lying in the grass in the isolated valley and Shali was sitting at her side. Instead of being puzzled by the complicated fastenings of a gown, he lifted the hem of Rianna's nightdress from her bare feet then bent to circle her ankle with kisses, seeming to leave a ring of sparks in his wake. He edged the nightdress higher, paused again to press his cheek to the side of her calf, linger there a moment, kiss her and move the hem higher. His kisses followed its ascent, leaving a bright path that seeped into her skin and lit a warm glow beneath.

Rianna's senses weren't sleeping though her mind was and couldn't discern that the messages stirring her ardor were caused by real, not phantom, caresses. Her consciousness didn't perceive the reality, but her ears heard the soft sound of his boots then the whisper of his garments falling to the floor. Shali straightened, as in the dream, unable to resist the lure of her lips. He leaned close to kiss her tenderly then lay his cheek to hers for a moment. Rianna felt his hair, soft and thick, brushing her temple; she turned her face to nuzzle it, to absorb its scent of sky and mountains. He whispered in her ear; and though he spoke his own language, she knew the meaning of the musical words was love. Dropping one more kiss on her forehead, Shali moved away.

Rianna felt his fingers lightly brushing the inside of her leg, travel slowly to her thigh, pausing while his lips explored her texture then move higher to trace a shimmering path. A new sensation began to suffuse her being, a tingle turning her flesh into warm fluid. As Shali's caresses delicately persisted, the tingles merged into a subtle, sweet aching. Ripples of sensation radiated through her body. The impulses increased, enticing her through the layers of slumber and nearer to awakening. Rianna became aware of her increasing consciousness at the same time she wanted to remain asleep and continue the dream, the exquisite feelings, to a promise of fulfillment she couldn't yet imagine, but sensed was awaiting her.

When Rianna's eyes opened, something warm was gently, but firmly, covering her mouth—a hand that stopped her startled cry before it had a chance to begin. Then she saw, in the moonlight beyond the hand, Shali's face was real.

"I promised I would come as soon as I could," he whispered as he took his hand from her mouth.

Rianna unthinkingly reached for her blanket to pull it up and preserve her modesty. She discovered the blanket had already been tossed aside and her nightdress, as in her dream, was at her waist! She was stunned. Shali watched her, his hand still poised as he gauged her reaction, wondered if he must again cover her mouth to stop her from crying out. Finally, Rianna understood that Shali had colored her dream with reality. Caught by surprise, already in the midst of a situation she'd been taught was unthinkable, her memories of the happy afternoon were crowded from her mind by a lifetime of forbidding admonitions. Yet the desire Shali had already aroused in her wouldn't allow Rianna to turn him away.

In a turmoil of conflicting emotions, all she could think of to say was, "Coraquenque will awaken!"

"Coraquenque woke up some time ago and went to her husband," Shali whispered.

"People have been walking back and forth past my bed while I've been sleeping?" Rianna was confused.

"Only me, *chinita*, to tell Coraquenque her husband was waiting near the old Incan road."

"But if you stay here, what will they think we're doing?" Rianna breathed.

"I doubt they'll give us much thought." Shali's voice had a sharp edge.

He was inclined to say more, but instead, considered Rianna's attitude. He'd persuaded Manco to take advantage of this last night near Lima before they returned to the mountains. Because Manco's too brief meeting with Coraquenque had stirred his passion, he'd agreed to risk approaching Nicasio's house. Shali had come eagerly to

Rianna's room still fired with the afternoon's desires, thinking the pledges they'd shared in the secret valley had finally overcome Rianna's inhibitions. Anticipating her happy surprise at his keeping his promise and coming so soon, that she'd welcome him to her bed, he was chagrined; but it didn't occur to him to turn away.

Resigned to patiently wooing Rianna past her fears, he whispered, "I'll help you forget what you've been taught about love." Then he bent to bring his lips to hers.

Shali's mouth moved searchingly over Rianna's, tenderly fondling rather than kissing her. With the tip of his tongue he delicately outlined her mouth. Then he gently nibbled her lips, coaxing out the tension to make them ready for his kiss. He was aware that her increasing passion was overcoming her reticence and he let his mouth at last settle on hers. The pliant caressing of his lips demanded nothing, though it reawakened the enticing sensations of before.

Rianna closed her eyes. The sweet aching returned and grew into a longing she couldn't have voiced if she'd been inclined. It was better not to think too much, she decided, best not to decide anything, easier to let the sensation overtake her. When she became aware of a feeling of emptiness waiting to be filled, Shali's lips were brushing one nipple; and she caught her breath at the tremor that shook her. Afraid her sudden tension was due to alarm, he withdrew whispering soothingly in Quechua.

He sat at her side without touching her for a time while he considered what to do. Finally, he decided to carefully continue to try to win her.

Rianna opened her eyes and saw him sliding into bed. Echoes of old teachings hissed at her to flee; but the sensation of the hard, warm body snugly alongside hers was winning over the voices of her past. Shali was lying on his side watching her face, measuring her conflicting emotions. But all she could see were his eyes, filled with desire reflecting the shimmer of moonlight. Without Rianna's consciously choosing, her hand reached out to touch his shoulder. Her fingers ran along its strong curve to his arm then down his side to his waist. She felt him shiver and looked at his face.

Shali's eyes on Rianna didn't waver though his mouth was soft with kisses he was waiting to give. The impulse to touch him more intimately floated through her thoughts, but fled; her fingers sliding over his hip stopped.

"Does your touching me this way mean I haven't come so far, taken this risk for nothing?" he asked quietly. She withdrew her hand. Disappointed, he commented, "I came prepared to be patient. I knew I'd have to teach you; and I'm willing, if you'll let me." He paused, waiting for some sign of encouragement and, seeing none, said in annoyance, "I'm the same man you wanted so ardently in the valley this afternoon." Then he got out of bed.

Shali began to pace the room with a soundless, lissome grace that reminded Rianna of a jungle cat. The moonlight made him a silhouette of broad shoulders and firm, sleekly moving muscles, long, lean legs. When he paused to gaze out the window, his profile was stamped with strength, the tilt of his head at first revealing uncertainty then regret and finally a determination that renewed her wariness of him. As unconscious of his nudity as an animal was of its fur, Shali turned to face Rianna.

"I think you want me as much now as you did before, but you're afraid to admit it," he said as he came closer. He stopped at the bed and looked down at her a long moment, noting that she'd retreated to the far side and was holding the blanket up to her shoulders like a shield.

"You won't need this," he muttered, snatched the covering from her and, with a flick of his wrist, tossed it to the floor.

"Have you come to love or to conquer me?" she breathed.

Shali put one knee on the bed and regarded her silently a moment before he answered, "To love you, I must first conquer your past however tightly you cling to it." He reached over so casually she didn't move away. When he caught her nightdress with both hands and, in one quick movement, pulled it over her head, she was so surprised for a moment she didn't move. During that moment, he threw the garment aside and firmly pushed her shoulders to the pillows.

"We have hours until dawn comes and I'll have to leave," he said quietly. "You needn't decide during that time whether you love or even like me, but one thing you'll learn before I go is that your body is a thing of beauty and can be a source of great pleasure."

Shali gripped both of Rianna's wrists in one hand and pinned them against the pillow above her head while he lay one leg over hers. She tried to wriggle free; but he watched her struggle calmly, holding her with such ease that after a moment she gave up to look helplessly at him and demand, "You said before you wouldn't force me into anything; but what are you doing now, if not planning to ravish me?"

"This afternoon I said there might be times you'd question my purpose, but I never thought this moment would be one of them. Your body is already so aroused you'll discover I won't have to force you." He kept his voice low, but she could hear the undercurrent of his anger as he added, "If I were to leave now, your unblemished virtue wouldn't soothe the pain of spending the rest of the night tossing in frustration." Then he leaned closer and said more gently, "You promised to trust me. Do it tonight, *chinita*."

Before she had a chance to answer, he bent his head and his mouth claimed hers. Expecting his caresses to be as lightly enticing as before, Rianna was stunned that Shali's lips were hard and moved ruthlessly against hers in a challenge to deny the forces he knew were pulsing through her. Rianna's passion, waiting just beneath the fragile surface of her reluctance, ignited; and her smoldering blood burst into a fire that blasted away her reason. He gambled and released her wrists. When instead of fighting him, her arms slipped around his back, he felt as if the wheel of the heavens shuddered.

Shali's lips left Rianna's to trail kisses down her throat to her bosom, between caresses whispering the ancient lilting love words of his people. His mouth bathed her breast in fire; but his lips teased her nipple with unerring delicacy until she seethed with the impulses racing along her nerves.

He lifted his head to glance at her face, his eyes gleaming with the knowledge that he'd won her at last, then lowered his head to surprise her with a line of gentle nips on her stomach, a ring of kisses on her midriff. Her fingers wove into his hair as the tip of his tongue flicked the curve of her waist.

Shali rose to kneel beside Rianna and run his fingers over her body, stroking her flesh with so tantalizing a touch she trembled; but he ~ressed her unhurriedly, bringing the urges racing through her into sharp focus. She caught her breath and he withdrew to cover her mouth with his, muffling any further sounds.

Finally, he raised his head and whispered, "Now can you say I'm forcing myself on you?"

She stared up at him silently a moment while her mind gathered its scattered thoughts.

"I want you to admit you desire me," he insisted. "If you won't, I'll stop now."

Rianna could see in Shali's blackly gleaming eyes that, despite his ardor, he would go, if she told him to; and she knew she couldn't endure the pain this would leave her with.

"Yes," she breathed. "Shali, I want you."

Shali bent to kiss her softly with a lingering tenderness that was a promise, before he moved over her. Rianna's breath quickened and she tensed with anticipation.

He pressed his lips to her shoulder at the side of her neck, caressing her a moment before he whispered into her hair, "Don't try to guess at what you think will come." He moved slowly, sinuously, teasing her as he murmured, "I wouldn't like it if our love-making always followed the same pattern and neither would you."

Shali raised his head and nibbled around her lips' perimeter. Then his mouth brushed her parted lips with caresses so elusive she reached up, mutely asking for him. He captured her mouth in a kiss so intense the fires smoldering in her sprang high to engulf her mind with flame and she wasn't aware of Shali's body shifting to poise over her. His caresses swept Rianna's senses to new heights until she caught her breath at a sudden sharp pressure, a quick stab of pain.

He paused to kiss the corners of her mouth. His breath gently brushed aside the tendril of hair that covered her ear and he whispered, "Whatever may happen in all the tomorrows to come, that will be the only pain my body will ever give you."

Rianna opened her eyes to look into Shali's. A shaft of silver light coming from the window made them a swirl of luminous shadows for a moment before the moon was covered by a cloud. Shali's hips began to move slowly, persuasively. In his growing desire, his eyes gleamed blackly, seemed to become more slanted, until Rianna's vision became a shimmering blur.

The supple rhythm of his body scalded her senses with waves of sensation that became a steadily growing hunger blotting out everything but his breathless whispers. She didn't need to understand the music of his words. They were a fiery song answering the calls of her own spirit.

. Each time it seemed Rianna couldn't bear the magnitude of the impulses racing through her, Shali knew it; and though his body throbbed with the fervor that welled up in him, he paused or changed his rhythm to deliberately begin again and arouse her more. He brought Rianna to the brink of ecstasy then held her back, until he felt as if he reached to her through a tunnel of his own shattering nerves. Her quick, little breaths became gasps of mounting pleasure; but Shali still waited. Not until he felt a tremor deep in her being and knew her body would wait no longer did he allow his own fire to overtake him; and they were propelled into an explosion of ecstasy that consumed them with its power.

When Shali's mind began to function again, he felt as if he'd become one of the wisps of smoke that drifted into the night after a fire had been quenched. It wasn't until his heart had resumed its normal beat that he became aware he was still lying on Rianna; he moved to her side to enclose her in his embrace. She laid her head on his shoulder and he turned his face to burrow into her hair.

Noting that she was trembling, he whispered concernedly, "Did my passion frighten you and I, after all, fail in my purpose?"

Rianna tilted her head to look at Shali. "If I'd known how it could be, I would have stayed with you in the garden the first night you came here and come out every night after."

He turned to kiss her forehead and his lips remained. She felt his body relaxing, lengthening; and he lay quietly for so long a time she began to wonder if he'd fallen asleep.

But as Rianna closed her own eyes, the question that had been haunting Shali's silence became his whisper against her forehead, "Must you remain in Alonso's company?"

Rianna's wistful answer came from against his neck, "As long as Alonso won't return my father's money to me, there's little else I can do. I have nothing."

Shali's fingers under her chin gently tipped her face to his and he said quietly, "You have me."

chapter
10

The sky was as black as when Shali had first come to Rianna's room; but he could perceive from the stillness, the sense of waiting in the garden beyond the windows, dawn would soon be coming. He lay a moment more, listening to Rianna's quiet breathing, absorbing the sensation of her body in his arms, the warmth and perfume of her. Knowing he couldn't delay longer, that Coraquenque must be back in the house and he and Manco out of the area before light, Shali carefully withdrew his embrace and got out of bed.

Making no more sound than the shadows his movements disturbed, Shali found his clothes and dressed quickly. He returned to Rianna's bedside to gaze down at her while he fastened his knife sheath at his waist then bent to touch his lips to her forehead. Finally, he reluctantly straightened and left as silently as he'd arrived.

Floating in the shallows between wakefulness and slumber, Rianna was aware of Shali's touch; but drowsily assuming his kiss was the prelude to other caresses, she waited without moving. When the lips that had already discovered so many ways to lure her into ecstasy didn't reach again into her darkness, she lifted her hands invitingly. Discovering nothing, she felt for him beside her. Not finding the body she'd become as comfortable with as her own heartbeat, she quickly sat up to peer through the room's shadows.

For a moment Rianna wondered if the hours they'd shared had been a dream. Was it possible for fantasy to be so vivid, for her to imagine subtle details of the art of love if she'd never had the experience? Yet there was a difference in the way her body felt, as if it no longer was her own secret, as if her flesh now knew things she hadn't even dared think about before.

She lay back, trying to sort out her memories; and the scent in her pillows banished her suspicions of having dreamed the night away. The fragrance spoke of a grassy valley swept clean by the mountain winds, blended with a faint musk her instincts recognized as coming from the lush heart of a rain forest. It evoked remembrances of Shali's hair brushing her shoulder as he'd kissed her throat, his taut, lean body sinuously bringing her senses to explosions of delight that even in memory made her tremble. From the empty darkness of her room she could again see fathomless black eyes looking down at her slowly being lit by passion, hear the Quechua love words he'd breathed.

When a soft rush of air brought the garden's fragrance, like flower petals showering on the bed, Rianna quickly turned with Shali's name on her lips.

"It's only I," came Coraquenque's whisper.

"Did they . . .?" Rianna began.

"They left safely." Coraquenque's weary murmur discouraged other possible questions.

Rianna heard her friend's door softly close. She lay silent, but for the pulsing music Shali had made of her heartbeat, waiting for the spell he'd seemed to have cast on her to return. Instead, the echoes of the fears he'd banished came to circle her with a soundless chant: Shali is the son of an ancient people, whose way of life is steeped in traditions as foreign to Castilians as the Andes' soaring peaks were distant from Madrid's grassy plateau. Rianna silenced the ghosts with her certainty there was nothing left in her being that could deny him if he returned to her room the next night, the one after or a hundred nights from this.

If he returned.

The words were as ominous as the notes of a cathedral's bells tolling a funeral mass; and Rianna sat up in bed, rigid with tension. Like a serpent inexorably twined around a tree limb, a new possibility insinuated its way into Rianna's mind and tightened its hold. Maybe the union of their bodies didn't have the same meaning for Shali as it did for her. Perhaps the Incan concept of love was so different from hers she couldn't imagine the implications it carried in his mind. Rianna worried that Shali might not return at the same time she wondered, if he did, what kind of future was possible with a lover who was a soldier in a guerrilla army hiding in the mountains?

Recognizing that her turbulent thoughts drove away all hope of sleeping, Rianna got out of bed and, pulling on her nightdress, lost count of time while she paced, as Shali had earlier stalked while he'd wondered if their worlds were so far apart even love couldn't span the space between.

Sudden shouts, the rattle of hooves on paving stones, a horse's defiant trumpeting, was followed by a man's piercing cry. Rianna's first thought was for Shali—had he been captured and dragged back? She heard again the horse's angry shrill of warning, drumming hooves, several human shouts. Rianna rushed to the door and threw it open. Dawn was beginning to tint the garden with a gold light, but the commotion was coming from too deep in the foliage for her to see what was happening. Then Coraquenque was in the doorway at Rianna's side, peering anxiously into the violet shadowed paths.

"You said they'd left safely," Rianna hopefully recalled.

"They wouldn't have turned back," Coraquenque said slowly then, remembering how Shali had appeared when he'd rejoined Manco, as if he'd left part of himself behind, she wondered if he might have taken so great a chance as to return. She knew it wasn't in Shali's nature to love or hate halfway, that his emotions flared so high as to make him dangerously impetuous.

Coraquenque turned away. When she came back a moment later, their dressing gowns were over her arm. "I don't think it would be unreasonable to ask what this noise is about at such an hour." She held out Rianna's robe.

"Especially on a Sunday morning," Rianna commented as she thrust her arms into the sleeves then hurriedly tied the gown's ribbons. "It's enough to awaken the entire house."

"We would have been awakened, if we'd been sleeping," Coraquenque dryly remarked as she fastened her robe. She hurried after Rianna still tying the sash.

Holding their hems immodestly high, they ignored a curving path and ran directly across the lawn. The sounds were coming from the far side of the garden; and Rianna's fear for Shali increased. The panting girls burst through the bushes that surrounded the fishpond and stopped abruptly.

A white horse was rearing and kicking at Nicasio's guards, who were trying to get near enough to throw a rope over its head. Nicasio was shouting directions to no avail, while Alonso stood back looking faintly amused at their efforts.

"Wayra!" Rianna breathed. She hurried to Alonso's side and begged, "Don't let them hurt that mare."

Wayra's heels caught the morning light as she sent one of the men into the shrubbery and Nicasio fearfully scuttled back. Alonso chuckled at Nicasio's flight. "It appears more as if that beast will win this contest," he remarked then, as Wayra's lunges turned her rump toward him, muttered an oath. Catching Rianna's wrist, he hastily retreated to a safer distance.

Rianna saw a whip arc over a guard's head and tried to tug her wrist from Alonso's grasp; but he threw an arm around her waist, pulling her back. "Let me go to her! I can stop her!" She squirmed to free herself.

Rianna's body, soft and uncorseted, moving against Alonso, sent a provocative thrill through him. Her tumbled curls, scented silk, brushed his cheek. Sudden desire momentarily distracted him from the scene until Rianna demanded, "Let me go, Alonso! How *dare* you hold me this way!"

Aware of Nicasio's reproachful look, several nearby guards' staring, Alonso released Rianna; but before he could say a word of explanation or apology, she'd dashed toward the horse.

"Wayra!" Rianna whispered then paused to say more forcefully, "Come to me."

The horse's ears swiveled; its dark eye turned; and taking one quick snap at her tormentors, Wayra rushed past them to Rianna.

"Get back, Rianna!" Alonso cried.

"That horse is wild!" Nicasio exclaimed.

"Santa Maria!" one of the guards breathed fervently.

But Wayra stopped in front of Rianna and, as if relieved to find a friend at last, lowered her head to gently lay her face against Rianna's chest. Rianna rubbed her cheek on Wayra's forehead, murmuring soothingly.

"Get away from that animal—it's crazy!" Nicasio exclaimed as he rushed toward them. He veered aside as Wayra's hindquarters came up and her hooves flashed out. Nicasio approached from another angle and stopped a wary distance away. "Doña Rianna, I *beg* you. Stay away from that creature!"

Stepping around to Wayra's side, but still keeping an arm over the horse's glistening shoulder, Rianna said calmly, "If I do, how would you propose to catch her? The horse's dislike of you and your men is as obvious as her friendliness for me."

"I don't know this animal or where it came from," Nicasio began.

"I'd say some enemy left it in your garden hoping it would kill you," Alonso commented, eyeing Wayra from an area out of the reach of the horse's kicks. "I think you'd be wise to send one of your men for a crossbow before this creature decides to attack again."

"A crossbow! *Madre de Dios!* This horse is as gentle as a kitten with *me*!" Rianna exclaimed. She stretched out her arms as if she would shield Wayra with her own body. Recalling one of the most frequent reasons Alonso had said it was impossible for her to go riding, she said, "You've told me there were too few mounts available for me to go riding." Rianna noted Nicasio's quickly hidden scowl, which confirmed her opinion Alonso had lied. She added, "I can ride this horse. Obviously, it's useless to anyone else."

"I won't have you even trying to mount that animal. It's a killer!" Alonso argued in seeming concern for her safety, though he was angry she'd revealed his lie.

Rianna, meanwhile, had climbed up on the stones that surrounded the fishpond. To Alonso's horror, she caught Wayra's mane and swung up on her bare back.

Afraid to approach should the horse attack them and Rianna fall off to be trampled during the scuffle, Nicasio waved his men to back away. "Doña Rianna does seem to have a way with this mare," he admitted as he watched her lean forward to put her arms affectionately around Wayra's neck.

"It isn't your horse or any of your men's, Nicasio?" Rianna pointedly inquired.

Thinking if Rianna had her own animal Alonso no longer could prevent her from riding with him, Nicasio quickly confirmed the mare wasn't his.

"I know this horse doesn't belong to Alonso, so it seems I can claim it," Rianna said firmly as she slipped off Wayra's back. She picked up the broken cord Shali had used to tether Wayra.

"That animal should be destroyed," Alonso declared. "Nicasio, send one of your men for a crossbow as I already suggested. I won't have Rianna—"

She spun around and spat, "If anyone harms my horse, I'll go to Governor Pizarro himself to report the crime; and though I'm a woman, I think he'll listen to *that* charge. Everyone knows how valuable horses are in Peru as well as the penalty for stealing, much less destroying, someone else's."

Alonso was livid with rage, but he couldn't answer Rianna as he wished in front of Nicasio and his men. Leashing his temper, he said, "If you want to be killed or crippled, I suppose I can't stop you."

Rianna's eyes flared with triumph as she commented, "I must think of a name for my new horse." Turning to Coraquenque, she inquired conspiratorially, "What is your people's word for wind?" She hoped that Coraquenque grasped her underlying meaning.

"Wayra," Coraquenque gave the expected answer.

"That's what I'll call her—Wayra," Rianna seemed to decide. She stepped around Wayra and began leading her away from the fishpond, the men still gaping at the mare's docility in the girl's hands.

After they were far enough away, Coraquenque said under her breath, "The way Shali knotted this rope tells me Wayra is yours now."

"I was afraid he'd been hurt and Wayra had wandered back," Rianna sighed in relief.

"Shali loves Wayra," Coraquenque said quietly. "He would only give her to someone he loves."

Rianna's spirit soared with even greater joy. Now she *knew* Shali would come back to her. Whatever their differences, however many problems the future held for them, it was enough for her at the moment to know he loved her.

Since the scene Alonso had caused in the marketplace, Rianna had pretended to sleep late in the mornings so she wouldn't have to see him before he left the house. Today she not only was obviously awake, but it was Sunday, when no business could be conducted in Lima. Aside from attending church, Nicasio and Alonso would spend their day at home. There was no way Rianna could avoid them unless she again locked herself in her room, which was impossible because Wayra wouldn't tolerate the stableboy's approaching to even feed her.

It was Nicasio's habit to attend early mass and have a late breakfast. Though Alonso accompanied him to the cathedral, his motives weren't pious. The city dignitaries, even Francisco Pizarro himself, attended this service. Alonso liked to pause outside the church after mass to chat with them and court their favor.

Rianna's terror of priests had lessened only enough so she didn't get hysterical when she saw one, but she still couldn't bear sitting in a crowd sprinkled with them, and she couldn't go to the cathedral. She'd never blamed God for the crimes against her family committed by those who called themselves priests; so after she'd bathed and dressed, she prayed in the solitude of her room. Today she wasn't sure if she should ask forgiveness to have spent the night with Shali, though they weren't wed, or if she should give thanks he loved her and was safely out of Lima. She wondered, too, what Shali's god, Viracocha, would have thought of their love, but she was too shy to ask Coraquenque.

Rianna had just risen from her meditations when Beatriz tapped on her door to let her know they'd all returned from church. Steeling herself for the anticipated tension of the day, Rianna left her chamber to accompany Beatriz to the dining room. Coraquenque followed on silent feet.

Nicasio and Alonso were already in the dining room when Rianna turned into the corridor leading to it. From his place at the table, Alonso could see Rianna walking down the hall; the desire she'd earlier awakened in him kept his eyes riveted on her.

171

From a series of narrow windows in the passageway, rays of sunlight angled. As she walked through them, her golden curls twined with ribbons made a flame that shimmered, faded, flared again. The ivory damask dress was cut too simply to be fashionable, yet its bell-shaped skirt emphasized the gliding grace of her walk. The tight bodice had but one row of small pearls sewn to a finely pleated gold ribbon along the square neckline, but the cream of Rianna's throat needed no jewels or lace to call attention to its beauty. While elaborately decorated, slashed sleeves were the vogue, hers were damask tubes pointing to the delicacy of her hands. Alonso wondered why this child of a common merchant should have the carriage and refinement of an aristocrat. But added to Rianna's natural beauty, he uneasily noted, was a new composure. How could she have acquired this quiet poise overnight, he wondered, or had it been developing so gradually he'd never noticed?

Nicasio's heated glances at Rianna didn't escape Alonso. He was sure Nicasio would be more eager to find a way to accompany Rianna on a secluded ride since that horse had appeared from nowhere. Alonso didn't trust Coraquenque or even Beatriz to be proper chaperones. Rianna had made friends of them both and he thought they would be likelier to aid than guard her. He wanted Rianna more than ever; and the greed for Incan gold, that had distracted him for so long, receded a little to be matched by desire. He wished he could take her away from all these watchful eyes now.

As Rianna stepped into the room, Alonso realized he'd been gawking like a country lad would at a noblewoman in a passing carriage. Annoyed at himself, his greeting was acerbic, "Is this Athena, whose charm calmed wild Pegasus?"

Rianna fixed Alonso with her golden gaze, but said nothing until after Topa had seated her. "If Wayra were a magical horse, I could fly on her wings wherever I please. That I'm still here proves she's an ordinary mare and I an ordinary woman." She glanced at Nicasio. "Good morning, Captain."

Hoping he could find some favor in Rianna's eyes, Nicasio said, "Though that horse isn't Pegasus, neither are you an ordinary maid, Doña Rianna; and you do look like Athena today."

"Thank you, Captain," Rianna replied as she unfolded her napkin.

When she made no further comment, Nicasio, still hoping to charm her, said, "I beg your pardon, Doña, that no one on my staff is able to approach your horse and so you must tend it yourself. I wish I could think of some remedy."

"I find the task of feeding and grooming Wayra a pleasure, so there's no need to apologize on that account," Rianna assured, but added in a less gracious tone, "It's a shame you don't allow Incas into the stable; because I think Topa, who in no way resembles a Castilian man, might be able to approach Wayra. I fear the task of cleaning her stall may tax my strength too far."

"It certainly isn't the job for a lady," Nicasio agreed. He thought over her suggestion, decided Topa had so far proved reliable and might be trusted not to steal a mount and fly. "You may be right about Topa and perhaps his appearance wouldn't excite the horse's aversion to men."

"I could go to the stable with Topa to see if Wayra objects," Rianna pressed.

Not knowing Topa had already prepared mounts then sneaked them out for Rianna and Coraquenque the previous day, Nicasio turned to look at the Incan boy and asked, "Would tending Wayra frighten you? If so, admit it now. Horses know when someone fears them and often take advantage of it. In Wayra's case, you probably would be trampled."

Topa approached his master's chair. He knew Rianna's arranging for him to have access to the stable was deliberate, that she was offering him a chance to escape. He kept all hint of happiness from his features and said impassively, "I've never been allowed to tend a horse, but I haven't been afraid when I've held yours and waited for you to come into the courtyard each morning."

Satisfied Topa would serve Rianna's purpose, Nicasio turned to her and smiled. "Topa will be at your service whenever you find it convenient."

"I'm very grateful, Don Nicasio," Rianna replied with obvious relief. Her using his personal name was an indication of how pleased she was by his thoughtfulness.

Alonso, irritated that Nicasio had won Rianna's smile while he himself had angered her, decided to change the subject to one that not only would absorb Nicasio's attention, but would exclude Rianna from the conversation.

"I'm glad the matter of that horse has been disposed of," he said as if he were satisfied with the arrangement. Then he addressed Nicasio in a conversational tone, "Did you notice Francisco Pizarro wasn't in church this morning? I wonder if he's ill. Perhaps he's gotten one of the fevers so common in this land."

Nicasio brushed a napkin to his lips before he replied, "If anything threatens Pizarro's health, it isn't disease. Maybe he's learned of another conspiracy against him and finally has the good sense to stay home where he'll be safe from attack."

"Finding those three robes hanging from the gallows with his, Velasquez and Picado's names attached should have made all three of them nervous about public appearances," Alonso commented. "Pizarro should pay attention to what his secretary writes over his name about his former friend. Picado ridicules the deceased Almagro's soldiers and stirs their tempers more."

"Those men are so poor a dozen of them living in one hovel must share a single cloak," Nicasio said. "Picado infuriates them, but those who have brought complaints to Velasquez go away muttering that he isn't a judge, but only an echo from Francisco Pizarro's lips. Stories about Secretary Picado's hoarding gold in his house even the Crown doesn't know about angers the men more."

"If Pizarro *had* to have Almagro executed, he should have conducted a public trial instead of rushing the case through in secret. Then Almagro's men could have understood their commander was disobeying orders and trying to usurp Pizarro's power. Governor Pizarro should have placated his old friend Almagro's son with a promotion, not dismissed his soldiers so they had no income and nothing to do except chew over their complaints."

"Pizarro should have reassigned Almagro's men to scattered areas after the execution, but he wouldn't listen to his closest advisors and surely not to me," Nicasio said regretfully. "Diego Almagro will never be promoted higher. His father's betrayal of Pizarro and his Panamanian mother's blood prevents that."

Alonso thought Nicasio was right, but he was sure Almagro's son must be bitter. "I think Diego's quiet demeanor only shows he's biding his time. He may seem to avoid contact with conspirators; but I'll wager he knows each detail of every plot they hatch and has, so far, not seen one that merits action. Mark my words, Nicasio, if a scheme comes to his notice he thinks might succeed, he won't run to Pizarro to warn him.''

''Secretary Picado has already told Pizarro about a plot some priest said he'd heard in the confessional, but the all-powerful Francisco Pizarro said it was just a story and disregarded it,'' Nicasio said sarcastically. He shrugged helplessly. ''What can I, a mere captain, do except follow the orders I'm given? If Pizarro is attacked, my men and I will defend him. If he's killed,'' Nicasio crossed himself fervently as he spoke, ''I'll try to maintain order until the new *licenciate* comes.''

''The *licenciate* should have been here already,'' Alonso reminded, but he wasn't sad that the still unnamed official the Spanish court would send to assist Pizarro in governing Peru hadn't arrived. Alonso hoped the *licenciate* never came to Lima, because it was rumored his assignment could include enforcing new laws the Spanish Crown had decreed to curb the cavaliers' behavior toward the Incas. If Alonso would gather his fortune, he knew he couldn't do it by treating the Indians humanely.

Nicasio sat back in his chair and sighed. ''As if I don't have enough to worry about, I've learned Manco Capac has been supplying weapons to Almagro's followers. I guess he and Shalikuchima have finally captured enough weapons so he can give them back to Castilians who want to create new chaos among us. I wonder how I'm supposed to prevent that, as I've been ordered. It's impossible to find Manco or Shalikuchima and we seldom can capture one of their soldiers. Whenever we manage to trap one alive, he won't say a word no matter how long he's tortured. They all die without disclosing even their names. It's too bad we can't catch Manco. I'd recognize his face and make certain he was subjected to the most exquisite torment. If it took weeks, he wouldn't die until I'd learned where their stores of weapons are hidden and how to get Shalikuchima.'' Noting Rianna's shudder, Nicasio turned to her and apologized, ''Forgive me for discussing such distressing matters, Doña. My excuse is concern for the safety of us all.''

Rianna was horrified to hear of Incan captives being tortured as her sister had, but she had no idea how Coraquenque's heart twisted when her husband was threatened by name. She didn't know Shalikuchima was Shali. Still, she couldn't hide her pallor or disguise her sudden disinterest in food.

"I appreciate your concern, Don Nicasio, yet I think I must lie down awhile. Such talk makes me feel rather faint," she said weakly.

Alarmed at Rianna's sudden paleness, both Nicasio and Alonso began to rise to go to her assistence; but before either of them took a step, Private Sarabia burst into the room and hurried to Nicasio's side.

"Captain Montesinos, Francisco Pizarro has been killed!"

Nicasio leaped to his feet. "I knew this would happen! Quickly, tell me how it came about!"

"A mob broke into Pizarro's house and surprised everyone there except Herrada, who had turned traitor. Alcantara was the only one who had time to put on his mail and that was because his and Chavez's attendants kept the conspirators at bay," Sarabia said in a torrent of words.

"And Chavez?" Nicasio asked. "What of the cavaliers who usually visit Pizarro after mass? Where were they?"

"Chavez was killed trying to dissuade the conspirators; but many of the cavaliers, having no weapons, fled through the gardens when they learned what was happening. Alcantara, a few cavaliers that stayed and their pages held Herrada's men back from Pizarro's chamber door; but Pizarro hadn't time to even adjust his shield straps. When Pizarro saw Alcantara staggering from his wounds, he threw his shield aside and wrapped his cloak around his arm to use in its place. Herrada saw several of his men fall in the fray, cried it was taking too long and pushed one of his own men against Pizarro. Pizarro ran him through; but before he could free himself of the man, he was wounded in the throat. As he fell, Herrada and several others plunged in their swords. Now the conspirators are running through the streets shouting 'The tyrant is dead' and 'Long live Almagro.' "

"I must regain order," Nicasio declared and hurried to the doorway. At its threshold, he remembered his guests and turned. "I'll order the gates locked and leave guards for you, but the insanity of this sort of thing is contagious and I don't know what will happen next. Though my house isn't in the city, you must stay behind these walls.'' Nicasio turned and ran down the corridor with Sarabia at his heels.

Alonso sank back into his chair and put his face in his hands while he considered what he might do. He wished he knew how extensive this revolt was so he could judge more accurately which side might win. Gonzalo Pizarro would surely come as soon as word reached him. He was said to be courageous and to have the best lance in Peru, but Alonso thought he and his men were too far away to come quickly enough. Alvarado in the north with a large body of soldiers was unlikely to let Pizarro's assassination go unpunished. Order might be restored even more quickly if the Inca Manco Capac could be prevented from supplying Almagro's faction with weapons.

"What are you thinking of, Alonso? What will come of this?'' Rianna's fearful questions finally broke through his concentration.

"Almagro and his rabble can't hold Peru against men like Alvarado and Gonzalo Pizarro,'' Alonso said slowly. He was silent a moment before he made the decision he'd been considering. "I'm afraid Lima will become a battleground and it would be wise for us to go to Cuzco at once. Captain Holguin is near Cuzco with a large force. He should be able to keep that city safe.''

Rianna thought it was more logical to remain behind these solid walls than expose themselves to attack by making a journey to Cuzco. She reminded, "Nicasio is a captain too. Aren't we safe in his house?''

Alonso had gotten to his feet and was pacing agitatedly. At Rianna's question, he stopped and glared at her. "What does a woman know of such things?'' he growled. "Start packing immediately. If the mob doesn't attack, we'll leave for Cuzco tomorrow morning.''

Rianna was appalled. If they left so hastily, how would Shali know? She got up and approached Alonso. "You don't care about my safety or even your own. You know the *licenciate* will be sent for; and you think, when he comes, he'll stop adventurers like you from robbing and enslaving the Incas,'' she accused. "You want to steal as much as you can while it's possible!''

"That was my purpose in coming to Peru,'' Alonso said with a calm that angered Rianna more.

"I'm not leaving Nicasio's gates so I can be killed by a mob,'' she declared. "Give back my father's money and jewels and I'll take my chances here."

Alonso's hand flashed up to deliver a slap that sent Rianna flying backward against Coraquenque. Then he came closer to grip her arm and say, "I've seen the looks you and Nicasio have been exchanging. I know why you want to stay with him. You seem to have forgotten it was I who rescued you from the Inquisition and protected you since. Whether you realize it or not, Lima is now the most dangerous place in Peru. You'll come with me to Cuzco if I must bind your hands and feet and carry you over my saddle." Alonso thrust her away and stalked toward the door, saying over his shoulder, "I have preparations to make, but don't think I'll be so busy you can slip away."

"Would you send Nicasio's dogs after me?" Rianna asked contemptuously.

"Sanchez will watch so you can't leave," Alonso promised before he disappeared around the corner.

"This Sanchez isn't a guardian *I'd* choose. He has eyes as pitiless as a snake's," Coraquenque commented.

"It's possible Don Alonso is right about the danger of staying in Lima," Beatriz offered, looking frightened.

"He may be right about that, but certainly not this," Rianna said, gingerly touching the reddening patch on her cheek that marked Alonso's slap.

"A cold towel will ease the sting. No real harm has been done to your cheek, only your pride," Beatriz advised nervously.

"Do you think my pride matters nothing?" Rianna angrily inquired.

Coraquenque took up Rianna's napkin and dunked it in one of the silver pitchers on the table then returned to press it to her friend's cheek.

"I'll stay here a moment, Beatriz. Why don't you begin your own packing?" Rianna said more resignedly then sat in the nearest chair.

After the *dueña*'s footsteps had faded down the corridor, Coraquenque remarked, "That woman is supposed to safeguard you, but she watches Alonso strike you without saying a word of protest."

"Beatriz was hired to guard my virtue, not interfere with Alonso's disciplining me," Rianna said disgustedly.

Coraquenque frowned. "Is it your people's custom to strike one another so?"

"Not in my family," Rianna muttered.

"My people think it's as shameful for a woman to hit her man as the other way around," Coraquenque observed.

Rianna remembered how only last night, when Shali's love-making had caused her that one brief, unavoidable pang, he'd promised never again to give her pain and contrasted his behavior with Alonso's. If Incan tenets were really so foreign to her people, was it because Shali's civilization was more gentle? It was a violent age in Europe, she reflected; yet the Peruvians had no peace either. She wished Shali was with her now. There were so many questions on her mind; and it was his answers, not Coraquenque's, she needed.

Coraquenque patted Rianna's shoulder consolingly. "We'll leave this place before the violence reaches the captain's gates."

Rianna looked up at her friend. "If Shali and your husband don't know we've left so suddenly, they may not be able to trace where we go in Cuzco."

Coraquenque thought that, though Manco had said nothing last night about this coup, his contacts with Almagro must have told him about the plan. She was sure he'd have placed someone near Nicasio's house to keep watch in case they needed protection. Wondering if Shali himself were hidden nearby with a band of men, she blotted Rianna's tears and said quietly, "It doesn't matter when we leave. My husband will know it—and so will Shali."

chapter
11

Sanchez appeared in the dining room only minutes after Alonso had left. He offered neither greetings nor explanations, but merely posted himself inside the doorway; and Rianna knew the man was obeying Alonso's order to prevent her slipping away.

When Rianna went to pack, Sanchez followed and stationed himself near her bedroom door. Though it was dangerous outside Nicasio's gates and she believed Alonso meant to prevent her from doing anything foolish, her heart was in a fury that she should be watched this way.

During the day, Nicasio's men exchanging duties brought alarming reports about the turmoil in Lima. Topa heard their conversations and recounted them to Coraquenque who told Rianna. Many of Francisco Pizarro's partisans discovered they couldn't leave their houses; rebels were guarding their gates. Governor Pizarro and Secretary Picado's homes had been pillaged. Picado's house, as suspected, contained a large amount of gold. Though he'd fled to Treasurer Riquelme's home, he'd been captured. Rianna surmised that anyone not involved in the riots must be hiding behind locked doors trembling in fear; the city seemed to be in chaos with Pizarro's soldiers pursuing Almagro's partisans, rebels ambushing them in turn. She couldn't help thinking of Nicasio, possibly sprawled in some bloody lane.

The Brothers of Mercy, thinking the reverent Castilians would cease their battling at a display of the communion wafer, made a solemn procession through the city streets with the sacrament elevated over their heads so it could be clearly seen. When the monks approached the vicinity of combatants, the men paused from their battle and crossed themselves; but they only waited till the procession had passed then resumed fighting.

In a section of the city temporarily secured by the rebels, Almagro paraded on horseback escorted by well-armed cavaliers. The cry went up to display Pizarro's corpse in the marketplace, put his head on a gibbet; but Almagro refused. Pizarro's wife and a few faithful attendants took this opportunity to wrap his body in a simple cotton shroud and hastily take it to sanctuary at the cathedral.

Hearing all the stories of violence and desperation, Rianna wondered how Alonso could find the men he'd hired in Lima to accompany them to Cuzco; and she decided it was, after all, wise to leave the area. She was hurrying through the main room of the house carrying a load of items yet to be stuffed into her trunk when the door opened and Nicasio came in. Blood-smeared and sooty, he hurried to the dining room talking to Alonso as he walked. Rianna dropped her bundle and followed.

"The situation in the city is desperate," Nicasio said between deep draughts of wine. "Though many of Almagro's partisans have been arrested and imprisoned, it seems as if more are appearing out of nowhere."

"Maybe people, who were on the government's side or neutral, have decided Almagro and his men will win; and they're afraid of later being punished for not taking part in this," Alonso suggested gravely.

Nicasio put down his goblet, signaled Topa to refill it and started on the platter of food another servant had put before him. Though it was only cold sliced meat and bread, he seemed not to notice anything he was eating as he talked. "Despite Pizarro's mistakes, he was the governor appointed by the Crown. These revolutionaries have forgotten it was his courage that brought us through jungles filled with venomous snakes, treacherous mountains and disease-ridden swamps to this place of gold and made us rich. He's a hero, Alonso; but do you know how he'll be buried?''

"Very quickly, I should think," Alonso answered.

"A grave is being secretly dug for him in the back of the cemetery. As soon as it's ready, he'll be buried wrapped in that bloody shroud without even a coffin. The ceremony will be conducted in the dark so no one will notice and later mutilate the corpse. Can you imagine how his wife feels?''

Less concerned with the widow's heartbreak than with how the situation would affect his plans, Alonso nodded sympathetically, but promptly asked, "How much chance do *we* have?''

Nicasio wiped his mouth with a napkin and stood up. "The government is ready to fall. The rebels have called for us to surrender and recognize Almagro's authority," he said quietly. "I'm going to have to take all but two of my men with me. I'll give orders for the guards I leave to bar the gates and open them to no one except me or one of my men they recognize. Stay inside these walls, my friend." He gripped Alonso's shoulders a moment then turned to Rianna. "I'm sorry I can't leave you with better protection," he said as he bent to brush his lips to her hand.

When he straightened, Rianna whispered, "Go with God, Nicasio."

"And you," he said softly, turned away and hurried out.

Earlier, Rianna had been alarmed by the number of villainous-looking men gathering in the courtyard and Alonso had explained he'd hired them to go to Cuzco. Now that Nicasio had left with all but a pair of his soldiers, she was grateful for the presence of the men. Though they looked like brigands, she was sure that if a mob came to Nicasio's gates, they'd fight like demons not out of concern for her, but to preserve their own lives. Rianna didn't know that an Incan force hidden nearby was watching for her and Coraquenque's safety.

Sleep wasn't possible. Alonso, Rianna and Beatriz sat in the parlor silently wondering if a mob would bar their leaving in the morning. They were surprised when Private Sarabia, bloodied from multiple wounds, staggered into the room with news that the government had finally surrendered; Almagro had been proclaimed governor and captain-general of Peru. Before Sarabia collapsed, he whispered that all of

Pizarro's officers had either been killed or captured. He had seen Nicasio fall under a mace's blow and was sure he was dead.

Coraquenque and Beatriz cleaned and bound Sarabia's wounds, which though bloody, weren't serious. When he regained consciousness, Alonso questioned him more closely. Rianna didn't like Sarabia, but she begged Alonso to let him rest. Alonso didn't listen.

An hour before dawn Rianna, weary and depressed, went to the courtyard dressed for travel. She was stunned to see Sarabia being helped to mount his horse then learned he was frightened to remain in Lima and had insisted on traveling with them. He was so certain Captain Holguin would assure Cuzco's safety that Rianna's resistance to leaving faded and she mounted Wayra hurriedly.

The travelers left by the rear gates; and if anyone noticed that the old Incan entrance wasn't sealed as had been believed, no one commented about it.

The morning was obscured by a light fog and the sun's face was a pale, glowing blur on the horizon behind the clouds. As Wayra paced through the slowly dissipating vapor, Rianna gazed at the fog clinging to the horses' legs like shreds of gray veiling and hoped fervently that if any of Almagro's mob remembered Nicasio's house and came to loot it, they wouldn't notice the procession leaving by the rear gates.

It was the thought uppermost in everyone's mind and no one spoke even in a whisper. The horses' hooves had been wrapped to muffle their steps, and the only noises were the occasional clinks of the metal equipment the men carried as they turned onto the old Incan road.

By mid-morning, the group had left all traces of fog behind; and the sun blazed in a bright blue sky. Rianna recognized they were near the valley where she and Coraquenque had met Shali and Coraquenque's husband. Memories of that day floated through her mind and she recalled how Topa had managed to saddle horses and sneak them out of the stable almost under the noses of Nicasio's guard. Suddenly she realized she hadn't seen the Incan boy since Sarabia had come from Lima. She glanced around quickly to be sure then nudged Wayra closer to Coraquenque's horse.

"Where is Topa?" she whispered.

Coraquenque kept her eyes as steadily on the scenery ahead as if Rianna hadn't spoke and answered softly, "He left us."

"But when? How?" Rianna was surprised.

Coraquenque's shrug was almost imperceptible. "Several of Nicasio's Incan slaves are missing. As the trip goes on, more will disappear." Coraquenque tilted her head to let her shawl slip down to her shoulders as she whispered, "Don't worry; I won't be one of them."

"Why not take this chance to escape if you can?" Rianna urged then added slowly, "But maybe traveling in this wild country is too dangerous. Topa is so young to be alone out here."

Coraquenque was fairly certain Alonso's group wasn't alone, that unseen Incas were pacing them, but she replied, "All Incas learn as children how to survive if we get lost in the mountains or forests. Topa will be safe and so would I. This is our land, Rianna. We're as comfortable anywhere in it as we are in our own houses."

Rianna fell silent as she eyed the mountains and wondered at Coraquenque's quiet confidence that she could make her way among those ominous looking crags. "Now I know why Nicasio couldn't find Manco Capac and Shalikuchima," she commented, not knowing she spoke the names of Coraquenque's husband and her own love.

The Incan road followed the course of the rivers whenever possible and the procession moved through ragged ravines so deep they sometimes were surrounded by walls of granite so lofty the sky seemed like a painted ceiling in a giant's castle. Some of the Castilians glanced up at the heights and, dizzied by the movement of the soaring clouds, dared not look again. The enclosing rock walls didn't make Rianna feel trapped as she heard so many Castilians around her complaining. Rather, she felt as if the mountains held her in a protective embrace.

When the road led them up the side of a slope, she discovered wide, low steps cut into the stone. There were walls on the open side of the lane to protect travelers from thousand-foot drops. Coraquenque told her the roads had been used by royal messengers, officials and the king and his court when he'd toured the Incan empire. Coraquenque's voice held a plaintive note Rianna recognized as yearning for things past.

Rianna tried to imagine how a royal procession must have appeared winding its way among the crags and realized she had no idea of how Incas had dressed before the invaders had come. When Coraquenque began to reminisce aloud, Rianna was enthralled by her description of an army of shaggy llamas carrying bundles and baskets. Rianna saw, in her mind's eye, the king's elite guard marching along the road dressed in colorful tunics, their helmets, like their shields, decorated with fierce animal motifs, the golden javelins they held glinting in the sun.

The noblemen and their wives traveled in litters carried by servants, the women dressed in long cotton gowns in the warm lowlands, alpaca or vicuña in the chillier heights. Whatever the cloth, the dresses were decorated with embroidery, jeweled collars and belts, silken cords of elaborate tassels and fringes. The noblemen wore abbreviated tunics like the soldiers; but they also had long capes, which they threw back over their shoulders when warmth wasn't needed.

The picture Coraquenque vividly painted became a fantasy in Rianna's mind of bright colors in the sun, swaying plumes of long feathers and everywhere the gleam of gold. She hoped this splendor wouldn't be destroyed by the invaders.

During the days that followed, the travelers passed many deep ravines caused by past earthquakes; but they stopped to gaze doubtfully at a bridge suspended from vines over a canyon they must cross. Coraquenque assured Alonso it was safe. She pointed out the vines that were woven into cables the thickness of a man's body, the stout wood planks that made the floor, the huge columns of stone slabs supporting the span. Alonso realized there was no way to continue except to cross the bridge and ordered them to lead their horses one by one. Though the bridge's sides were protected by a network of vine ropes, it swayed; and many of the men, who'd appeared so formidable to Rianna in Nicasio's courtyard, kept their eyes fixed on the far side rather than glimpse the river rushing so far below. Others gloomily speculated what would happen if there was an earthquake while they were on the bridge. Worried that their horses would panic at the height, most took off their sashes and wrapped the cloth over their animal's eyes before leading them across the yawning chasm. They were surprised when Rianna led Wayra onto the bridge without a blindfold and the mare walked calmly across the span.

But Rianna barely reached the far side when a gasp of horror escaped the watchers. She turned to see that Beatriz, in trying to urge her already resisting horse onto the bridge, suddenly succeeded too well. The frightened animal abruptly trotted out, pulling her to the center of the span so the bridge swayed erratically. The *dueña* was too frozen with horror to control the horse, whose blindfold had slipped down. Its eyes rolled fearfully at the empty space below and it started backing at an angle. When its rump touched the vine webbing at one side, it stopped. It didn't know which way to go to escape the place, but was becoming more terrified each moment.

Rianna could hear the sharp, quick breaths the horse was taking and knew it was ready to bolt; but none of the men seemed willing to help Beatriz. Rianna pushed Wayra's reins into Coraquenque's hands and, gripping the hand-ropes on each side of the bridge, hurried out on the planks.

She knew Beatriz's fear was affecting her mount and urged the *dueña* to go on alone. Then Rianna laid her arm across the animal's withers and crowded close to its side, soothing the horse with her contact as she coaxed it to the center of the walkway. Though she was desperate with fear, she seemed calm as she talked quietly to the horse and stroked its neck. After the bridge stopped swaying, Rianna led the animal across the span until, nearing its end, the horse hurried the last few steps to solid ground. Rianna's heart was pounding wildly, but she ignored it to help Coraquenque calm Beatriz enough so the trembling *dueña* could be persuaded back to her saddle.

Alonso had been surprised when Rianna hurried out on the bridge. He'd admired her courage; but as she'd begun to lead the horse across, the wind had snatched the ribbon from her hair. Rianna's curls had spread like a golden offering to the sun, the riding skirt was blown against her body, clung to her legs and outlined the slender grace of her hips. Her seductive curves, the tossing of her hair in the wind made Rianna seem as wild as the mountains. Alonso was struck by an almost unendurable need to capture this shining creature and possess her vitality. He watched Rianna hurry past him with the horse and decided Beatriz's usefulness had ended. He would have to think of a way to get rid of the *dueña* before they reached Cuzco.

By the time Beatriz was back on her horse, the rest of the party had crossed the bridge. Coraquenque, watching Rianna gather up Wayra's reins and prepare to mount, suddenly asked, "Are there canyons like this in your land?"

"Spain has mountains, but I lived in the city," Rianna answered as she swung up to the saddle. "I don't know if their peaks are as high or their gorges as deep, but I think not. Why do you ask?"

"When you ran across the bridge to help Beatriz, many of the men turned away and couldn't bear to watch. Why aren't you as frightened as they?" Coraquenque inquired.

"I was *terrified*," Rianna confessed.

"Your fear was of a dangerous situation, but these men are afraid of the mountains themselves. You aren't. I've seen you look as calmly down chasms as you gaze at heights."

Rianna chirped to her horse to begin up still another steep path while she considered this. It wasn't until she reached the top of the slope they'd been climbing and paused to look at the lush valley below then raised her eyes to the grandeur of the snow-capped peaks that she knew the answer to Coraquenque's question. Her existence before had been like sleep-walking; something in this land had touched her soul and finally awakened her to life.

Watching Rianna's rapt expression, Coraquenque smiled, but said nothing.

The path widened and once again became a road on a stretch of tableland at an elevation where nothing could survive except a few stunted trees and yellow, matted grass. It was so desolate a plateau that even the brightly colored birds Rianna had seen everywhere else had vanished. Only a few large birds floated darkly against the sky.

Rianna asked if the birds were eagles and Coraquenque said they were condors, the imperial symbol. Rianna thought of the crest on the vicuña cloth and inquired what the jaguar meant. When Coraquenque answered it was the symbol of the Incan military commander, Rianna realized the crest was Shalikuchima's.

The stunted trees afforded no shelter from sharp winds that swept down from the higher summits; and Alonso called a pause so they could dismount and take out their cloaks. While the men passed flasks of rum to stop their shivering, Rianna walked closer to the plateau's edge to gaze at a storm gathering over the distant peaks. The rolling, purple clouds were charged with sudden, briefly shimmering lights; and though Rianna couldn't see the streaks, she knew it was lightning.

Despite the far-off storm, the sky over the tableland was blue and the sun shone brightly through the frosty air, turning the scrubby grass into a golden carpet. Rianna turned slowly, scanning the jagged, gray peaks surrounding the plateau and felt as if she were standing at the center of an immense diadem.

As beautiful as the area was, she couldn't ignore a sense of dread coming over her; and when Coraquenque approached, she asked uneasily, "Do you think that storm will come this way?"

"I don't know. They're unpredictable in the mountains," Coraquenque said and, indicating a hollow in the plateau, observed, "If it does come, we'd be wise to hide there. If we're caught by a storm on a narrow path winding down the slope, we could be swept off the side by a sudden flood."

When Alonso called that it was time to leave, Rianna hurried to his side and said anxiously, "Coraquenque thinks we'll be in danger on the road if the storm comes this way. She said we should wait and find shelter from lightning in that hollow."

"Stay on this windswept rock because of a storm that probably won't come? Don't be ridiculous," he scoffed.

"We're tired and need a rest anyway. Beatriz is exhausted. Even Coraquenque looks weary," Rianna insisted. "It's mid-afternoon already. We'd only lose a couple of hours if we made camp here."

"Beatriz is more ashamed than tired. She knows what happened on the bridge was her fault, that her foolishness endangered your life as well as her silly neck. I wish I hadn't taken her with us. She's become a burden," Alonso said vehemently. "As for Coraquenque, that Indian could walk twice as far as the horses and be less tired. She's looking for an excuse to delay us."

"Why would Coraquenque do that?" Rianna asked in surprise.

"This flat area exposes our position. If any Incas are on the neighboring slopes, they can see us," Alonso pointed out.

"I don't believe she's doing that, but wouldn't we be safer here from an attack as well as a storm? We would see anyone coming," Rianna argued.

"What a child you are!" Alonso sneered. "The Incas won't attack us here. Coraquenque only hopes to delay us so they can position themselves somewhere below."

"What makes you think that? Have you seen anyone watching us?" Rianna demanded.

"They're too clever to let me or any of my men see them," Alonso answered, his temper rising. "Haven't you noticed how many slaves are missing? No matter how I warn our guards at night to watch for slaves trying to slip away, almost every morning I count at least one less Indian. Where do you think they're going, if not to join one of these savage bands who live in the hills and murder travelers?"

Rianna couldn't argue that the escaped slaves would seek out other Incas and tell them about the Castilian travelers; but she was worried about the storm. Knowing from Alonso's expression it was useless to argue further, she turned away. As she approached Coraquenque, she said wearily, "He thinks you want to delay us so an ambush can be arranged."

Though Coraquenque was sure Manco had sent someone to follow them from Nicasio's house and protect her, she'd seen no sign of Incas. "I think Alonso's fear is making him think Incas are hiding behind every rock," she commented derisively, but dared say no more.

After they left the plateau, the road again narrowed until it finally became a steep, slender path winding along a cliff face. Rianna noticed Coraquenque often glancing uneasily at the sky. By the time they were halfway to the bottom of the mountain, both were relieved that Alonso seemed to have been right. The storm was veering in another direction.

The trail narrowed even more and was covered with sharp stones that threatened to lame the horses. The riders had to dismount and lead their animals single file.

This region had always been so desolate and untraveled the Incas had never bothered to cut steps in the rocks and there was no protective wall at the path's outer edge. Rianna only had to turn her head to see a drop of thousands of feet beyond the precipice. She concentrated her attention on keeping Wayra calm, because the mare, until now seemingly fearless, was showing signs of growing unease.

Finally, reaching an area where the path widened enough for two horses to walk, Alonso stopped the procession for a rest. Rianna could see tension was wearing on all of them. As Alonso passed inspecting their line, his face was pale despite the tan he was acquiring.

Rianna took a long drink from the waterskin tied to her saddle while she gazed into the distance at a pine forest that stretched to the high slopes of the next mountain. Then she stepped nearer the edge to look into the yawning abyss. At the foot of the cliff a river furiously rushed down the mountain slope to hurl itself into another, still deeper ravine. Even Rianna was made dizzy by the stupendous drop and she quickly stepped back.

"Finally, you're afraid," Alonso remarked as he returned to the front of the line.

Rianna said shortly, "Nothing less than a condor would fear this height."

"I had begun to wonder if you had the soul of a bird," he commented. Then, glancing at Beatriz whose face was set in a mask of terror, he added, "On the other hand, that woman has as much capacity to endure height as a mole."

"She's making her horse nervous," Rianna worried. "Maybe we should blindfold it again."

"I think we should cover Beatriz's eyes. The problem would be . . ." He stopped and stared incredulously at Rianna as the cliff began to vibrate then shouted, *"Everyone! Get off this mountain now!"*

Alonso's order wasn't necessary. The terrified men could hardly hold their panicking horses from running headlong down the cliff path. Pebbles tumbling from the ledges above became a shower of stinging missiles; and Rianna, wedging her back against Wayra's chest to slow the mare, found herself skidding and hopping precariously down the path because of the horse's pushing. She heard an animal scream; and though it was impossible to look back, she was sure one of the horses had fallen over the edge. Wayra needed no urging to keep away from the open side. The horse was clinging so close to the rocky wall her shoulder and hip were scraping small prominences. The ground's shaking jostled Rianna so violently she found herself leaning against Wayra more for support than to try to slow the mare.

One man, fighting to control his horse, suddenly lost the battle. Despite the blood staining the animal's foaming mouth, it gave one mighty heave against the bit; and the rein snapped. The horse passed Wayra and raced toward Alonso and Beatriz. Like Rianna, he was keeping his horse as close to the wall as possible while Beatriz, a step behind, was struggling with hers in the middle of the trail. When Alonso noticed the loose horse bearing down on them, he saw an opportunity to rid himself of the *dueña*. He covertly pinched his horse and it side-stepped. Beatriz stumbled into the path of the onrushing animal. Rianna saw Beatriz would be run down and screamed a warning. Beatriz took a step closer to the edge; and when the terrified horse dashed by, its glancing shoulder pitched her off the cliff. At Beatriz's wavering scream, Rianna cried out with horror and tried to slow Wayra; but another horse rushed by in a blur; and she knew from Wayra's desperate neighing that more animals were crowding from the rear.

Realizing there was nothing she could do for Beatriz, Rianna had no choice except to try to save herself. There was only one thing she could think of to do. She slipped around Wayra's side and swung up into the saddle. The mare half-reared then started down the cliff. Rianna saw a flash of Alonso cringing against the rock wall, but she didn't try to stop Wayra. She only prayed each time they approached a curve she could stay in her saddle, that the horse wouldn't slip on the loose stones and plunge off the side. But Wayra didn't race down the path as the other horse had, heedless of everything except getting off the mountain. As fast as the mare went, she seemed to calculate and adjust every move. Though the mountain stopped shuddering as abruptly as it had begun, the wild ride down the perilous trail was a horror Rianna thought would never end. Finally, Wayra leaped to level ground and raced into the small valley beyond. Rianna struggled with the still-excited mare until she finally slowed to a trot.

When Wayra turned back, Rianna was glad to see most of the group had survived, though many of the horses' packs had split open to spew their contents along the path. Some of the men trailed behind horses who, too frightened to answer their call, were so tired they could do no more than walk away. When Rianna saw Coraquenque leading her limping mount into the grassy area, she threw herself from the saddle and ran to her friend.

"It was a good idea to get up on Wayra and ride her down," Coraquenque panted. "I think I'm alive only because I followed your example."

Their embrace was interrupted by Alonso's sharp command. "Coraquenque, see to your mistress's belongings."

"Don't you have one human feeling? Can't you let us rest even a moment?" Rianna snapped.

"We have a lot of work to do," Alonso said. He caught Coraquenque's arm and pulled her away from Rianna then ordered, "Help the injured. Rianna can take care of her own gear."

Rianna couldn't disagree that many needed help, but she was angered by Alonso's roughness with Coraquenque. She gave him a black look before she turned to find the pack horse carrying her bundles.

As their fright began to subside, the men settled down to increasingly organized action. Some went back up the trail to retrieve what was possible while others sorted the supplies that had been saved. At Alonso's brusque orders, the Incas still with the group began to set up a camp for the night. Seeing there was little left for her to do, Rianna turned away to walk across the glade in the hope of calming her still-turbulent emotions.

She was saddened to think that three men had been killed, five horses had gone over the cliff and another was too badly injured to live; but she was grieved to think of Beatriz's death. The *dueña* had been her friend. The terror of the episode weighed on Rianna like a heavy blanket smothering her breath; and she wanted to escape the scene. She turned to a path that wound into the forest, carelessly paying no attention to her surroundings until she found herself on a rocky ledge with another chasm yawning before her.

With a little gasp, Rianna quickly stepped back then sank down to sit on a rock, put her face in her hands and weep. After a time, her sobs lessened and she felt calmer. The wind lifted her hair as if coaxing her to raise her head. Coming from the valley rather than the frosty heights, the wind was balmy; and it gently dried her tears.

Rianna got to her feet and slowly walked closer to the edge to look warily at the slopes in the dimming light of the afternoon. The wind swirled around her ankles and billowed her hem against her legs. It seemed to breathe fresh life into Rianna and the mountains gradually lost their terror. Once again she was enthralled by their spirit; and she closed her eyes to think not about the tragedy, but of the condors' soaring, joyous freedom.

"Incas have a song to express the feelings the wind in the mountains gives them," a low, softly accented voice said behind her.

Rianna wasn't startled by Shali's presence; it seemed right for him to be there. She opened her eyes and slowly turned to face him. His rough, peasantlike clothes were gone. He wore a jerkin and breeches of fine, dark red vicuña, a narrow belt of gold links. Soft, gray boots ending above his ankles were intricately embroidered with exotic black and gold designs.

"You weren't surprised when I spoke, yet now you seem so," he commented as he came closer.

"Your appearance is . . ." she began then stopped. How could she ask where a poor soldier got such clothes? It would sound as if she accused him of thievery.

"Are you all right after that earthquake?" he asked. When Rianna nodded, he put his arms lightly around her and murmured, "I was afraid for you, but there was no way I could help."

"It wasn't possible to help anyone," she whispered then, recognizing that the firm muscles under the silky feel of his clothes were a sensation more intoxicating than the mountain wind, she drew away. "How were you able to find us? How could you follow me here?"

"We're aware of everything that moves on our road," Shali replied obliquely. He noticed she was retreating not only from the brink of the ledge, but from him. "You weren't paying much notice to where you were walking or if anyone was following. It wasn't hard to keep pace with you after you'd left the others."

When Rianna's shoulders brushed the wall, she stopped backing up and asked, "If I'd been alert, would I have seen you?"

"No, *chinita*, not unless I'd wanted you to," he admitted.

Rianna gazed up at Shali and, trying to read the purpose in his bottomless eyes, could only feel the lure of his nearness drawing her.

Shali saw the questions on Rianna's face and knew, while he must evade them, he must also somehow put her more at ease. He wondered if every time he was with her he must think of a way to melt her resistance with even more care than he used to plan a battle.

"Coraquenque's usefulness as a spy ended when Nicasio was killed. She didn't have to come on this journey except for her promise to you. Her steadfastness should prove how seriously Incas regard giving their word." He paused to let Rianna consider this as he rested his hands on the rock wall beside her shoulders. Finally, he said softly, "I, too, made a promise and asked that you trust me. Will you?"

Rianna looked up at Shali, acutely aware that he was leaning closer, was about to kiss her and she still had a score of questions. Yet, when his lips began to warmly caress her mouth, when she felt the length of his body against her, the importance of her questions faded and disappeared. She felt as if she were one of the flowering jungle vines that must cling to the strength of a tree or die.

Shali stepped away from Rianna, took her hand and whispered, "Come with me."

chapter

12

Shali led Rianna through the trees without a word. Though he walked with a loose-limbed, easy gait, she noticed his steps were soundless and became conscious of even the swishing of her skirts. The snap of a branch immediately sent him into deeper foliage, she awkwardly hurrying after.

Though their only contact was his grasp on her hand, she could sense the wary alertness of his body. She looked up at his face. His black eyes were slowly scanning the forest; and his chin was inclined a bit, as if he were listening for the smallest sound. Perceiving nothing, still clasping her hand, Shali silently edged his way through the bushes then down a shadowy corridor of trees. After he'd led her between two crags, he finally stopped and turned.

"I thought that noise was an animal, but I had to be certain. I'm sorry if you were alarmed," he said quietly.

Rianna let out a sigh of relief.

"Sometimes you're so brave on the outside, but so frightened in your heart," Shali observed, the barest hint of a smile touching his lips. He put his hands gently on her shoulders and urged, "Step around me and look toward the next mountain."

Rianna did as he asked to see the setting sun glowing along the dark slope like a ridge of crimson fire that lit the valley with a rich, amber light. She felt arms sliding around her waist, Shali's chest against her back then his cheek resting lightly on hers.

"Do you see a building on that outcropping?" he murmured.

Rianna's eyes searched the area until she discovered that what she'd thought was part of the mountain were walls constructed by human hands.

"It was made for the same purpose as Nicasio's house, a resting place for travelers. None of your people have found it, so it's as it's always been." She felt his lips against her cheek as he kissed her then asked softly, "Would you like to see it?"

"Oh, yes!" she breathed. Then, thinking about it, she added disappointedly, "I've been away from the others too long. They'll search for me and may find you."

"They're not likely to find this place. Like you, they'll mistake it for part of the mountain." His lips again brushed her cheek as he murmured, "I can bring you back to them in the morning and you can tell them you were lost."

The pulse at Rianna's temple beat softly against his cheek as she whispered, "In the morning?"

Shali moved away and turned her to him. She could see, through the crimson streaks of sunset reflected in his eyes, the inner fires he controlled; and she wondered at the stormy emotions seething just beneath his surface calm. Shali cupped Rianna's face with his hands and bent to kiss her softly, unhurriedly. His lips parted to nibble at her mouth, sending a series of soft shocks through her nerves.

Against her lips he whispered, "Would you like to sleep in an Incan palace tonight?"

"A *palace?*" she breathed.

"When Manco Capac travels, it's one of the places he stays in; and I think he wouldn't refuse a soldier as loyal as I."

Shali drew away. His hands slipped from Rianna's temples then she felt his fingers weaving strongly through hers. When he turned to lead her up the slope, she willingly followed.

Rianna didn't know Shali had been guiding her along a path until they reached a bridge made of stone slabs laid across a shallow creek.

Beyond the stream she discovered stairs, hidden by cleverly placed foliage, a large stone platform in front of a pair of wooden doors she guessed were a half-dozen times Shali's height. The walls were granite ramparts that seemed as enduring as the Andes.

When the great doors began to silently swing open before them, Rianna backed away a step. "Someone else is here!" she exclaimed then stared into a long corridor lit by golden lamps placed in niches in the walls.

"The only person you'll see will be my servant," Shali assured.

"Your servant?" Rianna's hushed voice echoed in the stillness and startled her.

"Every officer needs an aide," Shali answered then added, "Certainly you realize by now my rank isn't the lowest."

Too intimidated by the echoes to speak aloud, Rianna whispered, "That you're an officer would explain some things."

Shali swept her up in his arms and started walking down the hall. He laughed softly as he went, a light-hearted, joyous sound. Rianna realized it was the first time she'd heard his laughter and it suddenly seemed as if all the cares that weighed her, the tragedies of the past, the uncertainties of the future, even the dangers had been locked outside the massive doors.

Shali set Rianna on her feet in an enormous room lit by a myriad of golden lamps. A small fire, set against the chill of the coming night, was dwarfed by the dimensions of the great stone fireplace at the room's center.

He said, "This is similar to what my home was like before it was destroyed."

Rianna was saddened to hear this; but because so many Incan houses had been burned or confiscated, she wasn't surprised. She decided to take this opportunity to ask one of the questions that had been on her mind, "Where do you live now?"

Shali glanced away, as if he hated to answer, "I can't talk about it."

When she turned to look at the room, Shali frowned. He was sure she'd concluded he lived in a rough, mountain camp and he was humiliated that his life seemed to be one of running and hiding like a thief. But Rianna was silent because there were so many questions she knew he couldn't answer. She was wondering if the conflict of their peoples, the difference of their civilizations, would always be a barrier between them. Finally, she turned her attention to the room and was caught with admiration for its spaciousness, quiet order and rich beauty.

Two walls were covered by tapestries that reached to the rafters. They were rich combinations of deep yellow and crimson with dark blue, white and black figures. She noticed the condor motif repeated in the designs along with serpents, boars and other animals unfamiliar to her. The remaining stone walls had niches holding lamps. The spaces between the niches on one of the walls were hung with gold and silver plaques of artfully designed sunbursts, flowers and birds. On the opposite wall, the spaces between the niches were empty, but for a number of shields obviously hung without regard for color or arrangment.

"The other decorations are placed with an eye to order and beauty. I wonder why these shields weren't more carefully arranged," Rianna murmured, thinking aloud rather than meaning to comment.

"Those aren't decorations, but war shields left by soldiers who stayed here," Shali answered, not wanting her to know they belonged to the small group of his own men he'd ordered to remain out of sight until after he and Rianna had retired for the evening. "Shields are placed on this wall so they can be close at hand even while the men lounge or eat in this room."

Rianna went nearer to study the shields and saw that one held the insignia of the jaguar carrying a condor. She touched it with one timid finger and asked in awe, "This is Shalikuchima's?"

"I suppose he was here at some recent time and left it," Shali replied, feeling awkward with his necessary deception.

"Why would he leave it?" she wondered. "Why would any of them leave their shields?"

"Maybe these were old shields and no longer wanted," Shali quickly suggested then firmly guided Rianna away from the wall to one of the brightly colored thick floor cushions that served as chairs. "Would you like to sit for a moment and rest after that walk up the slope?" he asked, wanting to get her mind off the subject of Shalikuchima.

Rianna looked at the inviting cushion and thought only of how much she wanted to be in Shali's arms, but she was too shy to say it. Her eyes moved to gaze at the floor, smooth, dark wood worn to satin by countless generations of noblemen's sandals and boots; and she said softly, "I don't think I want to rest."

"My servant has heated water. Perhaps, after that wild ride down the mountain, you'd like to bathe?" Shali inquired.

She realized she'd forgotten the earthquake and all it involved and reminded herself she was soiled by a layer of dust. But as Rianna walked with Shali through the corridor, she recalled, though his kisses outside had been tender, they hadn't been passionate. Nothing he'd said had told her he planned to make love. Was his invitation to spend the night in an Incan palace merely a way of allowing her to see this ancient place and introduce her to something of his people? At the same time Rianna was disappointed by this conclusion, she inwardly scolded herself for the desire thrilling through her she couldn't ignore. When Shali stopped walking and opened a door for Rianna, she passed him in sullen silence.

Rianna thought the room must be a sort of parlor. One of the walls was layered with reed hangings she assumed covered window-openings. Another had a series of varying size doors that suggested a cabinet. Instead of a wall, directly opposite where she stood was a flat linteled archway where slender, widely spaced columns were outlined on both sides by curtains of intricately knotted gold cords. Beyond them she could see a bathing chamber with polished white stone walls that glowed softly in the light of several lamps. Was this first room a bedroom, though it looked nothing like the one she'd had in Nicasio's house? She turned again to look at it. There were a pair of large cushions like those in the great hall and a small table. The fourth wall was covered by a blue tapestry with black and gold designs. A thick mat long enough to accommodate a man Shali's height and equally wide was covered with lustrous alpaca fleece. It was flanked by a table with legs only a few inches high.

Finally she asked in uncertainty, "Is that to be my bed?"

Shali gazed at Rianna a moment with a look in his eyes she couldn't decipher then answered curtly, "Yes."

Not realizing Shali was annoyed at her saying *my* bed, as if she intended to sleep alone, she thought she might have seemed critical of Incan furniture. Rianna followed him into the next room trying to explain, "It looks comfortable, but it's different from any bed I've slept in before." She faltered then added, "It's very low and I wonder if it's healthy to sleep in the drafts so near the floor."

Shali tersely replied, "The Incas are a healthy people." He indicated the steaming water in the tub that, as in Nicasio's house, was sunk in the floor and meant for the bather to stand in rather than sit. "There's no maid to attend to your undressing; but if you'll tell me how your garments are unfastened, I can help you."

Shali spoke with such cool courtesy Rianna raised her eyes and wondered if he realized it was almost impossible for her, unassisted, to get out of her clothes and was really just offering help. His attitude—one moment tender and inviting then distant and cool, almost as if he were angry, and now so dispassionately courteous he might really have been an attendant—was mystifying.

When Rianna didn't answer, Shali came nearer to face her and said shortly, "As you've already agreed you wish to bathe and it's obvious you can't undress without help, it seems logical I take the task upon myself."

"Will it be a task?" she inquired as coolly.

Shali gave no answer as he stepped around her to examine the hooks of her dress. "These seem not too complicated," he remarked as he pressed the edges of material together with one hand. He dug his fingertip under the first hook, flipped it open then the others one after another without pausing. The sash was undone in another second; and with a flick of his wrists, he brushed the dress from her shoulders. It fell in a heap around her ankles.

Rianna didn't realize Shali's annoyance had been caused by her previous remark, that he thought the old ghosts of her propriety had arisen and she would resist his love-making. Wondering at his mood, she said cautiously, "If you just unfasten everything, I can do the rest."

He ignored her and she felt the little tugs he made untying the strings of her petticoat. Then that, too, fell to the floor. Shali's voice, coming from low behind her, commented, "Your women wear so many layers of clothes I don't doubt a man's ardor might be cooled by the time he gets them off.''

Then his fingers were on her thighs picking at the tops of her stockings, easing them down her legs, making her tingle at his carefully discreet yet calculated touches. His fingertips brushed her legs so lightly as he rose she wondered if it was accidental. Without a word he undid her corset strings and cast the garment aside so vehemently she wondered at his temper. Not knowing what he planned, she felt self-conscious to stand naked before him; but when he stepped around to face her, his eyes were implacably fixed on her face. His expression was unreadable.

"Did Coraquenque show you how we bathe or leave you to your own invention?" Shali asked.

Confused, Rianna answered shortly, "She left me alone, of course. What is there to bathing?"

"I'll show you," he said with seeming dispassion.

"I'm not a child to be taught how to bathe!" she snapped.

Shali wordlessly took Rianna's hand and walked her to the edge of the water. "Stand there a moment," he directed and unclasping the links of the golden belt he wore, laid it on a table. When he pulled up his jerkin, Rianna caught her breath, wondering if he meant to bathe with her. She was struck mute at the thought; and she stared at him speechlessly, as he bent to slip off his boots.

Shali straightened, turned to a nearby table and poured water from a pitcher into a basin of ivory-colored cream. Then he stirred it with his fingers until it foamed. Rianna watched in fascination and growing desire as he liberally applied the soap to his body, seeming to be demonstrating what he wished her to do. When he looked up, she put out her hands as if requesting some of the foamy soap.

Shali scooped up two more handfuls of foam, but he put his arms loosely around Rianna and smoothed the creamy soap on her back. Each stroke of his lightly pressing fingers made her sway against his body and the slippery foam he'd covered himself with turned every move into a silky caress. His hands slid to her waist, then her hips, all the while he looked with seeming stoicism beyond her shoulder.

"Would Coraquenque have taught me *this*?" Rianna whispered.

Shali's eyes finally lowered to meet hers. They reflected golden glimmers from the lamplight as he murmured, "She would have taught you to soap yourself then step into the water to rinse." He bent his head to caress her shoulder, the side of her neck with his cheek.

She closed her eyes to say softly in his ear, "When we were in that great hall, you seemed so aloof and polite I'd begun to think you only intended to show me this place, that you didn't want me."

She felt Shali's warm breath against her neck as he whispered, "I want you with each breath I take; for I live every moment with this passion and never forget it, though I've tried."

His mouth slid up Rianna's throat, languidly across her cheek then rested lightly on hers. His tonguetip touched the perimeter of her lips, slowly traced their outline, making a tenuous tingling run through her. It urged her lips apart and he nibbled at her mouth teasingly even while she felt his body tensing against hers. She tightened her hold on his waist but his hands slid to her arms to loosen her embrace. Then he moved against her slowly, invitingly, arousing a sweet, hot ache in her. Yet, as Rianna's grasp on Shali tightened, he caught her hands and stepped away.

"Now we should rinse ourselves," he said softly.

"But," she began. His lips stopped her words with a lingering caress.

Still holding Rianna's hands, Shali guided her to the pool then backed slowly down the steps, drawing her after him.

When she was standing shoulder deep in the water, he bent to kiss her then murmur against her lips, "I'm too tall for you when we stand on the tiles."

Rianna felt his arms tighten around her hips, her buoyance as he lifted her. She blinked in surprise and noted his eyes intently watching as he moved against her. His body, sinuously persuasive, ignited a flame in her.

"Put your legs around me, *chinita*," he whispered and pressed his mouth to her shoulder. His lips wandered over her skin lighting little sparks in every pore he touched, while she obeyed him. He felt the tremor that ran through her, the sudden tension of her body; and as he tilted his head to again take her lips, he murmured, "Don't resist me because you didn't expect this. There are many things we have yet to share that will be unfamiliar to us both. We need to learn about each other, about ourselves when we're together.''

She looked into his eyes, obsidian shimmering with golden firelight, wondering at what he seemed to predict; and he said, ''Don't think about it, *chinita*. Just let your feelings take you where they will.''

Shali's lips were firm as they covered hers. The flame in her that had dimmed only a little leaped higher at his insistent caressing. Her senses swept forward, her mouth eagerly responding while his body again moved with supple effectiveness against her. Shali's embrace tightened and Rianna let out a little cry that was muffled by his mouth caressing hers with clinging hunger. His body took on a rhythm that filled her mind and banished thought while the fires in him flared with so sudden a force he couldn't suppress his soft moan.

He was dimly aware of Rianna's quickened breath, but its sound only matched his accelerating heartbeat. Her limbs were like flames coiling around Shali, binding them with approaching ecstasy until, almost lost in his own impulses, he decided to surrender the last threads of his control and was overwhelmed by a compulsion that dissolved his being in a burst of exploding rapture.

Finally serene, Shali felt Rianna's head sink to his shoulder. He buried his face in her hair, breathing its fragrance a moment before he felt her grasp on him loosen. He let her slide down until she again stood in the pool leaning against him, her cheek resting on his chest. Her breaths, sharp little pants against his skin, slowed and evened before he released her from his embrace.

Rianna felt Shali's hands at her temples lift her face toward his and discovered his eyes no longer were an enigma. She felt as if she could have walked through them into his soul.

''Are you still wary of all we can share tonight?'' he asked softly.

''I think I should stop questioning anything you do,'' she whispered.

''For the moment I only plan to dress and have the evening meal we've delayed,'' he said with an easy smile.

Shali took Rianna's hand and led her from the water. He shook out a length of soft cotton that lay folded on the table and enveloped her in the cloth. He noted her eyes following his every move; and as he turned to take a second towel, he commented, ''I've found I can often perceive *some* part of your thoughts; but now I can't begin to guess their direction.''

"I was thinking of what a gypsy once told me," she said.

"What is a gypsy?"

"A kind of people who wander about the land staying where they choose as long their mood allows," she explained. She came closer to look up at Shali. "The woman I was thinking of could see into the future. She told me that my love would be so unlike any other man I couldn't imagine him."

Shali let his towel drop and admitted, "I once saw a vision of you."

Mystified, Rianna asked, "You did? Really?"

"Yes, a thing I'd never experienced before and haven't since." He tossed his towel aside, as if he were discarding the subject as well, then gave Rianna a long, sleeveless robe made of the finest-spun, softest cloth she'd ever touched.

"But won't you tell me about this vision?" she asked.

"I'll describe it for you someday," he promised, not wanting to bring up the subject of her parents' death. He prompted, "Put on this robe."

Rianna found that the robe had neither fastenings nor a sash. Shali smiled at her confusion, as if the matter of closing the garment was of no importance, and slipped on a similar robe.

His arm lightly guided her into the adjoining room where he paused to raise his head, turn toward the door and say something loudly in Quechua. When the door to the corridor opened and Topa stepped inside carrying a tray of food, Rianna was stunned. She clutched at the front of her robe to hold it closed though Topa discreetly didn't look at her as he set the food on one of the tables.

Finally, Rianna found her voice and exclaimed, "Topa! Were you all along Shali's servant and another spy in Nicasio's house?"

Topa glanced at Shali's face to read his wishes then said, "I was carried from my village in a raid a few years ago to become one of the Castilian captain's slaves. After I left his house, Lord Shali found me in the mountains; so I gladly serve him."

"But he said you were his aide," she recalled.

"I would aspire to that honor when Lord Shali's present aide is promoted," Topa answered; then, looking at Shali to learn if he had further orders and noting there were none, he bowed his head and backed away.

After the door closed behind Topa, Rianna turned to Shali with a questioning look. "*Lord* Shali?" she inquired.

"It's an expression of respect," he replied.

"But Topa behaves as if his every breath depends on your word," Rianna said, watching Shali move across the room to the table beside the bed where Topa had placed the food.

"He's of humble birth and glad for the chance to become my aide," Shali flung casually over his shoulder as he lifted the cover on one of the food bowls to peer at its contents.

"You are not, I gather, of humble birth?"

Shali realized what he'd said, tensed briefly, almost imperceptibly, then straightened to turn and look at her. "Not many officers are."

"Or not at least so high ranking an officer?" she pressed. When he shrugged, she tried again. "What is your rank?"

"There's no equivalent of my title in your language, none I know of anyway," Shali replied. He looked at her speculatively a moment before stepping onto the low bed. In a movement whose ease was borne of habit, he sank down to sit cross-legged on the cushions and prompted, "Don't you want supper?"

Rianna came closer. "In bed?"

Shali reached for her hand. "Many pleasant things can be comfortably done in bed, which is why Incas, who can manage it, like them to be large. Come, *chinita*. The answers I *can* give to your questions will be the truth."

She joined him; and after he'd offered her a golden bowl of vegetables mixed with meat, aromatic with spices unrecognizable to her, she said, "You know I would never betray you."

Shali nodded and answered solemnly, "But for an oath I gave my king, who doesn't know you as well as I do, I would answer any questions you put to me." He motioned her to taste the food then poured a bronze-colored liquid from an urn into a golden cup. As he placed the goblet within her reach on the table, he warned, "This is more potent than your wine so drink it cautiously."

"What is it?"

"It's made much like your wine, but not from grapes." He lifted his own cup to his lips coaxing, "Taste it, *chinita*. A little at a time will merely warm you."

"You've already warmed me," she replied.

He said nothing; but pleased that she was finally beginning to feel free enough with him to become a little saucy, he glanced at her from the corner of his eyes as he sipped his drink. Rianna saw that his eyes were smiling before she looked away to sample the liquid in her goblet. It had an unfamiliar tang, and, as Shali had promised, spread a gentle warmth through her blood. The lingering flavor in her mouth was like smoky honey. Intrigued, she lifted the cup to try more; but Shali's hand stopped her.

"I don't want your mind to be blurred or your senses dulled by this," he said and suggested, "It's wise to eat something at the same time."

Rianna finally tried the dish he'd offered, found it savory, then sampled a mildly sweet vegetable, still another that was piquantly flavored. She found them to her liking, though their contents still were unknown to her. He explained the meat was from an animal called a tapir. The vegetables were tomatoes, sweet peppers, a root called *oca* flavored with an herb called *quinoa*. There were yams cooked in syrup the Incas made from maize, something called plantain prepared with cinnamon and herbs.

At the end of the meal, Shali sliced a piece of fruit, green-skinned though its flesh was rosy-hued. He put a bit of it into her mouth before saying, "You want to know about me, so I'll tell you what I can." He paused a moment, as if considering what he would say before resuming, "I was born and grew up in Tumbez, which is near our northern border. My father's family was well-placed in Ecuador, which was part of the Incan empire. Because of arguments between King Huascar and his brother Atahualpa, whose mother had come from Ecuador, Huascar looked with limited favor on us. While I was in Spain learning about your people, a disease swept through Tumbez. It was later said to have been a gift from the soldiers Hernando Pizarro had left in exchange for me. I came home to find that my mother and three brothers had succumbed to it as well as a third of the city's population."

"And your father?" Rianna asked softly.

"Like your parents, he was burned at the stake." Shali again fell silent a moment as if remembering before he continued, "I wasn't allowed into the plaza and wasn't sure what was happening until someone later told me. I only remember the smoke rising over the heads of the crowd. Someone, who witnessed the execution, said my father suffered silently until his last breath, which he used to curse the Pizarros. My family's home was burned then. Not long before you arrived in Peru, the house I'd had built was also destroyed."

Shali had spoken so dispassionately Rianna wondered at his seeming lack of emotion until he finished in a voice that trembled slightly, "We called your people 'children of the sun' when they first came because so many of you had red tints in your hair and blue eyes. We thought your coming fulfilled a legend, very ancient among Incas, that described such beings as our ancestors and godlike. We learned too late there was nothing benevolent about the Pizarros or their soldiers." He swallowed the last of the liquor in his cup and looked at her. "I hated all your people until I met you. Though I like the others I've observed as little as before, I'm as surprised to discover I love you as you must be. But, *chinita*, are my customs really so alien from yours?"

"After what you've experienced, I would think your *not* hating my people would be strange," she said then took the last sip of her drink.

Shali stretched out on his back and, after Rianna put down the cup, reached up to lightly caress her cheek with his palm as he said, "I wasn't speaking of revenge, but love. Are my ways too different from those of your people?"

"I can't know exactly what others of my people do. Intimacy isn't spoken about freely," she said.

Shali's eyes smiled wickedly as he commented, "For once I'm glad your people are so reticent about making love. I'll enjoy teaching you."

Rianna bent over him, her hair falling like a shimmering golden veil around his face as his lips reached up and caught hers. His arms sliding around her tightened to pull her down and press her to him. Both their robes had fallen open and the sensation of his hard, warm body under hers had an impact on Rianna's instincts that made her mouth crush then caress his lips with a new sureness that inflamed him even more.

Shali moved against Rianna's mouth so forcefully he caught himself, paused to learn if she would flinch from his aggressiveness. When her lips reached unshyly for him, gladness rushed through Shali in a torrent of desire so powerful he couldn't deny the urges racing along his nerves. His body undulated beneath her until she shuddered with passion; his mouth possessed hers as if his kiss were a challenge. She threw aside the last shackles of her caution and didn't surrender, but demanded.

When Rianna began to move, her entire body became a seductive caress; and Shali felt as if triumph were a pool of molten liquid rising in him. Rianna's hips swiveled and he couldn't prevent his gasp any more than he could stop the exquisite waves of fire flaring higher with each breath he took. He opened his eyes, hoping to distract himself and salvage his control; but vision escaped him and the impulses streaming through his blood impelled him on, whipped his senses to greater heights. He could contain them no longer. The full force of his passion leaped its last barrier and erupted in a sheet of fire that consumed him.

Rianna lay gloriously spent and unmoving while her ability to think gradually returned. When she realized what she'd done—*she'd* directed Shali's fire—she slipped away to lie beside him. The one thing, above all others, Rianna had learned about the behavior of men and women was that a woman was never to be in command. Yet she had crossed that forbidden line and had driven Shali to fulfillment almost as if his body were her slave. She cringed at what he must think of her now, though he didn't speak or move. She looked at him from the corner of her eyes and saw his were open and gazing at the ceiling. Abashed at the extravagance of her passion, face flaming, she turned on her side away from him.

Rianna was wishing she could think of some way to creep invisibly out of the room when she felt Shali nestle against her back. When he didn't move again, she wondered if he'd fallen asleep and automatically sought her warmth. She lay motionless, brilliantly aware of the sensation of him, almost afraid to breathe lest he awaken and, remembering her brazenness, turn away.

Then she felt his breath on her ear as he whispered, "*Chinita*, I want you again."

She turned slowly to stare incredulously at him as he said, "Now you at last understand your passion runs as deep as mine."

"I thought," Rianna began. She stopped, not knowing what to say.

Realizing what she'd assumed, he smiled in denial. "Though I needed a few moments to recover from my surprise, my joy at what you did will never dim."

Shali sat up beside her and shrugged off his robe then his hands under Rianna's shoulders urged her to rise a little so he could discard hers too. When he again leaned close, he looked appraisingly at her a moment before he said quietly, "There is in our forests a kind of flower that opens its petals when the sun touches it, closes as a shadow briefly falls then only a moment later blooms again. You will be that flower and I your sun and shadow."

Rianna stared at Shali a moment before whispering, "I don't think—"

"You worry needlessly," he assured then kissed away any more she might have said.

During the hours that followed, Rianna forgot her misgivings, everything she'd ever thought she'd known about herself as well as all Shali had taught her. She was commanded by the needs he evoked, possessed by forces of such power she was overwhelmed again and again. His kisses made garlands of embers around her limbs and bathed her body with clouds of sparks. Even the warm little breaths he exhaled explored her reaction and, when she responded, tantalized her more. His caressing hands, his entire body seemed pledged to entice her to completion though he withheld himself. Rianna was a flame swirling in the wind and Shali a sultry, restlessly seeking song; until finally, the blaze he'd so carefully nurtured in her burst through his smoldering control; and as the last shimmer of moonlight retreated from the mountains, he surrendered to ecstasy.

Then, sheathed by moisture and still trembling, Shali tilted his head so his lips were near Rianna's ear and he could whisper in Quechua. Though he realized the many ways he was telling of his love were lost on her, he knew it wasn't possible to say it in her language.

*   *   *

The sun's edge hadn't yet had a chance to rise over the dark slopes of the Andes, but streaks of golden light were already turning the morning mist into a shower of gilt as Shali led Rianna down the mountain to the ledge where he'd met her. He knew they'd delayed leaving their bed until it was dangerously late and now he dared not remain with her more than a moment.

He turned to take her into his arms one more time, inhale the fragrance of her hair and whisper into its silk, "I swear by my god and yours, I would take you with me if it were possible." He felt her nod and added, "I'll come for you as soon as I can."

Again Rianna nodded, but she clung to Shali so tightly he suspected she was weeping. He put his fingers under her chin, tilted her face to his and saw he was right. His regret deepened.

"I can walk no farther at your side, but I'll follow until you reach the valley," he promised. "I'll watch from the edge of the forest to make certain you reach Alonso's camp safely."

Rianna looked up at Shali through a blur of tears, but he stepped away and dipped his head to pull off a chain he'd worn around his neck. He slipped its fragile, shining links over her curls and directed, "Tell Alonso you were lost and found an old Incan hostel to spend the night in though, because of your wanderings, you can't remember its location."

"It's the one place in these mountains I'll never forget, but I'll tell him I was lost," she agreed.

Shali looked at her a long moment. He realized, if he kissed her mouth, he couldn't trust himself to leave; so instead, he bent to press his lips to her forehead. Then he murmured against her hair, "Tell Alonso you found that pendant in the hostel and thought it was pretty. It isn't so large a piece of gold he'll lust for it too much; but if he asks to see it, don't give it up. Wear it always and in plain sight. It will protect you, *chinita*."

Shali couldn't resist the impulse to briefly kiss her cheek before he suddenly turned and left, poignantly aware of her tears on his lips he carried away with him.

Rianna watched Shali's smoothly graceful steps as he moved over the rock strewn ledge until he vanished into the foliage.

"Even if I can't see you, I'll know you're always there," she breathed. She looked down at the pendant shining on her bosom. The design delicately worked into the gold was that of a jaguar bearing the royal condor.

chapter

13

Private Sarabia carefully scanned the small clearing he'd found to make sure none of the other men searching for Rianna were nearby. Then, certain she'd come this direction, he sat on a fallen log to wait.

He moved his sword so he could sit more comfortably, loosened his cloak and reached for the flask he'd tucked into the back of his sash so it would be hidden from the others. Rum wasn't what Sarabia preferred for breakfast, but it had kept him warm during the chilly Peruvian night while he'd searched for Rianna. He tilted his head to take the last swallow he had left, waited for the liquor to trace a warm path to his stomach then replaced the flask in his sash and considered the situation.

It had already been twilight when Coraquenque had discovered Rianna wasn't in camp; and Alonso, assuming she'd gotten lost, had sent the men out to hunt for her. The others had decided a woman would go for a walk in the forests surrounding the meadow where they'd camped and concentrated their search there. But during the journey, Sarabia had often noticed the joy on Rianna's face when they'd reached some lofty crag. He knew she loved the mountains so he'd headed for the nearby slopes. Though Sarabia had climbed every precipice, tramped through every gully he'd come across, had even called into several caves, he'd found nothing until just before dawn.

He'd been resting on a rocky ledge gazing at an outcropping of rocks when he'd been surprised to notice a splash of violet against the stones, the same color, he'd recalled, as Rianna's riding dress. Sarabia had been about to hail her when he'd seen she was with a man. An Inca.

The care the Inca used in leading Rianna down the slope had told Sarabia Rianna wasn't a prisoner. Amazed that she was apparently a spy, he'd withdrawn to hide among the rocks. He'd been stunned at the tender embraces Rianna had shared with the Peruvian and he'd watched until the Inca left her with obvious reluctance. After the Inca had vanished in the foliage, Sarabia hurried down from his vantage point then cut across the forest intending to tell Alonso Rianna was a spy and had an Indian lover.

Halfway to the camp Sarabia had changed his mind. How would Alonso reward him for this news? Sarabia was a soldier, not one of Alonso's cutthroats who could share whatever spoils Alonso might later gather. What good would it do to warn Alonso about a possible Incan attack? Sarabia had no idea where or when it might take place and was certain that, being a woman, Rianna was only a source of information for the Inca, not privy to his plans. The travelers were always aware the Incas could attack. If and when they did, Sarabia anticipated Alonso's turning to him, a military man, for advice on how to meet the enemy, which he'd give in any case. While Sarabia concluded that telling Alonso about Rianna's rendezvous with an Inca would benefit him nothing, he speculated that facing Rianna with this news might be a different matter.

Ever since Sarabia had first seen Rianna he'd thought her beautiful, but she'd paid no attention to the glances he'd cast her way. He'd assumed she was Alonso's mistress then later, because of her demeanor, had believed the story he'd heard about her being orphaned and Alonso's being her protector. During the trip from Lima, when Rianna had tended Sarabia's swordcuts, it had been frustrating to have so beautiful a woman dressing his wounds, and he'd felt as if he'd been drowning in the nearness of her. Sarabia had always been successful with women and hadn't been able to understand, even if Rianna was circumspect, how she could completely ignore him. He had tipped other young women from their virginal pedestals. Now Sarabia assumed the reason for Rianna's indifference to him was another lover.

Sarabia surmised, from the way Rianna had clung to the Inca and wept over their parting, that the affair wasn't a passing thing. She was in love with the Peruvian and Sarabia knew women in love were often willing to do anything to protect their lovers. He speculated happily on what she would give to buy his silence.

Rianna knew Shali was anxious to leave the area, that she should hurry back to Alonso's camp; but her steps were deliberately slow. She wanted to prolong these last moments with Shali despite their not being able to walk together.

Though Shali's movements in the forest were as soundless as the sun falling through the trees, she couldn't help listening for him. Unable to glimpse even a leaf quivering from his passing, she yet glanced from one side to the other. After the night they'd shared, she felt so closely bound to him she thought she could sense his nearby presence in the foliage pacing her.

Shali's love had driven away the nightmarish past at the same time he seemed to have stripped her of the inhibitions left from her sheltered upbringing. Rianna reflected on how Shali's careful nurturing of her desire had taught her body to trust the wild feelings he evoked, to accept the joy and give it back like the shining offering it was on the altar of their love.

Rianna wished they could spend a day doing the ordinary things Incas did in less violent times and she speculated on what life might be like for a woman at his side. Now that she knew he was an aristocrat, she was curious about the duties and pleasures such a rank involved. But, Rianna mused, it was possible the disruption Pizarro had caused in Incan affairs had already changed them. Even if the Incas could drive the Castilians from Peru, the empire of Shali's fathers might be forever lost.

A rustle in the foliage bordering a clearing brought an abrupt end to Rianna's musings. She stopped midstep to warily listen. Rianna knew, even if Shali had decided to approach carelessly, he wouldn't make that noise. Was it the sound of an animal so large it couldn't walk without crashing through the foliage or one so ferocious it had no fear of discovery? The knowledge that Shali would protect her was quickly followed by the reminder that the only weapon he bore was the knife sheathed at his hip; and Rianna was chilled to think of his being mangled by the unseen creature lurking nearby. She glanced suspiciously around the area and was about to hurry into the foliage to hide when the bushes parted and Sarabia emerged.

Breathless with relief, Rianna gasped. "Private Sarabia! I was terrified I was being stalked by some beast!" As Sarabia approached, she added, "I'm so glad you found me. I've been wandering around in this forest in circles, I fear."

"You've been going in as straight a line as an arrow's path. Don't bother to lie. I saw you with that Inca," Sarabia said quietly. He noted the fear that flashed through her eyes and added, "I've decided you aren't likely to know his plans, but I doubt Alonso would believe that. I've come to the conclusion we can make a bargain."

Desperate to learn a way to silence him, Rianna slowly asked, "What kind of bargain?"

"This journey has been long and boring for me, especially when I have nothing to look forward to at the end of the day like that Indian obviously enjoyed last night," Sarabia said slyly. Seeing the expression on Rianna's face changing, he knew she understood. He stepped closer to take her arm. "If you'll meet me whenever it's possible to be alone, I won't tell Alonso you have an Incan lover."

"Private Sarabia, I'm neither a spy nor a whore!" Rianna breathed.

"If you can spend the night with an Indian, I think you can pass an hour here and there doing the same thing with me," Sarabia said.

Rianna stared at him in dismay and anger not only because of his crude proposal, but because he'd said "Indian" in the same derisive tone as if he were accusing her of having coupled with an animal. Her lips parted to answer him sharply.

"Before you say anything, you should consider your situation," Sarabia advised coolly. "I can bring you back to Alonso and let him beat you until he realizes you have no information about the Inca's plans or I can take you here by force then return you to Alonso. What could you say to him?"

Rianna was so aghast at Sarabia's proposal she momentarily forgot

Shali's promise to remain nearby. Furious that the cavalier would think she'd agree to such a bargain, she wrenched her arm from his grasp; but Sarabia laughed softly at her show of defiance.

"What can you do?" he asked so calmly Rianna wasn't prepared for what he did next.

As expertly as if Sarabia had ravished many women in the past, he suddenly put an arm around Rianna's waist and simultaneously kicked her feet out from under her. Rianna landed on her back; and flipping his cloak over his shoulder, Sarabia sat on her.

Shali, watching from the foliage, had been too far away to hear the low conversation so he wasn't immediately alarmed. When the solider took Rianna's arm, Shali thought the gesture preparatory to leading her back to camp. Rianna's back was to him and he couldn't see her face; but the cavalier's expression appeared relaxed, even pleasant. Yet, there was a tension in the air that made Shali wary. The moment Sarabia knocked Rianna down Shali shot out of the foliage like a bolt. His soft boots made no sound as he sped into the sunlight, and Sarabia never suspected he and Rianna weren't alone until Shali's grasp on his hair lifted him away from her and cast him aside. The soldier reacted automatically by rolling then quickly springing to his feet. But Shali, having a set of rules about personal combat different from the Castilian's, was already mid-leap. His boots caught Sarabia in the stomach. The soldier gasped and doubled over. Shali's knee came up to meet Sarabia's face with a force that sent the Castilian crashing to his side. One well-placed kick to Sarabia's temple ended the short battle.

Rianna, who had meanwhile scrambled to her feet, stared for a moment at the soldier's inert form before she ran into Shali's arms.

"He saw us saying goodby and said if I didn't . . . didn't . . ." She couldn't finish.

Shali stroked Rianna's hair soothingly a moment then, reminding himself that they stood in a sunlit clearing and, if any other of Alonso's men were in the area they'd be seen, he stepped away. "I must hide this man and you have to go on your way," he said.

Rianna nodded and watched dazedly as Shali bent to pick up Sarabia's feet and drag him into the foliage. When he returned, she whispered, "What will you do with him?"

"Don't worry about that." Shali said grimly. He took her arm and turned her toward the edge of the clearing. "Go on to the camp, but don't dawdle as you were doing before. I'll still follow to make sure you're safe, but I'll have to get back as quickly as possible so no one finds that man before I've left this area."

"Maybe he'll regain consciousness if you come with me," she said nervously.

Shali shook his head, but didn't mention that the soldier wasn't likely to ever open his eyes again. He put his arms around Rianna for a hasty embrace before he left her to vanish into the forest.

Giving the bushes where Shali had deposited Sarabia one last worried glance, Rianna hurried in the direction Shali had pointed. Now, as he'd warned, she didn't delay. She ran through the forest in a terror that Sarabia would be discovered and the search for her would turn into a hunt for Shali.

When Rianna reached the meadow, she thought she now must certainly look the part of a lost waif. Her riding dress was torn, her face and hands soiled, her hair tangled with bits of twigs and leaves.

Shali, watching from the forest's green shadows, waited until Coraquenque raced out to the center of the meadow to meet Rianna before he turned away.

After Coraquenque stepped back from Rianna's embrace, she continued to anxiously grip her hands. "Where have you been? I was afraid you'd fallen down a canyon or been attacked by an animal!"

"Let me explain quickly while we're still alone," Rianna hushed then hurriedly told her friend what had happened.

Coraquenque's expression was wistful rather than surprised. "I know where that hostel is. I'm glad you had the chance to be with Shali, but I wish my husband had been there too. I would have taken that walk with you."

Rianna saw beyond Coraquenque's shoulder that Alonso had come to the edge of the camp and was watching. She slid her arm around her friend's waist and warned, "We must return now." It occurred to Rianna that Coraquenque seemed to have known in advance her husband wasn't with Shali, an unusual thing, because Rianna had observed the two men seemed to be always together. She would have liked to ask Coraquenque more, but they were too near Alonso.

"What happened to you?" he immediately demanded.

"I walked too far and got lost in the dark," Rianna answered.

"*Never* again go for a walk in the twilight," Alonso scolded. "That's when the predators start hunting." He stopped as his eyes fell on the pendant Rianna wore. "Where did you get that?"

"I took shelter for the night in an old Incan building and found it there." When Alonso began to reach for the pendant, Rianna backed away.

"I merely wanted to see the piece closer," Alonso said so hastily she knew it was a lie. He would have taken it. Rianna remained carefully out of his reach and he inquired, "Where was the Incan building?"

"How can I know after all the wandering around I did?" she snapped then, realizing he probably wanted to search the place for loot he could carry away, she added crossly, "It was a ruin and there was nothing left for you to steal."

Embarrassed that Rianna had guessed his purpose at the same time he was angered by her shortness, Alonso was tempted to slap her; but one of the men approached to report that everyone had returned from the search except Sarabia. Alonso turned to the man to bark, "Go out and find him! I would have thought a soldier would know how to get back," he added disgustedly as he turned again, intending to question Rianna further about the Incan building; but she had left. He saw her walking slowly toward her tent and decided she'd probably told him the truth about not knowing where it was. There was no reason he could think of for her to lie.

It was almost noon before the searchers returned with Sarabia's body. Rianna, bathed and changed, came out of her tent to hear what Alonso decided about the soldier's death. She was relieved when Alonso assumed, because there were no wounds on Sarabia's corpse and the men had found him at the bottom of a rock-strewn gully, he'd fallen during the night, probably because of sleeplessness and the empty rum flask they found on him. Rianna was glad no one questioned Sarabia's death, but she was awed that Shali had killed the soldier.

Alonso ordered a grave to be quickly dug and a hasty prayer

followed his burial. Then Alonso, muttering about having already lost half a day's traveling time, ordered them to resume the journey.

Shali, too, was in a hurry to leave the area, and his reason was the same as Alonso's—the pass into the valley of Xaquixaguana. The valley was a lush garden the travelers could easily cross in a day and enter Cuzco's gates. The pass was the last place suitable for a raid.

During the journey from Lima, Shali had noted that Alonso directed the pace of his group as if he had a schedule. Shali surmised Alonso wanted to reach the pass at midday when there were no shadows to help cover Incas hidden among the rocks. The Castilian had asked the right people's advice about the journey, Shali had to concede. Alonso's plan was the same as he would have made had their positions been reversed. Shali wasn't sure Alonso could make up the time he'd lost because of the earthquake and having to search first for Rianna then Sarabia, but he knew Alonso would try. Shali and his men had to arrive at the pass by dawn on the day he estimated Alonso would so they'd have time to conceal themselves.

Shali would have allowed Alonso's group to reach Cuzco undisturbed, but Manco Capac wanted to gather horses for his own troops and as many weapons as possible to pass on to Almagro's men. Shali understood Manco's dealing with Almagro's partisans wasn't inspired by friendship. The Incan leader hated one Castilian as much as another, but supplying weapons to the weaker of the warring factions encouraged the chaos the government had been plunged into. Manco hoped the Castilians would kill each other and save him the task, that when the new official arrived from Panama the situation would be past mending and the Incas could drive the invaders from Peru.

Shali would have preferred to attack Alonso's group before this last opportunity in the pass, but he hadn't had enough men. It had been arranged for more Incas to join his soldiers; but Shali knew, whether or not the additional forces met him in time, he would *have* to attack. Not even the commander of the Incan army could ignore Manco Capac's orders despite his being the king's cousin and friend.

While Shali persistently pushed his men forward, he left scouts behind who, noting the progress Alonso was making, could rejoin the main body of Incas and report the travelers' position.

Alonso, too, sent out scouts; but steep cliffs, yawning chasms or tumbles of loose stones left from rockslides made it impossible for the Castilians to parallel Alonso's column. Once in a while someone would see a horseman, who had climbed a cliff from the opposite side, overlooking the trail. Though Alonso knew such horsemen could no more descend this side of the slope than his own scouts could ride up and capture the strangers, he was worried about their presence.

Because there never was more than one watcher, who after a moment withdrew, Rianna assumed it was Shali or Topa keeping guard as Shali had promised. Rockslides and trees occasionally blocked the road, making Alonso curse at the delays. The men ordered to clear the trail glanced fearfully over their shoulders as they worked; but Rianna, convinced Shali and Topa were alone, assumed the obstacles were natural occurrences. When they came to a bridge they couldn't cross because the planks that formed its floor were gone, Coraquenque commented sadly, since Incas had been forced to flee or fight the Castilians, they couldn't maintain the king's bridges and roads they'd once been so proud of. She wasn't able to tell Rianna in front of the others that she suspected Shali's men had removed the planks to delay Alonso, who would have to follow the bank to a place where the horses could ford the river.

On the morning of the day Alonso hoped to approach the pass, they got up well before dawn so they could reach the pass at noon. The travelers ate a hasty breakfast then wearily prepared to leave.

By mid-morning, after having covered a stretch of particularly rocky ground, a number of horses, who had long ago lost their shoes, began to go lame. It was necessary for the animals to be led so the sharp stones cut into their riders' boots as well as the horses' hooves. Finally, the shoes had to be pooled; and despite the scarcity and value of the animals, a few had to be left behind. Some of the horses had to carry two men; even with double burdens, they could go faster and farther than men on foot.

An hour later the column plodded through a village Coraquenque said the Incas themselves had destroyed so the Castilians could obtain no food or comfort from it. Coraquenque's voice had a bitter edge as she remarked that many villages had been torched by the Incas, who had also destroyed fields of crops, orchards and storehouses before they'd fled. In larger towns, where there had been temples, anything made of gold or silver had been gathered and buried or even dumped into deep rivers and lakes to keep them out of the enemies' hands.

Throughout the afternoon Alonso pushed the travelers as hard as he could; but they didn't sight the pass until the sun was dangerously low. The weary men sent a representative to talk to Alonso, who resisted their plea to wait until morning to enter the pass.

"It's madness to try to go through so late in the day," the man named Fuentes finally declared in exasperation. "It's too easy to be ambushed."

"We can just as easily be attacked here in the shadows of the cliffs as in the pass," Alonso stubbornly answered.

"If we camp with our backs against the cliff the Incas can only approach from the open space we just crossed and we'd see them coming," Fuentes reasoned. "The pass's slopes could be filled with Indians hoping we'll continue." Fuentes hurriedly crossed himself as he added, "I swear I can feel their eyes watching us now."

"Manco Capac's entire army can creep up on us in the dark if we camp here," Alonso argued.

"Incas can't see in the dark any better than we can and don't fight at night unless they must," Fuentes insisted.

"They'd see our campfires," Alonso replied, becoming angrier with every point Fuentes made. He'd already weighed the risks of waiting against the dangers of immediately going through the pass.

"Many horses have carried double and even those that haven't are too tired to move swiftly under an attack. The men are exhausted and a weary arm has less strength. Look at how fast the light is fading," Fuentes complained more heatedly. "The hour is approaching when a man trying to take aim on an enemy can be most easily deceived by the light."

"Then instead of useless debating, we should proceed now before the light fails us," Alonso said. He added in a menacing tone, "I am your commander, Fuentes. We'll camp in Xaquixaguana Valley on the other side of that pass tonight." Alonso raised his arm and gave an emphatic signal for the men to begin forward.

Even Rianna's confidence had been shaken by the urgency of

Fuentes' arguments, but she became more uneasy as she neared the entrance to the pass.

The air was drenched in an orange light that made her feel as if they all were trapped in a bubble of amber. The golden-tinted cliffs rising high at either side seemed deserted, she thought as she nervously glanced around. The lengthening purple shadows could, as Fuentes had observed, hide Manco Capac's army in the many crevasses lining the stone walls.

Long before each rider entered the pass, his complaining voice was stilled; and the only sound besides the horses' hooves echoing eerily off the rocks was the wind's sighing in the peaks. Like Rianna, the men's eyes moved warily over every shadow; and the horses, sensing their riders' fear, shook their heads and snorted nervously. The sounds the animals made seemed out of place among the towering rocks. Nothing alive and vital was appropriate in the pass. Only the wind's moaning, like the lamentations of Incan souls who had perished before the onslaught of invaders, seemed suitable in the desolation.

It was the sudden thunder of hooves that chilled Rianna even more than the wild cries of the Incan horsemen who suddenly raced down from one shadowy slope. The speed of horses who had spent all day resting made the double line of Incas seem like a tidal wave sweeping down on Alonso's men. Exhaustion slowed the Spaniards' reaction; and their muskets had barely been raised, bolts only just fitted to their crossbows, when the torrent of Peruvians hit them.

Rianna turned Wayra to stare incredulously as the Incas seemed to race through their column having done little damage until, an instant later, a number of Alonso's men toppled from their saddles. Some of the second line of Incas snatched up the reins of vacated horses and sped by to join the first while others with swords or war axes paused only a moment to wreak whatever damage possible before they, too, raced on.

"They want our horses!" Alonso cried and turned back, shouting orders to his men to gather together and form a more solid front to the Peruvians.

Horses, too wearied by the day's hard traveling to respond quickly, moved awkwardly. Some protested, reared and tried to back away.

Animals stumbled; and men, desperate to prepare weapons, swore and struggled with their mounts.

More afraid to enter the scramble than to take a chance on the Incas attacking a woman, Rianna hesitated where she had turned. The Peruvians took advantage of the Spaniards' commotion to fire into the cavaliers and Rianna shuddered at the good use the Incas made of muskets and crossbows they'd previously stolen from their enemies.

Some Peruvians carrying ropes with a sliding noose were tossing the loops over horses whose riders had fallen or, too weakened by wounds, were reeling in the saddle and slipped off when their lassoed mount was tugged from the others. One Inca, noticing a Castilian woman helplessly watching the fray, turned an eager eye on her snowy horse and wheeled his mount in Rianna's direction. He was near enough so she could see his dark eyes calculating the distance between them as the loop of rope momentarily floated over his head. Then his gaze fell on the pendant she wore, the loop snaked back into his hand; and with a disappointed yelp, he turned away.

At a sharp note from a horn, the Peruvians suddenly retreated. They regrouped into a quiet line on the lower slopes. One man, whose bearing was proof of his command, made his way out of their ranks and, advancing through a third of the space that lay between them and the Castilians, stopped.

A voice Rianna instantly recognized called, "If the weapons of those who have fallen remain where they are, we will allow you to leave the pass!" Shali didn't bother with a threat of what would happen otherwise; the Spaniards knew.

Rianna heard the Castilians discussing their situation, some arguing hotly with Alonso not to leave their wounded behind; but she paid little heed. Her attention was riveted on Shali.

The horse he sat, a glossy black creature, seemed anxious to resume the battle; for it stepped lightly around, pawed a moment, then rose off its forefeet only to land, prance again and shake its head. The horse's movements kept the dark red cloak Shali wore swirling around him; and the last streaks of sunlight coming through the pass glimmered on gold trimming the red and green band he had knotted around his brow. She recognized the green wool jerkin and breeches as those he'd worn when he'd walked with her in the forest and she could almost feel again the silky vicuña covering the shoulder she'd laid her head against.

But was this fierce-looking Inca *her* Shali, who had tenderly kissed her, whose passion had captured her heart as surely as he now had captured Alonso's hired brigands?

Rianna heard Alonso agreeing to leave the weapons and fallen men behind, but the meaning of his shouts was momentarily lost on her. She stared at Shali as if mesmerized by the dully shimmering links of the golden belt she'd only a few days before playfully fastened around that taut waist, the sudden flash of the knife sheath that clung to a hip so recently pressed against her own.

The black horse reared once before wheeling away and Rianna watched Shali's receding back until he rejoined his men. Despite the threatening, suddenly alien appearance he presented, she would have urged Wayra to gallop after him, but for Alonso's hand suddenly catching Wayra's bridle.

"Are you so befuddled you'd run *toward* that savage?" he cried. Giving Wayra a wrench so Rianna turned to face the far end of the pass, he said, "Get out of here now or we'll leave you behind with the rest of their spoils." As Alonso spoke, he slapped Wayra's rump, offering Rianna no choice; the mare plunged forward.

Rianna didn't press Wayra to run faster, even after the mare had slowed to a trot; and only Alonso's presence at her side kept Rianna from turning back. As those left of Alonso's men slowed their mounts so they could funnel through the opening to the valley, Rianna took the opportunity to pause and look back over her shoulder at the Peruvians, who had dismounted to gather up the weapons they'd won.

When Alonso reached for Rianna's arm, she smartly slapped his hand with her riding crop.

"I only meant you to go on out of the pass. The way is clear now," Alonso explained as he shook his stinging fingers.

"We're safe enough here, I'd warrant, now that you've followed their orders," she snapped then added contemptuously, "If you're so frightened by Incas after your first scuffle with them you dare not pause even to take your wounded, I have to wonder where you expect to get the courage to steal gold from their temples."

"That was hardly a scuffle!" Alonso exclaimed.

Rianna wouldn't relent. She thrust the truth at Alonso as if she poked at him with a lance point of her own. "It was a trap you stubbornly rode into despite the counsel of wiser men. I have to wonder what the survivors of your gang of thieves think of your leadership now, how loyal they'll be the next time you decide to enter a dangerous place."

"You'll notice they all left the pass ahead of us," Alonso answered, seeming not at all abashed by Rianna's accusing him of cowardice. "If you think the men we left back there are alive, you're wrong."

"How can you know that?" Rianna flashed back.

"Shalikuchima's men never aim to merely wound."

Rianna's mouth fell open in surprise. "*Whose* men?" she breathed.

Alonso jerked a thumb toward the distant, crimson-cloaked figure, who had drawn his horse to the side of the path and was staring steadily in their direction. "That devil! He's watching us so closely I think we'd best leave before he orders his men to attack us again."

"Shali is . . ." Rianna couldn't utter the name of the feared Incan commander.

"Not 'Shalyis,' " Alonso mistakenly corrected her, "Shalikuchima."

Rianna looked blankly at Alonso a moment then again at Shali. Alonso was stunned when she threw back her head and laughed aloud.

"Shalikuchima isn't going to kill *me*!" Rianna cried.

Concluding she was hysterical after the violence she'd seen, Alonso kept a wary eye on Rianna's riding crop as he caught Wayra's bridle then turned the horse to guide it through the mouth of the pass. The trill of Rianna's laughter trailed after them, bouncing off the granite walls like golden bubbles bursting in the fading light.

chapter
14

Because Shali had promised to let the travelers go peacefully, Coraquenque insisted they could safely camp at the exit to the pass; but Alonso was afraid and gave orders to ride into the valley. When one of the exhausted horses went to its knees, Alonso had no choice. They established camp in a grove of trees beside one of the streams that ran through the rolling terrain to the river at the valley's center.

When Rianna went to the stream to bathe her face and arms, all she could modestly manage because of the men's nearness, Coraquenque followed.

"You haven't said a word since we left the pass," the Inca observed as she knelt to dip a cloth in the water. "Are you still upset about Shali's attack?"

Rianna, ready to splash a little water on her face, said sullenly, "Don't you mean Shalikuchima? Alonso told me the truth."

"Are you proud to be Shalikuchima's love or are you afraid?"

Rianna wiped the water from her eyes and turned to look at Coraquenque. "I'm too surprised to know how I feel." Her voice had a petulant edge she didn't bother to disguise.

"You're angry I didn't tell you," Coraquenque concluded. She sighed. "I'm sorry. I couldn't tell you."

Rianna coolly inquired, "Is your name really Coraquenque?" At the Inca's startled look, Rianna added resentfully, "Shali, you, all your people, even Topa, have so many secrets I can't know what to think about anything!"

Coraquenque hung her head. "My name is truly Coraquenque and I'm your friend."

Rianna sat back on her heels. She was angry at herself for feeling guilty she was making Coraquenque unhappy. Still too upset to stop, she grumbled, "I felt disloyal enough to my people to love a man, who was a soldier opposing them. Though what my people are doing is wrong, how do you think it makes me feel to learn he's one of the most feared of our enemies?"

Coraquenque was sympathetic, but said, "Shali is no one's enemy until they make him so." She held out a towel hesitantly, as if it were a peace offering.

Accepting the towel, Rianna had to admit, "He did tell me something about what happened to his family." She couldn't resist adding a little sarcastically, "Not all of it, of course, his personal life being a state secret."

Coraquenque ignored the sting in Rianna's tone and said, "Now that you've learned who he is, I can tell you more. What would you like to know?"

It suddenly occurred to Rianna that a man so renowned a hero among the Incas must be pursued by every girl in the land and it was at the tip of her tongue to ask about his romantic past. Pride overcame the impulse and Rianna shook her head. "Later, Coraquenque. I have too much to think about now." She got to her feet and turned to rejoin the others.

Coraquenque put her hand on Rianna's arm to hold her a moment while she whispered hurriedly, "Even Shali and I must obey the king's commands. My people aren't usually secretive or suspicious; but this is a *war*, Rianna. Shali intends to win it."

"Is that why Alonso said Shalikuchima's men never wound their enemies?" Rianna murmured to hide the tears in her words.

Coraquenque's own temper was rising. She held her voice low with an effort. "Tell me how a soldier in the heat of a fast-moving battle can choose to wound an enemy, who has no qualms about killing him."

Rianna fell silent as she remembered the battle she'd seen that day. She knew Coraquenque was right, but didn't want to admit it.

"There's something else you should consider." Coraquenque noted her friend's resentment as Rianna lifted her eyes, but she angrily continued, "One of the things you don't know about Incas is that our healers are wiser than yours. If you'd ever seen one of your soldiers die because your doctors did him more harm than good, you'd understand that anything except the most minor wounds is a death sentence. Even if a choice were possible to Shali, he wouldn't be cruel to kill his enemies. In truth, he saves them from a more lingering, agonizing death."

Coraquenque turned and walked away, leaving Rianna looking after her in chagrin.

Later, when Rianna lay in bed staring at the streaks of light the campfire made on the wall of her tent, she wondered how it was possible to put her thoughts in order when there was so much she didn't know and couldn't be told. Though Coraquenque's comments about Incan physicians had stung her, she knew the doctors in Europe killed more patients than they saved.

Coraquenque's careless remark that *even* she and Shalikuchima must obey their king piqued Rianna's curiosity. Rianna could understand how so powerful a man as the kingdom's military commander might sometimes be tempted to disobey his king; but why would Coraquenque say that about herself? She'd never hinted she had a particularly elevated place in Incan society. Was her mysterious husband so important?

Another distressing fact that plagued Rianna was Shali's willingness to risk her life by attacking Alonso's group in the pass. A voice in the back of Rianna's mind recalled how he'd defended her against Sarabia then argued that nothing, except orders from the king, would have caused Shali to put her in danger. The voice persistently asked if she thought the ability Shali had used to prevent Sarabia's raping her had been so easily won, if many previous battles hadn't already steeled him to the necessity of killing his enemies without hesitation. Rianna wondered why his capacity for violence seemed so different from that of other soldiers; but her inner voice immediately gave the answer—because she loved Shali, anything he did would always have more impact on her than the actions and motives of other men.

Despite the many questions spinning in her mind, Rianna couldn't erase the memory of Shali sitting on his horse at the side of the road watching her so intently while his men picked up the weapons they'd won. Had Shali realized someone would tell her who he is? Had he been wondering what she thought of it?

The knowledge that, even while he'd spent the night making love with her he'd planned to attack the travelers, faded in importance before visions of the Incan commander wearing a blood-red cape and a gold-gleaming headband, sitting on his restless horse while he confidently awaited Alonso's surrender. Threading through every image Rianna had of Shali was the passion that was like an insistent theme of a melody she couldn't forget. When her exhausted mind finally succumbed to sleep, she dreamed of a jaguar with obsidian eyes.

Daylight revealed that entering the valley of Xaquixaguana was like stepping into the fantasies Rianna had dreamed about Eden. Unlike the tangy mountain winds that whipped the spirit to wild yearnings, the breezes of Xaquixaguana seduced the soul with sensual delight.

The air held a perfumed invitation to explore the vistas of rolling hills so lush with blooming vitality Rianna felt as if her being couldn't contain the beauty. The fragrance of pines from the mountains, sunwarmed valley grass and varieties of flowers she'd never before smelled was a constantly changing bouquet. Calls of brightly swooping birds, the sound of whispering trees was music that lured eyes to go farther afield and, saturated with their discoveries, poured the excess into her soul.

Watching Rianna's expression, Coraquenque said softly, "This valley is like a lover. It possesses one's spirit as well as senses."

Rianna could think of nothing to answer. She stared through the distance at a building massed with banks of flowers, at low stone walls bordering a garden sheltered by blossoming trees.

Coraquenque followed Rianna's gaze. "That used to be a nobleman's villa, but now it's untended and overgrown."

"A nobleman's villa?" Rianna echoed.

"The valley is dotted with such retreats," Coraquenque advised.

"Does Shali . . ." Rianna began then, wondering if she *should* ask, fell silent.

"Shalikuchima's home was in the north. He needed a second house in this valley convenient to our capital while he attended court," Coraquenque said.

Rianna drew in a soft breath as a kaleidoscope of visions whirled before her eyes of Shali mingling with the royal court, an elegantly clothed aristocrat conferring with his king. She couldn't believe such visions were of *her* Shali. Awed, she wondered how she could ever walk at his side.

Sensing some of Rianna's thoughts, Coraquenque said, "It isn't possible for you to imagine, no matter how you try, what Shali's life was like before the invasion."

Rianna whispered, "I feel as if I'm a shepherd's daughter, who has suddenly found herself standing in rags before King Charles."

Coraquenque reached over to pat Rianna's hand as she reminded, "Even if you were to be presented to Manco Capac's court in so startling a fashion, with Shalikuchima at your side, any comments would be silenced."

Rianna discovered her awe at this new view of Shali suddenly made her shy as well as curious. She was aware her color was rising, but she asked, "What would an Incan nobleman's daily business be?"

"The noblemen are the king's administrators. They have different tasks," Coraquenque answered.

"And Shalikuchima's job is to conduct wars," Rianna concluded.

"He maintains the king's laws, which normally means little more than making certain the army is trained and ready. We're an orderly people not given to internal disputes," Coraquenque replied.

"Does he do something else then?"

"Shali governs a province or did, until it was invaded," Coraquenque advised.

"Doesn't he administer it though he must be absent?" Rianna inquired.

"Nothing is left for him to govern," Coraquenque replied sadly. "His principal city was destroyed. Shali's people had to flee except for the men who are fighting at his side. Now that you know the men who attacked us in the pass had memories of their burning homes, their wives and children fleeing to desolate places to hide inspiring them in battle, can you wonder at their willingness to kill their enemies?"

Rianna wordlessly shook her head.

Coraquenque said no more. She wanted to give Rianna a chance to absorb all the things she'd learned. Understanding that her friend wanted to know everything she could about the Incan way of life because of Shali, Coraquenque regretted not being able to tell Rianna the more intimate details about the court. She realized that, if she gave in to the temptation, Rianna would wonder how she knew so much; and Coraquenque couldn't let even Rianna guess she was Manco's wife.

Coraquenque inwardly sighed at how much Incan society already had changed. In previous days she'd have had no contact with the daughter of a gem merchant and certainly wouldn't have puzzled over how to smooth any girl's romance with Shalikuchima. But then, Shali'd had his love; and since Yupanqui's death, he hadn't seemed interested in women. That he'd found love again was a relief to Coraquenque, that his new love was as sweet and good as Rianna was a joy.

When the procession approached the swamp that lay at the center of Xaquixaguana Valley, Coraquenque guided them to the stone-flagged causeway through the quagmire. She told Rianna how the river's frequent floods had produced the swamp then fell gloomily silent as she noted weeds overgrowing the flags.

Because Alonso had made them rise before dawn and had kept them to as lively a pace as the horses could bear, the travelers passed Cuzco's gates late in the afternoon. Coraquenque pulled up a shawl then bowed her head so the cloth would shadow her features. Though the streets were crowded with Castilian soldiers and adventurers, she noticed many Cañars, the Incas' old enemies. If by chance any of them recognized her, they would gladly betray her identity. She inwardly shuddered at how the Castilians would torture her to learn Manco Capac's plans or, even worse, dangle her like bait before his eyes; so they could trap him.

Shortly after Manco had inherited the kingdom, his first wife had been captured by the Castilians, who had publicly stripped her, beaten her almost to death then put her out of misery with a barrage of arrows. Manco had loved the woman and had grieved her loss deeply. Coraquenque knew Manco would never allow *her* to remain in captivity without rushing to her rescue even if he knew he would die in the effort. But Coraquenque never forgot, no matter how much she loved her husband or how grieved she would be if he was killed, that Manco Capac was, until he had a son, the last of the kings. At his death the heartbeat of his entire nation's spirit would be silenced; and she couldn't permit that.

Despite the damage the invaders had done to the Incan capital, the grandeur of certain buildings marked them as being of special significance. Coraquenque was forced by Rianna's questions to occasionally glance at an edifice to identify it and explain something of its purpose. It was a task that depressed the Inca.

When Rianna noticed the temple of the moon and asked about it, Coraquenque was pained to see it had been looted of even the smallest of its silver ornaments and mourned anew that its handmaidens who, because they were among the most beautiful girls in Peru, had been dragged away for the soldiers' pleasure. At Rianna's queries, Coraquenque explained how the maidens, who had served the temple of the sun, had been forced from their apartments and the places had been made into barracks. These girls, too, were used by the soldiers. Coraquenque felt as if their suffering were her own, and she was depressed that the sacred flame it had been among the women's duties to tend had long ago been extinguished. The light's going out had always foretold a catastrophe, and the Incas were now fighting for their existence.

Lust for treasure had all but destroyed the temple of the sun, which once had been the pride and wonder of the land. Now it was a shell, its golden cornices and frieze torn away, the resulting holes plastered over. The plaster was a scar mocking the temple's desecration.

Incan families had been driven from their homes, their houses confiscated; homeless Incas wandered the countryside while their houses became stables, so ill-tended they reeked of dung. The streets smelled of garbage cast from other buildings and Coraquenque was quick to assure Rianna that Incan streets had always been kept clean. Coraquenque sadly remembered that the fragrance of flowers or food being cooked had been the only odors in brighter days.

Finally, unable to bear even glimpses of the city that had once been known as "beloved of the sun," Coraquenque abruptly refused to acknowledge Rianna's questions because she couldn't look again at Cuzco's ruin.

Wondering at her friend's unrelenting silence, Rianna turned to Coraquenque, saw tears trickling down her cheeks and asked no more.

Alonso led his procession of weary travelers to military headquarters and demanded to speak with whomever was in charge. An aide, assuming Alonso was only another arrogant adventurer, was ready to send him packing and was stunned to learn he was addressing the Earl of Avila's son. His attitude instantly changed to ingratiating subservience. He hurried into another room and a moment later reappeared to escort them to Captain Estudillo's office.

The captain was ten years Alonso's senior, a veteran whose military ability had carried him through many campaigns, while his lack of noble blood had delayed his captaincy until recently; and he knew he wouldn't be promoted further. His dark eyes had seen too much for him to fawn over an earl's son, though they warmed at his introduction to Rianna. The presence of a gently bred lady in Cuzco was a rare treat and he wondered why Rianna was in Falla's protection.

Estudillo invited Alonso to sit down, but led Rianna to the most comfortable chair and seated her himself. His gesture brought a sullen Incan slave to pour goblets of fruited wine. When Alonso complained about having been attacked by Shalikuchima in the pass, the captain delayed answering until after Rianna had tasted the wine and declared it to her liking.

"How did you escape?" Estudillo inquired with obvious curiosity.

"He wanted the weapons and horses of the men who had fallen," Alonso answered.

"Guns and horses—damn!" the captain said softly.

"Our lives are worth more than horses and guns!" Alonso exclaimed.

Estudillo sighed, "Yes, of course." He sank into the chair behind his desk and commented, "You're lucky Shalikuchima settled for only that much. Perhaps Doña Rianna's presence made him more compassionate. Though he's never turned from travelers when he can take *all* their horses and weapons, I've never heard of him or his men harming women."

"But aren't you going to pursue him?" Alonso demanded.

Estudillo raised his gaze to Alonso and inquired, "Where shall I begin? If I'd arrived in the pass with a full regiment a half-hour after this incident, I wouldn't be able to follow Shalikuchima. He's too clever at disguising his tracks." Estudillo took a sip of wine before adding, "I can't spare men for fruitless searches when Cuzco itself is so unstable. The city is recovering from Almagro's partisans trying to overthrow this government as they did in Lima. Captain Holguin had just restored order before I arrived a few days ago."

Disappointed there would be no attempt to catch Shalikuchima, Alonso coldly observed, "I was sure we would be safe in Cuzco. I thought law is maintained in this city."

"It is, as well as possible under present conditions," Estudillo answered, then asked, "Did you come to Cuzco to escape Almagro?"

"I intend to find a tract of land suitable for a plantation," Alonso lied.

Estudillo briefly wondered why an earl's son would emigrate to this war-torn land and realized Falla was in some sort of trouble in Spain. Estudillo could believe Falla wanted to settle on a plantation because of Doña Rianna's presence, but he wasn't inclined to trust Falla anyway.

"If you plan to stay in Peru, you'll be comforted to know Captain Holguin sent a message to the *licenciate* in Panama urging him to replace Governor Pizarro. I'd think, because of Pizarro's death, his title may be changed to viceroy," Estudillo advised, more concerned with reassuring Rianna than Alonso.

But Alonso no longer was thinking about Shalikuchima. The reinstatement of royal authority in Lima by a man who might insist on a more benevolent attitude toward Peruvians was the last thing he wanted. "I haven't heard the new official's name," Alonso prompted.

"It seems to be a secret. Not even I know it," Estudillo admitted.

"I suspect the man's identity will strike fear in the hearts of the adventurers who have abused the privileges King Charles awarded them in Peru."

Alonso nodded gravely, though his goals were the same—to steal all he could from the Incas before any new laws were enforced to stop him. He privately wished the new viceroy wouldn't survive the journey. Hoping to learn when the official might arrive, Alonso remarked, "If the viceroy delays coming, Almagro might become too powerful. I understand Juan de Herrada, his chief advisor, is a man of action; and traveling from Panama to Lima is dangerous even in more peaceful times."

"If Benalcazar will escort the viceroy through Ecuador, Alvarado can safely bring him the rest of the way. Alvarado has a large force in the north and he was loyal to Pizarro." Estudillo took a swallow of wine before saying, "Since the possibility of a rebellion in Cuzco has ended, Captain Holguin is considering meeting Alvarado and joining their forces, which would present a considerable threat to the rebels in Lima."

"It certainly would," Alonso agreed. He hoped the battle that might result between the government and the rebels in Lima would be lengthy or that the new viceroy would be a weaker man than supposed. Then bribes might sway him. Alonso wished he could learn this official's name. If he'd been acquainted with the man in Spain or knew his reputation, he'd be better able to plan what to do.

Alonso was silent for so long a time Estudillo, who had other matters to attend besides imparting information, grew restless. Finally, he asked, "Do you know where you'll stay in Cuzco while you search for the land you wish?"

Aroused from his mind's wanderings, Alonso replied quickly, "No, Captain. I came directly here to learn what I could of the situation."

Estudillo inwardly sighed with resignation. No matter how much a nuisance this earl's son might become in future days, his status demanded certain courtesies; and the lady with him couldn't be expected to live in a shack like an Incan slave. "There's an apartment in one of the native buildings that was converted into a temporary dwelling for visiting officials, which is now vacant. It has ample space for you, Doña Rianna and any servants you've brought. I can't promise how long you'll be able to occupy it because I can't be sure when someone else may arrive. Such accommodations are scarce."

After having glimpsed the condition Cuzco was in, Alonso had begun to fear they'd have to pitch their tents on the city's outskirts. He leaped at this opportunity. "That's welcome news, Captain. I accept your kind offer. I intend to make permanent arrangements as quickly as I can."

"Thank you, Captain. You're being very helpful," Rianna said.

Estudillo turned his attention to her. "Permit me to do one more thing, Doña Rianna. I'm sure you must be tired of having your meals outdoors. Please be my guest at dinner tonight," he invited then, remembering Alonso, extended the offer to him as well.

Alonso was annoyed at the attention Estudillo was paying Rianna, but he thought the captain might be useful to him later and he dared not show his irritation. Ignoring Estudillo's slight he accepted, though he was glad when Rianna demurred.

"I would be delighted to say yes at a future date, Captain," she said with regret, then explained, "The journey from Lima was tiring and the last several days have finally exhausted me. I would like to retire early tonight."

"I understand, Doña Rianna," Estudillo replied sympathetically, though he was disappointed. "I'll look forward to your company another evening."

"We shouldn't keep you from your duties any longer," Alonso said, wanting to get Rianna out from under the captain's eyes.

Estudillo brushed his lips to Rianna's hand and promised to extend another invitation soon. Finally, he instructed his aide to have someone guide them to their accommodations.

"Alonso seemed pleased that you refused the captain's dinner invitation," Coraquenque remarked as she opened Rianna's trunk.

"Captain Estudillo was attentive to me and Alonso didn't like it," Rianna replied. She paused to consider the matter then added, "I suspect Alonso was relieved I wouldn't be there to question the lies he'll no doubt tell the captain while he digs for more information."

Coraquenque pulled a dressing gown from the trunk as she commented, "Maybe some of those lies will be about you."

"If so, Estudillo didn't impress me as the kind of man who believes everything he hears," Rianna replied as she unfastened her skirt.

Coraquenque cast her a curious look. "Is the captain handsome?"

Rianna shrugged, stepped out of the skirt and stooped to gather up the garment. "He recently arrived in Cuzco and I think he doesn't approve of what he's seen so far. He seems to be a different sort of soldier from the others, more professional maybe, less interested in loot."

"That *is* different," Coraquenque muttered as she dug deep into the trunk searching for a nightdress.

Rianna approached and turned her back to the Inca. "Will you untie my laces?" While Coraquenque busied herself at this task, Rianna suggested, "Let's only unpack what we'll need for tonight. We're both too tired to do more."

Coraquenque agreed and smothered a yawn. "I think I'll fall asleep as soon as I lie down, even if my bathwater will be cold tonight."

"Cold!" Rianna turned to face her friend.

"When I filled the bath for you just now, the water started running cool toward the end. I suppose there wasn't enough time to heat it since we just moved in," Coraquenque said regretfully.

"You've had enough cold baths in rivers and streams during the journey," Rianna declared. "We'll bathe Incan style. Then we'll both be able to rinse ourselves off in hot water."

Coraquenque's brows lifted speculatively. "Did Shali teach you our bathing custom?"

Rianna vividly recalled exactly how Shali had taught her and was embarrassed by her rising blush. She turned away to hastily put on her dressing gown then went to the bathchamber without answering.

Coraquenque said nothing while they soaped themselves; but after they were standing in the pool luxuriating in the comfortable water, she commented, "You act differently since you learned Shali is Shalikuchima." Rianna glanced up then quickly looked away and Coraquenque sighed. "You're shyer about everything, more as you were in the beginning." She paused to think then said slowly, as if carefully choosing her words, "You behave as if he's changed into another person and you're ashamed of having accidentally loved a stranger."

"He seems like a stranger," Rianna said, still refusing to meet her friend's eyes. "How would anyone feel after they'd been so deceived?"

"You've been thinking many things about Shali; but instead of asking questions, you've decided you know the answers," Coraquenque concluded. "The deception was necessary; but the Shali you met in the marketplace is the same man who commands our army. Shali is Shali, whether he's in the royal court or standing on the mountainside with you."

"Is that why he uses two names?" Rianna inquired coolly.

"It's true Shali isn't his real name, but neither is it a lie. After his father was executed, Shali refused to use his name. Shali said he didn't deserve it until his father was avenged," Coraquenque explained.

Rianna was quiet a long moment before she said awkwardly, "I'm sorry, Coraquenque. I've been cross with you, but none of this is your doing. I'm just confused. Everything happens so fast I hardly have a chance to make up my mind about one thing before it changes into something else." She started up the steps out of the pool and Coraquenque followed. The Inca was silent until after they'd put on their robes and gone into Rianna's room. Finally, she said, "One thing that hasn't changed is Shali's love for you. He isn't a man who gives his heart easily; but when he does, he withholds no part of it."

Rianna sat on the edge of her bed and silently stared at her lap.

"I think your emotions are so powerful you're afraid to surrender to them," Coraquenque reflected. "You're fighting your own heart and creating your confusion."

Rianna put her face in her hands and said softly, "When I saw that villa today and you told me Shali had one like it in the valley, part of me wanted nothing more than to be there with him while another part of me was terrified at the thought of sharing his life."

"You're afraid that because you aren't an Inca, Shali's people won't accept you or that you wouldn't be able to accept us," Coraquenque concluded. She took Rianna's hands and waited until Rianna finally met her eyes before she said, "I'm an Inca and I've accepted you. Is there anything you've so far learned about Shali and me you think is objectionable?"

Rianna's eyes blurred with tears and she shook her head. "I love you both," she whispered.

Coraquenque smiled and put her arms around Rianna. "It isn't easy for me to know what to tell you about my people. So much is changing anyway. I often think of odd little customs that don't seem important enough to mention, so I don't. Then I sometimes think talking about what might seem important would, in a way, frighten you more; because you'll think I'm trying to push you into something."

"Tell me one of these 'odd little customs,' " Rianna urged. "I don't want to hear about royal courts or politics now."

Coraquenque smiled in understanding and recalled something she thought might interest Rianna. "Incas enjoy exchanging news with their neighbors; but because travel is so difficult in the mountains, they can't visit as often as they'd like. We discovered a way of singing that carries from one mountainside to another. Since words are difficult to perceive, the changes in melody tells what we want to say."

"You really can hold conversations?" Rianna asked in wonder.

Coraquenque nodded. "News passes very quickly from slope to slope."

"It's a lovely idea to speak to each other in song," Rianna commented, "but I wonder how the sound travels so far."

The Inca laughed softly. "We sing very loudly and the mountain air is thin and clear. We couldn't do it in the jungle. Perhaps one day you'll be able to hear one of these conversations and understand how it's done."

"I would like that better than having to appear before the royal court," Rianna said.

"You'd find that talking to Manco Capac is easier than singing across the mountains," Coraquenque remarked. She noticed Rianna's tension was lessening and decided to tell her friend about another way of communicating. "When official messages must be exchanged, it isn't always desirable for everyone in the countryside to understand what's being said; so the king has runners to carry dispatches. Young men are hand-picked for their fleetness and honesty and trained to become *chaquis*. It's an honor to be chosen for this task."

"I can see why they'd have to be trustworthy," Rianna agreed. "They must be very strong to run so far."

"Each *chaquis* runs no farther than five miles. There are buildings along the roads where another *chaquis* waits to carry the dispatch to the next post," Coraquenque explained.

They talked in this easy way for a little longer. Coraquenque discovered it was better to tell Rianna about odd bits of information like mountain-singing and *chaquis* than to worry her with politics. She decided Rianna could learn more later, when she felt at ease with Incas.

Finally, when their yawns became too frequent to hide, Coraquenque stood up. "After spending so much time in your company, it seems strange to sleep in a room down the hall tonight."

"Even in Nicasio's house our rooms were connected," Rianna observed then admitted, "I feel less safe here than in Lima. Even Captain Estudillo commented that in Cuzco the law isn't very secure."

"I noticed that while we were riding through the streets, which is why I brought this for you." Coraquenque produced a small, golden dagger. "It's more ornamental than deadly, but maybe having it will make you feel better."

Rianna leaned closer to the lamp to examine the dagger which, though daintier than the knife she remembered Shali's wearing, looked deadly enough. Its double blade was razor sharp. The light glanced off an intricate design of a bird on the dagger's handle and she commented on its beauty.

"The bird is a coraquenque. This dagger was made as a gift for me," the Inca explained. She smiled, adding, "The design is proof I've told you my real name."

"I believe you. Despite what I said, I never really doubted you're my friend," Rianna said quietly. "Thank you for giving me this. I do feel safer now that I have it."

She walked with Coraquenque to the door and they exchanged good nights. After Coraquenque had left, Rianna closed her door and was chagrined to discover it had no latch. Before she blew out the lamp, she laid the dagger on the table beside her bed.

Rianna knew the conversation she'd had with Coraquenque had gone a long way toward helping ease her mind about Incas. Her last drowsy thought before she fell asleep was Coraquenque's remark that she and Shali were Incas and they loved her.

*   *   *

Early in the evening Alonso had tried to extract more information from Estudillo. Failing, Alonso decided the captain had too recently arrived in Cuzco to learn the ins and outs of the situation there; or, unlike Nicasio, Estudillo didn't open lines of communication to many levels of the society his assignment had thrust him into. Having made this decision, Alonso relaxed his effort to gather information and enjoyed the captain's hospitality. By the time Estudillo's clock chimed the first hour of a new day, Alonso's cup had been filled many times with *chicha*, Incan corn liquor; and it took an effort not to stagger as the captain showed him to the door.

Estudillo watched Alonso mount and was relieved when his guest was successfully in the saddle. He quickly closed his door and didn't care if a dozen paces down the street Falla fell off his horse and lay there till dawn. Estudillo hadn't wanted Alonso's company, but Rianna's, for the evening. He'd deliberately served *chicha* hoping Falla, not being accustomed to its creeping potency, would quickly succumb and leave; yet, he'd been surprised at Falla's capacity.

As Alonso guided his horse through the street, he recalled the captain's warnings to be careful of Rianna's leaving the house without a male escort. Estudillo had complained about the number of cutthroats and thieves, how many soldiers were little more than brigands. The captain had promised Cuzco's lapse into near lawlessness would shortly end.

With the *chicha* adding to his courage, Alonso wasn't greatly worried about his safety. What piqued his interest was the knowledge that, behind so many windows overlooking the street, soldiers and adventurers alike were taking their pleasure with Incan women. Alonso reminded himself he, too, had a woman under his roof; and Rianna's situation finally was as he'd wanted it to be. There was nowhere for her to go, no one she could ask for help, not even the *dueña*. He saw no reason to wait another day to possess her.

Despite Rianna's physical exhaustion, she had so much on her mind her sleep was interrupted many times by confused dreams and mental wanderings. It wasn't only personal problems that made her restless, but what she'd seen on Cuzco's streets, the tragedies and injustices Coraquenque had told her about.

Rianna was wishing she could be back in that abandoned palace on the mountainside with Shali, isolated from the ugliness of what was happening in the cities, when she heard a horse's hooves on the cobblestones of the courtyard below. She brushed aside the mosquito net and got out of bed to look out the window. Alonso had returned. She supposed he'd been drinking; and remembering how long it had taken for him and Nicasio to quiet down when they'd come back to Nicasio's house in this condition, Rianna decided sleep would be impossible for some time. She relit her lamp and turned it low then pulled on her dressing gown to stand to the side of the window and gaze at the Peruvian sky glittering with stars, wondering where Shali was.

The sounds Rianna had expected—doors slamming, Alonso's shouting orders to servants to rouse them, the stamping of feet—never came; and she concluded this Incan building must have even stouter doors, thicker walls than Nicasio's house. She was surprised when her bedroom door opened and Alonso stepped inside.

Thinking nothing less than an emergency would warrant such an imposition, Rianna asked anxiously, "What's wrong?"

Alonso stared at Rianna standing in the circle of lamplight. Her hair was a burnished halo of spun gold in the flickering glow, her body a slender, enticing silhouette in the silk dressing gown. She was, en déshabillé, even more alluring than he'd anticipated. "Nothing is wrong," he said. "Nothing could be more right."

Rianna supposed what Alonso had said were merely the mutterings of a drunk because it made no sense to her. She assumed the house was new to him, and in his stupor, he'd mistaken her chamber for his. Annoyed, she reminded, "Your room is farther down the hall."

When instead of turning, Alonso started toward her, Rianna sighed and took his arm, resigned to having to show him the way. When she tried to turn Alonso toward the door, his feet remained as solidly planted as if they'd sent out roots.

Rianna disgustedly began, "It isn't enough that you must return in this state at this hour to disturb me, but—"

"It's my purpose to disturb you," he said and, peeling Rianna's fingers from his wrist, laid his hands at her waist.

"I've had enough of this foolishness. Find your own room." Rianna tried to brush his hands aside, but his grip tightened. She looked up in dismay.

"Leaving now would be the real foolishness after I've waited all this time," he murmured and dipped his head to kiss her shoulder.

Rianna tried to pull away; but Alonso was holding her too tightly. "You're talking nonsense. You're too drunk to know what you're doing," she said, becoming alarmed.

She was relieved when Alonso finally released her, but he only stepped away to unbuckle his sword and lay the scabbard on a table. Rianna decided she'd better try to escape and wondered, if she could get to Coraquenque's room, whether there was a lock on that door. When Alonso began to unfasten his cloak ties, she darted past him; but his hand shot out to catch her wrist; he spun her around to face him.

"What do you want with me?" she gasped.

"What I've always wanted," he replied and pulled her against him.

Rianna pushed her hands against his chest with all her strength trying to break his grip on her. It seemed impossible. She arched her back, trying to evade his mouth, but he was too strong. Rianna's heart seemed to be pounding in her ears as Alonso's lips took hers. She squirmed sideways, trying to free herself, but his mouth ground against hers; she felt as if she could hardly breathe. She thought of Shali's lips caressing her so tenderly and sensually. Alonso's tongue tried to force her lips apart and she clenched her teeth. Unable to endure another second of Alonso's wetly prying mouth, Rianna lifted her foot and, with the force of all the desperation in her, drove the sharp little heel of her slipper down on his instep.

"Damned wench!" Alonso flung her away and she bumped into a table. He bent to inspect his injured foot, but glanced angrily up at her as he snarled, "You act like you're such a lady and you're nothing— nothing! Why do you think I bothered dragging you all this way, stupid little minx?"

Shocked at his venom, stunned that he'd wanted not only her money but to make her his mistress, Rianna exclaimed, "You said you wanted to marry me! Now I can hardly believe I'd ever seriously considered it!''

"I don't want to marry you or any commoner," Alonso sneered.

"You're the one who's common, a common thief!" she shot back. "You said you'd keep my father's money and gems safe for me; but you never intended to give them back, not even my personal jewelry!"

Alonso stopped nursing his foot and straightened to glare at her. "There's only one thing I plan to give you."

Rianna began to back away. "I'll bring charges against you. I'll go to Captain Estudillo. He'll listen to me. You know he will."

Alonso paused and, to her shock, smiled. "If you were to step out on that street alone even in daylight, you wouldn't get more than a few paces from the door before you'd be carried off by someone. Would you rather be passed from one brigand to another than become my mistress?"

Rianna said contemptuously, "There's no difference between you and those others."

Alonso's face flushed with anger and he said menacingly, "Even if you reached Estudillo and he wanted to help you, I could make sure you didn't spend much time with him."

"What could *you* do here in Peru? Being the son of an earl in Avila doesn't mean so much in Cuzco," Rianna taunted. "It's the army that rules this city, not a civil government like Lima's. Captain Estudillo is in command of the military, not you."

"There's something more powerful than even the army. The Office of the Inquisition wields as much influence in Cuzco as it does in Madrid, as a great many Incas and even some Spaniards could attest, if they were able," Alonso coldly reminded.

At his words a hundred remembered nightmares rose up to chill Rianna. She felt as if she were trembling inside her skin and wondered how her voice remained steady as she answered, "The priests have no charges against me. You have no evidence, no proof; and the captain could testify in my favor."

"The inquisitor in Madrid didn't inquire of your family's neighbors and friends before arresting your parents. Your brothers didn't get a trial. Who did your sister get to tell her story?" Alonso could see the fear shadowing Rianna's eyes and he added triumphantly, "Their

244

conviction in Spain could taint your case here. You were released in my custody. If I marched you to the inquisitor here and said I've learned you're as guilty as the rest of your family, who would listen to you?''

"You wouldn't! Not even *you* could do such a thing," Rianna said, but she wasn't certain.

"I have a copy of the records of the case," Alonso said smugly. "My personal testimony would add details that aren't even in the records.''

Rianna felt as if a small, hot flame had suddenly sprung to life in her. "How would you obtain a copy of such records?" she asked in a tone that gave no hint of the fire beginning to spread along her nerves and consume her fear.

"It doesn't matter," he answered quickly, too quickly.

Suddenly Rianna realized Alonso had purposely gotten the records in case he needed to use them as a weapon against her. "*You* did it!" she breathed. "You brought charges of heresy against my family. But why? *Alonso, why?*"

Knowing he'd gone too far, he said hastily, "I never did such a thing! I had no reason! You're wrong!"

But Rianna's mind was flashing along the events of the past, connecting them in a way she never had before. "You owed Francisco a large gambling debt for a long time. You didn't pay him because you *couldn't*!" She looked up at Alonso, her eyes lit with the truth.''You owed others, too, didn't you? You kept my father's money and gems because you needed them that much. You'd run through your own fortune. You saw Peru as a way to make a new fortune and avoid disgrace. You won't inherit that precious title from your father unless you make amends. Is that it? *Is it?*"

Aghast at what Alonso had done, Rianna didn't know what more to say, what to do. She stared at him accusingly, seeing visions of Carlo being pitched into the well, Francisco sprawled on the ground, fires exploding through her parents' clothes to ignite their hair. A sob caught in her throat and she began to shiver.

Alonso came closer and caught her wrists. "That's not true, Rianna," he declared.

She wrenched her hands away. She wanted to say she hated him, but it seemed too small a word for what she felt. Nothing she could say was enough.

When Alonso again approached, she shuddered with revulsion and stepped around the table.

"These accusations are ridiculous," Alonso said, becoming afraid of the blaze gathering in her eyes. It reminded him of how she'd looked on the ship when she'd seen the priest. "Calm yourself and listen to reason."

But Rianna had stopped backing away. Her fingers trailing across the table had found the dagger Coraquenque had left. They closed around the handle.

Alonso saw it and said warily, "I won't try to touch you, Rianna. Let's sit down and talk this over. I'll prove how mistaken you are."

As Rianna stared up at him, the fires crackling behind her eyes rose to new heights. Hoping to capture Rianna, Alonso suddenly reached for her; but she reacted as instinctively as Shali had in his fight with Sarabia. The golden blade flashed in the lamplight and struck. Jacinta's screams echoing from the dungeons rang in her ears; and possessed by the memory of her sister's suffering, Rianna stabbed Alonso again then again before he fell.

She backed away, part of her horrified at what she'd done, another part of her triumphant. She stood there staring at him, at the blood running in bright rivulets over his doublet; and she was finally aghast. She began to tremble so violently she couldn't hold the dagger and it fell with a muffled sound to the rug.

Rianna suddenly thought of what would happen when Alonso's body was discovered. As surely as she would have been tortured into a confession of heresy, she would be tortured into confessing to Alonso's murder. Even if, by some miracle, she wasn't tortured, if she would be allowed to defend herself in court, the judge would condemn her after the records of her family's case were brought forward. The realization that she had no choice except to flee was like a searchlight in her eyes.

Though Rianna knew she'd have little chance of survival in the jungle, she couldn't bear to face a court of law and answer accusations for the death of the man who had murdered her family. She would rather die in the jaws of a predator than face the Inquisition again.

After Rianna had made that decision, she discovered, though she was trembling, her mind seemed to be functioning with more clarity than it had since she'd left Spain. Was it because she'd finally avenged her family and at last understood why Shali avidly pursued his enemies? She wondered briefly if she might somehow find Shali then decided it was impossible. Not even Coraquenque knew where he'd gone after he'd left the pass.

She realized she'd stabbed Alonso with Coraquenque's dagger and knew the Inca might be accused of Alonso's death. "No, they won't connect you with this, my friend," she whispered. "I'll make sure before I leave that you aren't blamed."

Rianna was grateful the Incas had made such thick walls and heavy doors in this building so no one else in the house had heard her struggling with Alonso and come to investigate. She wanted whoever found Alonso's body to see the evidence she'd leave of her own guilt.

Rianna took off her bloody dressing and nightgowns and dropped them beside Alonso's body. She wiped off Coraquenque's dagger and laid it aside so she wouldn't forget to take it with her. Though she loathed touching Alonso, she forced herself to pull from his sleeve the little dagger she'd learned he always carried. She smeared it with his blood and dropped it on her garments.

Wishing fervently she could take Wayra, but thinking the horse would only die with her in the jungle, Rianna went to her trunk and dug out one of her riding costumes, which were the sturdiest of her clothes. After she'd dressed, she plaited her hair in a single tight braid and put on her boots.

Rianna caught up the length of vicuña that carried Shali's crest to use as a blanket, and with only Coraquenque's little golden dagger as a weapon, she let herself into the courtyard.

After Rianna stepped into the street, she saw that Alonso hadn't been merely trying to frighten her with his warnings of brigands. She fled into an alcove between two buildings and waited in the darkness scarcely daring to breathe until several burly men passed. Then she crept warily from shadow to shadow, often having to slip into doorways to hide from other rough-looking men, who wandered through the streets.

Rianna peered down a narrow, dark alley, saw it ended at the wall of foilage that was her goal and turned into it. Despite the danger of being discovered, she broke into a run. The echoes of her footsteps on the cobbles behind was her only farewell as she fled into the jungle.

chapter
15

Coraquenque had found she couldn't sleep. The Inca lay quietly staring into the darkness reflecting on her past.

After the royal court had been driven from Cuzco, for a while Coraquenque had traveled to other Incan cities searching for refuge only to find the Castilians already had marched through or were expected soon. She'd been a lady of the court, who had never seen violence; and she'd been shocked by the cruelties inflicted on her people. Because of their society's structure, the Incas had no reason to steal or lie; and they hadn't known how to deal with the avarice and deception of the foreigners. They'd almost lost the war before they'd been able to reorganize and rally against their enemies. During the interim, Coraquenque had lost family, friends and home; but she'd won Manco Capac's heart.

No queen had ever loved her king or been more devoted to the survival of her people than Coraquenque. She'd been proud to become consort of the king, though they were watching their kingdom slowly crumble like kernels of maize under the millstone of the invasion. Instead of doting servants seeing to her needs, Coraquenque had learned how to ride a horse, cook over a campfire and wash the king's laundry in a river, to flee on a moment's alarm and live in the mountains like a bandit, sometimes even pretend to be a blind beggar and spy. Because of the violence and fear Coraquenque had to live with every day, she'd lost two children through miscarriage. She'd seen so much blood, suffering and destruction, her heart seemed to have grown a callus to protect it from breaking; and she'd sometimes wondered if she'd forgotten her gentle heritage, if Incan royalty was a long-ago dream.

Returning to Cuzco had stripped off Coraquenque's shields and her wounds reopened. She speculated that if she went to Rianna to explain how she felt and begged her friend to leave Cuzco with her now, Rianna would understand and agree. Finally, she slipped out of bed to go to the window and gaze at the mountains silhouetted against the star-shimmering sky and wonder what she should do.

Coraquenque saw Alonso enter the courtyard; but the building's heavy walls, stone plastered over on both sides, absorbed most sounds within the rooms themselves. While Rianna struggled with Alonso, made her desperate decision and fled, Coraquenque was reflecting on the situation between Shali and Rianna.

She applauded Shali's finally having found a woman; because his emotions, like Manco's, were too powerful to keep bottled up. But where other men would have bragged at least a little about their high rank and the honored place they held in their king's trust to a woman they wanted to win, Shali had avoided revealing anything about himself he hadn't been forced by circumstances to disclose. Coraquenque knew this was only partly necessitated by the war. Shali wanted to be certain Rianna would come to him because of her own, fairly made decision; and he'd been trying not to influence her with his background. Because Rianna knew so little about Shali and the Incas, she was like a young bird teetering on a branch, whose instincts urged it to take its first flight while it hesitated out of fear of the unknown.

Coraquenque knew, if she could tell Rianna she was Manco Capac's wife and speak frankly about her marriage, Rianna could see a future spent with Shali under any conditions would be more satisfying than living alone even among her own people. If Rianna agreed to leave Cuzco, Coraquenque could take her to Machu Picchu. But once Rianna had seen the city, would Manco allow her to leave if she eventually decided she couldn't adopt the Incan way of life? Coraquenque would have to tell Rianna this, too, was a possibility.

While Coraquenque dressed, she decided to tell Rianna she was the wife of a nobleman, whose name and rank she'd fabricate, if necessary. She could describe Machu Picchu without mentioning even the direction it lay from Cuzco. Then, if Rianna refused to leave Cuzco and was ever subjected to torture, she still couldn't tell the Castilians anything specific.

Though a little starlight squeezed through the narrow window at the end of the hall, the corridor was so dark Coraquenque had to run her fingertips along the wall and count doors until she reached Rianna's. She tapped softly. When there was no answer, she slowly pushed the door open and was shocked when her eyes fell on Alonso sprawled on the floor. She quickly stepped inside and closed the door.

Coraquenque saw Rianna's crimson-stained nightclothes beside him and immediately assumed Alonso had tried to rape Rianna and been stabbed for his trouble. But where was Rianna now? Coraquenque's gaze flew to the bed's tangled linens. Was Rianna unconscious or dying beneath them? Coraquenque's heart seemed to stop as she walked swiftly past Alonso to the bed and tossed the blankets aside. She was relieved, but baffled, not to find her friend. Coraquenque hurried back to Alonso's side and stooped to pick up Rianna's dressing gown. Alonso's dagger fell from between its folds. She gazed at it thoughtfully a moment then at the gown. Some marks on the dress appeared as if Rianna had hurriedly wiped off the knifeblade. Confused and apprehensive, Coraquenque raised her eyes to carefully scan the room for other traces of blood that might be Rianna's. She walked slowly into the bathing room dreading what she expected to find. She wasn't aware she was holding her breath until she sighed with relief. There were no signs of Rianna's having been harmed. It occurred to Coraquenque that, if Rianna had used Alonso's knife, she would have had to have taken it from him first, which wasn't likely. But why would she have done that when Coraquenque had left her little dagger laying on the table within easy reach?

Suddenly Coraquenque knew the answer. Rianna had deliberately taken the Incan knife with her so she'd be blamed instead of Coraquenque. The Inca went back to Alonso, knelt at his side and searched for his pulse. Surprised to find life was still beating in him, she looked more carefully at his wounds. Though they'd bled freely, she discovered they weren't very deep. She judged that if he were placed in the care of an Incan healer, he would likely survive.

Coraquenque *had* to find a hint of where Rianna had gone. Feeling no sympathy for Alonso's condition, she slapped his cheeks sharply to bring him back to consciousness. When his eyes fluttered open, she asked coldly, "What did you do to Rianna?"

Alonso was yet too dazed to understand.

"Did you hurt Rianna? Where is she?" Coraquenque demanded.

Recognition slowly came back to Alonso's eyes and, with it, remembrance. "Didn't do a thing to her. Don't know where she is," he mumbled then begged, "Get help for me. Get a doctor!"

"What made her do this?" Coraquenque gave Alonso's shoulder a wrench that made him gasp with pain. "Tell me now or I'll make sure these wounds open further," she warned.

"Nothing, nothing! Just told her she could . . . heresy . . . inquisitor . . ." he slurred and fainted.

Coraquenque sank back on her heels, eyes blurred with tears. Alonso had threatened Rianna with the inquisitor, the one thing that could so terrify Rianna she'd leave the house without telling even Coraquenque where she was going. The Inca understood why Rianna would have thought only of her certain condemnation and flight. That it had even occurred to Rianna to protect Coraquenque from blame was a shining tribute to their friendship.

Mad with fear, Rianna had fled into the jungle, Coraquenque concluded and knew there was no chance for her friend to survive there alone. There was only one way she could think of to save Rianna. She had to find Shali so he and his men could search for her.

Alonso moaned and Coraquenque looked down to see he'd again recovered consciousness. His lips formed the words, *help me*. Coraquenque said pitilessly, "Your devil can take you."

Then she left the room and carefully closed the door.

Coraquenque silently made her way to a servants' entrance at an obscure corner of the building. After she'd let herself out, she moved as cautiously through the courtyard as if a thousand eyes were watching for her and she must elude them all. Slipping into the stable, she immediately hid behind a grain bin. A boy was supposed to always be posted in the stable, but she had no idea where he was. Scarcely daring to breathe, she listened for any sound that might reveal his location and heard nothing. After a moment, she rose from her hiding place and, seeing no one, crept silently down the aisle between the stalls toward Wayra's. Each time she passed a vacant stall she glanced inside and finally saw the stableboy sleeping on a fresh pile of straw. Relieved to know where he was, she continued soundlessly toward the white mare, who was watching her progress from her stall's doorway.

Coraquenque recalled that Wayra listened to no one, but Rianna and Shali. Praying that the white horse had become well enough acquainted with her during the long trip from Lima to obey, Coraquenque entered the stall.

She had only put on Wayra's bridle and was reaching for the saddle when she heard the stableboy's boots coming down the aisle. Knowing she was only a second from discovery, Coraquenque caught a handful of Wayra's flowing mane and leaped up on the horse's bare back.

"Stop! Get down from that horse!" the boy shouted as Wayra stepped out of her stall.

"We're going to find Rianna, your friend *Rianna,*" Coraquenque told the mare in Spanish and squeezed her legs against Wayra's sides.

The stableboy reached up for the bridle, but Wayra lifted her head out of reach and sprang forward. As the horse brushed by the boy, her shoulder dashed him aside.

"Damned Incan bitch! They'll draw and quarter you for this!" the furious boy screamed as Wayra shot into the courtyard.

Though Coraquenque hated to gallop Wayra on the slippery cobbles, she had no choice; and as they raced through Cuzco, she comforted the mare with promises of finding Shali and Rianna. By the time they were approaching the city's gates, the mare was running at full gallop; and the soldiers, who had stepped into the street to try to stop what they assumed was a runaway, changed their minds and scattered.

They stared incredulously at the white horse that flashed by and finally, realizing its rider was an Inca, lifted their muskets. The volley came too late. Horse and rider had vanished into the darkness, leaving the sentries cursing that a mere Incan girl had stolen a horse from under their noses.

*　　*　　*

It was impossible for Rianna to continue running after she'd entered the jungle; but though wetly clinging vines caught at her skirt and roots protruding from the mossy earth made her stumble, she didn't stop. Memories of her prison cell in Madrid made the moonlit foliage less ominous by comparison. Recalling the other prisoners' madness seemed to lessen the threat of wild creatures prowling the shadows. Every time Rianna had a mental vision of Father Nuñez accusing her family of heresy new strength flooded her weary limbs; and she continued plodding until dawn began to lighten the darkness.

A rocky clearing in the undergrowth revealed a pond fed by a spring and Rianna knelt at its edge for a drink. Exhaustion overcame her. She sank to lie down and immediately fell asleep. The sun had swung over the treetops and was shining in Rianna's eyes when a bird's screeching startled her awake. She splashed handfuls of water on her face then got up to find something she could eat.

Rianna returned to the pond carrying several wild bananas she'd plucked and sat down to breakfast. For the first time since she'd fled Alonso, the enormity of her predicament dawned on her finally clear mind.

"I must have been mad," Rianna told a brilliantly feathered parrot on a nearby branch. The bird tilted its head to the side, as if listening. Rianna drew up her knees and folded her arms around them. The parrot lifted a foot to scratch under its wingtip as if it were resigned to Rianna's murmuring as she tried to organize her thoughts. "After what Alonso did to my family, his threatening to make me endure another inquisition was like a nightmare." Rianna shuddered at the thought and whispered, "Something snapped in my mind when I killed him." She paused and her voice began to tremble as she mused, "If I'd told Coraquenque, she'd have left with me. Maybe we could have found Shali. I must have been insane. I've killed Alonso, I'm lost in a Peruvian jungle and I can't believe any of it happened."

The pressure of Rianna's pent-up emotions burst free in a torrent of sobs that made the startled parrot take flight. She laid her cheek on her knees and gave in to her weeping until she was drained of tears. Still, Rianna stayed curled up hugging herself against the world.

Finally, when she lifted her head, her eyes fell on a tiny, fuzzy monkey that sat near the edge of the water. It was staring at her with a worried expression on its wrinkled little face.

"I suppose I have no choice now, do I?" Rianna quietly asked the marmoset. The monkey's frown seemed to deepen at her words. "I can't go back to Cuzco and I don't think there's a village around here. You may like to live in this jungle, but I don't know how I can. Probably I should go back to the foothills. If only I knew where the mountains are."

There was only one way she could think of to see past the jungle. She had to climb a tree. She sighed and got to her feet. At the movement, the marmoset scampered away. Rianna eyed the trees, rejecting palms as too smooth to climb. She shuddered when she noticed a fat snake coiled around the branch of a *cinchona*. She finally chose a sturdy looking tree whose branches seemed close enough that she might step from one to another as she ascended.

Though Rianna slipped and caught herself many times, tore a hole in her skirt and almost screamed when she discovered a sloth among the branches gazing at her from half-closed eyes, she managed to struggle high enough to see the Andes' distant peaks to the north. One of the branches broke when she put her weight on it; and in her struggle to get back to the ground, she almost fell.

Rianna plucked another small bunch of bananas, took a long drink of water and set out to the north. During the previous night, fear of the Inquisition and its torturers had kept her from thinking about the jungle's dangers. Now she noticed snakes in the trees she hurried under, a hairy tarantula on the path she leaped over to avoid. But the jungle was beautiful. It had more kinds of orchids than she'd known existed and many forms of life that were new to her. Caterpillars, so cleverly disguised by nature, some spotted ones appeared at first glance to be dead leaves while fuzzy white ones looked like plant pods. What seemed to be shell-like blossoms growing in colorful bouquets on fallen trees drew Rianna's admiration until she went closer and saw the exotic flowers were really clusters of fungus.

When Rianna found that a swampy area lay in her path, she paused to consider whether to try to cross it or take the time to skirt it. Though it appeared to stretch endlessly to right and left, if she looked straight ahead, she could see its far side; and she decided to cross. But before venturing farther, Rianna used Coraquenque's dagger to saw a branch from a tree. Then, using the branch to test the ground before she stepped stepped on it, she cautiously began making her way across the bog.

The heat in the mire was like a giant, wet hand bearing down on her so oppressively she felt she could hardly walk. Water in stagnant pools exhaled putrid vapors that seemed to poison the air and cut off Rianna's breath. She held a fold of Shali's vicuña cloth over her nose and mouth while she tested the moldy soil ahead with the branch. Often she found that places she'd been about to put her boot in had no substance and knew she would have sunk from sight in the mud. Animals, even birds, seemed to shun the place; for there was no sign of life except clouds of flying insects that plagued her with their stings. There were too many of them for Rianna to drive away and she concentrated on picking her path through the swamp as fast as possible to escape them. Upon reaching solid ground, Rianna made a quick dash to elude any following insects. Aware the sun was rapidly falling, that it soon would be dark, she began to search for a safe place to sleep.

A mud cliff covered with green and scarlet macaws perching in its vines offered a gaping hole where she thought she might not be seen by a prowling nocturnal animal; but when she warily stepped into the opening, she quickly leaped back outside. The roof was covered with bats. Rianna discovered a grove of trees clustered with marmosets; remembering the harmless little creature who had studied her by the pool, she climbed up to one sturdy bough and wrapped the vicuña around her to settle down for the night like a leopard relaxing after a feast. She hoped if predators came near, the marmosets would awaken her with their alarms. Rianna's last waking thought was the fervent wish she wouldn't fall out of the tree.

During the next several days Rianna became more adept at finding places to sleep. She confined her meals to fruits or vegetables she recognized as having been served at Nicasio's house or as those the Incas had gathered during the journey to Cuzco.

When she began to grow listless, she thought it was because she was lonely for human company. Later in the day, she couldn't shrug off the fact that her face was becoming oddly warm. She realized she had a fever and wondered if it was from breathing the fetid vapors in the swamp or if the insect stings had carried venom.

"It can't be too much farther to the mountains," Rianna assured herself repeatedly as she doggedly plodded on.

After leaving Cuzco, Coraquenque had first turned Wayra toward the marsh at the center of Xaquixaguana Valley. Manco had tried to hide there during his first attempt to escape the Pizarros and been recaptured only because he'd never had a chance to get into the undergrowth. Coraquenque knew Shali disliked swampy areas; but it was near enough the city for him to remain close to Rianna while he could stop any small groups of soldiers or fortune-hunters who had the horses and weapons Manco had ordered him to collect.

She rode Wayra as far into the marsh as she dared then trilled the call of the bird she'd been named for. The notes were of a pitch that carried far, especially in the night air; and she knew if Shali and his men were in the swamp, she'd be heard. When there was no answer, she went to several other areas to repeat the calls, but still got no response.

Coraquenque wondered if Shali had brought his men to the ruins of his old villa, which was more isolated than the retreats of other noblemen. Since it had been razed, the Castilians had forgotten it; and no one else went there. It lay in the same direction as a valley she knew of that was tucked in the foothills to the north, another place Shali might camp.

Shali's villa was surrounded by a high stone wall so the cavaliers had concentrated their attack on the entrance. The doors that once had protected the property had been pulled down and some of the facing stones torn away, Coraquenque noted as she led Wayra through the gateway.

One walk around the courtyard to let herself be seen was all that would have been necessary if Shali's men had been concealing themselves in the ruin; but no one hailed her. Only Wayra's hooves clattering on the cracked paving stones broke the silence. The house's walls were steaked with soot and the roof, doors, everything flamma-

257

ble inside had burned. She could tell from the heavy veils of undisturbed spider webs Shali had never returned after that awful day.

Coraquenque remembered how the villa once had been, white and gleaming in the sun, surrounded by a garden shaded with great old trees. Flowering vines twined around the tree trunks had made a network of fragrance to float over the stone benches. Coraquenque looked at the place where a large bronze and stone fountain once had sent its tinkling music from golden spouts and saw it had been destroyed with axes. Even the roof that had shaded the walkway along the house had been pulled down. She sighed, remounted Wayra and left.

Coraquenque rode hard through the night's last hours. By dawn she was as tired as Wayra as they plodded through the foothills. Though she saw no one while she threaded her way through a narrow, curving passageway, she knew that if Shali and his men were near, sentries were watching. Before she reached the end of the rocky corridor, she paused to give the trilling call of her namesake. Relieved to get an answer, she chirped to Wayra; and they walked confidently through the entrance to a valley.

Amaru and Ruminavi immediately came to greet Coraquenque with the same respect they would have shown Manco Capac's wife in the royal court.

"Where is Shali?" she immediately asked, looking beyond their shoulders at the other men who were moving among the tents.

Amaru tilted his head in a gesture that showed Coraquenque Shali was up on a slope. "If his father hadn't been Shalikuchima, he would have been called by the name of an eagle, your highness."

"He's always walking along the hillsides, my lady," Ruminavi observed.

Coraquenque was about to ask Amaru to fetch Shali when she heard loose pebbles falling. She turned to see Shali coming down the nearest slope. He leaped off the incline and trotted to Coraquenque's side, who waved away his beginning bow.

"What's wrong?" he quickly asked.

"Rianna has run away. We must find her," Coraquenque said urgently.

Shali's face mirrored his shock and for a moment he couldn't speak. Then he demanded, "What did Alonso do to her?"

"It was what he *tried* to do that earned him several wounds from my dagger," Coraquenque dryly observed.

"But, if you were there, why did Rianna run away?" Shali looked perplexed.

"I'd loaned her my dagger. She stabbed Alonso several times and fled out of terror of the inquisitor," Coraquenque explained.

Shali's eyes reflected a mixture of emotions. "What about Alonso? Is he dead?"

"He wasn't when I found him."

Shali's gaze briefly swept Coraquenque. "You look as if you've ridden all night. Come to my tent and rest while you explain." He lifted his head and called, "Topa! Take care of Wayra!"

Coraquenque said nothing as they walked toward Shali's tent. She knew, from the sharp edge to Shali's voice, how worried he was.

Coraquenque gratefully reclined on the layer of thickly quilted alpaca that was Shali's bed when he was in the field. He paced agitatedly in the small tent while she explained what had happened in Cuzco.

"Only Viracocha knows where we should begin the search!" he exclaimed after Coraquenque had finished. "Rianna has only your dagger for protection, no food, not a blanket?"

"She took that piece of vicuña of yours; and since she always wore the pendant you gave her, I suppose she has that. I know of nothing else that was missing. I doubt she even had the presence of mind to take a waterskin." Coraquenque was solemn.

"I wonder if she even survived the night," Shali said huskily.

"Don't say such things!" Coraquenque declared then added more quietly, "Rianna is very resourceful and I think she has a chance."

Shali finally stopped pacing and swore, "I hope Alonso's flesh rots off his bones before his doctor's leeches can bleed him to death."

Coraquenque said bitterly, "I already cursed his soul to his devil."

But as if Shali hadn't heard, he turned to stand silently in the tent doorway for several minutes thinking. Finally, he tilted his head to look at the sky. "The weather is fair. If there are no storms . . ." He turned to face Coraquenque. "There's a small stretch of jungle that starts at Cuzco's limits then goes toward the mountains. Rianna might try to reach the foothills.''

"She may hope to find you there," Coraquenque agreed.

"We can't search everywhere. We *have* to choose one area and that seems likeliest. I only hope we're right.'' Shali's hand was gripping the tent pole so tightly his knuckles went white as he raised his voice to call, "Ruminavi, order the men to break camp immediately!" After the officer had hurried to obey, Shali turned to Coraquenque. "You're tired. Stay here and rest. We'll come back for you."

"If I stay, you'll leave a squad of men to guard me; and you'll need them all for the search," Coraquenque replied. She got up from her resting place and said firmly, "I *am* going with you on this search, you'd best have Topa start dismantling this tent.''

Shali flashed her a glance that showed how much he objected to her decision, but he couldn't argue with his queen. He left the tent and hailed Topa.

Though Rianna's fever had steadily risen, she dared not stop walking to lie down during the day. She knew it would mean certain death. Any of a number of scavenging creatures would attack if she were to fall asleep and lie motionless too long, and the horror of being overwhelmed by flesh-eating insects kept her on her feet. When Rianna became aware of the terrain's gentle incline, she knew she was getting nearer the foothills. She was encouraged and dreamed of vistas of shady pines, a wind coming from the mountains to cool her burning skin. Her heart sank in disappointment when the jungle's tangled undergrowth gave way not to hills with mighty peaks rising beyond, but to a dismal forest.

Rianna told herself the mountains *must* begin soon and tried to walk faster; but her normally steady pace had become awkward, uncoordinated from her growing weakness. She stumbled often and sometimes fell. When she did, her body made no more sound than her footsteps on the thickly matted avenues under the trees.

In contrast to the teeming life of the jungle, Rianna saw nothing alive in this place. Except for the occasional splash of water dripping from one leaf to another, the silence was broken only by her heartbeat and labored breathing. The trees were so tall their foliage blotted out the sun; the only light filtering to the forest floor gave the humid atmosphere a sickly green aura. Nothing except moss could survive at the base of the huge, gnarled trunks.

"I'd thought it was only passing insanity that made me run away," Rianna mumbled as she plodded through the misty light. "Now I suspect it wasn't temporary. I'm still mad. I'm not doing any of this right." She paused to pant, look at the surrounding gloom and inquire, "What sane person would choose a place like this to die in?" She resumed her staggering steps, realizing she'd finally admitted what she'd secretly been thinking all day.

"Secret?" she asked aloud then laughed bitterly, "What is in this dismal solitude except secrets? I can scream every secret I've ever known and they'd be as safe as in the confessional. No one can hear me anyway, not even a bird."

Rianna was silent a long time as she dragged her feet through the moss thinking this would be where her life would end—a delirious dream in a rain forest.

"I'm losing everything, after all, even Shali," she muttered. "I've tried so hard; yet something, someone always prevents me from getting what I want. Is there some reason I'm so cursed? What did I do I'm being punished for? Nothing I know of—or maybe I'm already so ill I can't remember." She fell silent as she recalled the past. Finally, she realized with a shock she'd momentarily forgotten stabbing Alonso.

"So that's what all this is about," she whispered. "But why are other murderers rewarded with gold for their killings? Thieves of Incan gold, bloody hands, will go back to Spain to live in luxury while I'll be dead in this place."

Rianna continued mumbling disjointedly as she staggered along until a cool draft suddenly bathed her fiery face. Surprised, she lifted her head to stare in disbelief. She'd reached the end of the forest and a rocky slope lay ahead.

"At least I can die up there in the clean wind with the sun on my face," she muttered in a voice that had faded to a whisper. She paused to consider the meager strength she had left and dazedly wondered if she could climb a little distance up the slope. "I *have* to," she panted then began forward.

The base of the slope was covered with loose pebbles; and Rianna often slipped, fell on her knees and gashed them. She didn't care. The thought of escaping the odor of moldy earth, decaying trees and slimy pools of fetid water to lie on a dry slope with a cool wind bathing her feverish face gave her strength to reach out and grip one of the coarse shrubs growing on the hillside, pull herself to her feet and struggle on.

Rianna's legs seemed to be dissolving, her fever-laden breath felt like a flame she expelled; and at last she collapsed facedown on the gravel. She lay motionless, panting for a time before she tried to move then discovered she could summon only the strength to turn her head. The impulse to weep brought not the sobs she'd expected, but a moan broken by gasps. She was appalled; the fever had burned away even her tears. There was nothing left to do except wait until her life's spark flickered out.

The wind from the mountains chilled her, but she welcomed the shiver it evoked. The fragrance of pine, a faraway valley of emerald grass, the clean clarity of snowy peaks reaching into a turquoise sky was on the wind. It was the scent that had been caught in Shali's hair on a day that seemed to have happened so long ago her befogged mind remembered it like a dream. She dimly decided that it was the memory she'd take with her to eternity.

Shali divided his men into groups of two or three so they could cover more area in their hunt for Rianna. Coraquenque remained at Shali's side while Amaru, on foot a few steps ahead, hacked a path through the foliage for the horses. The knowledge haunted Shali that, if Rianna were in the area and alive, she would hear Amaru's noisy progress and call; but the only sounds were monkeys chattering and birds screeching.

Several days later, the searchers regrouped at the narrow river. There was no news to exchange. Though they knew the jungle grew so fast her path would have been covered with new creepers if she'd gone that way only yesterday, Shali was gripped by so great a fear he couldn't keep its shadows from his eyes. He directed some of his men into the swamp and others back to the jungle, the rest of them into the rain forest where he and Coraquenque continued their search.

As Shali and Coraquenque walked their horses through the gloom, they spoke little. Any effort to cheer each other would ring so false it would have discouraged them more. They peered down the aisles of dripping trees fearing to see Rianna's body sprawled on the mossy forest floor while both knew she could have been swallowed by a bog or dragged away to some beast's lair without having left a hint of what had happened.

Abruptly, Wayra stopped walking and lifted her head to test the air with flaring nostrils. Shali wondered if the mare had scented a stalking animal. Wayra's body was rigid with tension as she stepped nervously around. She reared once and Shali dismounted from Chuncho to catch Wayra's bridle.

"What do you think is bothering her?" Coraquenque anxiously asked.

Shali watched the mare carefully a moment more. Her ears were pricked alertly, her eyes aglow—with fear or excitement? "Get down from Wayra. Hold Chuncho for me," he tersely directed.

Coraquenque hastily slid from the saddle and handed Shali Wayra's reins. He pulled them over the horse's snowy head and let them dangle loosely from his hand. When Wayra realized Shali was offering her a choice, the mare turned her head to the north as if urging him in that direction.

Afraid to even hope Wayra had sensed Rianna nearby, Shali quietly said Rianna's name over and over. The mare became more excited each time she heard it. He flashed Coraquenque a glance as he swung up into Wayra's saddle and advised, "I'm going to let her take me wherever she chooses. Follow with Chuncho, but don't try to ride him." Then Shali chirped to Wayra and she cantered briskly away.

Wayra carried Shali to the edge of the forest and paused at the bottom of the first of the hills that formed the foot of the mountains. The horse glanced distractedly around, as if she were confused; and Shali raised his eyes to scan the area then the slope. There seemed to be nothing on the hill except rocks and clumps of scrubby bushes. Then his attention was caught by a flicker of light coming from behind one of the low bushes, a tiny gold flame dancing on the slope.

Suddenly he realized the sun was reflecting something shiny. A stone whose surface had been polished smooth by the wind and rain? Or was it possible the glimmer came from the pendant he'd given

Rianna? Afraid to hope too much despite the rising excitement in his heart, he turned Wayra toward the slope.

Though the mare's hooves slipped on the loose gravel and her shoes struck sparks against the rocks, she eagerly scrambled up the hillside. Shali caught his breath to recognize a splash of scarlet and gold beyond the shrubs ahead. It was the vicuña cloth Rianna had carried like a talisman all the way from Madrid. Shali's heart was pounding so hard with a mixture of hope and fear he thought its beat must be echoing off the mountains as he leaped from the saddle and ran to kneel at Rianna's side.

He turned her over, gathered her shoulders in his arms. Rianna's eyes opened and gazed blankly up at him.

Still caught in delirium, thinking she was once again in the valley where she'd lain across Shali's lap while he'd promised to return to her, she mumbled, "I know you'll be back. I do trust you."

"I'll *stay* with you, *chinita*. I'll never leave you again," he whispered into her hair.

Though Rianna didn't understand the Quechua words Shali had used, her fading consciousness accepted him as part of her dying illusion.

Coraquenque, leading Chuncho up the slope, approached, saw Shali rise from behind the shrubs holding Rianna's limp body and paused in apprehension. Was Rianna dead? But when Shali lifted his eyes, Coraquenque saw the joyous light that filled them. Her breath caught with a sob of relief and she hurried toward them.

chapter
16

Rianna opened her eyes to a rainbow of blurred shapes. Still too drowsy to question anything, she gazed steadily, unthinkingly at the bright colors until her vision cleared and focused on a mural of fanciful birds and idealized flowers. She realized the figures were embroidered on a tapestry then snuggled a little deeper under the edge of a softly quilted blanket and reclosed her eyes. Like a returning nightmare came memories of a gloomy forest, her collapsing on a rocky hillside, the feverish dream of Shali she'd thought would be her last view of life.

A tapestry? A blanket?

Rianna's eyelids flew open to stare again at the tapestry. Then she noted she was lying on a thick mat, a bed like the one she and Shali had used at the royal hostel during the journey from Lima. Rianna slowly turned to her other side and discovered the wall that should have been at the opposite end of the room from the tapestry didn't exist. The chamber was open to a wide terrace edged by a low, protective stone wall. Beyond the wall was a breath-taking panorama of snow-topped mountains lit by the sun. She was startled to realize she was looking almost level at the peaks as if the room itself were on the summit of a mountain. A thin veil of smoke momentarily obscured the view. She was incredulous. Had that been a *cloud*?

The effort it took for Rianna to sit up left her trembling with weakness. The blanket had slipped down, and she noticed she was naked, chilled in a room bright with sunshine. Rianna pulled the blanket up around her shoulders then, wrapped in a cone of quilting, tried to gather her wits while she studied her surroundings.

Above the opening to the terrace, rolls of heavy cloth were tied against the ceiling. She concluded they must be untied and let down at night to form the fourth wall. Rianna tried to imagine how it would be to lie in bed with the moonlit mountain peaks and the star glittering sky looking down on her and decided she'd prefer to leave the hangings tied up—if she'd be given a choice.

A plastered wall to her right held niches filled with lamps, vases and ornamental figures of silver and gold. At the opposite side of the room beyond a partly open door she saw an Incan bathchamber.

Was this a hostel like the one where she and Shali had spent the night? But if that place had seemed palatial, this was magnificent, she thought wonderingly. Even the air was pleasantly perfumed with a softly tantalizing, but unfamiliar, fragrance. This observation confirmed that this wasn't merely a hostel, not unless an entire procession of travelers with a great quantity of servants had found her. But who could they be?

Wanting to have a better look at the terrace and what was below, Rianna tried to get to her feet and found it impossible. The fever had drained her of strength. Shakily gathering the blanket more closely around her shoulders, she continued to wonder who had found and brought her to this place. She hadn't been near the Incan road. At least, she hadn't thought so. Rianna's lips parted in surprise. *Was it possible her delirious dream was reality?*

"Shali?" she said aloud. Her hesitant voice was absorbed by the spacious room. Suddenly afraid that a stranger, maybe someone who wanted her alive to use as a hostage, perhaps even the Spanish authorities pursuing her for Alonso's murder had found her, Rianna cried out, "What is this place? Who brought me here? Shali, was it you?"

*　　*　　*

Shali, who had just returned to Machu Picchu after an exploratory patrol, was giving his report to Manco Capac. When he heard Rianna's cry from the next room, he forgot his report and even his king. He stopped in the middle of a sentence, turned away and went out on the terrace that was a walkway adjoining the suites. When he stepped into Rianna's chamber, he found her huddled in the blanket on the bed-mat, staring as intently as if she didn't recognize him. Her eyes, wide with apprehension, were as bright a gold as her hair. He remembered he was dressed as she'd last seen him during the battle at Xaquixaguana Pass. Realizing that memories of the violence added to Rianna's recent troubles alarmed and confused her, he quickly began to unfasten the belt that held his sword and the dagger at his waist.

Rianna's slowly recovering mind was stunned at the vision of the tall Incan commander on the threshold. For a moment, everything that had happened since the last time she'd seen him was erased from her memory; and she was bewildered. She watched as he tore off the crimson cloak, even undid the gold-embroidered headband. "Shali?" was all she could finally whisper.

Then Shali had crossed the space between them, was kneeling on her bed-mat. The familiar scent of the mountain wind in his hair, the welcome warmth of his body, the strength of the arms enclosing Rianna finally confirmed his reality and banished her questions. As long as Shali was with her, she was safe. It no longer mattered where they were or how she'd gotten there.

"You should rest. The fever left you very weak," Coraquenque's voice gently reminded.

Rianna felt a large cushion being tucked behind her. Shali released Rianna and coaxed her to lean back against the cushion, which allowed her to sit up without effort. As if Shali couldn't bear to break their physical contact, he took both her hands in his. Rianna gazed at him a long moment, filling herself with the presence of this man she'd feared she'd never see again.

Looking at them, Coraquenque knew how much they loved each other. The obsidian eyes of the Incan commander even the Pizarros feared above all others unabashedly glowed with the knowledge that, but for his king and queen's presence, he would have again taken Rianna into his embrace.

Shali glanced at the couple over his shoulder and apologized in Quechua for having left them without permission. Manco answered that he understood then approached Rianna's bed.

Rianna had recognized the apology in Shali's tone, the forgiveness in Coraquenque's husband's reply; and she wondered if Shali was prompted by courtesy, Coraquenque's husband's superior rank or both. Rianna finally noticed how changed Coraquenque's appearance was. Instead of the threadbare blouse and skirt Rianna was so used to seeing on her friend, Coraquenque now wore an ankle-length dress of white vicuña trimmed with red and gold embroidery. Her hair wasn't bound in its usual chignon, but was brushed back from her face and held by a fillet of scarlet fringes trailing a ribbon of tassels from each temple to her shoulders.

Except for his features, nothing about Coraquenque's husband resembled the peasant Rianna had seen in Lima's marketplace. He wore a long robe of lustrous vicuña finely sewn with blue and green featherwork at its shoulders and hem. A gold belt studded with emeralds girdled his waist. Fastened around the crown of his head was a scarlet-fringed fillet, more elaborately knotted than Coraquenque's and threaded with gold.

Rianna turned her questioning gaze to Shali. When he said nothing, she looked self-consciously at Coraquenque's husband and said softly, "I'm sorry I don't know how to address you. I never learned your name."

His eyes warmed with humor as he said in excellent Spanish accented with Quechua, "You need not apologize. It was my order that prevented your learning my name. I'm Manco Capac."

Rianna was shocked into speechlessness. *Coraquenque, her former slave, was the Incan king's wife?*

Coraquenque smiled at Rianna. "Now you understand why I was secretive about my husband."

Rianna listened while Coraquenque spoke to a servant, who had trailed after the royal couple into the room. When Coraquenque again turned, Rianna said in a voice diminished by awe, "If I were presented to the king and queen in Spain, I would make a very deep curtsy; but I don't have the strength to get to my feet."

"You also aren't dressed for a curtsy," Coraquenque reminded dryly. At Rianna's chagrined expression she added, "It seems unsuitable for you to worry about making gestures of homage to me after I had to help my attendant disrobe and bathe you. She, of course, didn't know how to unfasten your Castilian garments though I'd had considerable practice while I was your slave."

"My slave," Rianna said faintly and flushed hotly at the memory.

Coraquenque's eyes were warm with humor. "Don't trouble yourself about that. You were a very considerate mistress and you still are my friend."

The servant, who had left at Coraquenque's orders, now returned with another attendant. At Coraquenque's nod, one of the servants put a low table beside Rianna's bed-mat, while the other man ladled steaming broth over wild rice into a golden bowl then poured hot, frothy chocolate into a goblet. He set the food on Rianna's table and, bowing, backed away from his king and queen.

Coraquenque urged Rianna to eat and regain her strength. Then Coraquenque explained how she had come to Rianna's room, found Alonso then taken Wayra to find Shali so his men could search for her.

After Coraquenque had finished, Rianna laid down her golden spoon and said quietly, "If you hadn't come, I would have died."

"You were so ill my healer and three assistants took turns watching at your bedside for several days and nights," Manco confirmed. "The healer dared not say you'd live until after the fever had broken. Even so, he warned that you won't walk by yourself for several days."

Rianna thanked him for providing so much help then looked at Coraquenque, who was urging her to drink the chocolate. "You found Alonso alive? I didn't kill him?"

"It's the fervent wish of us all that his death was slow and agonizing at the hands of one of your doctors," Coraquenque answered bluntly.

"If he survived their treatment, he won't live through mine when we meet again," Shali vowed.

Rianna lowered her eyes and recalled, "What Alonso said when I resisted him proved he'd brought the charges against my family to the Inquisition. He killed my family because he wanted to steal from my father's house and shop. He desired me, but the money was more important to him.''

"If you killed him, our law would call it justice," Manco commented.

"Rianna shouldn't talk about that now," Coraquenque observed. "We should discuss happier things, her future."

"My future?" Rianna glanced self-consciously at her friend. "I have no idea what you expect of me or will allow me."

"We'll grant you the same freedom as everyone else. We'll respect your beliefs and ask you to do the same. We expect you to obey our laws," Manco advised. "Though I'd normally never allow a Castilian this choice, *you* may return to your people, if you wish, after you've recovered. You'd have to travel in a sealed litter so you'll never be able to say where this city is even if you're tortured."

"Thank you, Your Majesty," Rianna replied, feeling highly honored. She commented, "I didn't even know if this was a city or a hostel."

"You're in my palace in my new capital," Manco advised, "and you should address me as 'my lord' or 'the lord Manco Capac.' "

"My lord, did you mean I could live here in the palace?" Rianna breathed.

"Until you've recovered," Manco answered. He glanced at Shali then added, "If you want to make other living arrangements, you may. If you decide to return to your people, understand that the way the war is going may determine when you'd be able to leave here."

Rianna realized the conflict could force them all to flee or seal themselves in the valley. She nodded solemnly then said, "May I ask a favor, my lord?" Manco nodded and she inquired, "After I'm well, will I be permitted to move about in your city?"

"I said you would be free to do all the things my people are."

"Then my lord, I must ask a second favor. May someone teach me your language?" she requested.

Manco's eyes narrowed thoughtfully. "There are a number of my people who understand Spanish. Would you prefer someone you aren't acquainted with teach you?"

Rianna wished her tutor could be Shali, but she was too shy to ask for the military commander. She felt herself getting flushed and she said hastily, "Whomever you wish, my lord."

Manco noted her rising color and understood. "I think your teacher should be someone who's already familiar with you and your ways. Except when I have need for him, Shalikuchima will act as your teacher.''

Rianna said a silent prayer of thanks and glanced at Shali from under her lashes to see if he agreed. She didn't realize that though he was Manco Capac's cousin and friend, he couldn't object even if he were inclined.

"All of us who know your language will help you," Coraquenque promised.

"That will be very helpful," Rianna replied then hastily added, "My lady."

Coraquenque recalled, "When Sarabia took me to Nicasio, you saved my life. Now I've had a part in saving yours. You and I have worked together, confided in each other, laughed and wept together. We're friends in a very special way. Don't call me by a title unless others besides my husband and Shali are present." She laid her hand on Rianna's shoulder. "You're still weak and our visit has tired you. We should leave so you can rest."

Manco Capac raised an eyebrow at Shali who, at the gesture, began to get up. Coraquenque quickly spoke in Quechua to Manco, who considered her comment then nodded to Shali to reseat himself. After Manco slid his arm around his wife's waist, they left the room.

Rianna looked up at Shali and reminded, "You're supposed to interpret for me. What did she say to him?"

Shali explained, "Manco wanted to hear the rest of the report I'd been giving when you called; but Coraquenque asked him to hear it later. She suggested there was something else for him to do."

Still unused to the idea of Coraquenque's royalty, Rianna sighed at this additional reminder. "I suppose a queen who's been absent for so long must have many responsibilities to catch up on."

"Manco and Coraquenque were the assistants who took turns with the court physician watching over you while your life was so endangered by the fever, so they haven't had much opportunity to be together." Shali's lips tip-tilted in humor as he admitted, "Now that it's certain the fever hasn't damaged your mind, Coraquenque wants to spend some time alone with Manco."

Rianna fell silent, as she considered the reason they'd all been so concerned about her recovery. Finally, she said, "You were afraid I'd awaken a lunatic?" Shali nodded solemnly and she asked, "Did you watch over me too?"

"Except for last night, when I had to take a patrol to investigate something. I'd only returned a short time before you called," Shali answered.

Rianna shuddered at the possibility she might have awakened to a continuation of the madness she suffered in the forest.

Shali understood and reassured, "That danger is past and Coraquenque was wise to warn you shouldn't think about such things. She also was right about your needing rest."

Rianna hated having to admit, "I'm a little afraid of being alone. I guess I feel this way because I was so ill."

"And, no doubt, because you were alone in the jungle for so long," Shali replied. He bent to kiss her eyelids closed then took her hand and said softly, "Go to sleep, *chinita*. I'll stay with you."

Rianna preferred to remain awake in Shali's company, but her struggle not to fall asleep was soon overcome by her body's weakness.

Shali watched Rianna's features relaxing and knew when she slipped into slumber. He sat beside her nearly an hour before his own weariness began to weigh on him. He'd slept only in snatches since Coraquenque had ridden Wayra into his camp and they'd searched for Rianna. After spending all last night in the saddle investigating a rumor that cavaliers had been seen near the entrance to Machu Picchu's valley and found it false, he still was tense. Shali knew that, despite how tired he was, there was little chance of his falling asleep once he'd decided not to; so he finally stretched out on top of the quilt.

When he felt Rianna turn in her sleep to instinctively nestle closer, he frowned and recovered her shoulder with the blanket. If there had been any possibility of his cat-napping, it vanished with her nearness. He was amazed that, despite his weariness, one small, unconscious gesture from Rianna could so deeply stir him. Though he normally would have been overjoyed to feel this way about a woman, destiny had thrust him into a situation that prevented him from obeying his instincts. He viewed his immediate future as cheerfully as he would the prospect of having to cross one of Peru's deserts barefoot and without water.

During the days and nights he'd watched over Rianna while she was unconscious, Shali hadn't been able to bear the idea of her mind's having been scarred by the heat of her fever. Instead of dwelling on the possibility that when she awakened she might not be the same as before, his thoughts had traveled along another path.

Of all the Incan cities the Castilians didn't know existed, Machu Picchu, Manco Capac's stronghold, was the one place they must never learn about. Shali hadn't previously asked Rianna to come there because he'd thought Manco Capac wouldn't allow her to leave. Now that unavoidable circumstances had brought her, Manco's decision that Rianna could leave in a sealed litter had surprised Shali. He knew the war would dictate how soon Rianna might have to decide whether to stay forever or return to her people. If the situation changed suddenly, she might have no choice except to remain.

Shali understood how difficult it would be for Rianna to make a decision. Because she'd apparently been happy in Madrid before Alonso's scheme had changed her life, Shali realized her civilization must have redeeming qualities he hadn't considered, in light of what the Castilians had done in Peru. He knew the Incan way of life was very different from Rianna's homeland. She might not be able to adjust to the change. Then, marriage to him could become like a prison for her; he had no wish to be Rianna's jailer. As much as he loved her, he didn't want to spend his future worrying she might one day regret deciding to remain at Machu Picchu.

Shali sat up and folded his arms around his bent legs and, as he had so many times since he'd carried Rianna into this room, considered his own course. He knew he must be careful to answer her questions about the Incas without subtly interjecting his own opinions. As soon as Rianna was able, he must take her into the city and even to the valley below so she could acquaint herself with his people and their daily affairs.

He sighed as he considered what would be for him the most difficult aspect of his task—restraining the sensuality of his nature. Passion had so heady an influence on Rianna; it might be the one certain way he could win her. But he resolved not to allow love to blind Rianna to other factors she must consider in making her decision.

Shali rested his chin on his knees and grimly anticipated his torment at being almost constantly in Rianna's company yet denying himself even her affectionate touch. Though the surface of his eyes hardened to the opaque glimmer that defeated even his closest friends' efforts to read his thoughts, Shali's vulnerable mouth revealed his inner pain.

During the following mornings, after Shali had attended court and conferred with Manco Capac, he changed into one of the jerkins and breeches Rianna had become accustomed to seeing him wear and went to teach her Quechua. The meanings of the words he introduced Rianna to frequently piqued her curiosity about their background; and the lessons became conversations where Shali encouraged her to repeat the terms and use them in phrases. Rianna enjoyed her lessons as well as Shali's company; and the time always came too quickly when, after the midday meal, he left so she could rest.

But Rianna noticed Shali no longer sat on the corner of her bed-mat, as he had when she'd first awakened. He seated himself on a cushion nearby. Sometimes he'd tentatively lift his hand, as if he'd impulsively started to reach out to her then stopped himself. Shali occasionally paused during a conversation and stood up to walk around. Rianna knew he was often standing immediately behind her, sensed he was gazing down at her and wondered what he was thinking. While she recited the list of words he'd added to her vocabulary the day before, he frequently lowered his eyes to stare unseeingly at the floor as he listened. She didn't know he couldn't bear to watch her lips moving without reaching over to capture them with his kiss. After she'd finished, he'd say nothing for a long moment before his dark lashes finally lifted; but the eyes that met hers were unreadable.

After Rianna had regained enough strength, Coraquenque and Manco came with the healer to encourage her first steps. Shali had to help Rianna to her feet, then lend support while she walked. Through the cotton of Coraquenque's borrowed robe, the sensation of Shali's arm around Rianna's waist, of finally being close to him was so wonderful her face was alight with emotion when she looked up at him. Shali's returning glance was momentarily unguarded and Rianna was electrified by the naked longing she saw in his black eyes before they quickly looked away. Neither of them noticed Coraquenque studying them and correctly assessing the situation.

After everyone had left for the night, Rianna lay staring into the darkness puzzling over Shali's newly inhibited attitude toward her. Rianna was too weak for anything more than affectionate gestures, but Shali used to be generous with kisses casually dropped on her forehead or shoulder, brief embraces whenever they'd been alone. Now he didn't even hold her hand. Rianna had wondered if Manco didn't want his commander to love a woman of his enemy's people and had forbidden her to Shali, but she'd rejected this. Manco was very cordial toward her and Coraquenque had always encouraged the romance. Rianna decided Shali had some reason of his own to avoid contact with her and the inevitable question sprang to mind. Did Shali have another woman at Machu Picchu? Rianna never asked him about what he did during the hours he spent away from her, but she wondered.

After a sleepless night of speculation, Rianna had little appetite for her morning meal. She was staring unseeingly at her food trying to think of a way to tactfully learn even a hint of Shali's purpose when she was surprised by Coraquenque's unannounced entrance.

"I thought, as long as you had the strength to do a little walking last night, you might enjoy having more than a sponge bath this morning," Coraquenque said.

Rianna didn't notice Coraquenque's eyes running over her untouched breakfast. She was looking doubtfully at the covy of servants who had followed their mistress into the suite as she replied, "A bath would be wonderful, but do we need so many attendants?"

"You can't do much for yourself yet," Coraquenque noted then gestured to a maid, who held up a dress for Rianna's inspection. "I thought this would suit you; but if you don't like it, I'll have another brought."

Rianna's eyes lit at the sight of a long gold-colored gown embroidered with white and scarlet flowers. As the maid unrolled a crimson sash deeply fringed with gold threads, Rianna breathed, "But this is vicuña. This cloth is only used by the nobility and I'm not even an Inca."

"The gown is one of several of mine I had altered," Coraquenque explained. "They'll do until a wardrobe of your own can be made."

"But I can't pay for a wardrobe," Rianna began.

"You've forgotten Incas don't have money," Coraquenque reminded.

"All these things are gifts." She turned away to direct two of her maids to help Rianna into the bathing chamber.

Rianna quickly learned so many attendants were necessary because she wasn't expected to make the smallest effort. In their vari-colored dresses, the maids reminded her of a flock of brightly feathered birds busily going about their tasks. One maid soaped Rianna's body while another lathered her hair. A third stood by watching; and when Rianna merely lifted her hand to wipe away a fleck of lather on her cheek that had dropped from her hair, the third maid hurriedly brushed it away with a cloth, giving her a reproachful look for even trying. The attendants, who led Rianna to the bathing pool, accompanied her into the water to insure her safety. After a maid had finished rinsing Rianna's hair, they promptly led her out of the pool and blotted her dry. Then Rianna was taken to a mat and directed to lie down while an attendant massaged her.

"This will help get the blood into your muscles and bring back your strength," Coraquenque observed. "I find such a treatment very soothing at any time. I hope you enjoy it too."

"It's such a pleasure I feel sinful," Rianna mumbled drowsily.

"A bath like this has nothing to do with sin; but then we, of course, don't think of such things the way your people do," Coraquenque observed. "You'll have to go through an even more elaborate bath next week."

Rianna turned her head to look questioningly at her friend.

"It will be the Day of Wedding, a very important event. Everyone at Machu Picchu will be there," Coraquenque said.

"But I can hardly walk across my room. How will I have the strength to attend a wedding?" Rianna questioned.

"There will be little walking and less of anything else for you to do. After all, you aren't getting married," Coraquenque answered.

Rianna fell silent as two maids helped her to her feet then patted her with perfumed powder. As a third attendant began to painstakingly comb her hair dry, she asked, "Who is so important the entire city will celebrate their wedding?"

"Every man who has reached the age of twenty-four, every woman who is twenty is getting married," Coraquenque replied then explained, "I've noticed your people are wed couple by couple; but among the

Incas, there's one marriage a year for everyone in the kingdom who's reached the age. That's why the ceremony is so important. It's the heart and soul of our continuing existence. Afterward, there's a joyous celebration throughout the land.''

As Rianna considered the custom and her surprise lessened, the idea of a mass marriage began to appeal to her. ''Every family must have a member getting married or know someone else who is. I can see why there'd be a great celebration,'' she said slowly then asked, ''But what if someone doesn't want to be wed?''

''We're a passionate people, Rianna,'' Coraquenque replied. ''We choose our partners long before we reach the age our law requires we marry.''

''Marriages aren't arranged by the couples' families?'' Rianna inquired.

''Parents must approve their sons and daughters' choices, but they almost always do,'' Coraquenque replied. She walked around Rianna inspecting the mass of golden ringlets her hair had become and gave the attendant additional instructions.

While the maids dressed Rianna, she was gloomily thinking that her fears about Shali's status may well be justified. Though she didn't know his exact age, she was sure he must be in his late twenties. Perhaps Coraquenque's insistence on her attending the ceremony was her way of telling Rianna Shali was already married.

After she was dressed, a maid at each elbow escorted Rianna to a mirror made of a polished sheet of gold. Despite her inner misgivings, she was stunned by her changed appearance. In the exotic dress and with a gold and crimson headband circling her brow, Rianna exclaimed her thoughts aloud, ''I look like a blond Inca!''

''Different garments can make even inner changes,'' Coraquenque remarked as she studied her handiwork.

Expecting to be returned to her bed-mat, Rianna was further surprised when she was led to the terrace, where a pile of cushions had been arranged in the sun. Coraquenque directed the maids who guided Rianna to recline on the pillows, gestured another servant to arrange several of the cushions more comfortably, then withdrew to appraise the picture Rianna made.

''Are you comfortable?'' Coraquenque inquired.

Still dazed by the thought that Shali might be married, Rianna struggled to regain her poise. "I'm very comfortable," she finally managed. "But why have you bothered with all this?"

"I thought you might enjoy having your lessons with Shali here for a change. To do that, you must be properly clothed," Coraquenque replied.

To think of Shali now wrenched Rianna's heart. "I need to talk to you," she began.

"I'm sorry. There's something else I must do now," Coraquenque said quickly. "We'll have to talk later."

"But I need to ask you something about Shali."

Aware there was difficulty between them, Coraquenque had already decided to help all she could by smoothing their way; but she wanted to avoid injecting herself into the situation. She advised, "You must ask Shali whatever you need to know. He'll answer your questions, Rianna." She turned away as if to start toward the royal suite then paused to again briefly face her friend while she added, "He'll be here soon."

Rianna regretfully watched Coraquenque and her attendants walk down the terrace then disappear through their own door. After their lively bustle, the silence they'd left behind made Rianna feel even more wretched than before.

If Shali were married, surely Coraquenque must already know what was troubling Rianna. Maybe the question of fidelity didn't bother Incas. Maybe this was one other way their customs differed. What if Incas were polygamous? Rianna knew she couldn't bear to discuss it with Shali, if this were true.

Remembering Coraquenque's saying everyone at Machu Picchu would come to the ceremony on the Day of Wedding, Rianna reasoned, if Shali were married, his wife must attend. Rianna's pride made her decision for her. She wouldn't ask questions of anyone. If she had enough determination and was prepared for the worst, she wouldn't weep over Shali in front of everyone—especially him.

After having helped Rianna walk the previous night, Shali's memories of loving her had become an ache that nagged him even through the morning's royal audience. The court's discussions involved little other than arrangements for the mass marriage, which only sharpened his frustration with reminders of how much he would have liked to take part in the ceremony with Rianna at his side. After Shali outlined his plan to post soldiers throughout the city in case any of the merry-makers had too much *chicha* and caused a disturbance, he had had no more to do; so his mind returned to thoughts of Rianna. By the time the audience was over, Shali was so distracted from court business he didn't linger with the other noblemen, but quickly returned to his suite. As he changed clothes, he reminded himself that, even if Rianna were already fully recovered, she hadn't had time to learn enough about his people to decide if her future lay with them. He must allow her that chance not only for her sake, but his.

After the way his desire had flared up the previous evening when Rianna had merely leaned on him so she could walk, he reasoned he must not torment himself more by touching her at all. Having renewed that resolution, he walked down the corridor to her room feeling numb.

But when Shali stepped into Rianna's room, he was undone. The vision she made reclining on the cushions dressed in the garments of his people had a devastating effect on him. He walked slowly through the apartment looking at how the sunshine set her curls alight and made golden shimmers of her eyes, wondering how it would be possible to teach her his language today. He frowned, thinking he could hardly remember a word of it himself.

Rianna was surprised by the grim set of Shali's features. Had something angered him? She watched as he leaned his forearms on the terrace wall to gaze at the mountains a long, silent moment.

Finally, she ventured, "Coraquenque brought these clothes for me, but maybe you think I shouldn't dress like an Inca."

"How could I object when you're so beautiful in them?" he quietly answered. But he kept his eyes fixed on the mountains.

"Are you angry about something?" Rianna hesitantly asked.

Shali slowly turned to face her. She had gotten up and was leaning against the wall looking at him uncertainly. He said, "I was thinking I'm not in a mood to give you a lesson in Quechua today."

Rianna knew there was more on his mind than he was admitting, but she didn't know what she dared ask. Instead, she replied, "I don't feel like having a lesson anyway." She turned to look at the splendor of the mountains, the lush green sweep of the valley below. After a moment she commented, "I've never been on the terrace to see this view. It's breath-taking, but how does one get up and down. the slope?"

Shali was observing it was Rianna who took his breath away, but he said, "There's a road, but it's very steep for defense purposes."

"The city is built like an eagle's aerie," Rianna observed then added, "With Manco's presence, I should more properly say it's a condor's aerie, shouldn't I?"

"Coraquenque has explained the imperial symbol is a condor," Shali noted.

"She also told me the meaning of your family crest." When Shali said no more, Rianna began to feel as if she were smothering in the prolonged silence. She said awkwardly, "If you have something else you want to do this morning, don't feel that you *must* stay with me."

Shali turned his head to gaze at Rianna's profile, thinking it would be wise for him to leave her company when he felt this way. At the same time, he knew he was as helplessly captured in the golden web of her hair as a jaguar in a trap. He replied lamely, "I have nothing else to do."

Rianna sighed and said wearily, "It would be pleasant to sit in the garden and I should visit Wayra. But I've become tired just standing here. Will you help me back to those pillows please? I can't imagine how Coraquenque expects me to attend the ceremonies on the Day of Wedding."

Shali's heart melted with tenderness and he turned to scoop her up in his arms. Trying to ignore how much he wanted to kiss her—merely lovingly and without fire—refusing to look down at her face while she was so close, he stared straight ahead as he answered, "Coraquenque wants you to learn something more about our customs by attending the wedding. Because it happens only once a year, you might not see the next one if you decide to leave us." Shali walked the few steps to the pillows as he added, "You'll be stronger next week and there will be few places you'll need to go; but someone can carry you, if necessary." Though Shali had knelt to put Rianna on the cushions, he hated to release her. He finally lowered his eyes to look at her face as he added quietly, "Probably I'll do it."

"Don't you have other obligations?" she asked, wondering about the possibility of his having a wife of his own to escort.

"Nothing that will keep me constantly occupied," he answered. Unable to bear his emotions any longer, he drew Rianna closer. He could feel her trembling against him and wondered if it was from love or weakness left by her illness. "I shouldn't do this," he finally said and withdrew.

Alarm flashed through her eyes and she was afraid to ask, "Why?"

"Holding you that way stirs impulses I can do nothing about," he replied.

"Because I'm unwell? Or do you have another reason?" she prompted.

Shali stood up and backed away a few steps. "Both," he answered then turned and left without another word.

Rianna stared at him striding down the terrace in the sun, aghast that he'd seemed to confirm her suspicions. After he'd vanished around the corner, she threw herself face down on the pillows until the arrival of a servant bringing the midday meal.

Realizing the tray was, as usual, set for her and Shali, Rianna didn't want to even see the dishes. She surprised herself with how much Quechua she'd mastered when she directed the girl to take the food away.

Now Rianna hoped Coraquenque wouldn't remember her request to talk about Shali. She didn't want to discuss him even with her friend. She had no idea that the maid who'd brought the food, had gone directly to her queen to report Rianna's refusal to have lunch and that Shali wasn't with her. Neither could Rianna know that later that afternoon Shali asked Coraquenque if someone else could take over his role of tutor for the next few days. Coraquenque decided Shali and Rianna's difficulty couldn't be resolved if they had no contact and she refused his request.

During the long and sleepless night, Rianna considered her situation with a clearer mind. If Manco Capac sent her with an escort to the isthmus so she could, as Francisco had, get on a ship for Spain without the authorities in Cuzco or Lima knowing she'd left, it would be difficult, though not impossible, to reestablish her life in Madrid or even another city under a different name. Yet, Rianna knew there was a certain fondness growing in her for the Incas. She decided it would be foolish to not even consider remaining at Machu Picchu, despite Shali's presence. She didn't know her resolution was exactly what Shali wished, that she would look at the Incan way of life for its own values and not as something she would try to accept because she loved him.

The next morning Rianna faced Shali with an attitude as crisply business-like as his. Though there was no laughter about her awkward efforts to pronounce a difficult word or put together a phrase, there was also less temptation for him to reach out to her. Rianna seemed to have withdrawn from his reach and built an invisible wall between them. Shali assumed she understood how he felt and was trying to help him. Rianna told herself repeatedly it was better to know that circumstances made his love impossible by her standards, if not his.

Though Rianna didn't confide in Coraquenque and Shali had always been reserved about romantic matters, the queen knew the couple hadn't mended their problems. She decided that, if the matter wasn't settled during the celebration following the marriage ceremony, she would have to think of some way to resolve it herself even if she had to resort to trickery.

Early on the morning of the Day of Wedding, after a bath as elaborate as Coraquenque had promised, one of the queen's personal attendants remained to help Rianna dress. Coraquenque had again provided Rianna with a costume; but it wasn't one of the queen's that had been altered. It had been made for Rianna.

She gazed at her image in the gold mirror with mixed emotions. This was to be her first appearance in public and the entire royal court would be present. She wondered if Coraquenque should have chosen a dress with more subdued tints. This gown and its matching headband heightened the color of her hair and eyes and seemed to emphasize she was an alien among the Incas. The gown was a narrow, brilliant blue tunic that softly skimmed her hips and ended at her sandletops. Gold and copper feathers woven into the cloth formed a sunburst at its neck while the hem, a repeat of the feathers, was edged by a narrow blue fringe. The maid paused only for occasional breaths as she complimented Rianna's appearance, but Rianna wondered what Shali would think.

Having surprised herself by regaining her strength during the previous week, Rianna had told Coraquenque she was strong enough to attend the ceremony without assistance. Coraquenque had insisted the ritual would be lengthy, the celebration afterward even longer and she'd already arranged for Shali to be her escort. Rianna didn't want to be a burden to him if he was, as she suspected, married. She went out to the terrace and leaned on the wall to look at the mountains wishing the day had already ended. Then she would know not only if Shali was married, but if the Incas would accept her.

When she heard a smart tap on the door to the hall, Rianna reluctantly turned and was surprised that the maid had admitted a stranger. His royal blue tunic, the black cape thrown back over his shoulder announced he was an army officer; but the gold helmet with a long scarlet feather rising from its crest, the crimson armlet he wore revealed a high rank and noble lineage. Wondering at his purpose, she walked slowly into the room. He met her at its center. She looked up into dark brown eyes that regarded her with open interest.

"My name is Ruminavi, Lady Rianna. In your people's army I would be called a colonel. I am to be your escort." It was said carefully, as if he weren't accustomed to using her language, though he was fluent enough.

Rianna gazed up at the Incan officer wondering if Shali had declined to escort her. Or had Manco decided Shali shouldn't? "You're very kind, Colonel," she replied.

He stepped aside and took her hand to lead her to the door. "I'm not being kind, Lady Rianna. What I had anticipated to be a favor for another has instead become my pleasure. No one told me how beautiful you are."

As Rianna stepped into the hall, she blushed. She glanced up at the Inca and smiled her thanks.

Her rising color meant nothing to him, though he sensed her nervousness and said, "As all my people, I'm frank; but I don't want to make you uncomfortable with anything I say." He took her arm and started to lead her down the corridor.

"The situation makes me uncomfortable, Colonel. If anything, your compliment gives me encouragement," she replied.

"You're worried about meeting so many strangers?" he inquired.

Rianna nodded. "I know only three Incan men—Manco Capac, Shalikuchima and a servant named Topa. Aside from maids, I know only one woman, your queen."

"If the king and queen accept you, we all will" Ruminavi observed. "Yet, Lady Rianna, if you were a stranger even to Manco Capac, you would be admired by every man who will see you today." He looked at her and smiled. "Your cheeks again become the tint of a rose. It's a sign of distress in you, is it not? Now I must ask forgiveness for embarrassing you with the truth."

Two guards opened the palace doors to reveal a litter and two azure-robed bearers waiting at the base of the steps. Ruminavi scooped Rianna up in his arms.

"I can walk, Colonel," she protested as he carried her downstairs.

"I don't mind," he said then invited, "Call me Ruminavi, if you will."

Rianna was silent until Ruminavi had gently deposited her on the cushions. Then hoping to learn if Manco or Shali had sent him to fetch her, Rianna inquired, "Whose litter is this?"

"Everything in the kingdom belongs to Manco Capac," he answered evasively.

"I meant to ask who sent you for me."

"Pardon my ignorance of your language, Lady Rianna. If you'll speak more slowly, I'll make fewer mistakes," Ruminavi advised.

Because he said no more, she assumed Ruminavi must have meant Manco sent the litter. She said, "If I'm to call you Ruminavi, please call me Rianna. After all, you're an Incan nobleman; and I'm not Inca, or even of noble blood."

Ruminavi inclined his head and directed the bearers to pick up the litter.

Machu Picchu's streets were crowded, but the throngs parted at the officer's approach. Rianna was conscious of the stares she drew to be borne in a litter as if she were an aristocrat. She glanced under her lashes at the Incan officer walking smoothly beside her. He seemed not at all disconcerted to be escorting a foreign woman. When they arrived at the plaza, the bearers carried the litter to an area reserved for the nobility. After they'd set it down, Ruminavi turned to Rianna.

"There will be no need for you to get out of the litter except at the beginning of the ceremony. Until then you may be more comfortable to remain where you are," he advised.

Rianna scanned the richly dressed people around her. Many women were in litters the same as she, while others were seated on cushions in the grass. Some men, strolling and talking as they waited for the ceremony to begin, glanced at her then stared a moment before looking away. Several gave her flirtatious looks. She tilted her head to regard Ruminavi.

"Are you to stay with me?" she asked.

"Yes," he answered then observed, "The admiring glances I foresaw have already begun."

"Would it be improper for you to sit with me?" she inquired.

In answer Ruminavi lowered himself to a cushion at Rianna's side. "No one will come closer while I'm here. If you were alone and a man approached, he would only want to meet, not offend, you. But none of them, not even I, can know the customs of your people in these matters."

"They are different," she assured him. "No woman would sit alone like this with a man in Spain."

Ruminavi's brows raised a trifle and he commented, "If a man and woman can be considered alone, though they sit in the full sight of thousands, I must wonder how any of your people become acquainted enough to marry."

Rianna couldn't help smiling at his remark. "One reason I'm here is to learn if your customs are agreeable to me."

"I can see why at least one of yours would not be agreeable with *me*," Ruminavi observed solemnly.

Rianna made no comment yet, in that moment, she was again reminded of how wide the gulf was between her people and Shali's. She wondered if she ever would manage to bridge it at the same time her resolution to not hope too much Shali was free failed her. Rianna scanned the faces in the crowd as anxiously as if her heart beat for one purpose—a glimpse of him. Her pulses raced with anticipation at the same time dread, that another woman might be at his side, turned her hands to ice. But when the fanfare announcing Manco Capac and Coraquenque's arrival sounded, Rianna still hadn't glimpsed Shali.

Manco and Coraquenque were borne into the plaza on separate, open litters that were plated with gold and silver and flashed so brightly in the sun Rianna had to glance away. The litters, lined with bright plumes from tropical birds, were preceded, flanked and followed by a corps of guards, who wore ornate ceremonial swords and carried lances decorated by gaily colored streamers that fluttered in the breeze. They were clad in sky blue tunics with black capes that flowed over their shoulders to their knees. On their heads were helmets that sprouted a row of scarlet feathers like a short brush. A crowd of attendants followed the litters.

"We must stand and bow until we're told to sit down," Ruminavi instructed as he rose. He took Rianna's hand to help her out of the litter.

Though she dipped her head, she kept her eyes up so she could look at the royal couple who stepped from their litters.

Manco Capac wore a wide emerald collar and a robe of such finely spun vicuña it had the sheen of silk. Gold ornaments shimmered around his scarlet fillet, but his long mantle of brilliantly colored feathers was like a rainbow running from his shoulders to trail behind his heels. Instead of a fillet, small gold pieces formed a garland across Coraquenque's forehead then hung in ribbons down her temples to her jawline. Rianna was newly awed that this couple had taken turns sitting at her bedside while she'd suffered through her fever.

She knew without Ruminavi's prompting that the tall, spare man with white hair whose uplifted arms obviously invoked heavenly approval was Villac Umu, the priest Coraquenque and Shali had mentioned on occasion.

After he'd finished the prayer, the crowd was allowed to sit down. Manco had already made an offering of flowers, perfume and spices to Viracocha at dawn, Ruminavi informed Rianna. The king had only left the temple in time to come to this ceremony, which was a continuation of the ritual. When Manco signaled the couples that were to be married could approach, Rianna finally noticed there were so many she couldn't see the end of the long line they formed.

"Because of the war, many people have traveled here from cities in other provinces hoping to be specially blessed by being wed by the king instead of their governors. Of course, many of them no longer can be wed by their governors, who were killed by the invaders,'' Ruminavi explained as the first bride and groom approached their king and knelt. "The style each couple is dressed indicates their province. I can see some of them are from very distant places."

Although the brides and grooms all wore flower wreaths in their hair, Rianna observed there were differences in the way each couple dressed, that each bride and groom were from the same province. "Are there none who marry outside their own provinces?" she asked.

"There are many kinds of people in the kingdom with different languages, customs and even religions. Manco Capac's father united them in our empire; and though they've learned our ways, we haven't insisted on them giving up theirs except for some which are too barbaric to allow," Ruminavi explained. "Intermarriage is not normally allowed and not usually sought."

"The queen gave me reason to believe such things weren't impossible," Rianna said slowly, thinking of her and Shali.

"In the case of one such as you, who is an exile from your own people, the law would have to be lenient. If the king and queen favor you, as it appears, I'm sure you could marry almost any man who asks for you and gains royal approval for himself," Ruminavi advised. His eyes moved searchingly over Rianna's face a moment. "An alliance between you and Lord Shali is rumored. Is it true?"

Rianna lowered her eyes. "It seemed to be, but now . . ." Her voice trailed off sadly.

"If you decide you won't be wed, I would like to know."

Rianna looked up at Ruminavi in surprise. His expression wasn't flirtatious, but as if he'd asked an honest question.

Reminding himself how different their customs were, if her background dictated a man might not sit alone with a woman even in a crowd, Ruminavi quietly explained, "Lord Shali is my friend and I wouldn't approach you as a man if you were still promised to him. Would you tell me if you and he decide to part?"

Rianna gazed at Ruminavi a long moment before replying, "I'm not even certain I'll stay at Machu Picchu."

Ruminavi's dark eyes clouded at her oblique answer then softened as he said, "You still think I am too forward, but an Incan man attracted to a woman tells her. There is nothing wrong in this; I am saying no less than I'm thinking." He sighed, knowing she still had misgivings. "Perhaps, as this day goes on, we can become better acquainted so you will regard me as a friend. We both can learn later if anything more is possible or even wanted between us. Meanwhile, please continue asking any questions you wish about Incas or me."

"I will," she promised and turned her attention to the marriage ceremonies.

Manco Capac appeared to say little to each bride and groom other than address them by name and join their hands then pronounce them wed; but Rianna soon learned why. There were so many couples waiting to be married the ritual continued all morning and into the afternoon, despite the brevity of the individual ceremonies; and she was grateful for the litter. She was also glad for Ruminavi's company. He passed her pieces of fruit he'd had the foresight to have the servants pack and meticulously answered any question about the ceremony she put to him. The question Rianna most wanted to ask she hadn't the courage: Did Incan men take more than one wife?

It was late afternoon before Manco had proclaimed the last union. Although Rianna was certain the king must be exhausted, his straight back and erect head revealed no hint of it, as Villac Umu came forward to join him in another invocation to Viracocha that ended the ceremony.

Ruminavi made the litter bearers wait so the crowd of noblemen could thin before they tried to leave, but Rianna still didn't catch a glimpse of Shali. After she was back in the litter, Rianna puzzled over where Shali had been during the ceremony. She wondered if he hadn't come at all and, though it seem unlikely, if he might not attend the celebration in the palace garden.

When Ruminavi returned Rianna to the palace, he left her at the door to her suite, advising he wouldn't return for an hour so she could refresh herself after the long ceremony. She knew this was a custom that allowed a little time for Manco and Coraquenque to rest. She wondered if Shali might take advantage of her solitude and come; but when there finally was a knock on the door, she opened it to find Ruminavi holding a cluster of pale gold flowers

After he'd stepped into the room, he held out the blossoms to Rianna. His eyes revealed amusement at her hesitation to take the flowers and he said, "Every woman will wear garlands on her head except the queen. As part of my assignment is to make you feel as comfortable as possible among my people, I am fulfilling my orders by giving these to you."

Still wary of his intentions, Rianna asked slowly, "Where does custom dictate I wear them?"

He smiled knowingly and stepped behind her to tuck the sprig into the back of her headband. Ruminavi felt drunk with the perfume rising from Rianna's shoulders, the silk of the golden hair that brushed his hands and made him want to dig his fingers into her curls; but he said, "You need not be worried about my doing anything forward or improper by Incan standards. I told you I'm Shali's friend. Only if you told me your relationship with him had ended would I approach you as a man."

"But I still have to take your word about whether what you do is personal or a custom," she pointed out.

"You can ask anyone whatever you wish about my behavior." Ruminavi stepped away and took Rianna's arm to lead her to the door. "I cannot prevent myself from liking what I see in you, but I wouldn't be here if I couldn't be trusted with a woman."

After they'd entered the garden, a page immediately came to direct them to the king and queen.

"You must be very favored to be called to them so soon," Ruminavi commented.

"And you?" Rianna inquired.

Ruminavi wore a slight smile as he answered modestly, "I am of some small account."

Rianna knew all eyes were on them as Ruminavi escorted her across a large, paved area to where Manco and Coraquenque were seated. She bowed as deeply as Ruminavi; but when she raised her eyes, she saw that the formal solemnity their faces had held in the afternoon had melted into warmth. Despite their gorgeous costumes, they were the friends she'd known from the first.

The party was extensive and the guests' numbers great so there were only a few minutes to exchange greetings and a few casual remarks; but Rianna realized that Manco Capac's calling her to him before everyone else was an unspoken command to the royal court to accept her. The nobility dropped their previous reserve and, eager to introduce themselves to Rianna, especially where the king could see them, discreetly worked their way toward her. Ruminavi introduced them to Rianna then, after a moment, expertly fended them off and guided her to a seat under one of the wide-spreading arbors that had been made of lush tree branches interwoven with fragrant shrubs and flowers to perfume the air. He sent a hovering servant for a cool drink then settled back more comfortably on the cushions and regarded her with satisfaction.

"You can see they have not only accepted you, but make you welcome," he pointed out.

"I have to wonder if they're sincere or only doing it because the king's attitude ordered them to accept me," she commented.

"It all is the same in the way Incas think," Ruminavi assured. "Some of them may become close friends if you stay long enough with us. Others will not. None will oppose you."

Rianna was silent as she considered this. "If what you say is true, your court is quite different from what I've heard about any court in Europe."

Ruminavi accepted the goblet the servant handed him and sent an attendant to get food before he again turned to her. "Perhaps Incas are more obedient to their rulers," he commented then warned, "Sip this drink slowly until after you've had something to eat. It is very potent."

Rianna had recognized the bronze liquor she'd shared with Shali at the hostel. "I've already sampled this," she replied. She lowered her goblet and looked at Ruminavi so steadily he put down his cup.

"You have a question you're very reluctant to ask," he surmised.

"It's a personal question," she warned.

Ruminavi shrugged. "If I can answer, I will."

Rianna gathered up her courage and said, "I've learned a man must marry when he's twenty-four. I suspect you're older than that so you've somehow avoided the marriage law. Or is it possible Incas can take more than one wife, as I've heard some people in the world do?''

"If a man's means allow him, he can marry more than one woman. Some noblemen do while others choose not to,'' he answered slowly. "As you guessed, I'm three years beyond the marriage age, but not wed.'' He took a sip from his goblet and, as if he considered his answer fully given, fell silent.

Thinking Ruminavi was a handsome man, who seemed to have the qualities necessary to attract women, Rianna's curiosity was piqued even more. Hoping his reason for remaining single would support her hope that Shali, too wasn't married, she asked, "Why haven't you wed?''

"I spent my twenty-fourth birthday freezing in a mountain pass in Ecuador waiting for a Castilian troop movement we were going to ambush. I had been fighting your people for seven years and I needed a horse more than a wife.'' Ruminavi sighed at his bitter memories then looked up at her. "I'm still fighting, but it seems as if it never will be different.''

"What about Shali?'' The words were out before she could stop herself.

Ruminavi looked at her from narrowed eyes. "I said I would tell you about myself and the customs of my people, but I haven't a right to answer personal questions about someone else.'' Ruminavi's eyes traveled beyond Rianna's shoulder and he observed, "Shali's coming.''

Rianna started by this news, immediately turned. Expecting to see Shali approaching, she was confused when she didn't.

"He just arrived,'' Ruminavi prompted.

Rianna's eyes shot to the doorway and saw a man silhouetted against the lamplight coming from inside the palace. He was wearing a long cape, a helmet like Ruminavi had worn that afternoon with a long, slender feather rising from its crest, curving slightly from its length. As he stepped into the light, those standing near him turned to stare.

"Everyone is wondering at Shali's absence this afternoon, if he was on a mission for the king or disobeyed him by not coming,'' Ruminavi said.

"Disobeyed?" Rianna whispered in surprise. It was unthinkable for any Inca to disobey the king for even the most important reason. It was an insult regarded on the same level as betrayal to their enemies.

"I've heard gossip about it all day," was the most Ruminavi would say.

Suddenly Rianna knew the nobility hadn't stared at her merely because she was Castilian, but because they thought some quarrel between them was why Shali had spurned the day's ceremonies and arrived late for the celebration. Rianna was momentarily annoyed at the way gossip flashed through the palace and even the city. Did every Inca in the valley know about each breath she took? Then it occurred to Rianna that, if Shali had wanted this much to avoid her, was willing to risk his king's displeasure, even punishment, he must have wished to irrevocably demonstrate he didn't want her. Tears sprang to Rianna's eyes and she moved as if she would stand up; but Ruminavi's hand caught her arm and held her back.

"Shali always knows what he's doing," Ruminavi said to her beseeching look.

It was true Shali appeared as self-assured as ever while he moved down the path, Rianna observed and tried to calm her racing heart. He was in uniform; maybe he had been on royal business; maybe they all were wrong. Hope rose in her like a bright bird's flight. Then she realized she'd never seen him dressed so, not even in Xaquixaguana Pass; and she watched avidly as he walked smoothly through the shadows flickering with torchlight to the paved area.

Shali's tunic was the same royal blue as Ruminavi's, but its hem was embroidered with gold that flickered in the firelight. His dark cape flowed down his back almost to his heels; and its movements, as he walked, revealed glimpses of its wide border carrying the red and gold of his family crest. Scarlet cords, seemingly knotted decoratively around his upper arm, denoted with their short fringe that his was the highest of military ranks. Aside from the wide, gold wristlets and his belt of linked gold disks, he wore no jewelry. He also, Rianna noted, wore neither sword nor dagger. Was it a sign of his subjection? She wondered fearfully again if he were, in his disobedience, surrendering himself for punishment. But Shali's attitude, as he bowed before the royal couple, was that of dignified respect, not fear or penitence.

After Shali rose, he spoke to Manco so quietly Rianna doubted anyone except Coraquenque could hear. There was a short conversation among the three, which ended with Manco handing Shali a bejeweled goblet as a sign to everyone watching that, far from being in the king's disfavor, the commander was being awarded the honor of drinking from Manco's own cup. Rianna let out an audible breath of relief as Shali inclined his head to the royal couple and backed away a few steps. He straightened to look at the crowd, which hastily resumed its conversations then, moving his eyes over the guests, located Rianna and Ruminavi and started toward them. Ruminavi quickly rose when Shali approached.

Rianna's grasp of Quechua wasn't enough to tell her more of Shali's brief conversation than that, at its end, Shali thanked Ruminavi for escorting her through the day and dismissed him. Ruminavi wished Rianna a pleasant evening and promptly left them alone.

Shali's eyes were speculative as he looked down at her silently a moment. Then he turned to the torch that lit their arbor, took it from its holder and, turning it upside-down, jammed it back into the holder to snuff out its light.

"I prefer not to be on display for those who are still watching what we do," he explained. When he sat down, his eyes' black surfaces reflected only the faint, golden glimmers coming from the distant palace doorway.

"I was afraid something was wrong," Rianna finally admitted.

"Your Quechua has so improved you understand gossip?" he asked quietly.

"Ruminavi told me something about it. I figured out the rest," she murmured, lowering her eyes.

"The gossip was wrong," Shali advised. "We had placed a man in Cuzco and Captain Estudillo caught him spying. The man escaped, but got a bolt from a crossbow in his back. He managed to get to Machu Picchu late last night. I've been sitting with him all this time hoping he would regain consciousness and tell me what he'd learned. Fortunately, he did; but he's again lapsed into unconsciousness and the healer says he'll die."

Rianna thought of the sullen Incan slave in Estudillo's office, who had served them wine, and wondered if that man had been the spy. She asked slowly, "What was the news—or can you tell me?"

"Almagro was caught and beheaded in Cuzco. What was left of his army has either been executed or banished. Gonzalo Pizarro has gone back to Cuzco and it looks like he thinks he should govern Peru now," Shali answered. Rianna was silent so long he finally asked quietly, "Did you think the gossip that I'd disobeyed the king and was about to be punished was true?"

"It didn't seem likely, but I didn't know," she answered slowly.

"What did Ruminavi say besides repeat rumors to upset you?"

"As he was ordered, he answered my questions about your people, made me comfortable and was pleasant company," Rianna said. "He didn't mention the rumor until just now when everyone was staring at you so intently I got suspicious and he couldn't avoid my questions. It was then I realized they'd been staring at me all day for the same reason. They thought you avoided the ceremonies because I was there."

Shali took off his helmet and laid it beside him. As he ran his hand through his hair he said, "I'm sorry if your name being linked with mine distresses you, but even palace servants gossip." He raised his eyes to hers and she saw the dark fires rising in them as he commented, "They couldn't say much about our behavior as you were obviously too ill to take part in anything provocative until now. In any case, a pretty woman draws gossip," his hand slid over hers on the cushion as he spoke, "and you're so beautiful dressed that way even Ruminavi, who's always appeared to have a hide as thick as an armadillo's, seems to have dropped his shields."

Having already taken heart from what Ruminavi had said about how he'd eluded marriage, thrilling to the touch of Shali's hand, Rianna momentarily forgot her suspicions. "I felt like an impostor to wear this; but if you like me dressed this way, I don't care if the entire royal court objects."

Shali's emotions blotted out his decision to stay away from Rianna. His fingers moved over her wrist and ran lightly up her arm to her shoulder. His hand slid to the back of her neck as he leaned closer. "I've wanted to hear you say something besides reciting lessons for a long time, *chinita*, a very long time."

His mouth took hers and the sweet aching he'd forced himself to endure became unbearable longing as he caressed her lips. He momentarily forgot his previous resolution and that others might see. His free arm slid around Rianna, drawing her closer; and he felt as if the contact lit a torch in him. His lips caressing hers found the response he sought; but Rianna, too, had momentarily forgotten everything except Shali. Her hands wove under his cape, around his tight waist; and she melted against him.

Finally, Shali's lips kissing the corner of Rianna's mouth whispered, "I can't leave this party until after Manco and Coraquenque; but when they go, will you leave with me, *chinita*?"

Lost in the sensation of his lips fluttering over her skin, she murmured, "Where?"

He dipped his head to kiss the side of her neck and, feeling the light texture of his hair brushing her cheek, she wanted to weave her fingers into it, turn his mouth to hers for another kiss.

Thinking that if they stayed in his suite, Amaru or even Ruminavi might knock on the door with a message or an emergency of some kind to report, Shali whispered, "I think your room would be best."

The suspicion that Shali might already have a wife suddenly flashed like lightning in Rianna's mind. She pulled away. "Why must it be *my* room?"

Shali gazed at her, for a moment too startled to reply. His lips parted; but before he said a word, another voice spoke rapidly in Quechua.

"If you think there was gossip before, your kissing in this dark corner has multiplied it many times."

Rianna turned to stare up at the face of an Incan girl, whose almond-shaped eyes burned with angry fire. Rianna hadn't understood the words, but she knew what the expression on the girl's face meant. The dark eyes stared pointedly at Rianna's hand now lightly resting on Shali's waist. Rianna quickly withdrew her hand and assumed the worst. *This must be Shali's wife.*

Suya was thinking her long wait for Shali to recover from his grief over Yupanqui had been wasted. She said bitterly, "*This* woman certainly can't remind you of Yupanqui."

Shali's temper had flared at her words and he snapped, "You were my sister-in-law, Suya, never my wife."

"And obviously, never to *be* your wife," she said sharply. Suya paused to take a breath and realized she'd gone too far. In a moment Shali would unleash his anger and humiliate her before the court with his words driving her away. She made an effort to calm herself and said, "I didn't come for this purpose, but to tell you Manco Capac is leaving now and wants to speak with you before he retires."

"Now that you've spread me with poison as well as delivered the message, please go; so I can try to explain to Rianna," Shali said tightly.

Suya spun around and walked stiffly away.

Shali turned and found that Rianna had vanished. He stared in dismay at the place where she'd been. Then he muttered a soft oath, snatched up his helmet and got to his feet to go to the royal suite.

chapter
17

As Rianna rode through Machu Picchu's streets, she regretted having let Coraquenque persuade her to go down to the valley. She realized she was drawing as much attention as Coraquenque. Though the Incas showed their queen every deference, they seemed to be used to her laying aside her royal trappings and moving casually among them. The blond Castilian woman they'd heard Lord Shalikuchima had brought to the palace was another matter. Rianna was tired of being peered at and whispered about and she was glad when they finally guided their mounts through the city gates.

Coraquenque drew her horse to the side of the road and paused to point out, "Many generations ago Incas cut layers from the mountain slope so the land wouldn't be so steep. As you can see, we use every place we can make reasonably level to grow crops."

Rianna lowered her eyes to the rows of flourishing plants lining both sides of the road down the slope. Despite her mood, she had to admire the industry of the Incas, who had turned mountainsides into terraced gardens. The air rising from the valley carried the warm, green fragrance of growing things. It reminded her of the scent of the night in Lima when Shali had first come to her. Not wanting to remember, she lifted her eyes to the peaks surrounding Machu Picchu and found herself recalling the glorious night they'd spent in the hostel. She decided she *must* think of something besides Shali or she would weep.

Rianna said the first thing that came to her mind, "I'm still amazed at your going down the mountain without guards."

Though Coraquenque was acutely aware of her friend's tension, she replied, "I'm safe among my people and only Incas are in the valley."

"I can see from here the valley isn't completely cultivated. There are forests," Rianna hurriedly went on. "Aren't there any dangerous wild animals?"

"When I was a child, I wandered freely in the forest and am familiar with the animals' habits." Coraquenque signaled her horse to resume walking and moved ahead. "I promise we'll be safe. I have a special reason for being careful I'll tell you about later."

Curiosity piqued, Rianna nudged Wayra to catch up. "Why are you behaving so mysteriously?" she inquired. "I've sensed it in you all morning."

"I'm surprised you've thought of anything besides your own unhappiness with Shali," Coraquenque remarked.

Rianna glanced up at her friend's bluntness and said tightly, "I don't live and breathe only for him, not anymore."

Coraquenque let out an exaggerated sigh. "So you've decided this morning to cast Shali aside. At the celebration last night I noticed you seemed to like him well enough." Coraquenque looked at Rianna from under her lashes. "Why won't you talk to me?"

Rianna shook her head, but said nothing.

"I've seen your attitude toward Shali shift back and forth several times since you came to Machu Picchu, but you've never said a word about it to me." Coraquenque had overlooked the one time Rianna had tried, but Rianna forgot to remind her as Coraquenque added enticingly, "Still, I'm planning to tell you something important to me that no one else knows yet."

"What is it?"

"Incas don't have money, but we're very good at trading. I'll trade with you now." Coraquenque looked at Rianna and said slowly,

"Maybe your difficulty with Shali is something you don't understand about Incas and I can explain."

The anger Rianna had held before her like a shield suddenly was swept aside to bare the pain she'd been trying not to show. Tears bulged in her eyes and she said brokenly, "I don't know how to say it without insulting a custom among your people."

"I think I've voiced my disapproval of some of your people's customs often enough to give you the right to criticize mine once in a while," Coraquenque reasoned.

Rianna choked back her tears to exclaim, "I can't bear to become a second wife!"

Realizing her friend had learned some noblemen took more than one wife, Coraquenque said, "There are ways to avoid that. You'll notice I'm the only wife Manco has."

Rianna blinked furiously, but her tears dropped to her cheeks and sparkled in the sun. "But Shali is already married. Why didn't anyone, not even you, tell me that?"

"Because it isn't true," Coraquenque answered promptly.

Rianna was stunned. "Since we came to Machu Picchu, he's been acting so strangely. A woman came to us last night, angry I was with him."

Coraquenque stopped her horse and turned to put her hand over Rianna's. "Why haven't you asked him why he's behaving this way?"

"I can't share him," Rianna muttered.

"I don't know what Suya said last night, but Manco sent her to tell Shali he wanted to talk with him. Suya's not Shali's wife or his lover," Coraquenque said firmly. Aware Rianna's suspicions hadn't faded, she sighed. "Shali was married to Suya's sister, Yupanqui."

Rianna lifted her head to stare at Coraquenque. A thousand questions flashed through her mind and she exclaimed, "You must explain this to me!"

"He's told you nothing?" Coraquenque demanded. When Rianna shook her head, the Inca concluded, "And you didn't ask."

"I know you don't like to talk about someone else's personal affairs, but *please* tell me about Shali," Rianna begged.

Coraquenque considered the plans she'd made for Rianna's day and decided she must speak. "Shali and Yupanqui had a son, who wasn't a year old when Shali came back home to find everyone slaughtered by the Castilians. Shali went to his own province to grieve. He remained there for some time, shutting himself off from everything. After Manco's brothers were dead, Manco assumed the Incan crown; but the Castilians captured him. Shali roused himself from his grief to rescue Manco, but it wasn't until Shali's province fell to the invasion and his ancestral home was put to the torch that he finally threw himself into the battle. Then fighting seemed to become a compulsion, all he lived for; and I'm not sure he'd taken *any* woman since Yupanqui's death before you came. But I know, if he did, it wasn't Suya."

As Coraquenque related each incident, Rianna felt Shali's torment as vividly as if it were her own; and after Coraquenque had finished, she was breathless with vicarious pain. "But why hasn't he told me any of this?" she whispered.

"I know he loves you, but I didn't realize until now how much," Coraquenque reflected. "The power of his love for you has put the past so completely behind him he thinks of it no more."

Rianna's emotions were so piquant she couldn't speak. Coraquenque understood and was silent, giving her friend time to absorb this information and adjust her conclusions.

It wasn't until they'd reached the bottom of the mountain that Rianna finally said, "I'd thought *I* had suffered more than people should be asked."

"These are evil times. We all have suffered," Coraquenque replied sadly. "Suya lost her sister and her husband. She's longed so much to remarry she doesn't realize she loves, but isn't in love with, Shali. Manco lost his brothers and his first wife." At Rianna's surprised glance, Coraquenque nodded, as if to confirm her own words, then went on, "My family is dead. Because Manco and I had to flee from city to town to village, I've lost two children by miscarriage."

"How can you bear it?" Rianna exclaimed.

"I suppose we've kept our sanity because we're strong. Maybe we've moved faster or sooner than those who were killed or maybe it's simply that Viracocha decreed our survival. We know many things will change for us no matter how this war ends. We don't want the changes, but part of our strength is that we've had to change within ourselves because we love life too much to give it up. The future looks dark for my people, yet we plan to live in it and, if possible, flourish."

Rianna suddenly realized, "My past is much like the Incas' at Machu Picchu. That's why you thought I could live among you, isn't it? That city is like Noah's ark keeping afloat in this secret valley while the rest of the world is inundated by war."

"I don't know about that Noah, but I understand an ark is a big boat," Coraquenque said. "Yes, Machu Picchu is a place to be safe while we fight the storm outside our valley." She fell silent for a time before she remembered, "I was so occupied with making you tell me what your problem was I almost forgot to tell you *my* news."

"I'm relieved to learn about Shali and I feel less like an alien among your people now," Rianna said. "But I want to hear your news, which I suspect is happier."

A smile played around the corners of Coraquenque's mouth as she said, "I'm going to have a child."

"A baby! Oh, Coraquenque, after all this sadness, how very wonderful!" Rianna dropped her reins and leaned over to catch her friend's hands.

Coraquenque leaned closer to hug Rianna. "Let us hope it's a boy so Manco's crown will at last have an heir," she said against Rianna's cheek.

Rianna drew away. "You said no one else knew this? Surely you told Manco!"

Coraquenque shook her head. "I saved the news as bait to make you tell me your problem."

"You were *that* worried about me and Shali?" Rianna surmised and was touched by the depth of Coraquenque's concern.

"I *couldn't* allow Shali to lose a second love. I *had* to do more than stand silently by," Coraquenque explained.

As their conversation revolved back to the expected royal child, Coraquenque turned her horse off the road to follow a path where the trees grew so thickly on each side their branches twined overhead, making the trail seem like a tunnel of foliage. Sun filtering through the leaves turned the air to a soft aura of green shadows. When the trees stepped back from the path, they formed a crescent around a series of rocky ledges. A stream fell so gently over the rocks it seemed like a curtain of crystal droplets suspended in the green-gold light that only brushed the pool at the base of the ledges. Flowers clustered in depressions the waterfall had made in the rocks as blossoms festooned the vines clinging to the trees. The little clearing's floor was carpeted with fine, silky grass.

Rianna dismounted and turned slowly to gaze at her surroundings.

"Manco found this place and brought me here," Coraquenque said, her voice softened by memories of love.

Rianna looked up at her friend. "The king is more romantic than I'd have thought."

"I didn't marry him because I wanted to be queen," Coraquenque advised. She looked at the waterfall and the pool then at Rianna speculatively a moment and suggested, "Why don't you take a swim? The ride from Machu Picchu was warm and dusty and I can tell you from experience the pond is very refreshing."

"I suppose, if it's secluded enough for a king and queen, it should be for me," Rianna conceded.

Coraquenque looked up at the treetops and observed, "The sun is almost above us. I'll gather something from the forest for lunch while you bathe."

"You can't go off by yourself, especially in your condition!" Rianna exclaimed.

Coraquenque waved Rianna's protests aside. "I know this area well. Take your bath and don't worry about a thing. I suspect this afternoon will be one we'll both enjoy very much." She turned her horse and left without giving Rianna a chance to argue.

Rianna watched apprehensively until Coraquenque disappeared down the trail. Then she turned to Wayra and loosened the saddle girth so the mare could be more comfortable while she grazed.

Despite Coraquenque's assurances, Rianna glanced nervously at the forest all the while she undressed; but when she finally stood naked in the green light, her hesitance vanished. Rianna had never been undressed outdoors and she felt so alive and free thoughts of her previous troubles dissipated. The breezes moving over her skin were delicious as she stepped into the pond.

Rianna waded farther into the water and found it only reached as high as her waist. She discovered she could walk behind the waterfall and gaze at the world through its crystal shimmer. A sunshaft touched the center of the pool and made a rainbow. She hurried out from behind the fall and stood in the middle of the glowing band of colors, closed her eyes and made a wish.

When Shali entered the glade, it was how he found Rianna—an ivory statue wearing only a tumble of golden curls, standing in a rainbow with eyes tightly closed, making a wish that came true when she opened them and saw him standing on the grassy bank. She was so surprised she couldn't speak. She even forgot she was naked.

Remembering how they'd last parted, that Rianna had fled from him, Shali was afraid she would be angered by his intrusion. Though he couldn't tear his eyes from her, he said softly, "I didn't know you were here."

Rianna wasn't sure if he were an illusion her longing had caused and didn't answer. Unmoving, she only gazed at him.

The sight of her standing so still, like a startled woodland creature, as innocently unaware of her beauty, caused a tender, yet piquant desire to rush through Shali. He struggled to recall his purpose then explained, "One of Coraquenque's attendants gave me a message to meet her here at noon."

Finally, Rianna whispered, "Coraquenque went to find something for our lunch."

Confused by this news, Shali glanced in the direction he'd just come. "I didn't pass her." He turned again to Rianna and realized Coraquenque had arranged this. Hoping fervently that Rianna would stay where she was, he stepped out of his boots. Shali kept his eyes steadily on Rianna, as if he would hold her with his will while he discarded his jerkin and breeches. When he stepped into the water and walked slowly toward her, he still wasn't sure what she would do.

Shali laid his hands at Rianna's waist and began, "Suya isn't—"

His touch finally confirmed his reality and Rianna put her fingers lightly against his lips. "Coraquenque explained on our way here. I know I shouldn't have run off last night without giving you a chance to tell me anything, but I'd thought you were going to say Suya was your wife. I didn't want to hear it."

Shali kissed her fingers away and his slow smile became part of the rainbow surrounding them. He leaned closer, intending only to kiss her tenderly; but at the sensation of her lips under his, he found he couldn't. His palms, hungry for the feel of her skin, slid around Rianna's back then up to flatten against her shoulders and drew her so tightly to him her breasts were warm mounds crushed against his chest. His mouth took hers with all the passion he'd kept precariously banked for so long.

Rianna gave herself over to the impulses Shali's urgently moving lips awakened in her, the heat of the hard body she was clasped against. She felt the exultation that swept through him, the way he trembled for the moment until he forced himself to release her.

Shali gave his desire a firm command to wait, slid his arm around Rianna's waist and turned toward the grassy bank. But he found that her steps through the water were too slow for him. He swept her up in his arms and with a few long strides made their way swiftly to shore. He knelt to lower her to the grass and she didn't release her hold on him. Before he could do anything, while she still was sitting, she tilted her face and recaptured his lips.

Rianna's mouth was as eager, as hungry for his touch as Shali was for hers; and she kissed as if she would devour him. Her fire overwhelmed Shali. He lost himself in her kiss, in urges so intense he wasn't aware she was lying down until he felt his own weight against his arms around her back. He didn't release her. It wasn't necessary. He sank into her being and felt as if a streak of fire rushed through his flesh setting him alight.

His mouth crushed hers with all his old sureness, possessing her breath, even her soul. His control was so rapidly being consumed, as he moved against her, she felt as if he were a drum pulsing in her heart. Approaching the brink of ecstasy, she gasped; but he didn't hear. Only when he felt her legs, like flames, wrapping around his did reason sound one last alarm that forced him to tear his mouth from hers.

"It's been too long, *chinita;* I want you too much," Shali whispered urgently.

Rianna's eyes opened to gaze up at him. His were hard and bright, like obsidian in the sun. "Don't stop; don't wait," she breathed.

Shali's body tightened with the passion that surged over him at her words, but still he made an effort to withhold himself. She moved provocatively; and fire flashed along his nerves, searing his mind so all thoughts fled before it. The commands of his instincts were too powerful to resist. Poised at the edge of endurance, his hips moved without his direction, driving him to an even greater intensity, unleashing impulses that compelled him toward ecstasy. He didn't even hear the moan that burst from him as the explosion in his body shattered his senses.

Shali lay quietly for a time as his mind slowly gathered its fragments and brought him back to awareness. The perfume of the earth and grass mingled with Rianna's hair. The touch of the sun's warmth on his back, the moist little body beneath him, the sounds of the waterfall's whisper and Rianna's heart singing under his.

"I meant to stay away so my love wouldn't hold you at Machu Picchu if you wanted to leave," he murmured.

Rianna turned her face to kiss the side of Shali's neck, nuzzle his hair. "My desire for you became like that fever I got in the jungle. How could I think clearly to decide anything when it stopped my ability to reason?"

Shali moved to her side and put his arms around her. She laid her head on his shoulder as he wondered, "If passion fulfilled makes us want more and the lack of it gives the same result, how will we be able to reason at all?"

"I love you too much to bind you to a wife who might someday have to leave your people even if she wanted you," Rianna answered. "It would be too bitter for us both."

"We think the same then," he murmured, "I the Inca, you the Spaniard."

"Love is the common tie between all of us, every living creature," she said softly. "It's the fear they won't be loved that makes some people need to conquer others. Whether a man's impulse is to love or to conquer marks the difference between men like you and Alonso."

"There was a time when I thought, to win your love, I had to conquer all you'd been taught," Shali recalled then added wryly, "Now I have your love; but because I'm an Inca, the same challenge is before me."

Rianna leaned over him and said, "It's for me to lay aside my past. You need not conquer anything."

Shali's fingers lightly caressed her temples as he reconsidered his situation. It mattered nothing how he or she said it or which language they used. It was his heritage struggling against Rianna's just as surely as the war beyond Machu Picchu's valley was one to decide the supremacy and even perhaps the survival of the two peoples in Peru. The challenge had been given and accepted and Shali had never taken challenges lightly.

"Tomorrow, then, I'll introduce you to my people, a side of them you haven't seen before," he promised.

"And this afternoon?" she asked, as she felt his fingers weaving into her hair.

"Today I'll start acquainting you with Shalikuchima, as I think he's never been known before," he murmured and drew her mouth to his.

When they'd shared their first kiss in Nicasio's garden and Rianna had confessed not knowing that Incas kissed at all, Shali had said it was possible Incas did more than her people in love. Now that their first urgent thirst for love had been appeased though not quenched, he had the time and inclination to show her how to sip from love's goblet.

There was not, in all the vineyards of Spain, the cellars in France or all Europe so great a variety of flavors as Shali's being held. Where before they'd been swept into love like a wild fire racing before the wind, now he ignited separate tongues of flame he chose to fan then put out only to kindle others, bank them and begin again somewhere else.

Shali aroused Rianna, made her keep pace with him then restrained her with his own will. He invited, teased and seduced her, eroding away her control of herself until she cried out that he was her master and learned, when he surrendered to their mutual frenzy, there was no master.

Shali taught Rianna words of love in Quechua, while he demonstrated their meaning. He took her spirit into the molten pool at a volcano's heart then, like the fiery liquid at its core, shot up in a cloud of sparks to the crown of the Andes and soared beyond. The soul of the jaguar was his, the heat of the sultry jungles; and through him,

Rianna discovered she contained a sensuality that once would have made her incredulous

And after the passion Shali had evoked in Rianna, she learned there was yet an innocence left in her, a sense of delicacy that responded with a flood of poignant tenderness when he made love again as if it were the first time for them both, a sweetness almost naïve as he whispered in courtly Castilian then, even more eloquently, in Quechua and brought fulfillment that left them at last serene.

The sky was a sheet of orange silk lit to flame by the torch of the setting sun, the glade darkening with violet shadows when Shali, unable to release Rianna from his touch even to return to the city, lifted her to sit before him on Chuncho's saddle. She leaned back against his chest, content that the hands guiding Chuncho's reins also held her soul.

They and the black horse became an outline against the crimson sky while Wayra, following, was a flame as they made their way unhurriedly up the terraced slope. From a distant mountain peak came the trilling cry of a lover's message to his beloved on another summit and in its call were echoes of the song Shali's heart sang to Rianna.

chapter
18

Rianna awakened to the morning and Shali. He was sitting cross-legged on a cushion beside her bed-mat; and his eyes, powdered with luminous reflections from the sun, were contemplative as they steadily watched her.

"What are you thinking?" she asked.

"I was just watching you sleep," he quietly answered. His eyes softened with a different warmth as he leaned closer to kiss her. When the light caress began to gather power, as they'd known it would, he surprised her by withdrawing.

It was then Rianna realized he was already dressed in the royal blue tunic, the crimson and gold insignia that was his uniform as military commander. His scarlet feathered helmet lay beside him. She sat up slowly.

Noting her disappointed look, Shali's eyes took on a glint of pleasure as he asked, "Do you want me to spend the day here in your arms?" Rianna's rising blush gave her answer. Though he would have preferred to do just that, he said, "Since I have business to attend and you want to learn about the way I live, I thought you should come with me."

"You want me to attend the royal court?" she breathed, awed at the prospect and wondering how she could dress so quickly; for last night Shali had dismissed the servant Coraquenque had loaned Rianna

"Manco canceled today's audiences. He's too distracted by Coraquenque's news of their coming heir. I'm going to the royal suite for a private meeting with him. You can have breakfast and dress while I'm gone." In one smooth movement Shali rose and held out his hand to help Rianna up.

She pulled on a robe as he watched then walked with him to the door. "Where do you plan to take me on this business of yours?"

Shali bent to brush his lips to hers, left them tingling despite the casualness of his caress. He understood the reason for her question and advised, "Tavi will show you how the wife of a nobleman dresses as she goes about the city."

"The wife of a nobleman?" Rianna echoed.

"If you're to learn about the kind of life you'd lead, you might as well dress the part," Shali reasoned. He stepped into the hall and closed the door behind him, leaving Rianna wondering who Tavi was.

It didn't take long for her to find out. The attendant had been waiting in the corridor for Shali to leave; and after a discreet delay, Tavi tapped on Rianna's door then entered.

"I am to be your personal maid," Tavi said in slow, but clear, Castilian as she made a graceful little bow.

"Did the queen send you to me?" Rianna asked. "I don't remember seeing you among her attendants."

"Lord Shalikuchima chose me to serve you," the sloe-eyed girl answered.

"Shali did?" Rianna was surprised and pleased.

"My mother attended Lady Yupanqui and was killed in the invaders' attack in Xaquixaguana Valley. When you came to Machu Picchu, he remembered I spoke your language and sent for me," Tavi explained. "I'm sorry I was so long in arriving you had to borrow the queen's maids. I spent the time traveling from the lord's province where my family lives."

"You came from Tumbez?" Rianna was amazed that Shali had ordered a maid from so far away. "I'm surprised it didn't take longer for you to get here."

"Lord Shalikuchima's sending a messenger so great a distance was an honor to me. I left the same day the *chaquis* arrived," Tavi said.

"I think you'd better not call him Shalikuchima. He forbid the use of his father's name until your enemies are driven away. No one calls him Shalikuchima except occasionally the king and queen," Rianna advised.

"Thank you for reminding me. We continue to call the lord Shalikuchima in Tumbez, but not in his presence," Tavi said.

"Your attitude tells me Lord Shali is well thought of in his province," Rianna observed.

"We have great respect and affection for him, as we did for his father," Tavi agreed.

Rianna was silent a moment. It was obvious the people of Shali's province thought of him and his family in almost a proprietary way. She wondered what their opinion would be of his taking a Castilian woman, one of their enemy's people, as a lover much less a wife. If they resented her, would Shali's life be complicated by the disobedi- ence of his own fiefdom, though the Incas behaved politely toward her? Rianna gathered the courage to ask bluntly, "How do you feel about serving me? Do you know what I am to him?"

The girl lowered her eyes and answered, "It isn't for me to question Lord Shali's decisions, Lady Rianna."

"There are many things I don't understand about your people's customs and outlook. I'll need to ask many questions of you. Some of them may be a little embarrassing to us both," Rianna warned.

"So Lord Shali instructed me. I'll answer as well as I can," Tavi promised.

"This morning Lord Shali told me to behave as if I'm his wife. To do so will prove that we're lovers. What will be thought of this?" Rianna inquired.

The girl looked surprised. "Lord Shali's sending for me to serve you has already confirmed what you are to him."

Thinking that yesterday afternoon was the first time she and Shali had made love since she'd arrived, Rianna dryly observed, "Secrets aren't going to be easy to keep, I can see."

Tavi's confusion passed when she recalled how Rianna's people would be scandalized by her arrangement with Shali. She assured,

"You weren't born to your station in our society so you can choose your way of life among us as long as the king agrees with it. Lord Shali is cousin to the king and a very powerful nobleman. No one will speak against you because to do so would be criticizing Lord Shali's choice of you. Also, it's known you have the king and queen's friendship."

"Then no matter how they privately feel, no one will gossip anymore because Manco and Coraquenque are my friends and Shali is related to Manco?"

"Not exactly. I can explain something about my people now, if you'll permit me," Tavi offered. She waited until Rianna inclined her head in assent then said, "When the king decides something, the people don't bend to his will despite their own opinions. The king's decisions are law and his laws are sacred. To the Incan mind, there is no other way to think. No one will oppose you because they won't even think that way."

Rianna was silent a moment as she absorbed this then concluded, "If I remain at Machu Picchu, I'll have to accept Manco Capac's decisions in the same way."

"I'm not sure of that, my lady. You're different from the rest of us," Tavi said slowly. "Though you'll have to obey the laws, that you might have your own opinion may be something the king and queen like about you. Perhaps it will be useful to them on some future day." Tavi paused thoughtfully a moment then added, "Lord Shali is like you in this way, though he's an Inca. He's always been obedient, but not without question. I suspect the king likes this quality in him. Being unpredictable has served Lord Shali very well resisting our enemies."

"I can see how it would," Rianna agreed and thought of the times Shali's behavior had surprised or bewildered her.

As Rianna followed Tavi to her bath, she recalled what the maid had said about her not being born to her station among the Incas. "Must all your people be only what their families are? Has no one a choice?" she inquired.

"Occupations and titles are passed from father to son and, with them, one's status in the kingdom. Since a child learns from his parents' example, isn't it sensible for him to follow the occupation he already knows so well?" Tavi offered Rianna the basin of soap and inquired, "Is it different among your people? Can a man born in a peasant's cottage in your land aspire to become a magistrate or a governor?"

Rianna considered this as she soaped herself then had to admit, "He wouldn't know how." She was silent as she reflected that her father had developed the gem trade he'd inherited from her grandfather, who'd learned his craft from her great grandfather, that before the Inquisition had smashed their lives Francisco had been expected to carry on after their father. "I guess we aren't so different, after all," she commented then asked, "What is expected of your people at their work? Since you have no money, how are they paid?"

Tavi was thoughtful a moment. "Everything has changed since the invaders came; and I can't know, if we're able to drive them out, whether life will return to the way it was. I can only tell you how things were and we hope they can be again." Tavi took Rianna's hand to steady her as she made her way into the bathing pool then said solemnly, "We believe that wasting anything is wrong. Laziness isn't tolerated so everyone must do something useful, but our people were never given tasks that were beyond their ability. They never were forced to work until they were exhausted; there was always time to rest. If someone was ill or injured, his neighbors helped with his work until he recovered. Everyone paid the king a certain portion of his produce; but if there was an emergency, the king's officials made certain no one was hungry or wasn't properly clothed. Everyone knew what they were supposed to do and did it, what they could have and they got it. There was little reason to steal from someone else so theft was rare." Tavi's eyes grew wistful as she recalled. "There always was time to go to parties and plays. We liked to laugh, to sing and dance then."

"All of Machu Picchu had a party on the Day of Wedding," Rianna recalled.

"It wasn't the same," Tavi denied. "We couldn't enjoy the celebration with a full heart when we knew, at so many other places in the kingdom, Incas were starving and suffering."

Rianna was saddened to be reminded of this and said nothing more until she stepped out of the water and Tavi enveloped her in a drying cloth. Then she asked, "When someone in the kingdom has a special talent, can't he use it though it isn't the occupation he'd been born to?''

"Before our land was invaded, if someone had a special ability, he or she was brought to Cuzco for training," Tavi replied then asked, "Doesn't your king have officials he can trust to give him the news in their province so he can do such things?"

Rianna asked, "What if one of Manco's ministers was corrupt and didn't do his job properly?"

Tavi was surprised at the idea. "Why should he be so? There would be nothing for him to gain and everything to lose. He would be reported by one of the magistrates."

"Suppose the magistrate was bribed to keep silent?"

Tavi shook her head. "There's nothing to bribe the magistrates with. They answer to no one, but the king. To disobey him is unthinkable, the worst of all crimes. Isn't rebelling against your king a death sentence?"

"To be a traitor, yes," Rianna conceded then added, "But we don't think our king is God."

"Maybe that's because he doesn't behave that way," Tavi reflected. "Our king isn't only our lawgiver. He's kind and generous and sees that justice is upheld."

Rianna was silently thoughtful as Tavi dusted her skin with scented powder. Then, as she sat down to let Tavi comb her hair dry, she commented, "If I am to live by your laws, I must know what they are. Will you explain something of them so I don't accidently violate one and go to the dungeon?"

"We don't put criminals in dungeons or torture them as your people do. Most crimes are punishable by death swiftly dealt," Tavi advised. At Rianna's quick intake of breath, Tavi added, "Cases are carefully considered and exonerating circumstances modify the punishment. You must remember the laws are the king's. Breaking them is an insult to him. Everything belongs to the king and he shares it with us; destroying, stealing or wasting the king's gifts is forbidden. Of course, doing harm to or murdering one of the king's subjects is also forbidden."

"It doesn't seem likely I'd accidently commit any of those crimes," Rianna remarked.

"I think not," Tavi agreed. She smiled as she laid aside her comb and viewed Rianna's curls with satisfaction. "I can see why Lord Shali would love a woman as beautiful as you," she commented.

Rianna looked up at Tavi and noted the admiration in her eyes. "I hope all Incas are as generous as you," she said then got to her feet to follow the girl to breakfast.

Rianna became more acquainted with Tavi while the girl served her meal. Whatever Rianna asked, Tavi seemed incapable of lying, even withholding or diluting the truth. Rianna decided that, though many Incan philosophies were different from hers, they were appropriate to the Peruvians' way of life; and it seemed as if they'd been a happy, contented people before the invaders had come.

After Rianna finished breakfast, she noticed Tavi had laid out a dress, one Coraquenque had ordered made and Rianna hadn't tried on. She recalled Shali's promise that Tavi would know what an Incan noblewoman would properly wear for the day and approved the girl's choice.

The dress was a slender white shift, its weave so fragile it felt like gossamer sliding over Rianna's body. It had slim, elbow length sleeves and a simple round neckline. The skirt from hip to hem, like the sleeves, was embroidered with dainty yellow, gold and brown sunflowers. Ribbons of the same colors defined her waist and fell in a shower of tassels down the front of the skirt. It was pretty and elegant at once and Rianna liked the way she looked in it. She wondered at how quickly her eyes had gotten used to a style of clothing her countrywomen would have thought barbaric and, because of its clinging fit, immodest.

When Tavi turned away to approach a chest Rianna hadn't seen before, she assumed someone had carried it into the apartment while she was bathing. She speculated on what it might contain and went nearer. When the lid was thrown open, she was stunned by the rainbow the sunlight made over the gold and gems laying within. She quickly came closer to stare at the jewelry collection.

"Where did you get this?"

Tavi selected a necklace of finely detailed sunflowers, a pair of bracelets in a matching design and turned to Rianna. "I brought them from Tumbez at Lord Shali's order," she replied and stepped around Rianna to fasten the necklace. "It was all that was saved from his

house when it was burned. I have kept it safe for him since. Many of
these pieces have been in Lord Shali's family for generations.'' Tavi
slipped the bracelets on Rianna's wrists then stepped back to look
approvingly at her charge and inquire, "Does your appearance please
you, my lady?''

Rianna lifted her eyes to again gaze at her reflection in the golden
mirror and answered softly, "How could I not be? I'm dressed as
richly as Queen Isabella.''

Tavi corrected, "You're dressed like Lord Shalikuchima's wife
should be and as he ordered.''

"Such wealth is very impressive, but a little frightening too,''
Rianna said slowly then sighed. "How foolish and vacillating I must
seem. I loved him when I thought he was an impoverished soldier and
wondered then how I could want a man I supposed lived in the hills
like a bandit. Now I'm afraid of living in a palace.''

"You fear what you don't know about us. That's part of the reason
Lord Shali sent for me. Because I lived in his household, I can answer
your questions better than anyone else,'' Tavi replied. "Tell me what
troubles you. I'll give you the truth.''

Rianna turned away to gaze at the mountains beyond the terrace.
Finally, she declared, "I don't even know what a woman can expect
from marriage to any Inca, least of all a nobleman! Shali can have
more than one wife, something my people find unacceptable. I don't
think I could bear his taking another wife.''

"While Lord Shali was wed to Lady Yupanqui, he didn't seem
interested in other women, though he occasionally admired their beauty,''
Tavi recalled then concluded, "Many noblemen *prefer* one wife. I
think Lord Shali, like our king, gives his whole heart to a woman; and
there's no part of it left to offer another.''

"How did he behave when he lost Lady Yupanqui?'' Rianna inquired.

"He mourned her deeply and so long a time we wondered if he'd
ever want another love,'' Tavi answered then pointed out, "But the
king has not yet joined your hands in marriage. Until he does, your
union with Lord Shali isn't complete. That could make a difference in
his feelings.''

Rianna said nothing to this, but she felt less sure of her place with
Shali as well as the Incas.

Though she didn't hear Shali enter the apartment, she knew he had when Tavi suddenly dipped her head and backed away a few steps. Rianna turned to face him.

Shali's eyes ran over her approvingly. "You look very beautiful," he said quietly.

"Whatever I wear, I'll never look like an Incan woman," Rianna commented with an edge to her voice. Self-doubt forced her to add, "That is what you want, isn't it? You have me dress this way so I can be more acceptable."

Shali came closer to lay his hands along the sides of her face. "You worry too much about something that isn't important," he said softly. "*You're* what I want. I had you dress this way so *you* would be more comfortable." His eyes moved past Rianna's shoulder to Tavi. "You've done well, as I knew you would."

Tavi inclined her head and murmured, "Thank you, my lord."

Shali slid his arm around Rianna's waist. "Are you ready to leave?"

Rianna knew as she looked up at Shali that, whether it was wise or foolish, she loved him. As if he understood her thoughts, his arm around her briefly tightened reassuringly.

"Aren't you curious about where we're going?" he asked.

"I'm willing to go anywhere with you, yet I have misgivings about moving among your people," she confessed.

"You're finally saying exactly what you think though you'd rather not admit it even to yourself. You're becoming more like us," Shali advised.

"I've never lied to you—or myself," she said defensively.

"No, but you've often tried to soften the truth because you were afraid of it." He started toward the door, adding, "I can understand why you did it, *chinita*. Life was so harsh you had to protect yourself. But you don't have to face it alone now."

Rianna was silent as she remembered the grassy valley in the Andes near Lima where Shali had begged her to trust him. She felt his arm again briefly press her closer and realized he'd always tried to keep her safe. Whether or not the Incas accepted her or she them, Rianna suddenly realized Shali had always been like a lodestone pointing her toward the truth.

Shali took Rianna into the courtyard, where Topa stood with his stallion. Chuncho had been brushed and combed until his coat shone like polished ebony in the sun. The leather trappings glowed like dark satin and his bridle and saddle blanket were decorated with scarlet and gold tassels.

"Chuncho seems ready for a parade," Rianna commented.

"We're going to review my troops, so he should look his best," Shali explained while Chuncho nuzzled his cheek.

Watching them, Rianna said, "I'd always been told stallions were fierce and independent, but he's as affectionate as a puppy with you."

"Chuncho means 'forest creature.' I called him that because I found him alone in the jungle. I could see from the marks on him that he'd been beaten once too often and had run away; but he was helpless in the jungle, prey for too many kinds of beasts. He behaved as if he knew it and wanted help, though he had reservations about trusting me. Because my people had no horses until your people brought them to Peru, I'd never been taught how stallions were supposed to behave. I could only follow my instincts. Chuncho has a spirit no one can possess and I don't own him any more than he does me. I never tried to force him into anything; we just became friends."

Shali spoke to the horse softly in Quechua, patted his neck and mounted. Then he reached down to Rianna, and Topa helped her up to sit sideways in front of Shali. As he arranged his arms securely around Rianna, Shali assured, "Chuncho can be fierce to those he doesn't know, but he understands you're important to me, so he wouldn't hurt you."

Rianna didn't comment, but she was thinking Shali's description of the stallion's temperament was much like his own. Shali, too, had a spirit that couldn't be owned. Nor did he seem to want to possess anyone else's. He gave what he could of himself and expected no more than that from others. If, as with Chuncho, the exchange was compatible, it seemed to be all he asked. But, Rianna remembered, Shali had loved Wayra; and he'd given her the mare after he'd gotten Chuncho without really knowing if he'd see Rianna or Wayra again. Was it possible Shali could have the same attitude about a woman, if he happened upon another who appealed to him? Rianna couldn't prevent herself from worrying about it.

When they neared the plaza and she saw the lines of azure-uniformed soldiers awaiting them, she was snatched from her thoughts and exclaimed in surprise, "You do have a regular army!"

A smile colored Shali's voice as he said tolerantly, "Did you think only the palace guards had uniforms while the rest of the army were ragged guerrillas hiding in the mountains? The men who were with me in Xaquixaguana Pass didn't bother with uniforms or need all their weapons to attack Alonso's men, who are little more than a band of thieves. Tomorrow, though, we'll be going on a different sort of mission and we might face your regular army."

"Mission? Regular army?" Rianna asked in alarm and turned her head to look up at Shali. "What are you going to do?"

Shali's black eyes remained on his men as he answered, "We're going to a gold mine the Castilians captured from us. We're going to rescue a large group of Incan prisoners."

"Incas are forced to work in the mines?" she exclaimed.

"A dozen or so are chained together, all ages and physical states mixed. Those too weak to keep pace with the others must until they drop from exhaustion and die," Shali said grimly. "When an Inca is put to work at one of the mines, he knows he can't resist; because if he kills one guard, ten Incas will be burned at the stake as punishment."

Rianna shuddered. "I must wonder even more, when I hear such things, how your people can ever accept me, one of an enemy people they have so many reasons to hate."

"We don't hate all your people, only those who are killing us and trying to take away our land," Shali assured as he stopped Chuncho in the plaza.

An officer promptly stepped forward to offer Rianna assistance getting down from the horse. She looked into Ruminavi's eyes, remembered his previous request that she tell him if she and Shali decided to part and felt shy about putting her hands on his shoulders as he caught her waist and lowered her to the ground. His eyes flickered briefly with interest, but he immediately released her and stepped away. He greeted her formally then turned his attention to his commander.

Shali swung from the saddle, greeted Ruminavi then took Rianna's arm and turned toward his men. Assuming Shali would lead her to a place where she could wait while he inspected the soldiers, Rianna glanced up at him in surprise when he began to guide her closer to the first line of men.

"They might as well have a look at you too. If you decide to stay with me, you'll become acquainted with many of them," he advised under his breath.

"And if I don't stay?" she ventured

Shali didn't answer and not a hint of his reaction passed his features. She wondered if he were only masking his emotions before his men as he led her along the line then privately scolded herself for all the doubts that persistently crept into her mind.

"All male Incas of age are part of our military," Shali began to explain as if he hadn't heard her question and wasn't aware of her misgivings. "The smallest village used to have drills several times a month. Now, of course, they can't do such things in public as we can here."

"What about the people who, though not Inca, were under the empire's rule, the Araucanians, Huarpis, Chimus and others? Are they loyal to Manco and willing to fight the Castilians?" Rianna asked.

"It's true the empire includes peoples we'd conquered," Shali admitted then added, "but conquest never meant the same to us as it does to your people. We always negotiated with them first and tried to persuade their leaders they would benefit from Incan rule. If they weren't persuaded and we had to fight, we were willing to resume talks any time they wished. We never committed outrages against the citizens or their property; and after we'd won, they were allowed to keep their own beliefs, except for customs like human sacrifice or cannibalism. Their leaders continued in their offices, but as subordinates to the Incan king. They found our government more benevolent than theirs had been. Except for a few peoples too recently brought under our influence before the invaders came to have been educated to our way of life, the provinces are willing to fight our common enemy."

Shali led Rianna to an area from which they could watch the men and be out of their way, then signaled Ruminavi to begin the drills.

"And you're commander of them all, Incas as well as the other peoples?" Rianna questioned.

"Manco Capac is the commander and I his highest ranking subordinate in military affairs," Shali reminded, his eyes on the soldiers. "There used to be two hundred thousand in our regular army. We've been reduced to even I'm not sure how few."

"But how could that happen?" Rianna was aghast that an army the size of any in Europe could have been so decimated.

"The Pizarros' deceptions were something we weren't prepared to deal with. We always had standards to live by that made such trickery inconceivable to us. Also, because of the distances we had to travel, having no horses or firearms, we were always at a disadvantage. Not until Manco escaped the Castilian prison were we able to actually go to war. By then, most of our experienced officers had been killed."

Shali paused then commented grimly, "It may already be too late for us, as the legend foretold."

"What legend is that?" Rianna asked fearfully.

A stranger Rianna recognized as the high priest approached; and at the sound of his voice, Shali's gaze finally was diverted from his soldiers.

"It happened just before Huayna Capac, Manco's father, died."

Villac Umu's darkly arresting eyes were on Rianna as he continued explaining: "When the Pizarros' first expedition arrived on our shore, the landing was accompanied by a succession of strange events. Comets flamed across our skies and the moon was surrounded by fiery rings of many colors. There was a series of earthquakes and a lightning bolt struck one of the royal palaces, reducing it to ashes. An eagle, a bird too large and strong to ordinarily be bothered by other birds, was chased by several smaller hawks into the square at Cuzco. While it hovered over the plaza, the hawks killed it; and it fell almost at the feet of a group of Incan nobles. Though Huayna Capac never saw them, he swore that white-faced, fair-haired strangers would be the destruction of our empire, that they would destroy the Incas themselves if we resisted them. He died soon afterward. When Atahualpa was in Hernando Pizarro's hands, he saw similar heavenly events and knew in advance of Pizarro's sentencing him that he would be killed. It is said that night Atahualpa wept like a child for his people."

Rianna stared at the priest, not knowing what to say.

"You're the woman of Shali's vision," he concluded.

Rianna made a little curtsy in respect to the empire's most eminent priest. "I'm honored to meet you," she murmured.

"And you're as fearful of what I told you about Huayna Capac's prophesy as you're curious about Shali's vision," Villac Umu surmised. "After you're finished here, will you come to my house to share the midday meal? You'll learn the answers to many of your questions."

Rianna looked at Shali.

"Villac Umu is one Inca you don't have to worry about accepting your presence among us. He did that even before I met you. He came today to let you know it," Shali told Rianna then turned to the priest and said, "You've surprised me by coming now, but I often think you enjoy putting me off balance with your unexpected appearances."

Villac Umu smiled. "I do what's necessary and at the proper moment. As military commander you needn't anticipate the land's priest, only its enemies." He inclined his head and withdrew.

After the priest had left, Shali said, "Though I've known Villac Umu all my life, he's still a mystery to me. He is, though, a person to be trusted. You'll get used to his surprises in time."

"Is what he said about the prophecy of the Incas' destruction true?" Rianna asked.

"Villac Umu always tells the truth," Shali replied then returned his attention to the soldiers' drills, his attitude cutting off other questions she was anxious to ask.

Rianna noticed Ruminavi standing with some officers a short distance away watching her; and she wondered what he was thinking, if he'd heard any of the strange conversation with Villac Umu. Ruminavi's dark eyes revealed nothing of his thoughts and his expression was impassive.

When Shali and Rianna arrived at Villac Umu's house, a servant escorted them into the garden and said the priest would join them soon. The garden, like Manco's palace, was at the lip of the plateau Machu Picchu was built on and was protected by a low wall made of stones. Shali went to the wall and leaned his forearms on it as he gazed at the mountains beyond the chasm of the valley that surrounded Machu Picchu.

He was silent a long, thoughtful moment before he said, "Villac

Umu has purposely given us this time alone. He wants me to tell you about my vision.''

Rianna came a step closer until she was at Shali's side. "You really saw me before we met in the marketplace?"

"When I came home to find my house in Tumbez, all my city burning, I was outraged and disheartened at the same time. I stared at the fire feeling as if I would burst with frustration and anger. Then I saw the vision of you in the flames. You were weeping, seemed to scream in anguish then collapse. I'd never seen a vision of any kind or seen a woman of your people until then and had no idea who or what you were. I wondered if I'd finally gone mad. All I knew for certain was you were the most beautiful creature I'd ever beheld and in as much torment as I. Later, I asked Villac Umu about what I'd seen. He thought you were a human being, not a spirit, that at the moment of my vision you were suffering too because of some other fire; and our souls were somehow briefly united because of our emotions. When I spoke to you in Nicasio's garden and you told me about your parents being burned at the stake, I realized my vision was of you watching them die.''

He turned his head to finally look at Rianna. She was staring at him, stunned by what he'd said. Then she lowered her eyes. He saw her lashes fluttering, blinking back tears and knew she was newly grieved at this memory of her parents' death. Rianna finally looked up at Shali, her lashes starred by tears; and he wordlessly put his arms around her.

When Villac Umu stepped out of his door, that was how he found them, clinging to each other in the sunlight, surrounded by mountains and the arching blue sky. He silently waited until they parted before he approached.

Rianna didn't remember, until she and Shali were taking their leave, that Villac Umu hadn't said a thing about Shali's vision all afternoon. Then she realized Shali was right. The priest had always intended that Shali tell her and had merely provided the circumstances in which they could discuss it. She felt as if the priest had gently, subtly nudged them closer all afternoon.

Chuncho's movements, as he slowly paced through Machu Picchu's streets, formed a soothing rhythm in keeping with Rianna's finally peaceful heart. She leaned back against Shali's chest and admitted, "When you said this morning you wanted me to go with you through your day, I was upset because I didn't know what would be expected of me. But after talking with Villac Umu, I feel calmer."

"He has that effect on people. I'm glad we spent the afternoon with him, though I'd planned to acquaint you with the city so you could go about as you please while I'm on my mission." He sighed softly and added, "Maybe Tavi and Ruminavi can take you around while I'm gone."

"I would rather see it with you. Why not take me yourself tomorrow. Or will you be too busy?" she asked.

"I leave tomorrow at dawn."

Rianna looked up at Shali in surprise. "You're going *that* soon?"

His eyes lowered to meet hers as he said regretfully, "When we reach the palace, I'll have some preparations to make before I can come to you."

Disappointed, but not wanting to be a bother about it, she asked, "How long will you be delayed?"

"It's impossible to guess," he admitted as his arm around her tightened. He bent his head to brush her hair with his lips, adding, "I'll come as soon as I can."

While Rianna was bathing, Tavi inquired about her day; and she mentioned spending the afternoon at Villac Umu's house.

Tavi was obviously impressed at the priest's taking an interest in her mistress and said happily, "You have the king's approval, the queen's friendship and the high priest's support, a position any Inca would be grateful to hold. See how unnecessary all your worries were?"

"Now I have a new worry," Rianna sighed as she got out of the bath. At the maid's sudden sobering, she explained, "Shali is leaving tomorrow to free the Incas imprisoned at a mine."

Tavi wrapped Rianna in a drying cloth as she reminded, "Lord Shali is military commander. You must accustom yourself to his going on such assignments."

"Could *you*?" Rianna asked.

The girl was silent a moment before confessing she, too, would worry. Then she said, "Lord Shali has safely completed many dangerous missions. You must remember that."

"I saw him kill a man with a kick, how he led the Incas at Xaquixaguana Pass, but I can't help thinking this time could be different," Rianna admitted.

"Maybe your fear is magnified because you have so many other things on your mind," Tavi suggested. "Though you're less worried now about meeting our people, you still have to decide whether or not to stay at Machu Picchu forever. Forever is a long time to make a decision about and you want to make the best choice for both you and Lord Shali."

"You're right," Rianna agreed as Tavi helped her into a robe. "It's hard to decide anything when so much emotion is involved. I often feel so confused I begin to resent it. I shouldn't be asked to choose. I'm not wise enough."

"Sometimes things change and we're forced to do what destiny dictates so there's no decision to make," Tavi said.

Rianna agreed, thinking how convinced she'd been she had to stay with Alonso then been forced by circumstances to leave.

"You love Lord Shali and he loves you. If you make your decisions with this in mind, I think you must choose rightly," Tavi pointed out.

Rianna sighed. "I met you only this morning, but I feel as if we've been friends a long time."

"Maybe that's because you're used to being with people you had to be cautious of before you dared trust them enough to open your heart."

Rianna realized the girl was right again. She looked up at Tavi. "Perhaps you've given the answer to many of my questions. I've been looking at all of you suspiciously because I'd learned too much about lies and betrayal from others."

Tavi inclined her head in silent assent. "Now, my lady, would you like me to bring your evening meal? Or perhaps just some fruit while you await Lord Shali's return?"

"He probably won't have time to eat before he comes, so I'll wait for him," Rianna decided. She smiled wryly and said, "I have a taste for a glass of wine, but Incas don't make it. I guess that's one habit I'd have to learn to set aside if I stay here."

"When Lord Shali was in Spain, he learned to enjoy your wine. Now, when he comes back from a raid, he sometimes includes a shipment of this beverage among the weapons he captures. One of the llamas that came from Tumbez with me carried some of this wine at his request. Shall I get some for you?" Tavi offered. "Perhaps Lord Shali would like it when he comes."

Rianna had listened in disbelief and growing humor; and when Tavi was quiet, she smilingly commented, "So there is something he likes about Spain besides me, its horses and weapons."

Tavi returned the smile. "There may be even more he liked about your land, though how he feels about horses, weapons and other such things can't compare with how he feels about you."

Rianna blushed and advised Tavi to get a goblet of wine for her.

Later, Rianna recalled Shali's mentioning he'd never known what a Spanish woman looked like until he'd seen her in his vision. She wondered how he could have been to Spain yet never laid eyes on a woman. Speculations tumbled through her mind and she resolved to ask him. She went out to the terrace and looked at the mountains to see how late it was.

The snow on the peaks glowed orange with reflections cast by the sunset on the other side of the valley while the slopes were streaked with purple shadows. Rianna wondered what was keeping Shali. Thinking of his preparations for the next day renewed her fears about the danger that lay ahead for him. Telling herself, as Tavi had suggested, that Shali had been on many military assignments and had returned safely didn't reassure Rianna. Her impatience for him to come to her grew in proportion to her worry and she paced the apartment restlessly

The mountains wore a pale patina of moonlight before Tavi opened the door to Shali's knock. Rianna was surprised to see Topa, carrying an armful of clothes and personal items, following on his master's heels.

Shali immediately embraced Rianna. "I didn't take time even to bathe. I had Topa bring my clothes for tomorrow."

"I suppose you didn't have time to eat either," Rianna surmised. Shali admitted he hadn't and she said, "Tavi, could you see if anything is left in the palace kitchen so we could have dinner after Lord Shali's bath?"

"Have someone else get the food, Tavi," Shali quickly amended the order. "I'd like to talk with you about some things while I bathe."

"*While* you bathe?" Rianna echoed in surprise.

Shali's lips curved in a smile. "Topa will assist me, but I want Tavi to tell me the news from Tumbez." He bent to kiss the tip of Rianna's nose, explaining, "I've bathed many times before with female servants present." Noting Rianna's beginning flush, he added, "I'm not embarrassed about being naked."

"I'd noticed," Rianna murmured, her blush deepening.

Shali released her and turned away to signal Topa to follow him into the bath. Tavi approached Rianna.

"May I go now to find someone to bring your meal?" she asked.

Rianna nodded distractedly. While Tavi was gone, she decided to pour a goblet of wine for Shali and surprise him with it. When she brought it to him, he had already cast aside his uniform and his hands were full of soap. He bent a little so she could put the goblet to his lips.

"I'm glad you thought of it," he said gratefully.

Rianna watched while Shali resumed soaping his chest and remembered the night at the hostel when he'd coaxed her into bathing with him. He looked up, saw the golden sparks rising in her eyes; and the corners of his mouth tilted with the ghost of a smile.

"Since that night in the hostel, every time I've taken a bath I've thought of you," he said softly then promised, "We'll repeat it some other time."

"Am I so transparent that you read my mind?" she asked.

"It might make many things easier if you were," he admitted, "but what you were thinking just now is something that would reach out like a hand to touch me even if I didn't recognize that look on your face, *chinita*." He paused, gazed at her thoughtfully a moment then asked, "May I have more wine?"

Rianna brought it and Shali bent to sip from the goblet then turned his face to brush his lips to hers. He caressed her a moment without really kissing then straightened.

"That's all I dare now," he said then began down the steps into his bath. After Shali was in the water, he leaned his back against the pool's side, let himself sink deeper and closed his eyes. Though he seemed to be relaxing, he was thinking about how he would like Rianna to come into the pool with him.

Finally, he said, "Maybe you should move into my apartment." He opened his eyes to regard her as he reasoned, "It's awkward for me to go back and forth and we would have more time together. I have a larger suite than yours so we would be comfortable. But perhaps you'd rather preserve a certain amount of privacy."

"There's more than that to think of," she said softly, though her heart was urging her to agree.

"It's true my position often brings messengers to awaken me in the night. Officers come and go at sometimes inopportune moments," Shali pointed out. "Think about all these things; and if you want to move, *chinita,* let me know." He closed his eyes. Though he wished she would immediately answer yes, he was determined not to press her.

When Tavi entered the room, Shali opened his eyes to look at Rianna and warn, "I'm going to ask Tavi a lot of questions about Tumbez you'll probably find tiresome."

"If I get tired, I'll leave," she replied, thinking she would like to stay awhile simply to fill her eyes with Shali.

He began to talk to Tavi in Quechua. Rianna couldn't follow all of their conversation, though she understood enough to know it was about the situation in Tumbez and people he knew there. Finally, Rianna decided to get a cup of wine for herself and left them. Watching her go, Shali switched his conversation from Tumbez to Rianna. He wanted to know how Rianna had reacted to her day, what Tavi thought was troubling her and if she had confided in the maid.

By the time Shali had finished his bath, the servant Tavi had enlisted to bring their meal had arrived. After the dishes had been arranged on a low table set beside Rianna's bed-mat, Shali dismissed all three attendants.

"It would be more convenient to have our servants sleep in the adjoining room, as in my apartment, rather than have to send a guard down the corridor if we need them," he noted as he sat down on the bed. He patted the place beside him, inviting her to join him.

"Do you have rooms in your apartment for both Tavi and Topa?" Rianna inquired as she sat down.

"Several others as well, if I had a family or needed that large a staff," he answered casually, though he was trying to tempt her into moving.

She reminded, "You avoided making love so as not to influence me. Don't you think my living with you would influence me quite a lot?"

"I've changed my mind," Shali said. He put down his goblet and looked at her while he said evenly, "I'm going to do all I can to influence you—at least, all you'll let me, *chinita*."

Rianna didn't know what to say to that.

He smiled, as if they were discussing something of only passing importance, then began dinner.

Despite their physical closeness, the sudden silence was like a wall between them; and Rianna searched for something to say. Finally, she thought of her previous question. "I remembered earlier that you'd gone back to Spain with Pizarro to act as one of his interpreters." Shali nodded and she asked, "Yet you never saw a Spanish woman until that vision of me? How could you have seen none while you were in Spain?"

"I was *supposed* to act as interpreter, yet found there was nothing for me to interpret. I was little more than a prisoner," he replied. "I had comfortable quarters, but was locked into them and saw only various officials who came to visit me. I soon realized I was there merely as evidence Pizarro had reached Peru. That I quickly learned more Spanish surprised everyone; and a monk was sent to see how much I was capable of absorbing. I continued to learn, even to read and write, which was, I suspect, something of a miracle in their eyes. They seemed to think the Incas are a barbaric, unintelligent people. I was only a boy; so how could I explain that my language was more complicated than theirs, that my people are mathematicians, artists, physicians, astronomers and builders? I didn't know more about the customs of your land than you did about Incas when you first came here, but I learned more about them than that monk ever intended."

"Then you really do understand how I feel," she concluded.

"Yes, I know, *chinita*." Shali raised his eyes to hers. "The difference is you've been given a choice to remain with us or return to your people. I wasn't always so sure I'd be sent home; and if not, what could I have done about it?''

He took another sip of wine, noted that Rianna had finished her meal and was rinsing her fingers in a bowl of scented water. He moved closer, took her hand and lifted it to his lips. Eyes fixed on hers, he began to lick the water from her fingertips with a slow deliberation. He heard her catch her breath, watched her eyes become great orbs of light.

Feeling as if she were a candle softening near the heat of Shali's fire, that her ability to decide anything was melting and running into a shapeless pool of molten wax, Rianna whispered, ''Is this part of your plan to influence me?''

''Only a very small part,'' he murmured. ''If fortune is with me, I'll have almost a year before you'll need to decide. If you stay until the next Day of Wedding, because you have no parents, Manco and Coraquenque will have to arrange your marriage to someone.''

He turned his face into her hand and kissed it, his tongue making a spot of fire, like a star, burning into her palm. His mouth moved to her wrist then slowly up the inside of her arm to her elbow, where her sleeve stopped him. Shali raised his head, his face skimming over her bosom as he sought the edge of her robe and nuzzled it aside, pausing to kiss and nibble at her shoulder as he bared it. Shali moved to the other side, inching the robe off Rianna's shoulder until it would go no farther. His hands curved around her arms and, as if they couldn't bear to leave the touch of her skin, remained. He dipped his head to her waist, where a sash held the robe together.

His eyes, slanting against his cheeks, blackly glowing, looked up at Rianna while he undid the sash's knot with his teeth. Shali's face brushed aside the folds of material and his tonguetip caressed her waist, criss-crossed her midriff with kisses that swerved to circle her breasts. His hands around her shoulders tightened, drawing her down and under him as he leaned over her.

Rianna gazed up at Shali. A keen aching suffused her; but he slowly sat up to, with seeming calm, reach for the goblet on the table beside the bed and take a sip.

He returned to cradle her shoulders and lift her head to the goblet he held to her mouth. She merely wet her lips with the wine. Shali replaced the goblet on the table then, in one lithe movement, got to his feet.

Rianna avidly watched as he walked slowly, almost lazily to the wall that held the lamps and blew out all their flames, but one. The moonlight reflecting from the mountains beyond the terrace shimmered on his body when he untied his own sash and let the robe slide from his shoulders into a heap on the floor then returned to her. Shali knelt on the bed-mat and just looked at Rianna. His face was in shadow and she couldn't see his expression. She waited a long, trembling moment then, not knowing it was what he wanted, that she come to him, she got up to kneel before him.

Shali's hands on Rianna's shoulders lightly coaxed her nearer. Now she could finally see the passion that tightened his features and lit his eyes to dark fires.

He bent to kiss the soft curls that framed her temple. His lips moved over Rianna's cheek to her mouth and caressed it lingeringly, searchingly, for a moment before his hands slipped to her waist. Shali's arms curved around Rianna and pulled her to him. The sensation of suddenly being clasped against his hard body was like a flame igniting the sparks he'd lit in her. She clung to Shali, her body melting against his, while one of his hands moved to her hips molding her to him for the fiery moment his lips seemed to devour hers before he released her and moved away to sit on the bed-mat and again wait for her to come to him.

Rianna turned toward Shali like a magnet swings to the north. A dark glimmer went through his eyes as he watched her. When he bent closer, she expected their lips to meet with the same passion as before; but his mouth fondled hers with a restraint that was even more piquantly sensual. His hands at her waist didn't pull her to him, but ran lightly up her sides to the curve of her breast and rested there, while his mouth seemed to taste rather than kiss her. She tried to catch his lips, but they eluded her. Rianna's hands on his shoulders moved to the back of his neck and tried to draw his mouth to hers; but his strength mocked her efforts and he leaned a little farther away.

"I don't want to be hurried tonight," Shali murmured.

Again he put his mouth to hers, nibbling at her lips, lightly brushing them from corner to corner. Then his tonguetip stroked her mouth, coaxing it to soften, before he finally covered her lips with his. Rianna felt as if a current were streaming through her veins setting her blood on fire. His mouth grew harder, his kiss even more compelling, scalding her with its intensity until she felt as if she couldn't breathe. She gasped and didn't care, felt his shiver and knew he was further inflamed by the sound she'd made.

They sank to lie on their sides. Shali's leg curved around Rianna's hip drawing her to him, pressing closer. The hard warmth of his body was a fire dancing into her skin, merging with her. One hand weaving into her hair held her face to his, while his other hand resting on her hip lifted. His fingertips lightly, teasingly, ran along her side.

Shali knew the impulses rising from the depths of Rianna's body were overtaking her, that she was tensing to restrain them; and he whispered, "Don't try, *chinita*. Never think you have to withhold yourself from me."

Rianna opened her eyes and saw that Shali's were flickering with his fires as well as lamplight. "But you said you didn't want to hurry," she breathed.

"I won't," he murmured.

Shali's hips moved in lissome invitation and ignited a hot, new flame in her. She trembled; her senses rose to a higher level. Again he moved persuasively, slowly, this time not ceasing, deliberately compelling her to follow where he led. Rianna shuddered, but Shali didn't let her pause. Forces too powerful to resist overwhelmed her like a wall of flame burning away her reason, stripping her to the soul, until she cried out and was consumed by passion.

Time flashed by like a shower of sparks that slowly dimmed and died to leave her in peaceful darkness. The fires of Rianna's instincts seemed to have devoured all her sensations and minutes passed before she became aware that Shali was as before. She opened her eyes to look questioningly at him.

He said softly, "You've never been quite that way and I took pleasure from watching and feeling what was happening to you."

An airy, almost ethereal music drifted into the room from the terrace and caught both their attention.

Rianna turned her head to wonder, "What is that? A flute?"

"Panpipes. Someone on the mountain is playing to his flock,"

Shali replied. He listened a moment then said, "Maybe he's playing for himself more than for his animals. It's a love song."

"It doesn't sound like a happy love."

"The song is about lovers, who are separated and long to be together again," he explained

"It's beautiful," she murmured.

Shali drew away. "You'll be better able to hear it on the terrace."

Rianna was startled. "But you—"

He got up and offered his hand. "I'm not here merely because you're a beautiful female who excites me, but because we're sharing ourselves," he said as he caught Rianna's fingers and drew her to her feet. "I'm pleased you like our music and I can share that with you too."

Surprised that Shali was willing to pause in their love-making to listen to a shepherd's pipes, she went with him to stand at the terrace's threshold. His arm slid around her waist and drew her against his side.

The gently poignant music floating in the star-silvered night seemed to hold the essence of every lover's soul; and when Shali's fingers tilted Rianna's face toward his, the moonlight shimmered in her tear-glazed eyes.

"It's more than the music, isn't it?" he asked quietly.

Rianna was silent a moment before she admitted, "Tomorrow we'll be separated like the lovers in the song and you'll be in danger."

Shali knew, though his friends at Machu Picchu would mourn deeply if he were killed, they'd become too accustomed to his safely returning from missions to be alarmed before he left. Because his family, even Yupanqui, had died before he'd begun to fight in earnest, no one had ever wept over the possibility of his dying. That Rianna would weep for worrying over him endeared her to him even more.

He turned to draw her into his embrace and tilted his head to rest his cheek on her curls. A rush of tenderness flooded him while he soothed, "The guards at the mine are used to tormenting starving Incas in chains, not well-equipped and conditioned soldiers. It won't be so very great a danger for us, *chinita*."

She put her face against his shoulder and he felt her tears on his skin as she murmured, "You can't brush aside danger I know is real. I can't forget it or that I'll miss you just as that song speaks so feelingly of lovers parted."

He felt the shiver that ran through Rianna and murmured, "That song is a favorite of the shepherds and you'll hear it many times. You're getting chilled from the night. Come back inside where it's warmer."

Rianna looked up at Shali. "What will I do those nights ahead when lying in bed won't warm me because I'll be alone?"

"If you decide to leave Machu Picchu and me, what will keep you warm?" he whispered and bent to kiss her.

Intending it to be a tender gesture, thinking he'd banked his fires, Shali was surprised at the heat of the flames that sprang up in him. His arms tightened and clasped Rianna to him as his mouth eagerly caressed hers. He heard her breathless gasp and felt as if Machu Picchu was rocked by a tremor. Momentarily letting his senses fill with the wild need she'd awakened in him, he scooped her up in his arms and lowered his head to continue kissing her as he walked to the bed. But when he knelt to lay her down, he hastily withdrew and turned his face to the breeze coming from the mountains, breathing deeply while he waited for his temper to cool to a more manageable level.

Rianna watched Shali's dark lashes lower to cover the hard glitter of his eyes, the taut lines of his profile softening. When he turned again to her, his face was momentarily shadowed; and she couldn't see that his eyes were clear, he had regained his old control. He leaned toward her and she expected the swift return of his passions; but his mouth moved softly over hers, kissing her slowly, lingeringly, as if it were the first kiss he'd experienced and he was absorbing every tingle it sent through him. The warmth of his lips brushing hers renewed the aching he'd already aroused in her and she tried to capture them.

With a quick movement, he turned his head to brush aside her hair and follow the pattern of her ear with his tonguetip. She shivered and her fingertips on his waist tightened; but his mouth moved down her neck, over the slope of her shoulder and left a series of soft little nips on her arm. His lips paused at the inside of her elbow and his tongue marked it with fire then slid to her breast. His lips were so subtly enticing she shivered. The exquisite sensation grew in power until the impulses running through her gathered into a sweet ache low in her body. She wove her fingers into his hair, mutely asking for his kiss;

and he tilted his head to gaze at her a moment. She could see the knowledge of what he was doing to her in his eyes.

Suddenly she wanted to fling his teasing back at him, cause *him* the sweet torment he gave her.

Shali sensed Rianna's impulse and covered her mouth with his smile. He leaned only close enough so, when he shifted his shoulders, his chest lightly brushed her bosom. Her breasts bloomed with buds of fire, but the caresses were so tantalizing she arched her back to get closer. He wouldn't allow it; he moved a breath away to continue the provocative caresses even as he delicately licked her lips.

Rianna tried to pull Shali to her; but he reached up to grip her arms, drew them free of him then press them to the bed by her shoulders so she was helpless while he continued his seductive movements. When he felt her quivering, almost writhing under him, Shali let himself sink to cover her, knowing full well the sensation of his body against hers did anything but calm Rianna. His mouth finally claimed hers. Rianna's lips were warm and silkily moist and reached for Shali's as hungrily as if she would tear his soul from his body. He knew the demands of her mouth were an accurate measure of the impulses flashing through her; and though he felt his desire surge dangerously higher, he allowed his passion to scald his being.

Shali caressed her lips with a certainty that inflamed Rianna more. His mouth crushed hers, possessed even her breath; and not until he heard her whimper, did he tear his lips away and whisper, "You will have to take what you want from me."

Rianna's lashes flew open. She didn't know what to say. He withdrew and sat up to reach for the goblet on the table beside the bed. Though triumph gleamed in his eyes, she couldn't see them as he pretended to sip the wine, using the moment to rebuild his control.

Finally, he said tightly, "I've tried to coax you to reach out to me, but you never do that until after you're so maddened by desire you have no choice. A man likes to be touched and caressed too, at least this man does." He paused then finished firmly, "Now I want *you* to make love to me. If you won't, I'll leave you at dawn exactly as you are."

Rianna's body seemed to be occupied by another will that directed her to get up and kneel behind Shali, press herself against his warm back, incline her head to kiss the side of his neck while her arms slid around his lean waist. Her cheek impatiently brushed his hair aside; she traced the whorls of his ear with the tip of her tongue. As her fingers began to explore his chest, he leaned more firmly back against her. She caressed him more insistently, slid her hands over his taut midriff, saw his closed eyelids squeeze tighter as she measured the sensitivity of the side of his waist. When her fingers explored the joining of his leg to his body, he turned his face to nuzzle her cheek; and the texture of his hair brushing her temple was its own caress. Rianna's hand moved to the inside of his thigh and his body tensed at her touch. She felt as if the impulses delighting Shali sped along her own nerves. She even more avidly teased him. A small sound escaped Shali, as if he suppressed a moan; and he tipped his head back so it lay on her shoulder.

Shali turned his head, opened his eyes to look at Rianna. They were black and glittering with passion as he whispered, "Enough."

He lifted his head and turned to lie beside her, closing his eyes in an effort to rebuild the will she'd been rapidly eroding away. But Rianna bent over him and he felt her softly moving mouth begin to caress his lips, her teeth brushing his skin with maddening effectiveness.

"*Chinita,* stop *now,*" he said. The hard edge of his tone revealed how highly he was aroused. She withdrew and he tried again to regain his composure.

But her hands began to run over his body, clinging to his skin as he had so often done to her. Rianna's kisses followed the flaming path her fingertips had left; her breath felt like a shower of sparks on his skin.

"I must have a moment, *chinita,*" he whispered urgently.

She ignored the plea. She watched his face tighten, his body tense, begin to move with the waves of desire pulsing through him. He opened his eyes to stare at her accusingly.

"Isn't this what you wanted me to do?" she breathed.

His expression didn't soften and she moved away to lie at his side, knowing she'd driven him to the point of helplessness. Instinct told her he wasn't used to being swept away by another's will.

Shali was silent, motionless for a moment as he tried once more to lift his mind from his body's silent demands; but his nerves had already been captured by urges too compelling to resist. Suddenly he sat up and turned to kneel over her.

"I can bear it no more," he said breathlessly, the singing of his own impulses making him unaware he spoke in Quechua.

Though he wanted to restrain himself, he found, as soon as he was part of her, his desire soared into a compulsion, a frenzy that stopped his ears so he never heard the love words tumbling from his lips, that unfocused his vision until she became a golden blur beneath him. Uncontrollable forces gripped him, the surging of his body blasting away the last crumbling barrier of his will with the force of a lightning bolt that exploded from his depths.

He lay still at last, listening to the deep thunder of his own heartbeat, without the strength to lift his head or try to quiet his breathing.

With the gradual refocusing of Rianna's mind came the knowledge that Shali had never meant it to be this way; and she finally asked apprehensively, "Are you angry with me?"

Shali turned his head to gaze at her. Though his face was still filmed with moisture, dark fires were again rising in his eyes.

Stunned at their meaning, she breathed, "How can you be this way?"

He rolled over and propped himself up on his side to consider her question a moment before answering, "I was taught the situation, not the love-making, is right or wrong. I was never told being satisfied once was all I should expect." He reached out to tentatively caress her lips with his fingertip. "I have no barriers, no guilt about any aspect of making love, as I've come to realize your people often do. I've been free to find my own limits." He moved closer to brush his mouth to hers and whisper, "I've discovered, with you, I seem to have none."

It wasn't until the dawn shining from the mountains filled the apartment with crimson light that Shali rose from Rianna's side.

Topa, coming hurriedly to awaken Shali, found the commander already bathed and dressed, combing his hair while Rianna tied his sash. Tavi neared Rianna's door carrying their breakfast only to see them step into the hall ahead and begin toward the courtyard. She hastily put down the dishes and followed, noting with satisfaction that their arms were wound around each other's waists and her tall master inclined his head as he walked to speak softly into the ear of his love.

The courtyard was filled with soldiers already assembled and waiting. Shali turned to Rianna, dreading the moment of this parting more than he'd dreamed possible. An echo of the shepherd's piquant song floated through his memory and he realized he'd never before known the full meaning of it.

"Will you think about moving to my apartment, *chinita*?" he reminded.

Rianna nodded, but kept looking steadily up at him. Her wish that he could stay was a soundless plea in her eyes.

Shali bent closer to murmur wonderingly, "How is it possible, after what we've shared all night, that I still want you? I've never felt quite this way before."

"Not even with Yupanqui?" she asked softly.

He shook his head slowly then leaned down to kiss her lingeringly before them all. As if he dared not dally longer, couldn't bear the piquancy of his emotions, he suddenly turned away and walked swiftly to Chuncho.

Shali spoke tensely to Amaru, swung up into the saddle then signaled to the others and turned Chuncho toward the gate. Shali couldn't resist glancing back at Rianna, saw her lips soundlessly form the Quechua words for love and felt as if his soul left his body to embrace her again.

Rianna couldn't force herself to smile at Shali or hide the fear haunting her eyes. Despite his assurance the assignment held no extraordinary dangers, she knew he was wearing a thickly quilted doublet over the tunic that normally was his uniform because it offered more protection. She thought of the mail the Castilians donned for battle and knew Shali's doublet couldn't prevent a crossbow's bolt or a mace's spiked head from shattering his life.

After the soldiers had filed through the palace gates, Rianna hurried to the stable to get Wayra. She mounted the horse and trotted out of the courtyard into the city. The early risers of Machu Picchu were surprised to see a girl with long, golden hair, skirt pulled up to her thighs, riding her horse astride like a man through the dawn-washed streets.

But Rianna finally didn't care about the stares that followed her. She rode to Machu Picchu's entrance and watched Shali and his men descend the winding trail into the silvery mist rising from the valley floor.

chapter **19**

The pair of horsemen picking their way along the winding, rock-strewn path paused when one of them lifted his arm in warning.

"What is it now, Macizo?" his companion asked with forced patience. They had stopped several times since entering the narrow canyon.

Macizo turned in his saddle to look back uneasily. "I swear, Zangoro, I heard hoofbeats."

"It's the echoes of our own horses," Zangoro replied, though his voice had an edge that revealed his own misgivings.

"I hear them all the time, but these sounds only come once in a while. They're cautious and slow, as if someone trailing us doesn't want to get too close and occasionally by mistake lets his horse walk in a place he can be heard," Macizo insisted.

Zangoro reined his horse sideways across the path to study the way they'd come. "If it's Incas, who want to kill us, they don't have to be cautious; and they don't make mistakes in this terrain. This could be the opportunity we've been looking for. Maybe they want to talk."

"I feel like a fly caught in a web waiting for the spider to decide which part of me to eat first," Zangoro said gloomily. "I was a fool to agree to go on this job."

"The money Alonso offered was why we got into this," Macizo reminded then asked, "Do you think I should call out to them?"

Zangoro regretted agreeing to trek into the mountains looking for an Inca willing to carry a message to Manco Capac, but said, "Alonso is mad to think he can sell Manco that apparatus the Incas call an eternal light."

"The lamp is sacred to the Indians. Alonso thinks they'll pay a fortune in gold for it or he wouldn't have gone through so much trouble to get it out of the temple grounds in Cuzco. If he's caught trying to sell it to the Incas, he'll be arrested."

"He won't be in as much trouble as we will if Shalikuchima's archers fire on us in this canyon," Zangoro reflected. "Call to see if anyone is out there—and *please* sound as friendly as you can manage."

Macizo's frown deepened as he jerked his horse around to face the path they'd followed. Though he still saw nothing except the rock walls and scrub, he called in Quechua, waited a moment for an answer that didn't come, then hailed in Spanish.

One of the two riders hidden behind an outcropping of stones heard the shouts and threw back his monk's hood to listen more carefully. The sun fell on red-streaked brown hair, a face whose deep tan was as incongruous for a teaching monk as the bitterness clouding the amber lights in his tawny eyes. "Do you suppose they're Incas or Spaniards, Mariano?"

"You speak Quechua better than I, Francisco," Mariano said slowly. "Does it sound right to you?"

"One call isn't much to judge from, when they're using the dialect of the peasantry," Francisco commented. He waited for another brace of calls before deciding, "I think they're Castilians, but I wonder what they're doing in this wilderness." He pulled up his hood and arranged it well forward so its shadow disguised his sun-darkened face as he commented, "If they're honest, they won't mind the company of holy men; but even if they're up to mischief, they aren't likely to harm monks."

"If you're wrong and those riders are Shalikuchima's, we'll be fortunate they don't fill us with arrows the minute we show ourselves," Mariano grimly reminded.

"They have little reason to love Spaniards, but they tend to respect others' religions. That's why I decided we should wear these cassocks," Francisco advised then picked up his reins. "Are you ready, Brother Mariano?"

"As ready as I'll ever be, Brother Francisco," Mariano answered, though he wished the skirt of his robe didn't make the sword he wore beneath so difficult to get at.

Holding their crosses aloft in one hand and guiding their horses with the other, they nudged the animals back onto the path. Though Mariano was relieved to see his own countrymen ahead hastily crossing themselves at the sight of the crucifixes, Francisco was disappointed not to have made contact with the Incas.

"Monks, just what we need," Zangoro said under his breath. "Be careful what you tell them."

"I'll let *you* figure out a story. I just hope we aren't going to have to listen to sermons all the way," Macizo softly replied. He privately wondered if he were glad to meet the harmless monks or would rather have taken his chances passing Alonso's message to the Incas and have it over with.

"Their cassocks are from a teaching order," Zangoro advised. "I suppose they're missionaries."

Macizo didn't answer. The monks were too near.

"I'm Brother Francisco and my companion is Brother Mariano," the taller of the monks said as he made the gesture to give them his blessing.

Zangoro respectfully inclined his head a moment, then replied, "My friend is Ramon Macizo and I'm Juan Zangoro." While greetings were being exchanged, Zangoro decided having the monks with them could be an advantage. The Incas might be less likely to attack an innocent traveling party that included two monks.

"I'm surprised you're so far away from a settlement," Zangoro noted.

"God sent Brother Mariano and me to find the Inca, Manco Capac, and try to convert him. We hope to save the heathens' souls and end the bloodshed between our peoples," Francisco explained.

"That's a dangerous undertaking," Macizo commented.

"We believe it's less dangerous to do this alone than have a military escort, which would arouse the Incas' anger and fear," Francisco replied.

"We've made a vow and are doing God's work," Mariano sonorously added.

Zangoro considered this a moment then offered, "Perhaps you'd like to travel with us. It might be safer."

"Though your company is welcome, God will protect us all," Francisco reminded.

"Yes, of course," Macizo hastily agreed.

"May I inquire where you're going?" Francisco asked.

Macizo glanced at Zangoro, who said smoothly, "Our destination is the same as yours and our purpose similar. We're looking for Manco Capac or, at least, someone who will carry a message to him."

"A message of good will and peace, I hope?" Francisco inquired.

Zangoro had already decided to tell the monks the truth, but to make their cause seem inspired by charity, not profit. "Are you familiar with the meaning of the apparatus the Incas call the eternal light?" he asked.

Well aware of the lamp's significance to the Incas, Francisco decided a monk wouldn't be very enthusiastic about a pagan religious symbol. He said coolly, "The lamp that used to be lit at Cuzco as a sign the Incan empire would prosper?"

"The maidens of the sun temple tended the light constantly; because, if it went out before the ceremony the following year, it was an omen of disaster," Zangoro noted

"A deplorable heathen custom," Mariano remarked as he knew a monk would.

"Yes, indeed," Zangoro agreed. "But the light was extinguished when Pizarro captured Cuzco and the state of the kingdom now seems only to prove the validity of the Incas' beliefs. They hold great store in the lamp and are furious our people have it. The man Ramon and I work for thinks it's impossible to negotiate peace with people who are so angry and hopes offering Manco Capac the lamp as a gesture of friendship might cool his temper."

Francisco seemed to consider their reason, which he knew was a tale. So valuable an item would never be passed to the Incas unless a great deal of gold was also exchanged. Finally, he said, "I admire your courage in carrying this message to a hostile people and applaud your employer's good intentions; but I can't encourage paganism."

"Nor I," Zangoro agreed with seeming enthusiasm. "My employer only hopes an indication of friendship can open the door to peaceful negotiation."

"Perhaps emphasizing that the Christian God is giving them peace rather than their notion of a sun god might help," Francisco said thoughtfully. "Your employer must be very devout to go through so much trouble and not ask payment for so valuable an item."

"If you'd tell me your employer's name, I'll include it in my prayers," Mariano offered slyly.

Macizo decided Zangoro had told the monks too much of the truth already. Afraid to identify Alonso, he quickly said, "We apologize, Brother Mariano; but we can't tell you his name. Before we left Cuzco, we made a solemn vow to be silent."

Francisco inquired a little sternly, "This vow included even God's servants?"

"Forgive us, Brothers," Macizo seemed to plead.

"Surely you understand the necessity of our employer's wanting this unofficial gesture to remain secret," Zangoro said.

"Your employer hasn't gotten the government's permission to do this," Francisco concluded, though he realized their secrecy was to avoid being arrested for obtaining unreported gold from the Incas.

"It's a personal gesture," Zangoro said, his mind racing to find some explanation the monks could accept. "Our employer's son, his only heir, was badly wounded during the battle at Chupas and his recovery seemed hopeless." Once Zangoro had thought of the lie, he embroidered it with convincing skill. "Our employer begged God to spare him so the family name could continue and promised to try to stop this war. His prayers were answered and his son recovered. Now he hopes that giving the Incas this lamp and softening their anger is how he can fulfill his promise."

Francisco struggled not to reveal by word or gesture his contempt for the tale and finally managed to comment solemnly, "Your employer is an honorable man. I'll include his cause in my prayers. God will surely know who he is."

Francisco avoided mentioning Macizo and Zangoro's mysterious employer for the rest of the day. Despite his curiosity about the man's identity, he didn't want to appear so interested that Macizo and Zangoro would be suspicious he and Mariano weren't monks. Mariano understood Francisco's silence and followed his example.

Francisco's first concern was locating his sister; his second was killing Alonso Falla, the man who'd brought about the Alavas' downfall. He knew memories of that night in Madrid almost two years ago would haunt him the rest of his life.

Alonso had appeared nervous all evening. He'd taken his watch out of his waistcoat for so many surreptitious glances Francisco had begun to wonder if he'd wear out his pocket lining. Alonso had suggested they return to the Alava house much earlier than it was his habit to end an evening then had fairly pushed Francisco out of the fashionable gambling salon's door. Alonso's behavior had irritated Francisco, but aroused no curiosity; he'd assumed Alonso planned to visit a woman. When Francisco had entered his family's courtyard and seen Agustín sprawled on the cobbles, Cecilia weeping, Rianna and Jacinta struggling with soldiers, he'd somehow known Alonso was at the bottom of it; but coming to his family's aid had been his first priority. When Francisco had felt the lance tear into his flesh, he'd thought his life had come to its end. After the soldiers had left him for dead, Mariano, the Alavas' footman, had carried him to a deserted shepherd's hut in the hills, bound his wounds then returned to Madrid to get some of Francisco's clothes, and the emergency funds he knew Agustín kept in a strongbox in his study.

After weeks of hovering at death's threshold, Francisco finally had begun to recover and beg for news of his family. Mariano knew nothing could be done to save the Alavas after they'd been arrested, so he'd decided it was more merciful to tell Francisco they'd all been killed. Not until after Francisco was strong enough to bear the even more grisly truth did Mariano admit Agustín and Cecilia had been burned at the stake, Carlo drowned in the well and Jacinta had died of torture in prison. When Francisco learned that Rianna alone had escaped the Inquisition and had fled to Peru with Alonso, he had been wild to follow; but Mariano had restrained him until he had more strength. By then, Mariano had learned enough about Alonso's nefarious dealings to support Francisco's insistence that Alonso had destroyed the Alavas so he could steal their money and carry off Rianna.

Mariano had no family and was disgusted with the situation in Spain so he decided to accompany Francisco to Peru to hunt for Rianna. Already owing the man his life, Francisco couldn't refuse; but he wouldn't treat Mariano like a servant. They'd long since become friends and now pledged their partnership in whatever the future held.

They'd arrived in Lima during Almagro's revolt against Pizarro and had to wait until the turmoil had quieted before they could learn Alonso and his party had gone to Cuzco. Francisco and Mariano had followed only to discover Rianna and her maidservant had fled Alonso and vanished. That Rianna had stabbed Alonso gave Francisco little comfort. He could imagine why she'd done it.

Because Francisco had become so fluent in Quechua during his previous trip to Peru, he'd understood the gossip between Incan peasants in the marketplace and learned that a mysterious woman they described as having golden hair and eyes had suddenly appeared at Manco Capac's hidden stronghold. They called her a handmaiden of the sun and hoped she'd been sent by heaven to help the Incas resist their enemies. Francisco couldn't imagine how Rianna had managed to find Manco Capac, but he knew that description fit no one else in Peru, so he and Mariano decided to find the Incan king's secret palace. Francisco resolved that, if Rianna were a prisoner, he would try to find a way to rescue her. If that was impossible, he was determined to at least be with her.

The next day Macizo returned from a foraging trip to report seeing the tracks of a large body of horsemen. The Castilians hurried to examine the trail.

Francisco stooped to study the tracks then straightened to gaze into the forest a moment before looking at Zangoro and asking, "Are you aware of any Spanish commanders in this area?"

"No, Brother Francisco," Zangoro admitted.

"Though it's possible these tracks were made by adventurers, it seems unlikely in so remote a place," Francisco noted.

"No one we've heard of has come this direction," Macizo said then quickly added, "We did some checking before we left Cuzco."

"That was wise," Francisco agreed, though he realized Macizo and Zangoro must have made their inquiries in the same back-alley taverns as Mariano.

"If we're near the Incan stronghold, I think we should prepare ourselves for the possibility of attack," Zangoro warned.

Sure it would be informative to hear these brigands' confessions, Francisco offered, "Perhaps you would like to make peace with God before we proceed farther, my sons?"

"We confessed before we left Cuzco," Macizo hastily answered then more carefully added, "There are few temptations in this wilderness when even one's mind is occupied with a noble cause."

Francisco agreed, though he was disappointed. He was silent a moment, thinking that, if he and Mariano lived to reach Manco Capac and Zangoro and Macizo didn't, he might offer the Incas information about the eternal light in trade for Rianna. Finally, he said, "Perhaps you should tell Brother Mariano and me the message you're to give Manco Capac. If God takes both of you and Brother Mariano or I survive, your mission might yet be successful."

Mariano understood Francisco's purpose and urged, "It would be a worthy effort to lay before God's throne as your final deed in life."

Zangoro felt as if he'd been backed into a corner, though he knew the monks' offer made sense from a clergyman's point of view. Because he wanted to collect his pay, Zangoro carefully avoided mentioning Alonso's name as he said, "My employer couldn't know how long it would take us to find an Inca and pass his message to Manco Capac or if Manco would respond, so he arranged for someone to stay in an abandoned post house and wait. Manco's messenger is to meet with this man to arrange how the lamp can be transferred."

Francisco surmised they would then negotiate the lamp's price, but he asked, "Where is this post house?"

"It's a small one for Incan couriers," Zangoro replied. "It's less than a day's ride from where we are now."

"Please draw a map in the dust so we can describe its location if we need to," Francisco suggested.

Zangoro was reluctant, but reasoned as long as he'd already said this much, he must continue the pretense of being concerned about his employer's seemingly noble cause. He inwardly sighed as he unsheathed his sword and began to draw a map with its point.

Shali had ordered a scout to trail after his soldiers to make sure no one followed them back to Machu Picchu's valley. When the scout came galloping along the column of soldiers, Shali raised an arm to halt his men.

The scout stopped his horse so abruptly Shali was pelted by the bits of dirt spewing from its hooves. "Four Spaniards, two of them monks, found our tracks at the edge of the forest and are following," the scout reported.

"Surely they can't have followed us all the way from the mine!" Shali burst out then quickly asked, "Are you certain they're alone?"

"I circled around, but saw no one," the scout answered.

Shali turned to look at Amaru and said grimly, "Maybe that night we investigated a report about an intruder and found none we were mistaken. Perhaps he escaped and is returning with friends."

"Why wouldn't he bring Pizarro's army?" Amaru puzzled.

"Maybe they aren't sure they've found Manco's hidden city and want to take a second look." Shali remembered the scout's saying two of the men trailing them were monks and considered the religious zeal of the priest who had tried to convert his own father as inducement to being strangled rather than burned to death. He said angrily, "Maybe they think they're going to persuade Manco Capac himself to their beliefs. Whatever their purpose, they're much too close to Machu Picchu. We'll have to turn back and drive them away before they discover the entrance to the valley."

Shali reasoned that four men traveling in hostile territory would be horrified to find themselves circled by so large a force of Incas and would be likely to surrender without resistance. As they neared the area the Spaniards were in, Shali ordered his men to surround the intruders but not attack. He hoped to frighten them away.

Mariano, riding beside Francisco, saw the horsemen quietly advancing through the sun-dappled forest and put his hand on his hip, reaching by habit for his sword, only to suddenly remember it was under his cassock. He turned to Francisco to warn him, but Francisco had pushed back his hood and his sun-streaked eyes were shifting warily over the Incas.

"Zangoro, Macizo, stop your horses," Francisco said quietly. The sudden lifting of their heads, the tension stiffening their backs made him warn, "Don't do anything to rouse them."

The Castilians reined in their mounts and waited uneasily in the oppressive hush. Finally two Incan officers and a pair of guards nudged their horses forward. The guards had arrows fitted to their bows, but the weapons were held at an angle indicating they wouldn't shoot unless necessary.

Noting that Zangoro and Macizo had pistols in their hands, Francisco said grimly, "Don't raise those guns, whatever you do."

Zangoro glanced back at Francisco, his eyes frozen with fear.

"*Peace*, my sons, that's what we're here about," Francisco reminded.

The Incas stopped twenty feet away and sat looking silently at them. Francisco noted they carried a full complement of weapons and their quilted doublets were dusty and torn. He realized the smears on their uniforms were dried blood and knew they'd already taken part in a battle they seemed to have won. Though the officer nearest Macizo and Zangoro had noted their pistols were primed and cocked, he gazed at them as calmly as if he'd already decided they were too puny an enemy to worry about. Though the Inca said nothing and never took his eyes from the Spaniards' faces, Francisco felt as if he'd given an order to his subordinate.

"Lay down your weapons and you won't be harmed," the lesser officer said in heavily accented, but understandable, Castilian.

"If we put down our guns, you'll be able to shoot us at your pleasure," Macizo said tightly.

"We will not do it," Amaru answered.

"Have you forgotten our purpose is to talk with them?" Francisco reminded Macizo. "We have the chance now. Do what they ask."

"We're safer if we talk with our weapons ready," Macizo insisted.

"Why don't they lay down their bows?" Zangoro declared.

"Stay out of this, Brother Francisco. We know what we're doing,"

Macizo snapped and nervously ran his eyes over the Incas waiting among the trees.

"They're all around us," Francisco advised. "Your guns could kill only two of them at most. The others would fire on us then."

"I think that big one nearest us is the Inca we have to convince," Zangoro said. "If he knows he'll be the first to die, he might be more inclined to see our point of view."

Francisco began, "Don't be a fool . . ."

But Zangoro and Macizo had lifted their guns to aim at the officer. Simultaneous with their move, the pair of Incas raised their bows and so quickly fired their arrows Francisco saw only that suddenly their bowstrings were quivering. He looked incredulously at Zangoro and Macizo and saw their guns slide from their hands. He knew the arrows had already killed them though they slumped for a moment before falling from their saddles. Francisco noticed the Incas had immediately fitted new arrows to their bows and he dared not move a muscle as the officers nudged their horses closer.

When Francisco found himself staring into the narrowed eyes of the commander, he burst out, "They weren't going to shoot! Didn't you hear Zangoro say he only meant to frighten you?"

"Those two soldiers don't speak your language," the Inca answered quietly. "They reacted instinctively at a threat to me."

"Instinctively?" Francisco exclaimed.

"They train for a situation like this till their reaction becomes instinct," the Inca said.

"Is your life worth all of ours?" Francisco cried.

"My men think so," the Inca coolly replied.

"Who are *you*?" Francisco demanded.

"Shalikuchima."

Francisco's mouth snapped shut. He dared say no more. Mariano, too, was struck mute by this news as they stared at the Inca whose name was as feared as Manco's.

"My men will tie your companions to their saddles so you can take their bodies back with you," Shali advised.

"You'll let us go?" Francisco breathed.

"Amaru said we wouldn't harm you," Shali reminded them. "If you'll go south, in a few days you'll enter Xaquixaguana Valley and find Cuzco.'' When neither monk spoke, but only stared at him, Shali asked, "You are lost, aren't you?"

"No, not really," Francisco stammered. "We're just surprised you're offering us directions."

Shali's eyes took on a glint of amusement, but he inquired, "What are you doing in this remote area?"

Francisco finally regained enough composure to answer more calmly, "We have a message for Manco Capac."

The surprise that flashed through Shali's eyes was instantly quashed. "I'll take the message," he advised.

Remembering he was impersonating a monk, Francisco said, "I've made a holy vow to give the message only to Manco Capac."

Shali's eyes hardened, looking more than ever like volcanic glass. "Don't you realize, if you see where Manco Capac is, he can't allow you to leave and tell others about it?"

Francisco thought of Rianna, whom he now was certain was being held prisoner, and said firmly, "My fate is, as always, in God's hands."

Shali turned his eyes to the second monk. "And you?"

Mariano felt as if he were giving away his life, but he said as resolutely as Francisco, "I, too, made a vow."

Shali knew that, once one of these Castilian holy men made a promise to their God, they seldom betrayed it and he commented, "Maybe, if you can convince Manco Capac you'd keep a vow of silence about where he is, he'll let you go; but I doubt it." His eyes, carefully running over them, saw no weapons; and he turned away to give his men orders.

Francisco noticed Shalikuchima never had to raise his voice to summon even the most distant of his men. They seemed so attuned to his wants they anticipated him. When Shalikuchima merely turned his eyes to glance at one soldier, the man came swiftly to his side.

Francisco commented, "It appears he wasn't boasting when he said his men held his life in higher regard than all of ours."

Mariano remarked, "He wouldn't have to brag—even if he were inclined."

Shali paid the monks no further attention until his men were ready to leave the area. Then he asked Francisco and Mariano once again to give Manco's message to him. When they refused, he impassively directed them to ride behind him and two lesser officers, who flanked him.

They paced through the forest, which grew denser at every turn, until it was so tangled Francisco wondered that even the Incas could find their way. Because of the lush growth, neither he nor Mariano had any idea they were passing through the entrance of Machu Picchu's valley; and they were surprised when the forest ended as abruptly as if a line had been drawn that the shrubs and trees couldn't cross.

Ahead were rolling hills dotted by thatched roof cottages, cultivated fields and groves of fruit-laden trees. At the valley's center rose a vast plateau, like a mountain with its peak sliced off, with a city built at its crest.

Francisco gazed at the road that wound up the mountain's terraced slopes and breathed, "It's a city built in the sky! How beautiful it is! Look, Mariano, some of those lower clouds must be brushing the rooftops."

Shali glanced back at the comments he'd overheard, but his expression didn't change, and he never spoke as they rode through the valley and began up the road to the city.

The townspeople gathered in the streets to proudly watch the soldiers pass and stare curiously at the pair of strangers. Some of them called to the soldiers, asking the results of their mission. Although none of the men in the ranks dared answer, Francisco was surprised to see their stern commander turn his horse toward the crowd, bend to lift a shaggy-headed boy from the street, speak quietly to him, then set the boy back on his feet. Francisco saw the smile that momentarily transformed Shalikuchima's face and knew he'd given the child news of a victory. The boy ran into the crowd shouting happily.

After they'd dismounted in the palace courtyard, Shali led Francisco and Mariano, escorted by guards, into the entrance then to the great hall, where Manco and Coraquenque were seated on cushions conferring with several men.

Recognizing the scarlet and gold fillet on Manco's head, Francisco needed no urging to follow Shali's orders to bow low; but he noticed Shali's gesture of obeisance was as humble as his and Mariano's.

Manco Capac waved away the ministers he'd been engaged with, looked curiously at the strangers, but immediately asked the commander, "How did it go at the mine?"

Francisco listened with interest to Shalikuchima's report of freeing the enslaved Incas so they could rejoin their scattered families. Because the commander spoke in the most refined Quechua and Mariano couldn't understand, Francisco translated for him.

Though Francisco's whispers were barely more than a rising and lowering of his breath, Manco Capac was aware of them; and after he'd congratulated Shali on the success of his mission, he sternly asked, "Why have you brought these monks to our valley?"

"Your Majesty . . ."

Francisco began to get to his feet, as he spoke, but one of the guards pushed him back down, warning, "Speak only after the Inca Manco Capac commands you."

Manco again regarded Shali.

"They claim to have a message of so great importance they made a vow to give it only to you," Shali explained.

"And these wearers of cassocks *almost* always keep their vows," Manco remarked, sarcasm tinting his tone. His hazel eyes shifted to meet Francisco's and he said in Castilian, "You will explain yourself."

"I'm Brother Francisco and my companion is Brother Mariano," Francisco began.

"Your identity and titles are of little importance at this moment. I know what monks are," Manco interrupted. "Tell me this message you're willing to give your lives to deliver."

Francisco and Mariano exchanged fearful glances.

"You'll kill us?" Mariano whispered.

"What a sad reputation I must have among your people that you speak so," Manco commented then again urged, "Why have you come?"

Hoping to soften Manco's obviously unenthusiastic reception of them by telling him some of the events in the Spanish camp, Francisco began, "Gonzalo Pizarro has returned to Cuzco and the people are so enthusiastic about his leadership they wanted him to take the title of Procurator-General of Peru."

"*I'm* the only rightful ruler of this land," Manco Capac said coolly.

"Yes, Your Majesty. I realize such attempts to usurp your throne must rankle,'' Francisco quickly agreed, ''but I thought you'd want to hear what's happening among your enemies.''

''I haven't forgotten you're one of them,'' Manco noted ominously.

''But, Sire, I'm not!'' Francisco denied. ''I was in Peru some years ago and was appalled at what was happening. I complained so loudly and insistently my life was in danger. I had to leave by stealth and almost died traveling through Ecuador to Panama, where I took a ship home under a false name.''

Manco was startled by this declaration. His opinion of this visitor warmed and he asked more tolerantly, ''Why did you return?''

''It's a long story I'd like to tell you after I finish with the news I've brought, if you'll allow me,'' Francisco said.

''Continue in your own way,'' Manco Capac directed.

Francisco resumed, ''Pizarro refused the title, but that was just a trick to appear benevolent. He wants to rule Peru and knows he has to get rid of you to accomplish it. He also knows he has to do it fast, before Blasco Vela decides to come to Cuzco.''

Manco had leaned more attentively forward to listen. ''Who is Vela?''

''A knight from a place called Avila, which is near where I was born,'' Francisco explained. ''King Charles has sent him with a list of commands Vela is to enforce as Viceroy of Peru. These royal ordinances will free the enslaved Incas and insure they have certain rights.''

''This king of *yours* does not give *my* people their rights—I do!'' Manco declared then added bitterly, ''If I'm not my people's ruler and we must live under the reign of conquerors, we all are slaves, whatever *your* king decrees.''

Francisco lowered his head. ''I know that, Majesty; and I agree.''

Stunned at even one Castilian's acknowledging his right to the crown he'd inherited, Manco leashed his temper and coldly directed, ''Go on.''

''Those who have enriched themselves at Incan expense, don't want Vela in Peru. They've been trying to persuade him to their way of thinking since he landed in Panama; but he said he wasn't sent to debate or tamper with the laws he's bringing, only to see they're obeyed. He's just arrived in Lima and Pizarro is arming against him,'' Francisco said.

"I can understand why Pizarro and others like him don't want Vela to come to Cuzco," Shali, thinking of Alonso, commented. "I can also see why Pizarro would have to secure his place before Vela gets here."

Francisco said hesitantly, "Sire, Pizarro is gathering an army to search out and try to destroy you first."

To Francisco and Mariano's surprise, Manco Capac smiled sardonically. "You needn't fear giving me *that* news. One or another Pizarro has been trying to erase my family from the earth for the last ten years."

"But Gonzalo Pizarro has artillery at Guamanga and has appropriated thousands of Incan slaves to transport it across the mountains," Francisco advised.

Manco looked thoughtful. "We might free those Incas dragging Pizarro's artillery through the mountains and appropriate it for *our* use." At Shali's warning glance, Manco fell silent and regarded Francisco more warily. "Why have you come to tell me this?"

"It is, as I said, a lengthy story I was leaving to the last," Francisco answered.

Manco looked at Shali and noted, "I'm grateful for the victory you brought me, but I can see you're exhausted. Rather than hear all this now, you can go to your quarters and rest. We can discuss this conversation later."

Shali wasn't interested in the monks' personal mission and he was tired. He bowed and backed away, glad to have the opportunity to leave.

After Shali had left the great hall, he considered going to Rianna's apartment then remembered how distasteful a sight he must present in his blood-stained uniform. He decided he would bathe and rest then send Topa to tell Rianna he'd returned. Though Shali was so weary he felt as if his feet were encased with stone rather than his soft boots, his imagination pleasantly drifted over how it would feel to be awakened from a nap by Rianna's kiss.

Shali unfastened his cloak then his sword and dagger as he walked. When he reached his apartment, these plus his helmet filled his hands;

and he nodded to the guard to open the door. But as Shali stepped across his threshold, he was so surprised to see Rianna standing on his terrace that he dropped his equipment with a clatter.

She turned at the sound, a smile on her lips, and raced across the room into his arms.

"I saw your soldiers coming up the road from the valley," she said against his shoulder as she clung to him. "I was just wondering how long it would be until you got here."

"I brought back a couple of monks, who insisted on giving Manco a message, so I was delayed until Manco saw how tired I was and dismissed me." Shali dipped his head to breathe the scent of Rianna's hair. "A moment ago I was so weary I was dragging my feet. Now I'm beginning to feel alive again."

Rianna stepped back to look up at him. "I'll get a cup of wine for you or *chicha*, if you prefer, so you can relax while you bathe."

"If I relax, I'll fall asleep," he noted.

"I'll curl up alongside you and wait," she promised, not knowing she offered to fulfill his daydream of a moment ago.

Shali smiled and again drew her close. "I'll have a cup of wine and a bath now then, later, you," he murmured. After a moment he sighed and released her. "The wine is in—"

"I know where it is," Rianna said brightly. Her smile softened as she added a little shyly, "I learned where almost everything is while I was telling Tavi how to arrange my things."

Shali's lips parted in surprise.

"I hope you don't mind I didn't wait to tell you I decided to move, before I did it." Rianna said and lowered her eyes.

His hands tilted her face to his. "How could I be angry when you've done what I wanted so ardently I thought about it all the while I was away?" He bent to kiss Rianna softly, tenderly, then again put his arms around her and murmured, "I think the—"

"Commander, you're wanted in the great hall!"

Recognizing the voice of the guard, who had entered the room without knocking, Shali snapped, "From now on, you'll wait for permission to enter."

The soldier hadn't expected to find the commander with a lady in his arms but he said anxiously, "You must go to the great hall!"

"You're mistaken. Manco Capac just dismissed me," Shali answered.

"It's not a mistake, Commander," the guard insisted. "Those monks aren't monks! They were wearing weapons under their cassocks!"

Shali immediately stepped away from Rianna, a look of horror on his face. "Have they harmed anyone?"

"I don't know, Commander," the guard answered fearfully.

Already running, Shali snatched up his sword and was out the door. As he raced through the corridors toward the great hall, visions of Manco, Coraquenque or both assassinated by the men he'd brought gave his feet wings.

chapter
20

As Shali rounded the last corner, he saw that several noblewomen and their attendants had gathered in the corridor. Suya was among them, peering fearfully into the room.

"I don't think they've killed anyone yet," she said apprehensively.

"For their sake, I hope not." He brushed past her and into the room.

At Shali's entrance, Francisco shouted, "Shut that door! We don't want anyone else coming in who might get hurt."

Warning those in the hall to stay out, Shali closed the door then took in the situation at a glance. Manco had pushed Coraquenque back against a wall; and though the king was weaponless, he was standing in front of the queen to shield her and their unborn child. Two palace guards were sprawled on the floor while another was facing Francisco and Mariano with a sword. The pseudo monks were each holding another guard with a dagger to his throat.

"We didn't come here to harm anyone," Francisco spoke in Quechua so the soldiers would understand. "This all is a mistake."

Shali cautiously came a little nearer.

"One of the guards saw the sword under his cassock," Manco noted.

"He never asked a question, just raised his spear and tried to run me through," Francisco said quickly. "I almost died on a lance in Madrid and I wasn't going to chance surviving the experience a second time. He and the one who tried to stab Mariano are unconscious, not dead. Call off your guards, Commander, so we can talk."

"Tell me first why you carried weapons into the king and queen's presence," Shali demanded, coming a bit closer.

"How could we have discreetly taken them off with these skirts wrapped around us?" Mariano exclaimed. "We thought we would explain later that we'd posed as monks because we'd heard your people would be less likely to attack us."

"I'm glad you give us some credit for civility," Manco said dryly.

"What about that pair with you?" Despite the questions Shali fired at the men, he was trying to think of a way to overcome the intruders without getting the guards' throats cut.

"We met them the day before you found us. They thought we were monks too," Francisco answered.

"If this wasn't a plan to kill Manco Capac, why did you want to come to Machu Picchu?" Shali asked, inching his way nearer.

"That's close enough, Commander," Francisco said threateningly. Shali stopped and Francisco directed, "Throw away your sword."

"I cannot." Shali was adamant. "If you try to kill my king or queen, I'll have to stop you."

Francisco knew from the hard glitter in Shali's narrowed eyes that he meant what he said. "Then I'll tell you why we came here and let you make up your own mind, though I think we'd better keep holding these guards while I do it."

"Then talk," Shali snapped. "But you should know, whatever your reasons, raising a weapon to Manco Capac is a capital offense."

"We never threatened your king," Francisco declared. "We only defended ourselves from the soldiers."

"Manco Capac doesn't like his personal guards being attacked," Shali advised. "Neither do I."

"We saw how your men killed Zangoro and Macizo. They didn't wait to hear explanations," Mariano insisted.

Francisco said quickly, "Zangoro and Macizo told us someone wants to give Manco Capac the eternal light from Cuzco's temple, and they told us where a man will wait to negotiate the arrangements.'' Francisco noted Manco and Coraquenque's interest and continued, ''They told a tale about why their employer wanted to give it to Manco Capac, because they were convinced we were monks. I'm sure he really wants to sell it.''

''The lamp wasn't the reason you started on the trip to find Manco,'' Shali reminded.

''I'll trade information about the lamp for my sister's freedom,'' Francisco said tightly. ''I've come all the way from Madrid searching for her and I intend to take her back.''

Coraquenque stepped from behind Manco. ''We have no Castilian prisoners here.''

Shali felt as if an alarm were clanging in his ears.

Francisco said, ''Her name is Rianna Alava.''

''Rianna isn't a prisoner. She's my friend and Shali's love,'' Coraquenque said wonderingly. ''But she thinks you're dead.''

Francisco's startled eyes moved to look at Shali more appraisingly. ''Rianna loves you?''

Shali was silent a moment as he studied his prospective brother-in-law. ''How did you learn she was here?'' he finally asked.

''I heard gossip in the marketplace about a woman with gold eyes and hair living at Manco Capac's stronghold,'' Francisco answered slowly. ''I knew it had to be Rianna.''

Coraquenque said, ''The only thing that prevents Shali from marrying Rianna is her making a decision to adopt our people as her own.''

Stunned by this idea, Francisco exclaimed, ''That's only because she thinks she has nowhere else to go!''

Anger at this insult blazed in Shali's eyes and he took a sudden step closer. ''I don't have to force captive women into marriage. If Rianna wants to go back to Spain, she knows a way will be arranged for her.''

Forgetting that Francisco's people held a different view of such matters, wanting to reassure him Rianna was free to do as she wished, Coraquenque blurted, ''While Shali was gone, Rianna had her clothes moved into his suite. He couldn't force her to do that when he wasn't even here.''

Francisco paled under his tan. *Madre de Dios!* It's gone that far?'' In his shock he relaxed his grip on the soldier he held.

The guard dashed aside the dagger and spun around to kick Francisco's feet out from under him. The soldier threw himself over Francisco, but Shali sprang forward and ordered the guard to get up. After he had, Francisco found himself facing the point of Shali's sword. He looked up at Shali's narrowed eyes and thought his hour had come.

"If holding my king, queen and men at bay wasn't enough, the way you've insulted me should be, but . . ." Shali turned his sword aside and offered his hand to help Francisco to his feet.

Francisco got up and stared at Rianna's lover for a moment before saying, "In Spain, seducing a man's sister is cause for a duel."

"This isn't Spain; but if you insist, I'll comply later," Shali answered. "Now I think you should convince Mariano to put down his weapon and release that man he's holding. It would be safer for everyone here, especially Mariano."

After Shali had raced out of the door, Rianna had hurried after him; but she couldn't begin to match his pace, much less hope to catch up with him. She reached the great hall after he'd slammed the door shut. She stood anxiously staring at the closed entrance, unaware of anything but the danger he was in until Suya took her hand and drew her away.

"Shali does not want you to go inside," Suya said. She was surprised when Rianna merely answered that she understood. Suya gazed at Rianna silently a moment, assessed the fear on Rianna's face and finally said, "Shali knows what to do. Don't be afraid."

Rianna recognized that Suya, too, was frightened and trying not to show it. "And you?" she asked cautiously. "You love him too."

A sigh escaped Suya and she nodded. "Not in the same way as you. Coraquenque made me realize Shali was like a shelter in a storm, someone to hold on to when the days were too dark to see my way. I'm sorry for any trouble I caused you."

Rianna squeezed her hand in gratitude. "These times often make it difficult to understand even our own feelings."

"Perhaps now we can be friends?" Suya asked.

"I think it's possible now," Rianna agreed.

The other noblewomen in the hall had known of the rivalry between Suya and Rianna and had privately wondered about the result. After the conversation they'd just heard, they were satisfied not only that there would be peace between the women, but that Rianna seemed gracious enough to deserve the love of Shalikuchima and even the queen's friendship.

They all were startled by the muffled sound of Francisco's falling and Rianna hurried closer to the door to press her ear against the wood. After a moment, she stepped away and her eyes darted from one face to another. "I *have* to know what's happening!" she exclaimed as if begging for their approval.

They looked apprehensively at her. Lord Shali's instructions had been clear when he'd slammed the door on their noses.

"I just can't bear waiting!" Rianna cried and turned to tug at the heavy door. When she stepped into the room, her eyes were only on Shali. Grateful he was unharmed, she ran to him. "I had to know you were all right!"

Shali wordlessly brushed his lips to her forehead, then his arm around her waist turned her toward Francisco. He felt her body stiffen in shock.

Rianna's eyes widened in disbelief; she was too stunned to speak or move for a long moment. Then, with a sob, she ran to Francisco and threw her arms around him.

Shali saw the tears streaming down both their cheeks and wondered with a sinking feeling if Rianna might decide to return to Spain with her brother.

Mariano released the guard he held and put down his dagger.

"Is this possible?" Rianna managed between sobs. "I saw you fall with a spear in you! I saw the soldier pulling it out of your body! *How can you be alive?"*

Manco and Coraquenque approached. Though he still warily kept between his wife and the Castilians, he commented, "It seems he really is her brother."

"I knew it when he challenged Shali," Coraquenque replied. She brushed away her own tears and marched past Mariano to put her hand on Rianna's shoulder. "Come, both of you, and sit down. There is much to be said." She led them to the pillow-seats she and Manco had earlier occupied with their ministers.

Manco, noticing that Suya had ventured into the room behind

Rianna, waved for her to close the door. "Don't let anyone else inside. This is too private for servants to gape at," he directed then asked, "Will you pour *chicha* for us?"

Suya closed the door on the crowd growing in the hall then hurried to get the *chicha*. By the time she had handed small cups of the bronze liquor to the royalty, Rianna had managed to regain enough of her composure to stop weeping.

Francisco, seated beside his sister, was gently smoothing back her hair when Suya offered him their goblets. He looked up at the Inca; and his gaze, captured by the girl's dark eyes, lingered. He was surprised that, despite his emotional upheaval, a pleasant tingle ran through him.

Startled and confused by the snap of elation she felt, Suya hastily withdrew to stand a little away from the others. While Francisco explained how he'd escaped the Inquisition and come to Peru searching for Rianna, Suya avidly listened. She watched his every gesture and expression, even the way his lips moved as he spoke, and wondered about her reaction to him.

Francisco was aware of Suya's gaze and frequently raised his eyes to look at her. Each time he did he felt as if a current arced between them.

Finally, Rianna said, "I just *can't* absorb all this. It's too much."

Gripping her hands in his, Francisco said gently, "It will take a little time for you to get used to having a brother again, as I'll need time to accept your situation with the commander."

Rianna laid her cheek against Francisco's and whispered, "How can I tell you about how I've changed because of what's happened?"

"I know I've changed too in many ways," Francisco conceded.

"Do you remember what the gypsy said at my birthday party?" she asked then saw from his expression he did. She said softly, "It all came true, the evil she predicted as well as my finding a man unlike anyone I'd met. I do love Shali."

Francisco caught her eyes with his and admitted, "I know." He raised his head to look at Shali, who stood motionless and silent. "This has been a shock to me. Though I'll try to get used to the idea of my sister living with you, that your customs are different from mine, it won't be easy. Still, I withdraw my challenge and apologize for insulting you.''

Shali inclined his head to acknowledge the apology, but he wondered what Manco would decide to do about Francisco and Mariano, who had held him and Coraquenque prisoner. Shali could see the king hadn't forgotten the threat they'd presented.

Coraquenque realized Manco's anger had been inspired mostly by fear she'd be harmed and uneasily awaited his decision about Francisco and Mariano's fate. But suddenly, she smiled. Manco looked at her in surprise and she commented, ''This excitement seems to have awakened the prince I carry. I feel his first flutterings.''

In a quandary of happiness and concern, Manco asked, ''Isn't it too soon?''

''I think he's going to be a strong, lively child; and I'd wager, after he's born, he won't be willing to dawdle about anything,'' she said brightly then slyly suggested, ''Wouldn't it be wonderful if, when he first enters the world, the eternal light from Cuzco could be shining over it?''

Manco slowly turned to regard Francisco. ''You know now you needn't trade information for your sister's freedom. Tell me what you've learned about the lamp.''

''What will you do with Mariano and me?''

Manco was silent as he considered the necessity of Machu Picchu's location remaining secret at the same time he knew he hadn't the heart to keep Rianna's brother prisoner much less have him put to death. Finally he said, ''I offer you the same choice as Rianna, unless the situation changes so much none of us has a choice. If you want to leave, you'll be sent in a sealed litter to the isthmus where you can board a ship to Spain; but if you decide to go, you must never return to Peru.''

Francisco absorbed this silently a moment before he looked at Coraquenque and asked, ''Is that lamp *so* important to you?''

Her smile faded as she answered, ''It's sacred to us.''

''You've seen what our enemies are doing to the land,'' Manco put in then admitted bitterly, ''Some Incas have already decided they'll have to tolerate their conquerors, that driving them from our land is impossible. Even if they're right, all Incas will take heart if they know their rightful rulers still survive in this valley."

Coraquenque inquired, "Do you remember the gossip you heard about Rianna in Cuzco's marketplace?"

Francisco recalled, "Though the people, who were talking about her had to be careful so the soldiers didn't hear, they called her a handmaiden of the sun and thought she would help the Incas."

"Did they think I was sent by God?" Rianna breathed.

"It gives them hope for the future and, because of that, strength to bear the present," Manco said.

"Who can say in the longer view what this hope and strength might accomplish?" Coraquenque pointed out. "Maybe, because of it, generations from now Incas will still know what they are and go on trying to be what their ancestors fought to preserve. Who can be sure that even you, a stranger among us, doesn't have a purpose in this? The eternal light promises a future for the Incas. If no one in the kingdom can see it except us at Machu Picchu, the others will still *know* it exists, a bit of fire reaching toward the skies reminding us we're children of the sun."

"I'm sure the man who has the lamp wants a large amount of gold for it," Francisco warned.

"What is gold, that we can dig from the earth whenever we need more, compared to the lamp, which is irreplaceable?" Coraquenque asked.

Francisco inquired, "Is there anything I can use to draw a map on?"

Suya volunteered to find something and Manco nodded permission. When she returned, she was carrying a little pot of paint and had a roll of goatskin tucked under her arm.

As Francisco accepted the materials, their eyes met again; and when Suya backed away, she considered the feelings the tawny-eyed Spaniard evoked in her.

The last time Suya had felt this way had been when her husband was alive, she recalled. Even Shali's gaze hadn't aroused this current in her being. She watched carefully as Francisco bent over the map and wondered how it would feel to have that hand holding the paint stick clasp hers.

After Francisco had finished drawing the map that located the abandoned post house, Manco commented, "It's only two couriers' run from here."

"I know the place," Shali agreed. "It's a good area for a trap."

"This man, whoever he is, doesn't expect me to personally negotiate with him," Manco said. "Unless he tried to follow whoever I sent back to Machu Picchu, there's little he could accomplish by deception."

"They could capture whoever you sent and torture him," Francisco reminded.

"Most Castilians know there's little purpose in torturing an Inca to get information about you," Rianna suddenly recalled. "Nicasio admitted they died with their lips sealed." She paused and shuddered as she recalled Jacinta's screams floating through the prison in Spain then added, "Yet, I wouldn't want to send someone into a trap."

"Any Inca would be willing to risk torture and death to get the lamp back," Coraquenque insisted.

Manco was silent as he thought about the aspects of the situation. Finally, he said firmly, "Though my people are loyal and willing to bear much suffering for me, they *are* made of flesh and bone, nerves and blood. There's a limit to anyone's capacity to withstand pain. We're going to have to forgo the lamp, unless I can think of a way to protect whoever negotiates the exchange."

"I never heard you talk quite this way before," Shali commented.

"Do you think I haven't suffered with my people?" Manco asked.

"Of course not," Shali replied quickly.

"There have been many decisions I've hated to make," Manco admitted. "As much as I want the eternal light back, I don't think it's worth the risk. Perhaps this is part of Pizarro's scheme to locate Machu Picchu so he can destroy my stronghold before Vela comes. If Pizarro thinks he can fight me and win then almost immediately afterward attack Vela, his army must be formidable. I suspect we'd best concentrate on how to free the Incas, who are dragging Pizarro's artillery through the mountains, and get the guns for ourselves."

Rianna had been reflecting on the kind of battle that must result over the artillery. If thousands of Incas were needed to transport the weapons, how many Castilian soldiers must be necessary to direct the operation and guard the Incan slaves? Surely Pizarro knew, if Manco

Capac's spies learned about this plan, he would be tempted to attack. Pizarro's soldiers would be prepared. She knew Shali would certainly lead the Incan army into the treacherous mountains to launch the assault.

"If the situation is so desperate, maybe you should stop fighting, at least, until you've had a chance to get stronger!" Rianna exclaimed.

Manco and Shali looked at her in surprise.

"Forgive my sister's outburst," Francisco hastily said, giving Rianna a warning glance. "It isn't up to us, who aren't even Incas, to tell you what to do."

"There may be merit in her advice," Shali remarked. He regarded Francisco soberly. "You were recently in Cuzco. Did you notice Pizarro's preparations?" he asked then quickly added, "If you don't want to tell us, I can understand."

Francisco was silent, torn between loyalty to his own king and justice, which he considered on the side of the Incas. Finally, he said, "It's impossible not to notice Pizarro's preparations."

"They're *that* extensive," Manco concluded.

"It's as I'd thought," Shali admitted.

Coraquenque turned to put her hand on her husband's shoulder. "Cuzco was our capital city. The most revered of our temples stand there. You haven't seen lately the ruin it's in. Even if we can drive the Castilians from it, so much has been lost it will never be the same. We've been stripped of everything except the lamp. We need to keep *something* to remind us of what we are!"

Shali said bitterly, "Everything I had was taken from me, but I'm still an Inca who knows it."

"Are you saying, then, we should give up, stop fighting them and hide?" Coraquenque exclaimed.

"Manco Capac is the last of the royal line," Shali grimly reminded her. "If he's killed, we're ended as a nation."

Rianna looked at Manco and asked, "May I speak, my lord?"

Manco nodded wearily.

"If Pizarro successfully stormed Machu Picchu, killing you and Shali would be his most important objective," she said quietly. "Even if Coraquenque could escape and your child be safely delivered elsewhere, it would be many years until he'd be old enough to lead your people."

"Perhaps you should consider remaining at Machu Picchu while Pizarro and Vela kill each other. You'll be stronger than whatever is left of their forces," Francisco suggested.

"Meanwhile, the Castilians will destroy everything of ours outside this valley," Coraquenque said disgustedly.

"But what's here will be preserved and the Incas can fight again," Rianna said. "Think of the prince you carry. What he'll inherit may hinge on this one decision."

"Enough!" Manco Capac suddenly commanded. He stood up and took Coraquenque's arm. "The decision is mine alone. I'll retire now to consider it." Then he stalked out of the great hall, his personal guards hurrying after him.

"We should have kept silent. My sister and I have no right to presume to advise him," Francisco observed.

"We said too much," Rianna noted regretfully.

"Perhaps not," Shali said, looking thoughtfully at the doorway Manco and Coraquenque had disappeared through. He turned to Rianna. "My fatigue has gained ground and I feel as if an arrow has been shot through my forehead. Francisco, one of the servants can escort you and Mariano to suitable chambers."

Watching Shali and Rianna go to the door, Mariano remarked, "I wonder what Pizarro would think to see Manco Capac and Shalikuchima so distressed." He looked at the servant, who waited expectantly, then sighed. "Ah well, I have a headache too; but after this day's events, I'm glad I still have a head."

Then Francisco and Suya realized they were alone. He looked down at her uncertainly.

"If you aren't too tired, would you like me to show you around the palace?" she offered and was rewarded by his smile.

"I'd like that very much, Lady . . ." he prompted.

"My name is Suya," she said then added, "You needn't bother with titles."

As they left the great hall, Francisco reflected, "An hour ago I was a monk, who was in grave danger of being killed; and now I'm with a woman, who must be one of the most beautiful of flowers in this garden of Incan blossoms, escorting me around Manco's palace.''

Suya smiled and asked, "Where did you learn our language so well you can give such pretty compliments?"

"Atahualpa taught me a great deal of it," he replied.

Suya stopped walking and turned to stare at him. "King Atahualpa?" she breathed.

Francisco nodded solemnly and resumed walking as he explained, "After Hernando Pizarro captured him at Caxamalca, he whiled away many hours teaching me Quechua. He looked rather fierce to me upon first meeting him; but I learned he was a friendly and kind man. Even Pizarro liked Atahualpa. He taught him how to play chess and they played often. Atahualpa won frequently. I couldn't understand how Pizarro could play a comradely game, drink *chicha* and even laugh with Atahualpa then condemn him to death. But I was little more than a boy then and didn't understand how men can betray each other for politics and greed."

Suya looked up at Francisco and saw his eyes were clouded with pain. "Now that you're a man, do you understand?"

Francisco shook his head. "I think I never will. I suspect I don't want to."

"You aren't like them," she observed.

"If I were, Shali would have taken off my head back there," Francisco commented. He was distracted from his thoughts by Suya's hand creeping into his.

When he looked down at her, she offered, "Maybe tomorrow you would like to see the city outside the palace?"

"I'd like that very much," he agreed, feeling again the pleasant tingle that ran along his nerves when their eyes met.

When Shali and Rianna reentered his suite, he kicked aside the helmet, cape and scabbard he'd previously dropped and called, "Topa!"

The boy hurried into the room and, glancing at the things on the floor, swerved toward them.

"Never mind that, Topa. Prepare my bath," Shali directed then stooped to gather up the articles, sheathed his sword and laid everything on a table. Without a word, he walked out to the terrace.

Rianna followed, wondering if he were annoyed at what she'd said, worried about the Incas or both. He was leaning with his hands on the wall tensely looking at the mountains.

"Are you angry that I spoke?" she ventured.

His eyes flicked to her then back to the mountains. "No, but you should remember Manco is the king first, a friend after."

"You're worrying about Pizarro's plans?" she took another guess.

He sighed. "I'm trying to forget all of it."

Rianna concluded, "You think Francisco's coming may change things between you and me."

"That did occur to me," he admitted.

"Once, when I was a little girl looking adoringly up at my brother, it might have." She leaned closer to kiss the corner of Shali's mouth.

He straightened and turned to gaze at Rianna. "I should know better than to think Francisco can sway your opinions when I have so difficult a time doing it," he commented, though he wondered how much influence her brother would have on her opinion that she wouldn't admit even to herself.

"I *did* move into your apartment and I'm *not* going to move out because Francisco's come to Machu Picchu," she noted.

Shali slid his arms around Rianna and rested his cheek on the top of her head. "There are many things to worry about and I'm too tired to think clearly about any of them."

When Topa announced the bath was ready, Rianna told him they wouldn't need either him or Tavi for the rest of the afternoon; and the servants withdrew. Recognizing that wariness was added to the regret and fatigue in Shali's eyes, she answered his silent question, "I only want to be alone with you."

Shali's eyes lost their wary look; and his lips, softer than sunlight falling on a nodding flower, touched her forehead. Against her skin he whispered, "You have an Inca's understanding in that sun-maiden's body."

They bathed with the innocence of children, put on loose cotton robes, eschewing sashes to keep them closed and lay down.

Feeling so tired he thought he'd immediately lapse into sleep, Shali leaned over Rianna merely for a light kiss. But when their lips met, they unexpectedly clung. He felt a tremor deep within him, as if one of the Andean volcanoes had suddenly awakened. It evoked a quivering response in Rianna that was a heat making the edges of his spirit glow redly.

Surprised at his own passion, Shali withdrew a little and breathed, "This is insanity!"

Rianna, as startled as he, whispered, "It may be madness, but not folly."

Hesitantly, almost experimentally, his mouth reached toward her waiting lips; but the moment they touched, his desire, like a pool of molten lava, seethed higher. Despite his weariness, the kiss was like a live thing growing of its own volition, burning into their beings; and Rianna's gasp was an explosion of sparks behind Shali's eyes. His hands held her face to his, as if she might try to turn away; and he kissed her with a savage force that bewildered him, but wouldn't be denied. Shali tore his mouth from Rianna's and, with a quick, impatient gesture, pushed aside the folds of their robes.

"I want you *now*," he said, his low voice roughened by the fire overcoming him. He felt her arms around his back tighten, her hips tilt as she blindly sought him.

When she made a small sound of delight, a stream of flames raced through him; and he was caught in a firestorm so intense the last threads of his reason were burned away. But Rianna responded with a passion to match his, pulsing with their heartbeats, until their separate beings fused and exploded in a brilliant flare.

His body, at last serene, lay quietly on hers. He felt the throbbing at her temple slowing against his, heard her sigh as her breath evened.

"I don't know what possessed me," he finally murmured. "I never intended that."

"Nor I," she said softly.

Rianna felt Shali's body relaxing, lengthening, growing heavier on hers and knew he was drifting near slumber. She moved one hand on his back and he awakened with a start. He made a small movement, as if he would part from her; but her arms held him close.

"I'm too heavy," he began.

"Stay with me," she whispered.

He didn't move again and she burrowed her cheek into the hollow of his neck by his shoulder. She felt him again relaxing, heard his drowsy murmur near her ear, "There's nothing in life I'll want more than you."

Rianna gently threaded her fingers into the black shadow of his hair as she breathed the warm scent of his cheek. It still reminded her of high mountain valleys and sunny, vaulted skies.

"The scent and the touch of you is sealed in my heart and I am helpless to banish it," she murmured in Quechua, but he'd fallen into exhausted sleep and hadn't heard.

The full moon had risen high in the star-frosted skies, sheathing the mountains with iridescence, giving the moving clouds at their crests the glaze of crystal smoke before Shali awakened. Then the only sign of his stirring was his black lashes parting so the night gleamed darkly in his eyes.

"We still are the same," he quietly noted. "Did you, too, sleep?"

"No," she answered.

He lifted his head to look at her a moment and asked, "Wasn't it tiresome to lie unmoving for passing hours while I slept?"

"Not like this."

Shali laid his hands gently at her temples and touched his lips to hers. Though his heart sang with piquant tenderness, the wild impulses of before had been temporarily sated. He withdrew to lie on his side and, propping himself up on one elbow, gazed down at her.

"I've never before been like that. If Pizarro's army had broken down the door, they couldn't have distracted me," he admitted then added with wry humor, "If that's how I would always come back to you after a mission, it would be triumph, not the battle, that would endanger my life." His slight smile faded with his words when he saw the golden sparks relighting in Rianna's eyes. He said softly, "If we go on that way controlling nothing and you decide to leave Machu Picchu, you'll carry a small bundle with you."

Rianna's answer was to lay her fingers on his waist. She closed her eyes as she felt his muscles under her hand almost imperceptibly tighten with his renewing desire.

Shali touched her lips with a thoughtful fingertip and lingered to caress them until he felt the edge of her teeth brush his skin.

"It wouldn't be that way again," she murmured.

Shali didn't immediately reply. He was remembering the other times he'd been swept away by passion and forgotten about the possibility of a child—at the hostel in the mountains, by the pond in the valley, before he'd left on his mission. He wondered what Rianna would do if she learned she was carrying a baby but wanted to leave Machu Picchu. He wondered if Francisco's arrival might influence her more than she realized. Before her brother had come, she'd thought there was no one to go back to, that a life in Spain without an inheritance, family or husband offered little more than a struggle for existence.

Finally, Shali asked slowly, "If you were to decide you couldn't live with my people, would you leave though we'd had a child?"

Rianna said vehemently, "I don't want to think about such things now!" She turned her head away even as she tried to push aside the idea.

"Did you think that never occurred to me?" He turned her face again toward his. "To prevent accidentally binding you to me with a child, I must remember it every minute we're making love so I can restrain myself for a safer moment." Knowing that to speak of this now might make her withdraw, he carefully gauged the emotions behind her eyes and recalled, "Do you remember my saying I would influence you in every way I could so you'd decide to stay?"

Because Shali had never spoken like this before, Rianna suddenly was suspicious. He had, she reminded herself, already fathered a son by Yupanqui. "Does that mean you might not try to avoid our conceiving a baby?" she asked reproachfully.

"No." He turned away to lie on his back and gaze at the ceiling. "This afternoon, as several times before, it could have happened; and we must face the possibility. Would you return to Spain with an Incan child? How would you explain it?" He was silent for a long moment before concluding softly, more as if he were speaking to himself than Rianna, "Maybe you'd remain at Machu Picchu long enough to bear our son or daughter so you could leave the baby behind."

"Please, Shali, don't say such things!" Rianna burst out as she sat up. "I'm beginning to wonder if, while I'm caught in passion and helpless to refuse, you *would try* to begin a child."

Shali was discouraged; she seemed to have come to the very conclusion he'd wanted to negate. His eyes moved to look at her from their corners. Rianna's silhouette against the stars beyond the mountains buried its face in its hands. He said gently, "I promise I won't do it on purpose; but, *chinita*, there's always a chance it could happen no matter how I try to avoid it."

Rianna's silhouette lowered its hands and turned to look down on Shali. He recognized Rianna's uncertainty and grasped her arms to gently pull her closer. "Haven't you come to know me well enough to trust my promise?"

"I was foolish to say that," she apologized.

"Whatever I pledge, I'm not Viracocha," he said quietly. "If anything should result from our love-making, I want you to understand I can only do what's possible. I don't want you to condemn me later because of it."

Rianna nodded. "I know."

Shali wondered what she'd say if such a thing did happen, but he didn't want to think about the possibility himself. It was too painful. Shali sat up, sliding his hands under Rianna's arms, around her back, fingertips curving over the tops of her shoulders. He tilted his head across the space between and his mouth traveled slowly over the perimeter of her lips, brushing her skin with so light a touch she automatically reached for him, her body swaying closer; but his hands wrapped over her shoulders held her back.

"Are you certain you trust my promise?" he asked.

"Coraquenque taught me how sacred an Inca's word is by staying with me when she didn't have to, though she must have suspected she was carrying Manco's heir," Rianna answered.

Shali realized she wasn't convinced *he* would keep his word as faithfully as Coraquenque; but he noted, the fact that she was willing to put herself in his hands despite her doubts was a measure of her love. He wondered how he could dissipate any clinging suspicions she might have about his motives without also making the problem seem less important. There was, at the moment, only one thing he could think of to do. He drew her close and lay his cheek against hers while he considered his idea; but he was distracted by the sensations of Rianna's body warmly molding itself to him, her head turning, her mouth softly nuzzling his skin asking for his lips.

He moved away and stood up, drawing Rianna to her feet with him. Unaware of Shali's purpose, she gazed at him, waiting. Dipping his head, Shali let his kisses languorously trail along her neck then explore the curve at the beginning of her shoulder. He felt her move nearer; and his hands slid forward so his thumbs could make little circles on the sides of her breasts that matched the patterns his tongue was tracing in her ear. When he heard Rianna's breath quicken, he gently angled her shoulder toward him, let his kisses slide into her hair then down to the nape of her neck. With a quick, almost impatient gesture, his face brushed her curls aside.

Shali's nibbling lips slowly moved to the side of her neck and down her arm. His eyes raised to watch Rianna's face while his tonguetip lightly stroked the inside of her elbow then ran along her arm to her wrist and again paused before teasing her palm. Then he straightened.

Rianna looked questioningly up at Shali. When his fingers threaded into the hair at her temples, she tilted her face toward his, again seeking his kiss, her body swaying across the space between. This time he didn't elude her.

Shali's lips touched Rianna's at the same moment their bodies met. She wrapped her arms eagerly around him; and when his mouth took hers, she avidly returned the caresses his smoldering desire ignited to sudden life. His kiss challenged, commanded Rianna to find within herself passion to match his. A tremor went through her that answered his silent call and his desire rose even higher. When she responded with the same urgency, he felt as if a thunderclap rocked him. For a moment the power of his desire dimmed Shali's purpose and his mouth searched hers with a pliant heat that mocked any thought of denying the urges that drove him. His body seemed to shudder and Rianna clung to him, feeling as if she were possessed by his passion as well as her own. When she gasped, the small sound finally penetrated his reason. Shali tore his mouth from Rianna's to bury his face in her curls, to wait unmoving while his fire lowered to a smaller, steadier flame.

When he drew away, she opened her eyes and saw he was watching her. Though she wondered at the thoughts that left paths through the starlight reflected on his eyes, she recognized the meaning behind their silvery gleam.

Shali again leaned closer; and anticipating the ardor of before, she was surprised that he only nibbled at her. As his lips continued their delicately maddening caresses, she moved against them, trying to capture his mouth. Failing, she caught her breath in exasperation; and when she did, his lips firmly covered hers. A line of sparks streaked through Rianna's blood; but Shali's flattened hands grasped the sides of her temples to hold her still while, with prolonged tenderness, he kissed her eyelids, cheeks and forehead. The unhurried, lingering caresses reached a sultry depth she hadn't known she contained. Rianna became aware of a gently pulsing need that accepted the subtle sensations he offered in place of the wild impulses of before. She encouraged him by pursing her lips; but his tongue surprised the corners of her mouth with little darts of fire.

Because she'd stopped demanding, Shali released her, though his mouth still moved lightly over her face to her temple, as he turned her, then into her hair when her back was to him. No longer sure what he intended, Rianna leaned hesitantly against him only to feel his fingers slide around her sides to cup the swell of her breasts. While he fondled her, he tilted his head to flutter his tonguetip along her neck. A fresh stream of delectable sensations rushed through her. Every place he touched he seemed to leave clusters of tingling sparks that seeped into her body and set every pore alight. Aching with desire, wanting to burrow under his skin, she leaned even more tightly against him.

"Do you understand what I'm doing?" Shali whispered.

A little whimper of delight was his answer and he knew his purpose was lost on her. Resolving that it soon would be unmistakable, he shifted his grasp and lifted Rianna. Then, as if she weighed no more than a child, in an easy motion he knelt to lay Rianna on the bed-mat, continuing to cradle her in his arms as he bent to brush his mouth to hers.

He felt her trembling with need for his kiss and covered her lips with his, deliberately building her rising passion until she was so insistent he felt his own control crumbling. Shali released her and reached back for her hands to gently, but firmly, break her hold on him.

Rianna sank down to stare helplessly up at him. "You asked if I understand what you're doing,'' she recalled then added vehemently, ''I think your purpose is to drive me mad!''

Shali didn't reply, though a smile hovered at his mouth's corners as he bent over her. His lips moved languidly along her jawline and she tipped her head back while his tongue slid up her throat then over her chin to rest lightly on her mouth. But he kissed her only once, as if somehow in tribute to her persistently seeking passion before his lips left hers to circle her breasts with kisses. The shrinking spirals he was making finally concentrated on her nipples, whose crowns of sparks had begun to dim. He relit them.

At last he straightened. His eyes' dark fires revealed that the rising levels of his own passion equaled hers, but he gave neither of them respite.

Shali's tongue flicked down her body to her waist where he dropped a line of soft little bites on her abdomen before he suddenly moved to her feet. His tongue explored the sides of Rianna's ankles with piquant sensuality then lingered behind her knee. She trembled with delight as Shali kissed her thighs, his lips so subtly caressing that, when the edge of his teeth softly brushed her, it was a surprise. A sharp fire surged through her, but his hands moved to grasp her hips and held her still.

''Please, Shali, end this now,'' Rianna begged, not realizing she spoke in Quechua.

He withdrew, but said nothing. When her eyes opened to look imploringly at him, he moved to kneel over her hips; and a new streak of flame shot through her blood.

Rianna reached up toward Shali, certain he would tease her no more; but though his eyes were blackened by desire, he did nothing; and she wondered at his deliberate restraint. Torn by conflicting emotions, unable to resolve anything, she closed her eyes then felt Shali's weight shifting and him begin to become part of her.

She had no choice but obeyed her instincts and unabashedly reached for the fulfillment he offered. Shali's impulse surged forward to take her now without restraint, even if a child resulted from it. He checked himself, but couldn't prevent the shudder that ran through him she mistook for his surrender.

The supple motion of his body became waves of fire that seared her mind and emptied it of thought. Intently watching her, Shali knew she was at the edge of her endurance; and though his body throbbed with the forces racing through him, he paused, waited for her ardor to subside then deliberately inflamed her more. Rianna's sharp little gasps became breathless entreaties not to stop, but he did. When he felt her shudder, softly cry out and knew she could bear no more, he gave her release; but he kept his eyes open, fixed on her. Though he felt as if the world outside that room had fallen away, he leashed his own impulse.

Rianna's awareness returned gradually and with it came the stunning realization that, as she'd earlier accused, Shali had deliberately driven her to mindless begging; but he'd withheld himself. Her eyes flew open to stare at him in awe.

Shali's body was rigid with tension and filmed with moisture. He had tipped back his head and was breathing deeply. When he finally raised his head to look at Rianna, the intensity of the fires still burning in his eyes shocked her.

"You wanted to show me you'd keep your promise," she whispered.

He lifted one of her golden locks and, with his eyes steadily on hers, touched the curl to his lips in silent answer.

Coraquenque had said nothing more to Manco about risking dealing with a Castilian for the sacred lamp. She'd known there was no purpose in trying to persuade him. Whenever he was as troubled as he was over this latest round of problems, he'd always made it a point to decide nothing and had sought seclusion while he cleared his mind.

Immediately after leaving the great hall, as she expected, he bathed and dressed in the most simple of his garments. She knew he intended to go to the temple of the sun, to remain alone with the temple closed to everyone except Villac Umu until he could find peace. Coraquenque was certain that, because of the withdrawn mood Manco was in as he bathed and the gravity of the decisions he faced, he was likely to remain in the temple for several days and nights—maybe even a week—enough time for her to obtain the precious lamp.

Manco left for the temple at sunset, but Coraquenque waited until the shadows in Machu Picchu's valley had merged into solid darkness before she called Amaru, one of Shali's most trusted officers, and Hailli, the most devoted of her personal attendants, to the royal suite.

"You'll have to temporarily demote yourself, Amaru, to the rank of a common soldier; and we, Hailli, must disguise ourselves as virgins of the sun," she instructed. "No one else can know what we're about to do; for they'll report it to Lord Shali, who will disturb Manco Capac."

"*You*, my lady, will dress as a maiden of the sun temple?" Hailli asked in dismay.

Coraquenque patted her flat abdomen and noted, "There's not yet a hint of the child to betray I'm not a virgin. What would be more suitable than two temple maidens negotiating for the sacred lamp it's their purpose to attend? Bringing one guard for protection is reasonable."

Amaru, thinking with a shudder of what Lord Shali would say to this plan, asked, "What about the royal heir? You'd be placing him in as much danger as yourself!"

"We'll have to take every possible precaution to keep the heir safe. If we, at any time, have the smallest suspicion a trap has been laid or perceive a hint of anything at all being amiss that will endanger the heir, we'll forget the lamp and return to Machu Picchu."

"Royal lady, these invaders too often find the virgins of the sun temple so alluring they've—" Amaru stopped. It was too degrading to the queen to mention such despicable things as multiple rape.

But the queen was less reticent. "The maidens the Castilians took weren't acting as Manco Capac's messengers to negotiate for a precious holy object that could bring them a treasure in gold. I'll make it clear to the Castilians that no other messengers will be sent if we aren't allowed to return unsullied to our people. Then they'd be fools to satisfy their lust with us when they can have their choice of the women they've already captured," Coraquenque said bitterly.

"We might be followed back to Machu Picchu. This could be a plot to locate Manco Capac's stronghold," Hailli warned.

Coraquenque recalled, "When Manco Capac and I had to flee Tambo, we eluded capture many times. The Castilians, who wandered in the mountains fruitlessly trying to find us, can testify how well Manco taught me to cover a trail."

Amaru began to protest again, "But, royal lady, the danger . . ."

Coraquenque fixed him with the glare that had silenced many officials in the past and his words died on his lips. She commanded, "Quickly prepare what's necessary for our journey to the post house. I wish to be out of the valley an hour before dawn."

chapter
21

Hailli had never ridden a horse so Coraquenque and Amaru had to slow their pace to accommodate her. It was well into the following night before they approached the area Francisco had indicated on his map.

Amaru stopped on a ridge overlooking the post house where relays of Incan royal messengers once had rested. He dismounted and walked nearer the crest of the ridge to look over the situation. The building stood serenely in a clearing, its stone walls and thatched roof bathed in moonlight. Amaru returned and whispered that he wanted to investigate more closely. Coraquenque nodded then watched as he vanished in the darkness.

Hailli looked at her queen's calm expression and wished her heart wasn't pounding so erratically. Though she was afraid for her own sake, Hailli was terrified for Manco's wife and unborn child. It wasn't only devotion to the royal family that motivated her; it was love for Manco Capac.

Hailli's parents had served Huayna Capac, Manco's father; and she'd lived in the palace all her life. Though any of the royal sons would have been a good king, Manco Capac had always been the one Hailli had favored.

Like Atahualpa, he'd been intelligent and commanding even as a boy; but he also was warm and generous. Like Huascar, he was calm-tempered and thoughtful; but in battle Manco was, like his father, daring and courageous. After Manco's first wife had been killed, Hailli had felt as if his grief were hers. Her hopeless love hadn't been marred by envy when he'd married Lady Coraquenque. Hailli had worried as much as he each time Coraquenque had disguised herself and sneaked away to spy on the invaders of their land. When the queen had miscarried, Hailli had mourned as if the infants were her own. It was the same with this child Coraquenque carried now. Hailli couldn't bear the possibility of harm coming to it or the queen. Hailli thought the eternal light, however sacred, wasn't worth the risk Coraquenque was taking. Nothing, in Hailli's mind, was worth adding to Manco's painful memories.

Amaru returned to report seeing only a pair of Spaniards in the post house, who were amusing themselves with a game of dice. There was no hint of additional men or a trap. Coraquenque made the decision both Amaru and Hailli feared, to continue to the post house and, if all went well, negotiate for the lamp.

Amaru made sure they approached the building from an angle the Castilians couldn't see them; and because they'd wrapped their horses' hooves to muffle the sound of the animals' shoes, they reached the post house seemingly without being noticed. Amaru loosened his sword in its scabbard and fit an arrow to his bow before he kicked the door open. The Castilians sitting on cushions on the floor began to get up; but at Amaru's sharp command, changed their minds.

"There's no need for this," one of the men said in Spanish.

"What are your names and who is the man you work for?" Amaru demanded in Quechua. The men stared blankly at him. He asked several more questions to test them; and after he was satisfied they didn't understand, he said to the women, "We can speak our own language if we have something private to discuss."

One of the men commented in exasperation, "You'd think Manco Capac would send someone who could speak Spanish for this peaceful mission. How does he expect us to negotiate with them?"

Amaru said derisively in Spanish, "My people have seen too many peaceful missions become bloodbaths. Stay where you are and toss your weapons aside.''

The Castilians eyed the arrow lowered in their direction. They knew the aim of Incan soldiers was deadly, that this Inca could refit an arrow to his bow fast enough so he might shoot them both before either could stop him. They looked at his eyes, which seemed as pitiless as ebony beads, glanced at each other in warning then took the daggers from their belts and sent them skittering across the floor.

Amaru stepped aside so Coraquenque and Hailli could enter then, with his foot, pushed the door shut behind them. With the queen in the room, Amaru watched the men even more tensely.

"We are maidens of the sun temple." Coraquenque affected a heavier accent than she normally used to add to the impression she was a mere temple attendant.

The Castilians introduced themselves as Diego Seguidor and Ferdinand Porfiar and acknowledged they recognized the women's robes.

Coraquenque said bitterly, "No doubt because you have dragged others of my sisterhood from their convents in Cuzco." She paused to look at them sternly and warn, "If we don't return safely to Manco Capac, he will send no other messengers; and your master will lose the gold he seeks. I think harming us to find we have nothing worth stealing or satisfying your lust for an Incan virgin won't be worth your master's anger when you fail in this mission."

"We aren't thieves or animals," Seguidor protested.

"Maybe not, but others of your kind have behaved worse than wild beasts," Amaru said.

Porfiar sighed. "We have no weapons. There's nothing we can do."

Seguidor, who looked more frightened than his companion, asked anxiously, "How can we concentrate on negotiating with an arrow pointed at our hearts? For all we know, this building is surrounded by your army. Show some good faith and lower your weapon."

"We have no faith in you," Coraquenque replied.

"Amaru will keep his arrow aimed at your heart," Hailli burst out. Then, dismayed at her effrontery to speak in her queen's place, she fell silent.

The Castilians noted Hailli's seeming command and assumed she was of a higher rank than the other woman, but made no comment. Instead, Seguidor cautiously shifted his position on the floor and complained, "My body isn't used to sitting like an Indian. May I stand up?" At the Incas' silence he offered, "I'll stay well away from you."

The pair of Indians the Castilians had brought with them to the post house listened and watched the scene from their hiding place in the rafters. They were under orders to remain hidden unless needed, but they longed to plunge their knives in the Incan soldier holding their Castilian friends at bay. They were Cañars, the people who were sworn enemies of the Incas, who so hated Manco Capac they'd betrayed his first escape attempt from Cuzco and had helped recapture him. The Cañars had seen Amaru previously investigate the post house and had warned the Castilians then hidden before Amaru had approached with the women.

"Our orders are to make a bargain with you then take the message to our employer," Porfiar was saying. "He'll send his answer and instructions about exchanging the gold for the eternal light."

In rapid Quechua Amaru warned, "I would do *anything* for you, royal lady; but I'm a man, not a god. I cannot stand here with my bowstring pulled for several days while we wait. We must think of another way."

"Perhaps we could bind whichever Castilian remains with us," Hailli quickly suggested.

The Cañars in the loft had understood every Quechua word and knew these Incas were of the nobility because of the elegant dialect they used. Hailli seemed, as before, to have given an order; and the Incan soldiers addressing one of the women as "royal lady" made the Cañars glance at each other in surprise. They'd heard rumors that the Incan queen had sometimes disguised herself and spied on the Spaniards. Neither Cañar had ever seen Coraquenque and both assumed Hailli was she. There was no way to reveal this surprising discovery to their Castilian friends without exposing their position to the Incan soldier; but they knew what having Manco Capac's queen in their hands could mean to Alonso and the size of their own reward. No more than a couple of silent gestures were necessary for their agreement.

The Cañar, who dropped down on Amaru's shoulders, toppled him on impact. Amaru quickly freed himself then hooked his toes around the Cañar's ankle and sent him sprawling. But when Amaru leaped up, he saw a second Cañar had planted himself in front of the door and held a knife to Hailli's breast, while one of the Castilians had a cocked gun pointed at Coraquenque.

Amaru looked at Coraquenque then Hailli and cried, "What shall I do?"

The Cañar holding Hailli didn't realize Amaru had addressed Coraquenque and said, "If you do anything, we'll kill your queen."

Though Amaru would have without hesitance sacrificed both his and Hailli's life for Coraquenque, he was stymied.

"He addressed this woman as 'royal lady,' " the Cañar said in Castilian. "We couldn't tell you without revealing ourselves."

Amaru looked helplessly at their enemies and hung his head in despair and shame that he'd accidently betrayed Coraquenque.

Hailli suddenly realized the Cañars thought *she* was Coraquenque. She hoped, if they continued to think it, the queen might be saved. She said coolly, "It isn't your fault, Amaru. None of us could guess that pigs could climb to the rafters." When the Cañar holding her tightened his grasp, she looked at the Castilians and said loftily, "You'll get nothing from Manco Capac if you harm me. If I'm safely returned, you'll not only be paid for the lamp, but a ransom for his queen as well."

Coraquenque, listening to her maid's brave masquerade, thought of the child nestled in her body and dared say nothing to reveal her identity. She stood helplessly silent with tears flooding her eyes, hoping the Castilians would realize the practicality of Hailli's reasoning.

Hailli saw Coraquenque's glistening eyes and said softly, "Don't be afraid, my loyal servant. Manco Capac values you and Amaru and will pay for your release as well as mine."

The Castilians considered the situation a moment then ordered the Cañar to free the woman they mistook for Manco's queen.

Porfiar said, "You have a faster horse than I. You go to Falla and tell him we have Manco's queen, her maidservant and one of what must be his most trusted officers in our hands. He can decide what to do."

"What will you do if, before I get back with instructions or help, Manco sends his soldiers to learn why his wife's return is delayed?" Seguidor asked.

"I don't know how far these three had to travel to get here, so I can't be sure how much time Manco will allow them to get back," Porfiar answered. "If he's in the mountains, as I suspect, he must be at least a couple of days' ride away. He might wait another day or two to allow for a bargain's being reached. I think you'll have four or five days to get Falla's answer, but I can't be sure."

"Why don't we persuade the soldier to tell us when Manco expects them back?" Seguidor inquired.

Porfiar shook his head. "Even the maid would die under torture, rather than hint where the stronghold is. Do as I told you and ride as fast as you can. If you aren't back after five days, I'll have to go with the Cañars into the forest and hide from Manco and his army."

When Coraquenque heard Alonso's name, her heart sank. He would recognize her as Rianna's servant and friend and was sure to question her about Rianna's disappearance. Coraquenque wondered if Alonso wanted to avenge the wound Rianna had given him and would torture her to learn where Rianna was. She realized Manco might not emerge from the temple before Alonso or his agents arrived. Even if Manco came out sooner than she expected, no one knew where she'd gone. How could they help? Though she inwardly scalded herself with silent condemnation for having set out on this quest for the lamp, her expression never changed; and only Amaru and Hailli could begin to guess at her thoughts.

Coraquenque, Hailli and Amaru were locked in the windowless storeroom while Porfiar waited for Seguidor's return. Though the food supplies had long ago been removed when the Incas had abandoned the post house, the mice had remained. Because this generation of squeaking little creatures had no experience with humans and no fear of them, they often scurried boldly around the Incas' feet. Despite this, the Incas preferred being locked in the storehouse to being constantly under the Cañars' malevolent gaze when Amaru had no way to protect any of them.

Amaru reproached himself for addressing Coraquenque by title as he checked and rechecked the room for any means of escape. Coraquenque and Hailli, too, concentrated on how they might trick Porfiar, but he was too cautious. Only one Inca was allowed out of the storeroom at a time. A Cañar accompanied whoever went and the second Indian guarded those left behind. Dreading the thought of having to go into the forest with the Cañars if Alonso didn't get his answer back in time, on the last day Porfiar had promised to remain at the post house, the Incas took turns with their ear pressed to the door. They heard snatches of conversation and learned Porfiar and the Cañars were preparing to leave.

The Incas finally heard horses draw to a stop in front of the post house, the outside door open and many booted feet enter. They glanced at each other in alarm. More Castilians had arrived. When the storeroom door was opened and the Incas filed out, they faced Alonso and a dozen of his men.

When Alonso saw Coraquenque, his surprise was obvious. "I know this woman! One of Nicasio's men dragged her off the street in Lima. She was pretending to be a blind beggar." His fingers grasped Coraquenque's chin as he observed, "You seem to have risen in the world from a beggar to your queen's servant. Tell me, what became of Rianna?"

When Coraquenque remained silent, he gave her chin a painful squeeze.

Seeing her queen's flinch, Hailli exclaimed, "Stop it! She can tell you nothing!"

Alonso released Coraquenque and turned to Hailli. "I've heard about a golden-haired woman living in Manco Capac's stronghold. If that's true, the woman must be Rianna."

"None of us will tell you where Manco Capac is!" Hailli declared.

"So my little Rianna *has* found protection with the Incas," Alonso concluded, then added, "According to Spanish law, I'm Rianna's guardian; and it's only right that she's returned to me."

"Incas obey Manco Capac's law, not yours," Amaru snarled.

"Whether you torture or kill us one by one, we won't tell you where my husband is," Hailli said firmly.

"I might still find a way to get Rianna back, but I don't want her so badly I'm willing to forfeit the ransom Manco will pay for all of you," Alonso observed.

"You'll never find Manco or Rianna," Coraquenque declared.

Alonso surprised her by shrugging as if it really didn't matter that much to him. She couldn't know that, before he'd even approached the post house, he'd left several Cañars in the forest with orders to follow Amaru back to Manco's hiding place and learn where it was. Alonso was certain that, with all the artillery Pizarro would shortly amass, Manco would be defeated. Not only would Rianna be captured and again placed in Alonso's charge, but Pizarro would be grateful to Alonso for having made Manco's defeat possible. Pizarro then could concentrate on disposing of Blasco Vela. That, too, would give Alonso satisfaction. The knight from Avila had looked down on Alonso from boyhood; and since Alonso had become a man, Vela had often criticized his adventures.

Alonso signaled to one of his men, who pushed Amaru toward the door. Coraquenque and Hailli followed. They were allowed to watch from the threshold as Alonso again faced Amaru.

"You'll be my messenger to Manco Capac," Alonso directed. "Tell him to gather enough gold to fill a room the size Atahualpa did to ransom himself. That's my price for Manco's queen, her servant and the eternal lamp. My men and I will remain here with them until the gold is delivered."

"Once before your people took a wife of my king prisoner, but they killed her," Amaru said quietly. "Manco Capac will remember that. If you harm this queen or her servant, I know he'll think of nothing except revenge."

"Manco's first wife was being held by the army. I'm not the army," Alonso reminded as one of his men led Amaru's horse to their side.

Amaru's dark eyes shifted to regard the Indians who had guarded them and warned, "Cañars, especially, do not like Incas. Make sure neither of them harm my queen or her maid."

"*These* Cañars obey me," Alonso replied.

"If they don't, Manco Capac will kill you all," Amaru said grimly then turned to take his horse's reins. He paused to look one more time at Coraquenque and Hailli in the doorway. "I'll do what needs to be done," he promised them. Then he swung up into the saddle and, without another word or a glance back, kicked the horse into a gallop.

Coraquenque, watching Amaru speeding into the distance, squeezed Hailli's hand in silent reassurance.

Rianna took another step into Francisco's apartment then stopped to stare at her brother's changed appearance.

Francisco's previously shoulder-length hair had been clipped and its red-brown waves curved only to his earlobes. He wore tan vicuña breeches of the slender cut Shali often favored, a buff jerkin edged with a narrow strip of dark-green knotted fringe. Over the jerkin a belt of gold disks was linked at his waist and his feet were sheathed by soft boots. Uncertain what Rianna would say, his expression was wary.

"You look so different!" she breathed.

"That's what I thought when I first saw you dressed like an Inca," Francisco said defensively.

"Your hair—" she began.

He quickly explained, "Suya cut it for me. It's more convenient this way."

Rianna caught his hands in hers. "You certainly do look handsome. I'm sure your hair must be more comfortable like this."

Francisco smiled at the compliment and said, "Shali loaned me these clothes. He's taller than I, but someone shortened the breeches." Francisco paused then remarked, "I feel a little odd wearing the clothes of the man who seduced my sister."

Rianna was quiet a moment. When she raised her eyes to Francisco, they begged his understanding. "Incas feel differently about this than we were taught. Shali wants to get married. He's waiting for *me* to decide if I can accept a life with the Incas."

"In the meanwhile, you're living together," Francisco said tightly.

Rianna's first impulse was to answer sharply, which surprised her; she'd never spoken so to any male in her family. Realizing she'd changed more than even she'd known, Rianna said patiently, "It's Incan custom to have a mass wedding ceremony once a year. Before the Day of Wedding next year, I must decide to marry Shali or leave Machu Picchu and never return. It's very difficult to choose between everything I've thought of as home and the man I love. I'm living with Shali because we love each other and I'm trying to learn what life with him, an Inca, would mean."

Francisco recognized the emotion in her voice. He was quiet a long moment. Then his fingers under Rianna's chin gently tipped her face toward his. "Forgive me for seeming hard. Though much has happened to change me, I'm expecting you to be the same as you were in Spain. It's unjust of me." He drew Rianna into his arms adding, "You must tell me more about what has happened to you so I can understand." He put his arm around her waist and led her through his apartment to a pair of cushions on the terrace. He watched her gracefully seat herself then, as he awkwardly lowered himself to one of the cushions, commented, "Perhaps you can even tell me how to be comfortable living without chairs."

"It just takes a little time to get used to it," she advised.

"Like it will take a little time for me to get used to other things," Francisco commented.

"Do you think you can?"

Francisco realized from that one query how hard Rianna was finding it to answer the same question for herself. The depth of her dilemma indicated how she loved Shali. He finally admitted, "So much here is strange to me, but I've noticed many qualities about the Incas I like. I've heard about some ideas I can respect."

"You'll find that they don't lie," Rianna said.

Francisco raised his eyes to meet hers. "I'm learning that from Suya."

Rianna took his hand and said softly, "It's good for you to have someone explain things that I, perhaps, can't."

Francisco knew Rianna understood he was drawn to the Incan girl and was being tactful. He decided he didn't want to discuss Suya. Instead, he reminded, "The Incas are at war with Pizarro—a war they're likely to lose. If you were to stay, what of your safety, my sister?"

"If I decided to cast my lot with Shali, I would have to share that fate too," Rianna solemnly replied. "Just as if you stayed, you'd have to take the same risk."

Francisco was silent a moment until he said concernedly, "Our fates would be in God's hands, but I can't help worrying about such a future for you."

Rianna didn't know how to assure her brother because she had yet to make her own decision. To ease the moment's tension Francisco said, "Much has happened to you since you left Spain. Tell me something about it."

Rianna began to recount her adventures in more detail than she'd been able when she'd first seen Francisco in the great hall. She was assuring him that the fever she'd suffered hadn't left her with any after-effects when she noticed Suya walking along the terrace toward them.

Francisco got to his feet and offered Rianna his hand as he explained, "Suya has offered to show me the valley today."

"Last evening your brother heard someone singing a message on a nearby slope. He wants to know more about these calls." Suya spoke slowly, using the easiest Quechua words she thought Rianna would understand, as she had when they'd spoken in the corridor outside the great hall door.

"I know more of your language than I can speak, but I'm getting better at talking too," Rianna advised.

"Shali is a good teacher," Suya remarked then added, "I'm glad Francisco already speaks my language so well. I wouldn't be as patient as Shali, I think."

"I'm sure you'd be as good a teacher in Quechua as you are in explaining about your people to Francisco," Rianna replied.

Suya's dark eyes were warm as she asked, "If you're curious about the singing messages, maybe you'd like to come with us?"

Rianna knew Shali would be busy all day with military matters and Coraquenque seemed to have closeted herself in the royal suite since Manco had gone to the temple. Having nothing else to do, she happily answered, "Yes, thank you. I'll go if you won't mind waiting for me to change into something more suitable for riding."

Ruminavi walked through the courtyard while Rianna, Suya and Francisco were waiting for their horses to be saddled. Seeing them, he smiled and approached.

After Francisco explained how they planned to spend the morning, Ruminavi wished he could be included, but only commented, "That sounds pleasant."

Suya noted he wasn't in uniform and said, "You're off duty now. If you have no other plans, maybe you'd like to join us."

Though Ruminavi's interest in Rianna urged him to immediately accept, he glanced at her for a reaction then slowly said, "I go back on duty later, but I have no plans for the next few hours."

"There's a place not far up the mountainside that's perfect for singing messages," Suya said accommodatingly.

Remembering how Ruminavi had asked her to tell him if she and Shali decided to part, Rianna also recalled that he hadn't tried to press her in any way and had been good company. She knew he was hesitating on her account and commented tactfully, "If we were to meet any dangerous wild animals, your protection would be welcome."

Ruminavi smiled. "All we're likely to find on these nearby slopes are vicuñas or alpacas; but if anything more menacing appears, I'll gladly defend you."

Shali had previously arranged a meeting with Amaru to discuss tactics that might be used to capture at least some of the artillery Pizarro was having hauled through the mountains. When Amaru didn't come, Shali sent Topa to search the palace for him; and the boy returned to report Amaru couldn't be found. Shali knew only the most compelling reason would cause Amaru to ignore the meeting and decided to go to the officer's home near the city gates to see what was wrong.

After Shali learned from Amaru's wife that he'd said he was going on an errand for the queen, Shali emerged from the house wondering where Coraquenque had sent Amaru, why the officer hadn't spoken even to him about it. That Shali hadn't seen Coraquenque for several days didn't alarm him; because when Manco went to the temple to clear his mind, Coraquenque usually found her own kind of seclusion in the royal suite.

Shali was speculating if he should ask the queen about Amaru's mission when he glimpsed Wayra's snowy coat approaching the city gates. Shali raised a hand to wave to Rianna then saw she was accompanied by Ruminavi and lowered his hand. As Shali watched, Ruminavi reached out to touch Rianna's arm; and she tipped back her head in laughter. A pang went through Shali, which he quickly put down. He remained where he was. His eyes, narrowed against the sun, glimmered with dark lights, though he noted Francisco and Suya were with Rianna.

After they'd passed through the gates, Shali returned his thoughts to Amaru's mysterious absence. He knew Coraquenque had many problems on her mind and he finally decided she must have forgotten to tell him she'd sent Amaru on a task. He disliked intruding on her privacy to ask about a matter that probably was relatively minor. While Shali was thinking about all this, his feet led him to the city gates.

He stood in the entrance watching the two couples follow the road down into the valley, wondering where they were going. When he saw Rianna's head turn, incline toward Ruminavi listening to something he said, Shali considered the possibility of Topa's learning about this excursion from Tavi, Rianna's maid.

Rianna was aware that Ruminavi was taking advantage of Suya and Francisco's interest in each other to be paired off with her, but his conversation was pleasant and often witty. He pointed out birds and flowers and told her their names in Quechua then, as she stumbled through their pronunciation, assured her she would learn. At Rianna's urging, they all spoke in Quechua so she could practice; and though Francisco sometimes smiled at her struggle to follow the conversation, Ruminavi patiently corrected and prompted her. A light-hearted air ran through their conversation; but Rianna knew that sometimes when Suya and Francisco addressed each other, they deliberately spoke too rapidly for her to understand and used words unfamiliar to her.

When the little group reached a shallow valley scooped from a slope and paused, as Suya had promised, she explained something of the Incas' way of communicating from one mountain to another. She demonstrated how the inflections of her voice, the airy trills as well as a low, pulsating chant even without words could be eloquent.

When Suya stopped, Rianna, captivated by the exotic melodies the varying messages formed, urged her to continue; but the Inca said, "When there's no one to give an answer, it's like talking to myself. I don't know what more to say."

"I forgot it was *talking*. I was listening to the music of it," Rianna noted.

Suya smiled in pleasure and modestly lowered her eyes, though she looked sideways at Francisco from under her lashes and said, "If you would answer me, it would be easier."

"Me?" Francisco was startled. "I don't know how."

"I could teach you, but it would be better higher on the slope," Suya suggested.

Though Francisco welcomed a chance to be alone with Suya, he was reluctant to lend his voice to such calls. He looked from one face to another and finally said, "I don't think so."

Aware that Francisco was self-conscious about singing before them all, Suya coaxed, "Even our army uses this way of talking when they need to communicate quickly over a distance. Ruminavi knows how to do it. Maybe he could go with you and give you a start." She caught Francisco's gaze with hers, adding, "We need not sing long; and afterward, I can show you a place where strawberries grow wild."

Encouraged that soldiers used singing messages, but more intrigued by later being alone with Suya on a berry hunt, Francisco asked, "Would you be willing to help me, Ruminavi?"

Ruminavi wanted the opportunity to talk with Rianna, but decided they could be alone later when Francisco and Suya foraged for strawberries and agreed.

"I'll stay here and listen to the calls," Rianna decided.

She watched the three go on foot partly up the slope then Suya veer off to follow a trail separate from the path Francisco and Ruminavi took. After they'd disappeared, Rianna got to her feet to look at the valley. It was surrounded by mountains and reminded her of the place she and Coraquenque had met Shali and Manco near Lima. Rianna gazed at the Andes' granite spires and remembered how Shali had looked after he'd turned from her. That day, as she'd watched the wind ruffle his hair, she'd decided he was part of a world so different from hers she'd never understand him. Now, though Rianna knew more about Shali than any man, she was aware of depths in him she had yet to discover. She wondered if this was because Shali was an Inca or because he was a complex man.

Rianna turned slowly to look down the slope toward Machu Picchu and was surprised to see Shali leading Chuncho up the trail. In his free hand, he carried a single crimson flower. Though his eyes were on Rianna rather than the rocky path, his long strides were steady and smooth. It occurred to her he'd always known where he was going though his path had often puzzled her.

When Shali handed Rianna the flower, he said quietly, "I saw you leaving the city."

"Though I was with another man, you followed to bring me this beautiful flower?" she asked slowly.

"One has nothing to do with the other," he noted.

She looked down into the curving petals of the bloom then raised her eyes to his and said softly, "You are, as the gypsy predicted, not like any man I've ever met."

Shali lifted his head and turned at the sound of Suya's beginning song-message. He recognized Ruminavi's answering voice and remarked, "I would have thought he'd want to stay here with you."

"Ruminavi is teaching Francisco," Rianna said then added defensively, "He's just been good company."

"I said he could accompany you while I was busy. You needn't explain," Shali replied.

"Yet you don't like it."

Shali turned slowly to again face Rianna and quietly admit, "No. But I didn't come here because of that. There's something I want to show you later." He took her arm and invited, "Sit down and listen to the singing messages with me. I'll tell you what they mean."

After they were seated, Shali quietly waited for the singing to resume. When Suya began, Rianna listened to the melodious chant as if it were music rather than conversation. There was a long pause before Ruminavi answered. Suya resumed; and, after she'd finished, again there was a wait for Ruminavi's reply.

Rianna noticed a smile hovering over Shali's lips as he commented, "I think your brother and Suya like each other."

"What makes you say that now?" Rianna inquired.

"Suya isn't composing a conversation. She's singing a song often used to talk to a prospective lover who's shy. There's a choice of three answers for each question she asks—yes, no and maybe," Shali explained.

"But it's Ruminavi who's answering," Rianna noted.

"The pause between tells me Ruminavi is asking Francisco for *his* replies. They were yes, yes and maybe," Shali advised.

Rianna turned to stare at him in dismay. "But what were Suya's questions?"

"Maybe I'd better not tell you," Shali said lightly. When Rianna was silent, he turned to look at her more seriously and noted, "You have the same expression on your face now as Francisco wore when he discovered you and I are lovers."

Aware that she had no more right to criticize what Francisco might decide about Suya than he had to reproach what she did with Shali, Rianna blushed and said nothing. But she inwardly wondered what would happen if she, who'd been inclined to stay, and Francisco, who had wanted to take her from Machu Pichu, reversed their positions.

She lay back on the grass and, with the sweet scent of it enveloping her like an invisible cloud, stared up at the sky, using its brightness as an excuse for the moisture in her eyes, while she wished Shali could have been born in Madrid.

Rianna silently reminisced about parlors set daintily for tea, the sun slanting into a study lined with books, sleeping in a four-poster bed with a canopy over her. She thought of dancing at a formal ball, the feel of satin against her skin, lace tumbling over her wrists from her sleeves. She wished she could speak without first having to translate her thoughts into another language, to talk with people whose background was the same as hers and, so, automatically understood each nuance of her meaning. But to have even these small, comfortable things that meant home, she'd have to give up Shali.

Rianna looked at his profile, the lines of his lashes, the faintly amused tilt of his mouth as he listened to Suya and Francisco's song-messages and was torn by the decision she'd have to make.

Finally, Shali advised, "They're coming back."

Rianna sat up to note Francisco and Suya were holding hands, as if the song had sealed an agreement between them. Ruminavi was walking a few paces ahead of them. When he saw Shali waiting with Rianna, his dark eyes were impassive; but his smile had lost its warmth.

"We were teaching Francisco to sing messages," Suya happily announced.

A little sheepish that Shali had heard and likely understood the song, Francisco said slowly, "I guess I was beginning to catch on."

Shali smiled and replied easily, "I recognized your voice in the last several calls. You did very well."

Suya innocently asked the question Ruminavi longed to demand of Shali and didn't dare. "What brings you here?"

"Some time ago I mentioned to Manco Capac that I might like to build a house away from the city," Shali began.

Surprised at this, Rianna looked up at him. She saw his eyes glance warily down at her as he continued, "Manco knows I prefer higher land and recently offered me this valley. This is the first chance I've had to look it over; and I could only come now because Amaru seems to have gone on an errand for Coraquenque instead of keeping an appointment with me."

"You've needed time away from your work. I'm glad you came," Suya said brightly.

Though he was aware Ruminavi didn't agree, Shali pressed Suya's hand and commented, "It's been too long since I've seen you smile that way."

Suya admitted, "I'm happier today than I've been in a long time." Though she preferred to be alone with Francisco, she said politely, "I was going to take Francisco to hunt for strawberries. Would you like to come with us?" She looked at each of them in turn.

"I was thinking Rianna might want to look over this parcel of land with me," Shali answered.

Though Shali's tone was casual, Ruminavi knew the house Shali wanted to build was meant for him and Rianna. He said, "You might as well go ahead. I have to be back on duty soon and should return to change clothes. Thank you for inviting me, Suya." Giving Shali a cool glance, he went to get his horse.

The two couples watched Ruminavi start back down the path. Then Suya, eager to be alone with Francisco, caught his hand and laughingly tugged him off.

Watching them go, Shali quietly asked, "What do you think of this land?'' When Rianna didn't answer, he turned to look questioningly down on her.

"It reminds me of that valley near Lima, where Coraquenque took me so she could talk to Manco," Rianna replied. She turned to look up at Shali and inquired, "Did you ask Manco for this land because you knew I liked that valley?"

"I didn't ask him for anything. Maybe Coraquenque influenced his choice of this particular place," Shali answered. "It could be Coraquenque's way of tempting you to stay."

"She does know I liked the valley near Lima," Rianna concluded then asked, "Would you build a house for yourself if I left?"

"I'm not certain," Shali answered. He took her hand and began to walk as he spoke. "Where I live if you leave isn't something you have to consider in making up your mind to stay or go. That's why you asked me, isn't it? So you can add one more item to the many others that are already so confusing you it seems you can't make a decision?" When Rianna didn't answer, he said, "You're *afraid* of coming to any conclusion. It's all been a way of delaying while you've secretly hoped someone else would decide for you then tell you what to do."

Rianna turned to give him a sharp glance; but he continued walking, his hand pulling her along with him as he advised, "Returning to Spain to try to build a life by yourself wasn't so attractive an idea and you leaned toward remaining here with me. When Francisco arrived having only one goal, to take you back with him, you started to think differently. If you and your brother return to Madrid, you could almost pretend everything was as it always had been; you wouldn't have to take the chance of committing yourself to me and gamble everything on a new way of life in a strange land. But now it appears Francisco has gotten interested in Suya and is wavering. Now you're waiting to learn what *he* decides instead of making up your own mind."

"If I decide to go, I might have to leave not only you, but Francisco behind as well! How could I do that?" she burst out.

"If you stay or go because Francisco or I want you to, when you meet future problems, which you surely will, you'll resent not having made your own decision," he reasoned.

Rianna knew that, until the soldiers had arrested the Alavas and shattered her world, her parents had made all major decisions for her.

Since then, there really had been no choices open to her—circumstances had *forced* her to act—until Shali had brought her to Machu Picchu. Rianna stopped walking, lifted her eyes to his and cried, "But it isn't fair if the first real decision I make must be the most important of my life! Not only my life, but important to you and Francisco as well!"

"All decisions, even those that seem insignificant, affect your life. It's how the world works. You have to accept that," Shali advised. "In any event, you underestimate your brother. He's been through a great deal during these last couple of years. He'll accept your decision and still make his own choice."

"I just want everyone to be happy," Rianna said lamely.

"Do you think I'd be happy to see you go to Spain for the wrong reasons?" Shali inquired. He was quiet a moment before asking, "Do you think I want a wife who married me not because she loves me and is willing to accept what I am, but because her brother decided he loved a woman of my people and stayed?"

Rianna was stunned. She'd assumed Shali had committed himself to her without reservations of any kind.

Knowing what she was thinking, he put his hands on her shoulders and gently urged, "Sit down with me again, *chinita*. Let me tell you something."

She obeyed woodenly; and after they were seated, he said, "If you decide you can't live with my people, I'll understand. If the choice were mine, I know I wouldn't want to live in Madrid; but I have no choice. The moment I set foot on Spanish soil the Inquisition would brand me a heretic and burn me at the stake as surely as they would if I walked into Cuzco."

Rianna lowered her eyes. She knew he was right.

"The decision *must* be yours, *chinita*," Shali reasoned. He paused then admitted, "I love you as much as I can love any woman; but you should realize, if you decide to leave Machu Picchu, I won't die."

Rianna turned away.

Shali persisted, "Your leaving would cause me great pain; but I've already lost a wife and son, my province, home and everything in it. I've learned I could recover from that agony; so I think in time I'd recover from losing you." His fingers under her chin coaxed her to look up at him as he said, "There is a thing you should know about Incas."

Rianna gazed up at him, wondering what he meant.

"Because of the great difficulty we have traveling through the mountains, Incas have always warmly welcomed visitors then wept when they had to go. In truth, we've never known if those leaving after a visit might fall in a ravine or be caught by a rockslide; and we never would meet again. The only choice Incas have ever had was to make the most of every moment they're together, which is what I think you and I should do."

"Now you're saying I should forget making any decision and just enjoy being with you. How can I do that after what you just said?" she exclaimed.

Shali let out a breath and said with forced patience, "I don't mean for you to forget anything, but to go on in spite of all these problems, to try to salvage something of worth from the time we do have together."

All through the conversation Rianna had felt the knowledge creeping up on her that she'd been behaving like a little girl still looking for her father instead of a woman deciding what her own life would be. She resented knowing this about herself. Shali's advising her to take even another step along the path he'd been leading her, to have the strength to lay aside her problems and enjoy herself when *she* chose to, only added another faggot to her already smoldering fire.

Rianna sprang to her feet and cried, "How could I enjoy being with a man who's just told me he can manage with or without me—as if it really didn't matter all that much!"

Shali's eyes flashed with black fire as he stood up. Without a word, he turned away and stalked back to where Chuncho was grazing. Rianna, already sorry for her outburst, but not knowing what to say, hurried after him. He laid his forearms across his saddle and prepared to mount.

"I'm sorry. Don't be angry with me!"

At Rianna's apology, Shali turned his head to regard her silently a moment. "I'm not angry about a few foolishly impulsive words, but because you seem to have understood nothing at all," he said tightly.

She watched him swing up into his saddle, desperately trying to think of something she could say to stop him from leaving. She remained mute until he again looked down at her.

Shali recalled, "The first night we spent together I said, to love you, I would first have to conquer your past. Now I know, if I fail, it isn't a matter of whether you can live with my people or must return to yours. The real problem has been for you to conquer your fear of being a person."

Shali turned Chuncho and started the horse back down the trail toward Machu Picchu. He didn't look back; and he couldn't know Rianna ran after him a short distance, not really thinking she could catch him, not wanting to let him go.

chapter
22

Driven by his turbulent emotions, Shali rode down the trail at a reckless pace until Chuncho's having to leap over a wide crevice without guidance resulted in a slithering scramble in the loose stones on the opposite side that took them breathlessly near the lip of a deep ravine. Then, with a hammering heart, Shali dismounted to lead the horse awhile and make sure Chuncho hadn't pulled a muscle.

"You're wiser than I, my friend." Shali patted the stallion's black velvet neck. "You've kept your head as well as your footing, though I fell head over heels in love a long time ago and forgot my brain up on that slope."

He swung back into the saddle and resumed at a slower pace. Even after they'd reached level ground it was necessary to hold the stallion back and reserve his strength for the climb up the road to the city.

Shali's emotions were more difficult to control than Chuncho's speed; and when he reentered the palace courtyard, though the horse was calm, Shali's frustration had risen to an even higher level.

As the royal stable-keeper took Chuncho's reins from Shali's hands, he looked up into the nobleman's smoldering eyes, saw the fires barely contained behind them and, except for Manco Capac's direct order, would have avoided speaking. "His Majesty wants to see you immediately, Lord Shali."

"Did anyone say why?" Shali snapped.

The stable-keeper took a nervous step backward. "No, my lord, but it may have something to do with Amaru's return."

"I want to see Amaru myself," Shali muttered angrily and walked swiftly away.

Slapping dust from his clothes as he marched through the corridor toward the royal suite, Shali was startled by the sound of running feet. He turned to see Topa racing toward him.

When the boy skidded to a stop before Shali, he hurriedly ducked his head in hasty greeting. "The king is in the great hall."

"What's happened now?" Shali demanded.

"The queen has been captured. Amaru just told Manco Capac," Topa panted.

Shali's heart seemed to have stopped as he whispered, "Coraquenque captured?"

"And Hailli, her maid."

The words were hardly out of Topa's mouth when Shali spun around to race down the corridor toward the great hall. Topa hurried after him, but Shali had already entered the chamber and was in a low bow before Manco when the boy slipped into the room.

Manco seemed not even aware of Shali's presence. He was staring at Amaru, who was offering the king his sword.

"I let her fall into their hands, my lord," Amaru was saying in despair. "Take my rank and my life."

"You do not tell your king what to do," Manco answered coldly. "Nor could you disobey your queen. You acted according to her orders. I cannot, under the circumstances, fault you. Keep your rank, Amaru; as for your life, keep that too. I'm too short of good officers to lose you." Manco slowly turned to Shali and signaled him to rise from his bow.

When Shali lifted his head, he saw that, despite Manco's calm voice and stern expression, the king's eyes glistened with unshed tears. Overcome with sympathy for Manco as well as fear for Coraquenque, he didn't know what to say.

Manco saved Shali the trouble of making any remark; he quickly related what Coraquenque had done. Aghast at the results of the queen's adventure, Shali was silent for a long moment. Finally, he turned to Ruminavi, who had entered the chamber in time to hear the story and stood as if rooted just inside the doorway.

"Ruminavi, take a patrol into the forest outside the valley's entrance and make sure Falla didn't have anyone follow Amaru here." Shali fired off the order.

"Several Cañars tried to trail me," Amaru said. "I killed one of them and, I think, lost the others. They probably turned back."

"Are they on foot or horses?" Shali demanded.

"On foot now. The one I killed was guarding their horses while the others went into the underbrush hunting for my tracks. I took all three horses with me," Amaru said.

"That doesn't guarantee the Cañars returned to Falla. It would have been easier for them to follow the horses' trail and try to steal them back. If so, they might discover the entrance to our valley," Shali surmised. He turned again to Ruminavi with one terse order, *"Get them."*

Ruminavi glanced at Manco Capac, who inclined his head in approval, then hastily backed out of the great hall. They heard him already calling orders as he sprinted down the corridor.

Shali looked at Manco. "You're planning to pay the ransom?" When Manco nodded, Shali asked, "Will you let me go on this mission?"

"I'm going to lead it myself," Manco replied.

"Falla is the man who brought Rianna to Peru. That she told me so much about him might give me an advantage, should there be trouble," Shali persisted.

"Don't you think it's an odd coincidence that he's the one to have captured Coraquenque?" Manco worried. "Maybe he thinks, through her, he can still learn where Rianna is."

"Falla is an opportunist and it isn't coincidence that he'd steal the sacred lamp. What else of value is left in Cuzco for a thief like him to take?" Shali reasoned. "That Coraquenque went to the post house to negotiate for the lamp is unfortunate, but Falla has no reason to think she's in contact with Rianna now."

"You heard what Francisco said about the rumors circulating through

Cuzco that a golden-haired woman is living in my palace. Maybe he's torturing Coraquenque to find out if it's true." Manco's voice was sharpened by fear.

"Francisco only overheard those rumors because he speaks our language as well as we do. Falla can't understand a word of Quechua and isn't inclined to mingle sociably with our people in the marketplace. He's the man who beat us in Lima."

Manco's eyes clouded with fresh tears; and, uncertain he could contain them, he gestured impatiently to the several officers and servants in the room. After they'd withdrawn and closed the doors behind them, Manco brushed his eyes with the back of his hand and said, "You know I'm thinking of what they did to my first queen."

Shali lowered his eyes to hide the fear they held. In what he hoped was a reassuring tone, he said, "It was the *army* that killed your first wife. Falla's greed is greater than any interest he may have in Rianna. I don't think he'd risk losing the gold he wants by presenting you with Coraquenque's dead body."

Manco's emotions were a volatile mixture of anger and fear. He flashed, "Why did he send the Cañars to follow Amaru? Maybe Falla's offer to return Coraquenque for ransom was only a ruse to learn where I am. Pizarro would reward him handsomely for that information."

"That's true," Shali conceded. "But I think he would keep his bargain with you and, after he has your gold, tell Pizarro where you can be found." Shali paused to think over the matter again. If he were wrong, he knew he must somehow prevent Manco from personally finding Coraquenque's body the way he had his first wife's. Shali was certain Manco, in his grief, would throw away all thought of caution and, if there were a trap, charge right into it.

Again, Shali regarded his cousin and urged, "Let *me* bring the gold to Falla. If there's any chance of his trying to set up an ambush, he must not get the chance to kill you."

"Because, if they've already killed Coraquenque, they've also killed my heir, which makes me once again the last of the royal line?" Manco guessed Shali's reasoning. He grasped Shali's arms in affection and admitted, "You're right thinking I'd be so maddened by the discovery of Coraquenque's death I might act foolishly. But I *have* to go, Shali. I couldn't bear sitting here at Machu Picchu wondering if you'll return with Coraquenque alive or bring back a corpse." Manco released Shali and stepped away. "I'll compromise by agreeing to let you come along. While we're gone, Ruminavi will have to stay here to guard Machu Picchu."

Shali nodded reluctant agreement then asked, "Where are you going to get this gold or do we have so much here?"

"You're going to get it for me," Manco promptly answered. At Shali's perplexed look, he asked, "Do you remember how I persuaded Hernando Pizarro to let me out of Cuzco by promising to lead his soldiers to a life-size statue of my father made of solid gold?"

"Is there such a statue?" Shali asked.

"There is and more," Manco confirmed. "After I saw how well Pizarro kept his promise when he had Atahualpa executed, I decided it would be wise to hide everything valuable I could get my hands on. While Toparaca was suffering through his short reign as Pizarro's puppet-king, I deliberately acted subdued. But I and a small group of officers, all of whom since died in the battle at Tambo, were making caches of everything valuable we didn't have to travel too far and too obviously to reach. We dumped what the Castilians would consider treasures in the lakes and buried them in caves. Now I alone know where they are."

Shali was stunned. "But how could you have done this without my learning of it?"

"It happened before Yupanqui was killed, while you yet had a province to govern. You and I weren't as close then," Manco reminded.

"I thought you were mourning your dead brothers, but you were hiding gold?" Shali breathed in amazement.

"After Toparaca was dead, I deliberately put myself in Pizarro's hands. I wanted to learn about him and the way his people think. Surely you don't suppose I felt I had to go to Cuzco, *my* capital city, to beg the leader of my enemies permission to wear my own crown?" Manco asked.

"It seemed unlike you and was something I'd wondered about," Shali admitted.

Manco's lips curled in scorn as he remembered how well he'd deluded Pizarro until he realized what Shali's opinion must have been at his seeming foolishness to have walked straight into the hands of his enemy. He commented, "Despite what you must have thought of me then, you came to my rescue."

"You're my king," Shali answered simply.

"And you're my friend as well as my cousin," Manco said. He was thoughtfully silent a moment. "Choose the men to take with you and prepare to leave as soon as you're ready—this afternoon if you can. Come back to me then and I'll have a map ready so you can find the cave. You'll have little time to spare to reach the cave and return with the gold before we'll have to set out for the post house and get Coraquenque back, if that's still possible."

After Shali had left Rianna on the slope, all she was aware of was the pain of seeing him turn away angrily. She trembled as she watched Shali and Chuncho's diminishing figures turn a curve and vanish. Then she raised her hands, intending to bury her face in them, and noticed she'd clenched her fists so tightly the nails had dug into her palms and bloodied them. She quickly lowered her hands. Suddenly recognizing the gesture as only one more way to avoid the truth, she raised them again, stared at her palms as if her life depended on acknowledging this one small fact. Then she carefully, very deliberately wiped the stains on her skirt and made a decision.

She would not stay until Suya returned with Francisco. They'd ask questions about Shali's leaving that Rianna couldn't—no, she didn't *want* to answer.

Despite being afraid to ride down the slope alone, Rianna willed herself to approach Wayra. Her hands gathering up the reins confirmed she was still trembling, but Rianna resolutely mounted and turned the mare toward the trail.

In contrast to Shali's descent, Rianna slowly guided her horse with unwavering attention down the slope. It was, in truth, all she dared focus her mind on.

Later, after Rianna dismounted in the palace courtyard, she discovered that her steps were at last steady and she'd finally stopped trembling. She walked slowly through the corridors toward Shali's apartment wishing she didn't have to face him yet, wondering if she should move back into her old quarters, at least until her mind was more ordered. Dreading to face Shali's anger again, she forced herself to open his door and discovered he wasn't there.

Rianna walked through the suite; and by the time she'd confirmed that not only Shali, but Tavi and Topa, too, seemed to have vanished, she had decided to move out. She was thankful to be alone while she emptied the cabinets of her clothes and hoped neither Shali nor Topa would return before she was finished. The chore, Rianna soon learned, was far more difficult than when she'd packed to move in; for her work was hampered by having to look through tear-blurred eyes at the clothes she was folding and placing in neat stacks on Shali's bed-mat. When she heard the door to the hall open and close, she knew it was Shali's silent feet that had entered; and her pulses again started hammering at her temples. Hastily blotting her eyes as she hurried toward the next room, she almost bumped into him as he came through the doorway.

Shali stepped around Rianna without a word and, walking directly to his cabinet, tore the door open and began to toss articles of clothing on the bed.

Mistaking his purpose, she began, "There's no need for *you* to leave . . ."

Shali muttered distractedly, "I have to get the gold to ransom Coraquenque and Hailli."

Rianna's lips parted in shock. She watched him step out of his boots, hurriedly begin to undress before she finally managed to exclaim, *"Ransom Coraquenque!"*

Shali looked up at her in surprise. "The entire palace is buzzing over the news. Didn't you hear about it?"

"I haven't talked to anyone. Tell me what happened!" she begged, momentarily forgetting her own problems.

While Shali changed into his uniform, he hurriedly told Rianna how Coraquenque and Hailli had been captured. Speechless with horror, she followed him to the chest where he kept his weapons; and while Shali fastened a dagger at his waist, a sword at his hip and slung an arrow case over his shoulder, he explained what Manco planned to do.

Reaching for his bow and a handful of lances, Shali's eyes finally fell on the clothes stacked on his bed. He said nothing, but turned to stalk into the next room. Unaware of his glance at the garment piles, Rianna followed him.

He stopped at the door and shifted his burdens so one arm was free then, touching her cheek, he asked softly, "Why are your clothes on the bed?"

Rianna's plan to move out was like a tidal wave crashing over her head, drenching her with fresh pain. She wanted to, but couldn't, tear her eyes from his as she began, "I thought it would be better . . ." She stopped, listened to her heart's silent plea then whispered, "I thought you might not want me here. For a while anyway."

"Have you ever known me to run from a problem?" he asked quietly.

Rianna stared at him in surprise.

"I'll only be gone a few days," he said. "Please stay until I get back and we have a chance to talk."

"But I thought, if you didn't care—" Her words were stopped by his mouth caressing then briefly clinging to hers.

After a moment, Shali drew away. "I *care*," he said then turned to walk swiftly down the corridor.

Hailli stamped her foot at a mouse, that had paused from his trip across the storeroom floor to stare at her. She ruffled the skirt of her robe at the mouse that, rather than flee, sat up on its haunches to watch her with mild curiosity. "Go back to where you came from," Hailli persisted. "You offend the queen's eyes."

Coraquenque, sitting on an overturned basket with her hem bunched around her ankles, watched the contest with an amused attitude. "Your queen is becoming so accustomed to furry neighbors she's thinking of giving them names. You needn't bother chasing mice on my account, Hailli. They're used to having the run of this place; and since neither of us ever hurts them, they don't believe we're a serious threat anyway."

Hailli ended the contest by nudging the mouse with the tip of her boot so it retreated to the corner of the room to calmly preen its whiskers. "A show of resistance at least keeps them from walking over our blankets when we're sleeping."

Coraquenque smiled and didn't remind the maid that, when they were asleep, neither of them could see where the mice walked. Instead, she advised, "If Alonso or one of his men hear you refer to me as your queen or see you driving mice from me, our masquerade will be over." She sighed and added, "I wish we hadn't even begun this disguise. This pretense is only a bother; Alonso seems to be keeping his promise not to harm us."

"We can't be sure he'll continue to ignore us as he has," Hailli cautioned.

"Even the Cañars don't touch us," Coraquenque remarked.

"They would, but for Alonso's orders, my lady. The way they look at us terrifies me," Hailli admitted.

"It's Alonso's promising them a share of Incan gold that keeps the Cañars away," Coraquenque said then raised her head at the sound of a large band of horses approaching the post house.

Hailli hurried to her side and excitedly whispered, "Maybe it's our people coming with the ransom."

Coraquenque shook her head. "Wagons carrying gold would creak loudly enough for us to hear. Be silent until we learn who it is. We don't want to fall into the army's hands." She rose from her seat on the basket and crept soundlessly to the door. Pushing back her hair, she pressed her ear to the wood to listen.

The outside door opened; and when feet wearing heavy boots entered the post house, Coraquenque knew they didn't belong to Incas. She listened even more intently. Though she could hear the murmur of men's voices, she couldn't discern their words.

"What are you and all these men doing here in the middle of nowhere?" Captain Estudillo was asking Alonso.

"We were weary from our exploration and stopped to rest," Alonso answered. He had no intention of admitting he'd captured Manco Capac's queen and was awaiting ransom.

"It appears you've been here longer than overnight," Estudillo observed.

"There's no reason for us to hurry back to Cuzco or anywhere," Alonso said casually. He knew Estudillo was a meticulously thorough man, who from habit peered and poked into everything. He hoped the Incas in the storeroom had the sense to remain silent. If Estudillo saw them, Alonso would have to pretend he'd taken them as mistresses;

and though Vela hadn't yet come to Cuzco to enforce the laws he'd brought from Spain, Alonso knew Estudillo would disapprove of his keeping Incan women. Alonso didn't want to stir up Estudillo's already well-developed dislike of him. After Alonso had given Pizarro directions to Manco Capac's stronghold, he was sure Pizarro would hold him in such high regard Estudillo would be forced to show *him* deference.

Thinking he might distract Estudillo's ever present suspicions about everything that caught his attention, Alonso said, "I can't offer you the same hospitality I would in Cuzco, but perhaps you'd like a cup of the *chicha* we found in the storehouse?"

Having been in the saddle all day investigating reports of Indians in the area in the hope of finding a trail leading to Manco, Estudillo was more hungry than thirsty. He accepted Alonso's offer, but asked, "What else was in the storeroom?"

"Only mice," Alonso quickly answered. "They long ago got into the few sacks of grain that was left and ruined it."

Wondering about Falla's hasty reply, Estudillo observed, "Incas often keep nuts and dried fruit in pottery jars. The mice couldn't destroy that."

"The seals were dry and had cracked so the rodents smelled the contents and gnawed their way through the stoppers," Alonso explained. Realizing it was hunger prompting Estudillo's questions, he said, "One of my men shot a vicuña this morning and we roasted it. Would you like some of that, Captain?"

Estudillo had been pacing restlessly about and paused in front of the storeroom door as he considered the offer. "A bite or two would be welcome."

At that moment Hailli noticed the mouse had ventured from its corner and was studying Coraquenque's hem. Intending to push the rodent away, Hailli's foot accidently brushed the floor and her boot scuffed the wood.

Estudillo's ears, sharpened from years of listening for enemy soldiers, perceived the sound. He turned to look at the door. "Why do you keep the storeroom barred on this side?" he inquired.

"It was when we arrived. There was no reason to go in and out so we left it that way," Alonso promptly answered. He held out the cup of *chicha* he'd just poured and invited, "Sit down, Captain, and have a sip of this. Though it can't match our wine, this particular jar is surprisingly good."

Estudillo approached Alonso to accept the cup. "You found more than one jar of *chicha*? How odd. Incas are usually careful about leaving anything behind."

"Maybe this building was abandoned too hastily," Alonso suggested. "In any event, only a few jars weren't spoiled."

"It's quite good," Estudillo commented as he tasted the liquor. "Maybe I should take a jar of it back with me."

Alonso said hastily, "I couldn't refuse my men even a taste of it. You know how quickly it can be drunk. I'm sorry to admit what we're drinking now is from the last jar."

Estudillo was sure Alonso was hiding *chicha* from his men by pretending the storeroom was empty. He put down his cup and regarded Alonso smugly. "You can spare a jar or two for me, Falla."

"I'd give it to you if I had it, Captain!" Alonso declared.

When his voice raised so Coraquenque could at last hear his words, she quickly moved away from the door and motioned Hailli to get behind a large basket that stood in the far corner. Then Coraquenque blew out the lamp Alonso had allowed them and hurried to hide behind a sagging pile of grain sacks.

"I believe you would." Estudillo stood up and began walking toward the storeroom door. "But I heard a sound in there a moment ago and your attitude makes me think you're hiding something besides *chicha*."

Horrified that the women would be discovered, Alonso said, "It must have been a mouse. The place is overrun with them."

"The expression on your face tells me otherwise." Estudillo drew his pistol and cocked it. "Open that door," he ordered.

Alonso reluctantly went to the door to slowly slide back the bar. "There's no need for a gun," he said, hoping the Incas would hear him and hide. As he opened the door a crack, he was relieved to note the lamp had been extinguished. Perhaps the women wouldn't be seen. To insure their hiding, he said clearly, "There's nothing in there except mice, Captain." He opened the door wider.

Estudillo stayed where he was. "Light a lamp," he directed.

Alonso sighed and stepped into the storeroom to obey, thankful that the lamp he'd given the Incas had a low wick, capable only of a flickering glow that didn't reach the corners of the room.

Estudillo followed Alonso as far as the threshold and peered through the gloom to comment, "What a filthy place."

Hailli crouched in her corner behind the basket, like Coraquenque on the other side of the room scarcely daring to breathe; but when the mouse she'd previously chased poked its head under the dragging edge of her skirt, she quickly moved her foot to push it back. The basket quivered.

Estudillo saw even that small movement and demanded, "Who's there? Come out or I'll shoot!" When no one appeared, he repeated the order in Quechua.

Knowing she was trapped, it occurred to Hailli she might create enough distraction so Coraquenque wouldn't be noticed. With a silent plea to Oello Huaco, patroness of women, Hailli leaped to her feet and shot out from behind the basket. She dodged past Estudillo and darted by Alonso.

Estudillo whirled and rushed after her, pushing Alonso into the next room as he passed, shouting, "If that Indian escapes, I'll have your head on a gibbet!"

"Damn," Alonso said under his breath and, having no choice, followed.

After Coraquenque heard their feet race out the front door, she straightened and stepped from behind the grain sacks. Tiptoeing to the storeroom door, she peered cautiously around the corner and noted everyone was outside chasing Hailli. Coraquenque moved swiftly and silently into the main room, hunching down so no one could see her pass the window-openings as she desperately searched for a firearm, a crossbow, even a longbow. But there was nothing. She heard Hailli's scream and, standing aside from a window-opening, cautiously looked out to confirm what she'd feared. One of the Cañars had caught Hailli, who struggled fiercely in his grasp.

"Can't a man even have a mistress?" Alonso asked in seeming disgust.

"A virgin of the sun temple still in her robes?" Estudillo asked Alonso then warned the Cañar to hold the girl more firmly.

Realizing they might drag Hailli back into the post house and discover her as well, Coraquenque hurried to a window-opening in the rear wall. She glanced out to insure the commotion Hailli had caused had drawn everyone to the front of the building then lifted her robe so she could climb out the window. As soon as her feet touched the ground, she was running; and she didn't stop until she was across the clearing that surrounded the post house, when she took cover in the bushes on its far side.

While Coraquenque waited to catch her breath, she wondered if Estudillo knew enough about Incas to recognize that the pendant Hailli had insisted on wearing was from the royal house rather than the sun temple. She was sure Alonso wouldn't reveal what he thought was her real identity. Coraquenque realized Hailli had deliberately run erratically around the clearing instead of dashing straight into the bushes to give her a chance to escape. She thought of the child she carried and was tempted to creep away; but she couldn't bear to leave the faithful little maid in enemy hands without even trying to learn if there was some chance of helping her. Coraquenque speculated whether Hailli would be locked in the storeroom again. When night came, could she find some way to release her? She wished fervently that Manco and his soldiers would come now, sooner than Alonso expected.

Estudillo caught Hailli by the arm with one hand and with the other pushed the muzzle of his gun against her cheek. "Why were you hiding in the storeroom? Are you Falla's whore?" he demanded.

Sure she was about to die, Hailli squeezed her eyes shut and mutely waited.

"What is *this*?" Estudillo breathed as his eyes fell on the pendant Hailli wore then demanded, "Where did you get this?"

Hailli wondered if Coraquenque was far enough away, if the captain would believe anything she might think of to tell him. Hailli decided, as she looked fearfully into his face, she must do as Incas had always done when questioned by their enemies—remain silent.

"She's just a girl I found," Alonso was insisting. "If that jewelry means anything special, she probably stole it."

"Incas don't steal from each other," Estudillo said.

"There are a lot of ways she could have gotten that pendant. Maybe she found it. Why must you make a row over so simple a matter as a single piece of jewelry?" Alonso, getting desperate, asked more heatedly.

"Because you're lying to me, Falla," Estudillo answered coldly. He spat an order to his men, who quickly raised pistols and crossbows. "Now that those pigs you've hired realize we aren't here to play whist, I think you'd better tell me who this Indian is and why you're holding her prisoner."

"She's just a girl I fancied," Alonso said and, despite the weapons pointed at his men, added indignantly, "You've forgotten who I am, Captain. Pizarro won't be happy with your threatening the Earl of Avila's son."

Estudillo muttered an oath and turned his attention back to Hailli. "Tell me what's going on here and nothing will be done to you. Otherwise, I'll be forced to learn if you have as much determination to withstand pain as the others of your people."

Hailli's eyes revealed her terror, but she said only, "I am a maiden of the sun temple."

"Maybe I should personally see if that's true," Estudillo sneered.

Hailli flinched at his meaning, though she remained silent.

Estudillo looked again at the pendant that lay against Hailli's breast. "I just can't believe a temple maiden would wear such a piece of jewelry," he said slowly. "Only members of a family can wear its crest. It doesn't seem likely an Inca would encroach upon another's insignia, especially that of the royal family." He turned to Alonso. "I suspect you've somehow laid hands on one of Manco's relatives and I know he doesn't have many left." Estudillo considered the possibilities and was himself too stunned at his conclusion to immediately believe it. He breathed, *"Is it possible this is Manco's wife?"*

Alonso sneered. "What a notion! I got that pendant from a trader and, as it obviously was stolen, I didn't want to admit it to you."

Estudillo's eyes narrowed with anger. "You're still lying, Falla. Do you know what I suspect? That you've dressed this girl as a temple virgin and are holding her in so obscure a place to disguise her true identity. Only you forgot to take the pendant from her." He turned and called to one of his men to tie the girl to a tree that stood in front of the post house.

As the soldier began to drag Hailli toward the dead tree, she looked at the limbless trunk and suddenly renewed her struggle. Unlike Alonso's man, who had hoped to keep her unblemished for ransom, the soldier cuffed her sharply. Dizzy from the blow, sagging against the arm wrapped around her waist, Hailli's terror forced her to sob, "Are you going to burn me?"

"If you're who I suspect and won't tell me where Manco's stronghold is, you'll wish I had," Estudillo replied.

Seeing his plans slowly falling into ruin, Alonso was desperate to save at least some part of them. He sidled closer to Estudillo and asked under his breath, "Aren't you tired of risking your life for a mere captain's pay?"

Estudillo's lack of promotion despite his competence, always a sore point with him, made him respond crossly, "Why should it matter to you?"

"Come into the post house and we'll discuss it in more privacy," Alonso suggested.

Estudillo gave him a sharp look. His suspicions that Hailli was Manco's wife and Alonso had been holding her for ransom grew even stronger. He wondered if Alonso now intended to disclose the arrangement and offer a share of the ransom as payment for cooperating. Estudillo considered the possibilities. Only a very important Inca, someone of no lower rank than Shalikuchima, would be trusted to exchange gold for Manco Capac's wife. Estudillo knew, if he were to capture Shalikuchima, commandeer so large an amount of gold, then return with directions to Manco's stronghold, he would earn a promotion and a place high in Gonzalo Pizarro's esteem—or whoever replaced Pizarro if he opposed Vela and lost. Because this would be a legitimate reward, Estudillo decided it would be better than a share of stolen gold he must hide instead of spend.

Having worked her way through the forest to the front of the post house, Coraquenque heard Estudillo's threat to Hailli and caught her breath in horror. Watching the captain and Alonso return to the post house with a comradely attitude, Coraquenque's heart sank. She couldn't imagine how she could help Hailli escape, but she also knew she couldn't bear to leave her maid to Estudillo's torturer.

*   *   *

Rianna was afraid that the Cañars, who had trailed Amaru, were scouts for a larger force that would attack Shali and his men when they left the valley. She worried that one of the bands of adventurers searching the countryside for Incan gold might spy Shali and his men returning with wagonloads of it and ambush them. These possibilities plus Coraquenque's peril and the dangers to Shali and Manco when they went to ransom her haunted Rianna's days. She had frightening dreams of Shali in a gold glittering cave trapped by a monstrous serpent with a feathered body and a condor's head, visions of Coraquenque drowning in a lake of blood and Manco burning at the stake in Cuzco's plaza.

After the first couple of nights, Rianna dreaded sleep and spent long hours pacing. Finally too weary to remain on her feet, she curled up on the bed-mat and tried to immerse herself in memories of nights she'd lain in Shali's embrace until she drifted into a light sleep and dreamed of him. When her senses perceived a lean, hard body nestling against her side, she drowsily turned into his arms then suddenly realized it no longer was a dream. Shali had come home.

Rianna's eyes flew open; and Shali, remembering how they'd parted, wasn't sure what she would do.

Rianna asked anxiously, "Was there any trouble? Are you all right?"

Shali answered quietly, "I just finished giving Manco my report. We got the gold. On the way back, we met Ruminavi and his men. They'd caught the Cañars, but they're still patrolling the forest near the valley entrance to make sure we have no other unwanted visitors Amaru didn't see."

"I've been so afraid for you I was having nightmares. I'm still frightened Alonso has set a trap for when you go to get Coraquenque," Rianna admitted.

Shali gathered her a little closer. "Ruminavi said the Cañars seemed to know only that Alonso intends to keep his agreement with us though, if Ruminavi hadn't caught them, Alonso had wanted to tell Pizarro where Machu Picchu was."

"How can you be sure the Cañars told the truth?"

Shali's reply was grim. "Ruminavi can be very persuasive."

Rianna was silent for a time as she wondered how to bring up the subject of her and Shali's argument. All she could think of to say was, "And you and I?"

Shali's lips against her temple softly answered, "We can talk about it now if you want to, but neither of us would have much time to sleep. The darkness is already beginning to lift."

Surprised to hear the night was almost over, Rianna sat up to look at the sky beyond the mountains and confirm its blackness had taken on a deep sapphire tint.

Shali, too, sat up and explained, "Manco plans to leave as soon as the valley is light enough to drive wagons through the pass. We'd be able to reach the post house tomorrow night, which is several days sooner than Alonso expects. We'll have a chance to look over the situation while it's still dark and make sure there's no trap before we approach with the wagons in the morning."

"It will be light here in the palace an hour before the sun reaches into the valley below," Rianna observed then added musingly, "It's curious to think of Machu Picchu on this mountain having morning before the valley does. It's almost as if the sun must touch Manco before it reaches his subjects."

"That's why we build our temples on higher elevations when we can," Shali noted. "The sun's light and warmth makes life on earth possible so it's our symbol of Viracocha. Our king, who keeps earthly order, draws his power from Viracocha; so he's considered the child of the sun."

Rianna gazed up at him as she reflected on that concept then thought of how Manco, who absorbed strength from the sun during the marriage ceremony, passed its vitality to the couples being wed when he held their hands. It was as if he blended them with God in that moment of touching. Rianna wondered if, when Incas made love at sunrise, they realized it was like an extension of the same principle; but without Manco's presence, they were linked directly to their divinity.

The sky's beginning orange glow bathed Rianna's face with amber light. Noting her pensive expression, Shali asked, "Are the Incan ideas about God and king really too alien for you to accept or, at least, tolerate?"

Suddenly Rianna knew she and Shali had discussed their seeming differences enough times. All the words they could use again might only strengthen the barrier that had risen between them. It had finally come to trusting herself enough to make a decision. On the breathless brink of her own discovery, she said softly, "You've just returned from a dangerous task and in a few hours will leave on an even more perilous one. I don't want to spend those hours talking about problems."

Shali's wordless answer was to hold out his hands.

Rianna laid her palms in his and felt not the sharp current of excitement that usually went through her at his touch, but a rich warmth, a need for more contact. Rianna's fingers crept to Shali's wrists and his gaze intently fixed on her was like a light shining into her soul. To touch him became a deep hunger; and she ran her hands slowly up his arms, feeling as if she were absorbing from him an essence necessary to her life.

A streak of golden light, catching fire along the mountain ridges, reached into the room and seemed to settle on Rianna's face. There was a knowing in her expression, Shali observed, a wisdom he thought she, who wasn't an Inca, couldn't possibly understand. He wondered if, as Villac Umu had claimed, the link between their souls was so strongly forged Rianna could know, even without realizing it, the ancient rite of merging with the sun. Her tawny eyes were slowly becoming gold with the rising dawn; and Shali felt, if he looked into them much longer, they would engulf him. But he couldn't turn away. As if she understood the link between them had little to do with sight, she closed her eyes.

Rianna's fingers slid over the curve of Shali's shoulders and the sensation of his strength was magnified by her sightlessness. She threaded her fingers into the dense strands of his soft hair, beginning to explore his textures in a way she never had before; and Shali felt the rising power of the ancient ritual as clearly as if it were a column of light bathing them.

Rianna opened her eyes to see that Shali's had closed. Her fingertips lightly traced the spread of his lashes then the curve of his brow, making him feel as if each place she touched she left aglow. Her fingers followed the slant of his cheekbones and outlined his jaw then slipped to his chest to explore its firm curve, moved to measure the span of his waist. Her hands slid to his hips then across his flat stomach; and when she felt his muscles tightening, she lifted her hand to run her fingers lightly over the mound of his chin to his mouth. The roundness of his lips parted slightly under her exploration; so she knew, as he turned against her palm, he was asking for her kiss.

Rianna's lips replaced her fingers; and though Shali's restless mouth caressed her hungrily, it was their only contact. During that kiss, she felt as if every emotion he'd ever known was a stream of impulses pouring into her psyche. Finally, his arms circled her then drew her against him; and she opened her eyes to see that the room was shimmering with golden light, as if the air had become an intangible veil perfumed by the morning wind.

She laid her cheek against Shali's chest and felt his kisses warmly seeping through her hair, recognized the passion in his low voice as he said, "You seem willing to be distracted from your worries by making love. It would give pleasure to our bodies and bring us ease, but will your mind be satisfied later?"

Rianna considered this then answered, "You told me the only choice Incas ever had was to make the most of every moment they're together. You wanted me to think like one of your people. I'm doing it now."

She felt the joy that ran through him as vividly as if it bloomed in herself. Shali's hands at her temples turned her face so their lips met with an eagerness that quickened her heart to a sudden, wild rhythm. His chest against her bosom coaxed her to lie back; and after she had, her body moved closer to him, drawn by a magnetism she couldn't deny. As if he, too, were being driven by a power beyond his will, Shali's kisses held a sweet ferocity that bruised Rianna; but she wove her fingers into his hair to keep his mouth to hers while she softly bit his lips with answering abandon. Impelled by Rianna's passionate response, Shali's hands moved over her body with forceful sensuality. Discovering it wouldn't be too soon for her, he felt like a lightning bolt reaching toward earth for its explosion as he poised to possess her.

Though he was lashed by his need to take her now, the silent voice of his spirit firmly reminded him he had only one soul to give and she could change her mind. The tomorrow could exist when she might leave Peru. Torn between love for Rianna and the uncertainty of her decision, Shali opened his eyes and tried to gather his will for one last moment of his own choosing. When he saw Rianna's face, taut with desire, her eyes glimmering with tawny streaks, his reason began to fade. He felt her quivering beneath him and tried to strengthen his fading will by lifting his head to stare beyond the terrace. The arc of the sun's rim rising above the dark edge of the mountains was a reminder of how near the moment was when he must decide whether or not to complete the union like a ritual. Shali wondered how he could tell Rianna that to him, an Inca, this would mean the fusing of their souls. If the call of Rianna's homeland overcame her love of him, she would take his soul back to Madrid with her and leave him empty. He realized Castilian couldn't describe it and he didn't think she knew the words of his language that could make her understand.

She was gazing up at him expectantly and all he could think of to say was, "I must know, *chinita*, if I should temper myself to avoid the possibility of a child."

His reminder that, despite everything else she might decide, there was a future that threw its responsibilities back to today like shadows also recalled the fears that had haunted her before. Shali could die at the post house; and if he did, Rianna realized she'd have nothing left of him.

"I'll accept whatever the dawn is offering us," she said slowly.

The glow of the half-disk that sent its bright fingers into the room was a power seeping into his skin, gathering in his eyes, shining out at her. A shaft of brilliant gold light, like a hand reaching from the sun, touched her breast. Small puffs of smoke drifting from one of the drowsing Andean volcanoes threaded across the horizon, making the sunlight scintillate on her skin; and Shali began to run his fingers over her body again, this time caressing the streaks of light as if he were lovingly stroking an invisible harp that made a song of her senses. His kisses were the warmth that dappled her body, sparkled along her thighs and settled into her blood. The morning wind flowing from the summits became part of Shali's whispers, ancient words sealing his soul to hers.

She reached up to put her arms around him; and as she raised her shoulders, his hands slid under her hips, drawing her to him. Joy became ecstasy flooding them both, merging their bodies and minds with their emotions. He began to move slowly and her body eagerly answered. She opened her eyes to look at him and found his raptly watching, their dark depths seeming to flood with golden reflections from the sun, as if the dawning was happening within him instead of the sky. The rhythm he made was as sinuous as those the shepherds played on panpipes to their flocks; but the melody he made in Rianna carried a sultry sensuality that evoked a flurry of flames, rising ever higher toward her surrender.

Poised at the breathless moment before passion overwhelmed her, she felt Shali's triumphant smile against her lips as he whispered in Quechua, "My soul is yours." Then his mouth crushed hers and he twined his limbs more firmly around her.

As if they were two currents of the same golden light reaching back to their source, their beings broke all ties with earth and in a cloud of fiery sparks united with the sphere that absorbed their explosion.

Once separate flames now fused, part of the radiance shimmering over the valley, they drifted back to their bodies to lie tranquil within their oneness.

As Shali's awareness slowly returned, he knew his promise had been accepted and irrevocably sealed for all time. If Rianna's Castilian soul was less bound than his, it no longer mattered; he'd never want another love. He opened his eyes to see Rianna's were yet closed, her lashes spread against her cheeks like fans gilded by the sun. Wondering at the effect of their union on her, he moved over to lie at her side and draw her head to his shoulder. She nestled closer, her arm wrapping around his chest; and he silently prayed she was as much his as he was hers. He lay quietly thinking of how he loved her, watching the sun as it rose higher, until he no longer could delay the moment when he must dress and leave.

Even as the impulse to arise flowed along Shali's nerves, Rianna knew it as distinctly as if it were her own. She didn't cling to him as she would have in the past, trying to coax him to stay a moment longer. She watched as he dressed, inwardly wincing as he put on the quilted doublet he wore to battle.

As he took the weapons he'd previously lain aside, she got up and pulled on a robe so she could walk with him on the terrace.

Topa met them in the sun, took Shali's weapons, helmet and shield to free his hands then wordlessly left them alone.

Shali turned to face Rianna and his arms enfolded her. She tilted her head to share his kiss, hold him a little closer for a moment to renew the silent promise they'd already made. Like the women of other Incan soldiers, who were leaving on this journey, her soul no longer railed against their separation. When they parted, she knew as she watched him turn and walk swiftly toward the royal suite that when Shali went to join his men in the courtyard, even while he faced whatever this mission held for him, they would be together.

chapter
23

Manco Capac held up a hand to halt the Incan soldiers before the sheltering forest thinned too much. Shali nodded to Topa, who rode back along the column to relay the order; and the shuffling sounds of the horses' wrapped hooves stopped.

Shali tilted his head to scan the top of the ridge that rose beyond the forest's edge. Though the moon was only a sliver of pearl on the dark velvet of the sky, it cast enough light for his sharp eyes. He said softly, "I see two guards, but I'm sure there are more on the other side of the slope."

Manco swung down from his saddle and gazed at the crags a moment before turning to Shali. "I want you to scout the area."

Shali, too, had dismounted and, at this expected order, took off his helmet and began to unclasp the fastenings of his cloak.

Francisco slid off his horse and hurried to approach Manco. "I want to go with Shali," he said.

Manco's reply was immediate. "No."

"I can speak Spanish without an accent and fool them," Francisco said.

"If a Cañar finds you, it won't matter which language you speak," Manco replied grimly.

"After what Alonso did to my family, I have a right to do this!" Francisco protested.

"You will have to learn not to question my decisions if you want to stay at Machu Picchu." Though Manco spoke barely above a whisper, his command's impact wasn't lessened; and Francisco remained respectfully silent as he added, "Lord Shalikuchima will move more quietly than you can and isn't likely to be seen by anyone unless he wants to be."

Francisco inclined his head in obedience then backed away; but as he approached Shali, his disappointment was evident.

"I'm sure you could slip past the Castilian guards; but if Falla's posted Cañars in the forest on the other side of the ridge, you'd never get by them," Shali advised as he began to unfasten the belt that held his sword. "Besides, I know what to look for no matter what Alonso plans or the situation has become."

"Manco can better afford my loss than yours," Francisco said truthfully.

Shali pulled his sword belt loose and raised his head. "Manco needs information, not for either of us to be captured so Alonso is warned that we've come earlier than he expects." He offered Francisco his sword and asked, "Will you hold this until I come back?"

Francisco silently accepted not only Shali's sword, but his dagger, helmet, cloak and everything else the Inca had worn that might shine in the moonlight, make a sound or catch on a twig. "But you'll have no weapons," Francisco said in dismay.

"If I'm not discovered, I won't need one," Shali replied.

Francisco sighed then whispered, "Be careful, Shali. My sister's heart will break if you come to harm."

Shali nodded, squeezed Francisco's shoulder and turned away.

Watching him trot toward the edge of the forest, Francisco privately had to admit Shali's feet seemed to skim over the ground rather than disturb one leaf. When the Inca reached the base of the slope, Francisco saw him only for an instant before he melted into the deeper shadow cast by an overhanging rock. Expecting to glimpse him emerging from its far side, Francisco was amazed that he didn't. Shali had vanished.

Topa noted Francisco's baffled expression and approached more closely to whisper, "Lord Shali is there, right before our eyes; but I can't see him either."

"I hope none of Alonso's men do," Francisco grimly commented. "He didn't even take a dagger with him."

"Lord Shali's hands and feet are often the only weapons he needs," Topa said. His eyes fell on the bundle Francisco held and he noted, "He does you honor."

Francisco glanced in surprise at the boy.

Topa explained, "Not everyone is allowed to hold Shalikuchima's sword."

Francisco looked down at the blade that glowed softly in the moonlight. "I suppose not," he conceded, "but then I don't allow every man to hold my sister."

Topa couldn't prevent his grin, but he discreetly said no more.

The movements of each of the Castilian guards at the top of the ridge was limited and relatively predictable so it wasn't difficult for Shali to avoid them. After he'd made his way down the opposite slope and entered the forest, the task of eluding the Cañars was more complicated. He couldn't know if there were two or ten of them in Alonso's pay. Unlike the sentries on the ridge, the Indians had no prescribed areas to patrol and roamed the forest on feet as trained for silence as Shali's. Whatever orders Alonso might have given the Cañars, Shali knew, if they saw an Inca slinking around in the dark, they would likely remember only that Incas had been their enemies long before the Castilians had come.

Shali crept through the deepest shadows as noiselessly as a jaguar would pad, his ears and eyes sharpened to their highest acuity. It was only because of the soft outrush of the Cañar's breath as he yawned that Shali was warned a man was standing in the darkness only a few paces ahead. Shali stopped midstep. His eyes were all that moved as he noted a thicket of brambles on his left and to his right a marshy area that looked suspiciously like quicksand. To back away was to risk discovery. He remained motionless, peering through the darkness, trying to decide what to do until he realized that the Cañar's back was to him. Shali's fingers, running along the cords that held his tunic, found the knot he'd sought and nimbly undid it. Eyes still fastened on the Indian, Shali inched the cords free and twined the ends around his hands several turns.

Very carefully he crept closer until he was directly behind the man. Then he dropped the cords over the Cañar's head and jerked them tight. The Cañar's back arched and his arms flailed trying to catch hold of Shali, but he made no sound. He couldn't; his vocal cords had been smashed even as his breath had been stopped. Shali held him only long enough to be sure he was unconscious then let him slump to the ground.

The Cañar, Shali noted, was wearing a Castilian jerkin, breeches not unlike those Shali himself used for riding and Spanish boots—a hodge-podge of clothes of which only his headband and beaded belt were Cañar. Hoping to be mistaken for one of Alonso's Indians should any Castilian see him, Shali quickly stripped off his uniform and replaced it with the Cañar's garments. He dragged the man by the shoulders to the edge of the marsh and rolled him into the mealy fluid it contained then waited for him to sink. After all trace of him had vanished, Shali tied his uniform in a bundle and poked it with a stick, far enough under the brambles so it wouldn't be seen or stumbled over, but not beyond his retrieving it later. Then he straightened and turned away.

Unlike Amaru, who had left Coraquenque and Hailli in hiding while he'd almost directly approached the post house, Shali veered toward a ravine he knew cut through the forest behind the building. The depression was deep enough to form a natural corral for horses and he intended to learn from the number of animals how many men Alonso had with him.

When Shali crawled to the lip of the ravine to look in, he was disgusted and puzzled. There were far more horses than Shali would have anticipated even if Alonso had reason to fear Manco would attack rather than bargain for his wife. Shali slithered back from the edge, then got to his feet to move stealthily along the ravine's border, wondering if Alonso had brought so many men because he'd planned all along to ambush the Incas and only used Coraquenque as bait. It seemed out of character, from what Rianna had told him about the Spaniard; but, Shali reminded himself, Rianna had been frightened this was a trap. He was glad Manco had insisted on coming to the post house several days sooner than Alonso had expected and resolved he would learn what the Castilian intended before he'd let Manco ride in with the gold.

Shali was only partway to the post house, when he smelled the faint aroma of burning tobacco. Someone was smoking a pipe while he guarded the horses, Shali surmised, and moved in that direction. He was alarmed when he saw not Alonso's hired adventurers, but *soldiers* hunched around a barely glowing campfire. The unexpected presence of the army, added to the Castilians' numbers, complicated the situation in ways Shali could only try to guess. Reasoning that Alonso wouldn't have asked for military help to collect an illegal ransom even if he planned to turn the meeting into a trap, Shali concluded that the soldiers had stumbled across Alonso's men. As Shali backed away and melted into the foliage, he speculated whether the soldiers' commanding officer had discovered Alonso's plot or, unaware that Incas were to bring several wagonloads of gold in the next day or two, merely had stopped for the night. There was only one way to find out, Shali grimly decided. He had to get near enough the post house to hear what was being said.

As Shali approached the rear of the building, he was thankful for his impromptu disguise. He could approach the building openly and appear to be a Cañar loitering from his duties. Shali made certain he walked in a direct line with one of the window-openings so he could see who was inside—Alonso and an army captain, but not a hint of Coraquenque or Hailli. He sat on the ground and propped his back against the wall. Letting his chin dip to his chest, as if he were cat-napping, he wondered if his queen and her maid were locked in the storeroom or even the granary beyond the house. Shreds of conversation drifting through the window revealed that Alonso was trying to persuade the captain not to inform his superiors about the ransom, to divide the gold with him and capture whoever delivered it. Alonso argued that taking Shalikuchima would earn the captain a promotion, high favor in Pizarro's eyes and they still would have the gold for themselves. Shali recognized, from the captain's answers, that he was tempted; but Shali also grimly noted that there was no mention of where they'd imprisoned Coraquenque and Hailli.

Shali lifted his head, yawned and got to his feet more slowly than was his habit. If anyone could see him, he wanted to complete the picture of a Cañar who was weary of his patrol. Then, stretching lazily, he trudged around the post house toward the front to see if he might learn anything there.

As Shali rounded the corner, his eyes fell on the sagging figure of a woman tied to a tree. He stopped, wondered if he dared go nearer then decided he must. Whether she was Coraquenque or Hailli, she would take heart if she realized rescue was imminent. Shali approached slowly, as a Cañar might, who couldn't resist gawking at a captured enemy woman.

She didn't raise her head as Shali had anticipated. He concluded she must be exhausted and sleeping. Then, as he came closer, he saw the bloodstains on her robe, that the cloth didn't hang in folds, but shreds. Though he realized she'd been beaten, tortured or both, he dared not hasten his steps. He had to continue to play the role of a Cañar who already knew what had been done to her. But when Shali's fingers under the girl's chin tipped her head up, he was aghast; and he couldn't prevent his body's stiffening in horror. She was dead, not asleep, he knew now. Her face was so badly mutilated he couldn't even recognize her. Shali's eyes fell on the pendant still resting on her breast. The royal insignia. *Coraquenque*.

"Hey you! Cañar! Get away from that body!"

Shali glanced sideways. A soldier was watching him.

"If you think you're going to steal that pendant or get some grisly souvenir . . ." the soldier threatened.

Shali muttered an insult in the Cañar dialect and turned to walk sullenly toward the forest's edge. Though he appeared to crash angrily into the foliage, his unaccustomed carelessness was due to the tears blurring his vision. Once he knew the soldier no longer could see him, he paused to wipe his eyes. Then, knowing he must not give in to his grief, he lifted his head and walked swiftly through the brush. He didn't care if another Cañar saw through his disguise and tried to stop him. Now he'd welcome the opportunity to kill one of Alonso's men.

As Shali came trotting out of the darkness dressed like a Cañar, Incan lances raised and bows swung in his direction. He swept off the alien headband; and at his sharp, low command, the weapons were lowered. When he faced Manco, he didn't know how to tell his cousin he'd found his wife. Instead, Shali described the scene in the post house and recounted the number of horses he'd seen, that the army was there.

Manco demanded at last, "Did you see Coraquenque?"

Shali lowered his eyes and said quietly, "A woman was tied to a tree. She wore your insignia."

Manco was silent a moment. His fear was obvious. Finally, he breathed, "You didn't see her face?"

Shali raised his eyes. "She had none."

Manco turned and leaned his arms over his saddle, as if he hadn't the strength to stand alone. "Leave me," he commanded and would say no more.

Shali turned to rejoin Francisco, who stared solemnly at the king, wondering what Shali had said to him. Shali explained quickly.

"Maybe it was Hailli," Francisco said hopefully. "How can we know?"

Shali turned to Amaru and asked gruffly, "Did Coraquenque give her pendant to Hailli during the days you were locked in the storeroom with them?" Amaru shook his head. Shali concluded, "Then I doubt she would have done it later. There's no reason to think the Castilians would know its meaning anyway. No, I'm afraid the queen and Manco's heir are dead."

"What do you suppose Manco will do now?" Francisco asked.

Shali answered grimly. "He wants revenge."

Within the hour, Manco had recovered himself enough to give Shali brusque orders to have the men prepare to approach the post house.

"Have you decided how we'll conduct the attack so I may know how to deploy the men?" Shali asked. At Manco's silence, Shali realized his cousin was so shocked by grief that the thought of revenge, but not its strategy, filled his mind. Shali said quickly, "I suggest we send a few men into the ravine to drive the horses over their guards and into the army camp. That should scatter the soldiers and they may lose some of their weapons. When our men appear, many of the soldiers will stand and fight, others will try to get to the post house and their captain; but I suspect Alonso's men will mostly try to flee."

Manco gathered the shattered fragments of his composure and forced his mind to function. "The men who go to the ravine will have to kill the Cañars in the forest and the sentries on the ridge. Amaru will position half of the remaining men at the army camp; the rest will accompany us to the post house." Manco paused then added urgently, "Do it quickly, Shali, I want the horses stampeded before it's light."

Shali agreed the Castilians would be more confused in the semi-darkness before dawn, but he warned, "They outnumber us."

"But they don't have cannons here," Manco reminded. "If our soldiers need inspiration to fight, tell them to look at the body of their queen and remember how many Incas have been tortured and slaughtered."

Shali nodded and turned away. He gave orders to his officers even as he was tearing off the Cañar's clothes and tossing them contemptuously aside; and by the time he was finished speaking, his officers saluted their commander again dressed in his own uniform.

The eastern sky had barely lightened to indigo when Manco and Shali, waiting in the deep shadows of the forest, heard the first gunshots, horses shrilling in protest and fear then hooves drumming in the ravine. Incan victory cries, Castilian curses and death-shrieks, more gunfire followed; and the dust clouds that even in the gloom could be seen rising from the ravine exploded into the Spanish camp. Then the cacophony of full-scale battle assailed the morning air.

When Castilian soldiers burst from the underbrush at the rear of the post house, Shali raised his arm and turned to look at Manco. He waited until the Spaniards, pausing from time to time to turn and fire guns or crossbows at the pursuing Incas, finally reached the side of the building. Then Manco nodded and Shali dropped his arm.

The Castilians heard the thunder of hooves now coming from the forest and, distracted by their battle, assumed it was more of the stampeding horses. Not until the Incan riders burst from the trees did the Spaniards realize they were being attacked by still another force. When a battle cry rose from the Incas' throats, the Castilians turned and raced toward the shelter of the stone building. Only a handful of Spaniards managed to get through the door before the wave of blue-clad Incas overwhelmed the others.

During the dash across the clearing, Shali had hurled several lances; but as he neared the enemy, he unsheathed his long, straight-slashing sword. Well trained for battle by his former master, Chuncho never slowed his speed as Shali aimed him like a bolt into the thick of the Castilians. The stallion's shoulders brushed aside men as easily as if they were weeds and Shali's blade flashed one way then the other as he passed.

After he'd raced through the crowd, Chuncho turned in a swirl of dust; but Shali held the horse back for a moment so he could assess the battle. He shouted and gestured an officer to head off some of Alonso's men trying to sneak into the forest, then another officer to close the ranks of his men. Finally, he scanned the battle as he thought of what he would do next.

Manco was conspicuous in the midst of the fray, rapidly shifting the position of his shield to deflect the blows of one opponent while his other arm wielded a huge mace against a second enemy. A terrible force seemed to have taken control of the king; for even after the man staggered from a mortal wound, Manco savagely struck again and again. Suddenly, as if he snapped out of his blood-lust, he whirled to finish the other man with one blow. When Manco raised his head to choose another enemy, even across the distance Shali could see the fury blazing in his cousin's eyes in the moment before his deadly mace struck again.

Shali observed that Francisco had dismounted; and his blade was slashing and chopping at the Castilians with formidable skill, as he worked his way toward the post house door. Shali knew Francisco's one aim was to get Alonso and he wondered if Francisco was aware that a dozen or so Castilians had already gotten into the building. A battle cry, the sudden flurry of hooves distracted Shali. He turned quickly to see that a Spaniard, who had somehow caught a horse, was racing toward him ready to launch a spear.

Shali kicked Chuncho forward and ducked low as the missile whined past. The Castilian's mount crashed into Chuncho's hip, the shock of the collision making Chuncho swing around; but the same motion made an arc of Shali's flashing blade and the Castilian dropped from his saddle.

Francisco had finally gained the post house door. He was pretending to be one of Alonso's men seeking shelter and was shouting in Castilian, pleading to be let in, Shali noted as he turned Chuncho toward the building.

When the door opened and Francisco pushed his way inside, Shali and Chuncho came rushing through before the door could be reclosed. Chuncho's hooves shook the wooden floor as Shali wheeled him around and swung his sword to decapitate a soldier. Then, before Chuncho had stopped, Shali dove from the saddle to bowl over another enemy. The soldier, weighed down by mail, had only risen to his knees when he, too, lost his head. A Castilian wielding a battle axe forced Shali to retreat until his back was to the wall. Though Shali ducked and side-stepped to avoid the axe, he caught glimpses of Francisco facing a pair of soldiers with swords, Alonso on the far side of the room looking for a way to escape.

Shali's blade struck off the hand that held the axe then skewered the man. Turning to help Francisco, Shali was relieved to see that he'd meanwhile disposed of both swordsmen and was finally facing Alonso, who raised his sword to a position that told Shali he knew how to use it.

The shock of the blow dashing away Shali's blade numbed his arm halfway to his shoulder, but he quickly turned to a Cañar who held a crossbow. With the speed of a striking snake, Shali leaped up to kick the Cañar squarely in the face. The Cañar crashed backward; and drawing his dagger, Shali leaped on him to plunge the knife into his chest.

As Shali began to get to his feet, he saw Francisco sitting on the floor frantically struggling to get up; but his leg, streaming blood, wouldn't obey his commands. Alonso, standing over him like an executioner, had raised his sword. Shali hastily looked around for the fallen Cañar's crossbow.

Alonso said coldly, "You should have died two years ago, Francisco."

In the same apologetic Quechua he'd used in Lima's marketplace, Shali began, "I most humbly beg your pardon, exalted lord . . ."

Startled, Alonso turned. The blood-spattered uniform of the Inca who stood a few paces away was unmistakably that of a high-ranking officer; but the narrowed black eyes of the man wearing it matched those that once had looked at Alonso from under his own whip. "The peasant!" Alonso breathed.

Shali raised the crossbow. In Castilian he quietly corrected, "Lord Shalikuchima, Rianna's lover." Then he released the bolt.

At such short range, the missile could have passed through a war horse; but Alonso was so near the wall the bolt pinned him to the stone like a butterfly to a collector's board. Alonso's one short scream faded into the last rush of air escaping his lungs.

Shali threw the crossbow away then turned to help Francisco, who grimaced with pain as the Inca eased him to the floor. Francisco was silent, thoughtful, as he watched Shali slit open his pant leg to study the slash in his calf. Finally, he said, "At least this wound is one thing Alonso didn't do. One of the men I fought before and thought dead had just enough strength to take a last swing with his sword while I was facing Alonso."

Shali had pulled off his cloak and was tearing a long strip from it. He was silent while he worked hurriedly; but when he pressed the wadded cloth against Francisco's wound, he said, "I'm sorry I couldn't let you take revenge against Alonso."

Turning his head to gaze a moment at his family's murderer hanging limply from the wall, Francisco replied, "It's enough to see him dead. I guess you had enough reason for wanting to kill him too—what he tried to do to Rianna, feeling as you do about her." He paused then painfully propping himself up on an elbow, said, "We have a custom in Spain that a girl's father must give permission for her to marry. I'm the only male left of Rianna's family. If you want to marry Rianna, I'm giving you my permission."

Shali's dark eyes glanced up at Francisco. "Incas have the same custom and it's important to me you say that. The only problem now is if Rianna will agree." He busied himself tearing another strip from his cloak then asked, "Can you hold this to your wound tightly enough to slow the bleeding? I should go back outside."

"There's no need. We've won. The battle is over."

Surprised, Shali looked up to see Manco in the doorway. Then he realized he no longer heard sounds of fighting, just horses stamping, men talking or groaning.

"They're all dead or dying. Even their captain. I made sure of him myself. I'm certain it was his orders that . . ." Manco stopped, unable to say more.

Shali knew it would have been the captain who'd decided Coraquenque was to be tortured to death. As he pressed another wad of cloth to Francisco's leg he asked, "How many did we lose?"

"Far too many," Manco wearily replied then started at a crash that came from the storeroom. He quickly drew his sword and turned to walk warily toward the door. It was blocked by a chest that had fallen in front of it.

Shali arose to help Manco push the chest away. They were surprised to discover the door was barred from the outside. Was a prisoner in the storeroom? While Shali slid the bar aside, Manco raised his sword; but when the door swung open, the weapon dropped from Manco's nerveless fingers. He stared incredulously at Coraquenque poised on the threshold.

Too stunned to say a word, Manco opened his arms and Coraquenque flew into them. He pressed his face into her hair, kissing her temple, covering her face with kisses then finally just held her tightly to him.

"I escaped the soldiers once, but they caught me again when I tried to help Hailli," Coraquenque wept as she clung to Manco. "Forgive me for taking such chances with your heir, but I *couldn't* leave Hailli to them without trying to help her."

Manco held Coraquenque away a little so he could look into her face a moment then laid his cheek against hers and said brokenly, "When I learned you'd been captured, I never thought of the continuation of the royal line, only of losing you."

* * *

Shali watched as Topa, supporting Francisco by one shoulder, helped him through the post house's doorway. "Let him sit against the building," Shali directed then went to help Topa ease the Spaniard to the ground. After Francisco was sitting with his back against the wall, Shali inspected the makeshift bandage before straightening. "Don't move that leg and restart the bleeding or you'll leave a trail all the way to Machu Picchu," he warned.

Francisco nodded, but his eyes were fixed on the bodies in the clearing. "A lot of Incas died here today," he finally commented then, lifting his head to regard Shali, added, "I shudder to think how many others will be killed when you go after those cannons Pizarro is having brought through the mountains."

"If I could destroy the cannons instead of merely capturing them, few lives need be lost." Shali was quiet a moment before he said, "Whatever strategies I use to minimize our losses in that or the other battles to follow, many Incas will die."

"If one of them is you, who will guard Machu Picchu?"

"There are other officers."

Francisco persisted, "If you die, who will love Rianna?"

Shali let out a breath. "I'm not certain Rianna will stay," he admitted, then began to turn away.

"What point would there be in her remaining with a people who, if they continue fighting, are committing suicide as a nation?" Francisco asked. Shali's back stiffened and Francisco quietly inquired, "Aren't you tired of fighting?"

Shali turned to glare down at him. *"I am sick to death of it."*

Francisco pressed, "I should think, after seeming to have lost Coraquenque and their unborn child, her being found must seem like a miracle, a second chance only a divine hand could grant. Perhaps Manco will consider taking advantage of that chance."

Shali stooped to face Francisco and said bitterly, "If you mean he should surrender himself to the Castilians and agree to follow their religion, he won't do that. Nor would I. If you mean he should withdraw to Machu Picchu, he knows the Castilians will continue searching for him. They *must* kill our king before the Incas will stop resisting."

"They wouldn't search if they were convinced Manco was dead," Francisco suggested. "It seems to me this situation presents such an opportunity."

The idea was like a small explosion of light behind Shali's eyes. He silently considered it a moment before he said, "If Manco sees this as I do, he'll add your name to his list of noblemen if you stay at Machu Picchu."

"Don Francisco Agustín Luis Alava of Madrid, an Incan lord?" Francisco smiled faintly. "It seems unlikely."

"If Manco Capac commanded, it would *be*." Shali straightened and walked quickly to where his king was surveying the dead and dying with grim eyes.

"Francisco and I just were commenting on the losses," Shali observed.

"Amaru is among them," Manco said quietly.

"Another skilled officer, a good man and a friend." Shali sighed. "I'll have to tell his wife myself."

"Many wives will grieve when we return," Manco said then bitterly added, "Why did that king across the ocean have to send his people so far to kill mine?"

"They think they have a divine right to take what is ours just as they took everything from the Aztecs in the north. Now that once mighty people are so decimated they've become little more than slaves. Their leaders are dead, their government destroyed and they have no hope," Shali said as he turned level eyes on his king. "We've already been too weakened to fight a proper war. All we can do now is resist them in skirmishes like this. They'll continue to come with their cannons and we'll lose an entire generation of men. I must wonder who will father the next generation. Of those children already born or still in their mothers' bodies, I wonder who will feed and protect them, teach them what it means to be an Incan man if their fathers are dead."

"Don't you think that haunts my every waking moment and gives me nightmares while I sleep?" Manco angrily asked. "Don't you think I want to see that child Coraquenque is carrying grow up? I've already lost children and a wife because of this invasion! When I'd thought I'd lost Coraquenque too, I felt as if my heart was dead."

"I, too, have seen loved ones die. We all have," Shali reminded. "I don't want to lose even more."

"Should we give ourselves up to the enemy?" Manco demanded. "They'll grind us under their boots as they're doing to the Aztecs. The first thing Juan Pizarro would do is burn Coraquenque and me in Cuzco's plaza and make sure all Incas know the royal line is no more."

"Pizarro would stop looking for you if he thought you're dead," Shali offered. Manco's eyes flashed with the argument ready on his lips, but Shali quickly added, "Francisco has suggested a way."

Coraquenque, who'd overheard this, came closer. "What way?"

Shali looked at Manco, who nodded for him to continue. "There are many dead Incas here, but no live Spaniards to describe what happened. We could make it appear no one survived this battle. Among the Incas, surely we could find a corpse your size and age, whose features were destroyed."

Coraquenque said eagerly, "Amaru is one! His face was smashed by a mace."

Shali regarded Manco solemnly. "Do you remember how even we were fooled into thinking Hailli was Coraquenque? If you were to exchange clothes and insignias with Amaru's corpse—if you put your *borla* on his head, Pizarro would never guess the body wasn't yours. He'd have no one to parade through Cuzco's streets in chains or burn at his stake."

Manco said softly, "My *borla*, even my crown."

"A new one could be made," Coraquenque reminded then softly added, "In their separate ways Amaru and Hailli *did* die for us." She caught Manco's hands in hers. "We would be able to return to Machu Picchu until we were strong enough to fight again."

"My people would meanwhile have to live under our enemy's rule," Manco said bitterly.

"Are they living under your rule now or are they dying to preserve some small remnant of it?" Coraquenque inquired.

"This knight from Avila Pizarro fears so much, Blasco Vela, seems determined to enforce the laws his king has decreed, which would at

437

least prevent the Castilians from raping and killing Incas at their discretion,'' Shali advised.

"Word could be spread among our people that you and I are alive the same way it always has been since the invaders came, by messengers who wear our seal, but are dressed as beggars. Our people could pretend to surrender and withdraw to live quietly in the mountains while we become stronger,'' Coraquenque urged. Seeing from Manco's expression that he was seriously considering the idea, she said more quietly, "Alonso really did have the eternal light from Cuzco's temple and would have handed it to you if Captain Estudillo hadn't come. It's hidden in the granary. If we took it and lit it for the festival of Raymi, Incas everywhere could think of the flame burning at Machu Picchu and know everything isn't lost. It would be a flame of hope to burn in their hearts until we can take our rightful place again.''

"The fire that sears *my* heart is their king will think he's vanquished us,'' Manco spat. "Our greedy enemies, men like Alonso and that army captain, will think they've won.''

"Vela's laws will subdue their laughter, I suspect. In any event, it would be a shallow victory when those who are supposed to be conquered withdraw to the mountains and ignore conquerors who can't follow,'' Shali noted.

Coraquenque reached up to tenderly touch Manco's temples. "My husband, my king, does it matter what the Castilians or the entire world beyond that ocean thinks?'' she asked softly. "Or does it matter to us what our people *know*?''

Manco looked down at Coraquenque. In his eyes were echoes of the grief that had crushed his heart with agony while he'd thought her dead. He raised his gaze to look beyond her shoulder at the mangled bodies of the Incas who had died in this one small battle and reflected on the pain their families would suffer—all the others who would be killed in future battles until his people were no more. He thought of the Incas' plight if they had to live under Pizarro's rule, as the Aztecs did under Cortez's heel.

He said softly, "If Pizarro's cannons get through the mountains, he may defeat Vela.''

"An avalanche or two in the proper passes might prevent the

cannons from arriving, especially if the Incas who are dragging them disappeared in the confusion,'' Shali advised.

Manco said quietly, "We'd best find an Incan corpse that will fit into your uniform; because the Castilians won't rest until they think Shalikuchima, too, is dead.''

chapter
24

After Manco Capac had left Machu Picchu to ransom the queen, the Incas passing the city gates on their various errands soon got used to the sight of Rianna sitting on the lower section of the wall overlooking the road to the valley. She came each morning wrapped in a vicuña shawl to shield her from the dawn's chill; but as the morning progressed, she lowered the shawl; and her luxuriant curls were set ablaze by the noon sun that kissed her shoulders to the same golden tint as the Indians'. She remained until the last glimmers of light faded and the road descending to the valley was lost in shadow. The Incas knew Rianna was anxiously waiting for Shali and Francisco. They all were waiting for husbands, lovers, sons or brothers—and the king and queen.

While the Indians' curiosity about Rianna gradually faded, their respect for her steadfastness grew. Though she was of an enemy people, she was Lord Shalikuchima's love, friend to Manco Capac and Coraquenque; and they inclined their heads as they passed. The gesture was the same they would have made to an Incan noblewoman, though she often was too absorbed in her own thoughts to notice. People sometimes approached and waited silently until Rianna's tawny eyes focused on them, then they sympathetically offered a piece of fruit or a drink of water from the baskets and jars they carried. They were pleased when she accepted their gifts, surprised that she spoke their language, though the flow of her sentences was sometimes broken while she searched for a word. If they supplied the word, she warmly thanked them; and they continued on their way remarking on her courtesy. Descriptions of Rianna's beauty and faithfulness quickly spread even among the people of the valley, who had never seen her.

Rianna wasn't aware she was becoming a legend. All she knew was the Incas were kind to her, that they were friendly and their manners gentle. She wondered how she'd ever felt like an alien among them as she looked into the faces that passed, especially those of the children. Was she carrying a bud that would bloom into a child like one of these? A son or daughter with Shali's strong, but finely boned face, darkly tilted eyes and a thick shock of black hair? She lifted her gaze past the terraces down the road Shali had traveled and felt as if her spirit flew out over the valley in search of him.

She thought of how he'd looked riding at Manco Capac's side and her heart seemed to be a small bird beating its wings against her ribs. Though Shali's bearing alone proclaimed his rank as commander, his dark blue uniform with its gleaming gold trim, the black cloak whose folds spread over Chuncho's rump, blending with the stallion's velvet coat, but for its border of Shali's crest embroidered in scarlet and gold, stood out as vividly from the azure-clad soldiers as Manco's garments or Francisco's. Her brother had worn a simple green jerkin and black breeches; and Rianna wondered why, though he and Shali were nearly the same age, Francisco seemed younger. She decided it was because she'd never seen her brother ride off to a possible battle then suddenly remembered how he'd galloped into the Alava courtyard and shot one of the inquisitor's soldiers. But Francisco had been only a dark figure then. Her memory of Francisco's silhouette on the Alava wall impaled by a spear made her shudder and she turned her thoughts to the wagonloads of gold scintillating in the early sunlight that Manco took to Alonso.

Having to give Alonso gold in payment for Coraquenque, Hailli and the eternal light filled Rianna with cold fury not because the metal represented a fortune, but because the objects made from it were beautiful, many even sacred to the Incas; and it was being extorted from them by a greedy man who couldn't wait to toss it into a smelter. It surprised Rianna to realize she'd finally learned to regard gold as the Incas did, not for its value in coinage, but as a shining metal that could be formed into objects of exquisite beauty. She wondered if, when Shali had made love to her the dawn before he'd left, he truly had somehow combined her soul with his.

"It's getting late, Rianna. Won't you come back to the palace?"

Rianna glanced up at Suya in surprise then noticed the shadows growing deeper in the valley, the beginning shreds of mist forming at the foot of the mountains. She turned to see that Machu Picchu's towers were swathed in a rich, orange-gold light.

"It won't be dark for a while yet," Rianna said.

"Do you mind if I stay with you till then?" Suya asked.

Rianna looked at her and commented, "We might as well do our worrying together."

Suya perched herself on the wall beside Rianna, but she was silent a long moment before she finally admitted, "I would have come every day, as you have, but I thought you might not be pleased to know I love your brother."

Rianna smiled wanly. "Francisco wasn't happy when he learned I love Shali, but he's gotten more accustomed to the idea."

"I wonder sometimes if Shali and I are fools, both waiting to learn if you'll stay at Machu Picchu," Suya said frankly.

"I've wondered if we're *all* trapped by love that was never meant to be or maybe always was our fate." Rianna turned to regard Suya. "It's been difficult for me to decide what to do because everything is so different from all that I—and Francisco—have known before."

"Love, it seems, feels the same way to you as it does to me. We both are terrified they won't come back," Suya said softly. Her eyes were glistening with tears as she added, "I'm so frightened a trap has been laid for them I've even told Viracocha I won't ask for Francisco's love if only his life would be spared."

Rianna sighed. "I've said the same prayer to my God; but I've wondered if Shali's prayer is something quite different."

Suya blinked away her tears. "Why do you say that?"

Rianna stared at the terraces, like giant green steps cut from the mountain, wondering if she should confide in Suya. She decided the Inca could confirm or deny what Shali had done and finally asked, "Is it possible in your beliefs for lovers to combine their spirits almost the same way Manco Capac joins couples in marriage on the Day of Wedding?"

Startled by Rianna's question, which involved a ritual deeply private to Incas, Suya asked urgently, "How can you know about such a thing?"

Rianna whispered, "I think Shali did something like that the morning he left."

Suya's eyes were bright with excitement as she asked, "What exactly did he do?"

Rianna felt her blush rising, but she said determinedly, "It seemed as if he'd been timing our love-making for the sunrise. Just before we were swept away, he said, 'My soul is yours.' "

Suya breathed, "His love for you must be truly great for him to bind himself to you though he couldn't be certain you'd also be bound to him." Awed at what Shali had done, she was silent a moment then suddenly exclaimed, "I wish I'd done that with Francisco! If he returns safely, I *will* do it—whether or not he'll stay at Machu Picchu with me." Suddenly realizing what she was saying and to whom, she looked guiltily at Rianna from the corner of her eye.

But Rianna said with quiet vehemence, "If Francisco chooses to leave a woman like you, he's a fool—just as I'd be a fool to turn my back on a love like Shali's. What does all the rest matter anyway?"

Amazed at Rianna's sudden decision, Suya began to weep. "You'll be the sister I lost, different in many ways from Yupanqui; but you have the same heart."

Rianna put her arm around Suya's waist; but she was remembering Shali's saying to love her, he had to win her away from the past. She wondered if, having finally conquered it, he would return so she could tell him.

The two women sat on the wall clasping each other's hands, staring at the valley's deepening shadows. Suddenly a little cry escaped Suya; and she leaped from her perch, pulling Rianna with her.

Rianna stared at the double column of horsemen who had rounded the last curve in the road. She waited, hardly daring to breathe, until they entered the light.

Two azure-clad soldiers rode at the front of the column. Behind them were a pair of other soldiers Rianna assumed were wounded because they were wrapped in cloaks. Shali and Manco, Francisco and Coraquenque *must* be farther back in the line, she reasoned. Had they been hurt and were in the wagons? The fear growing in Rianna congealed her heart with visions of ragged wounds and dismembered limbs. Horror seemed to stop her breath as her eyes searched the riders to the column's end, to the wagons, still loaded with gold. There was no trace of Shali's uniform. Francisco's hair didn't catch red streaks from the sun. She couldn't see Manco's insignia gleaming in the light. There was no hint of Coraquenque or her maid. Only the soldiers and the gold. Always the glimmering gold.

Rianna's breath caught on the edge of a sob. It *had* been a trap, a successful trap; and everyone she loved best had been killed or captured. Her disbelieving eyes flew back to the head of the column to confirm that a soldier of low rank rode Chuncho, another officer Manco's horse.

Rianna hugged herself, as if to somehow protect her mind from the anguish battering at her sanity. *"It can't be!"* she whispered.

Suya turned to Rianna with tears streaming down her cheeks and cried, "None of them returned—*none!*"

Watching Rianna's strange reaction to his homecoming, for a moment Shali was baffled. Had something dreadful happened at Machu Picchu? Then he remembered he and Manco had changed into the uniforms of other soldiers, that Coraquenque and Francisco were wrapped in cloaks against the valley's chill.

"They don't recognize us!" he exclaimed and swept off his helmet to throw it aside. As Chuncho leaped forward, Shali called, *"Chinita!"*

Rianna straightened at the sound of his voice. She stood as tensely as if she were an arrow ready to fly from its bow. Recognition welled up through her shock; it became a torrent of joy. She started running down the terraces. The Inca riding toward her flung himself from his saddle to race to her on foot. When he threw his arms around her, she was beyond thought or speech. She clung to Shali's solid warmth and didn't know she was weeping, didn't even hear Francisco's call.

"I'm here, Suya! I just can't move as fast as Shali!"

Rianna's face was burrowed against Shali's chest and she didn't see Francisco limping through the shimmering light or hear Suya's cry, "I can! I can run, my love!"

Being locked in Shali's arms was all Rianna was aware of; the sound of his heartbeat was her world.

Shali bent so his cheek was against Rianna's shoulder, feeling as if his embrace must completely enclose her, even his head curl around her. He turned his face to breathe the scent of her hair then remembered the outcome of the battle at the post house and knew he must tell her.

Against Rianna's cheek, Shali whispered, "After what happened today, none of us except messengers will be able to leave this valley for a long time." He withdrew a little. Dreading the decision he knew she now must make, that this dream of his might be ending, he said quietly, "If you and Francisco don't leave tomorrow, you'll have to remain at Machu Picchu, perhaps for the rest of your lives."

Rianna turned her head to finally notice Francisco and Suya lost in their own embrace. Then she looked up at Shali and said, "Tomorrow at dawn I believe Francisco will be sharing the same promise with Suya as I plan to give you."

Shali's eyes, black as obsidian from his fear, began to glimmer with hope. Unable to believe the conclusion dawning in his mind, he whispered, "What promise is that, *chinita*?"

"When the sun rises over the mountains to look down on us lost in each other's arms, with the last breath I have before love overtakes me, I shall promise as you did before you left—*my soul is yours.*"

The magnitude of the emotions rising in Shali was a radiance that burst into his eyes. He wasn't able to speak for no words of any language could match the song his soul was singing. He put his arm around Rianna's waist and turned to begin walking with her toward Machu Picchu's towers, which beckoned to them with the last amber light of the day.